TILL THE SUN

Anne Bennett was born in a back-to-back house in the Horsefair district of Birmingham. The daughter of Roman Catholic, Irish immigrants, she grew up in a tight-knit community where she was taught to be proud of her heritage. She considers herself to be an Irish Brummie and feels therefore that she has a foot in both cultures. She has four children – three daughters and a son – and four grandchildren. For many years she taught in schools to the north of Birmingham.

An accident put paid to her teaching career and after moving to North Wales, Anne turned to the other great love of her life and began to write seriously. *Till the Sun Shines Through* is her sixth book.

For more information about Anne Bennett, visit her website at www.annebennett.co.uk.

By the same author

A Little Learning
Love Me Tender
A Strong Hand to Hold
Pack Up Your Troubles
Walking Back to Happiness

ANNE BENNETT

Till the Sun
Shines Through

HarperCollins*Publishers*

HarperCollins*Publishers*
77–85 Fulham Palace Road
Hammersmith, W6 8JB

www.harpercollins.co.uk

This paperback edition 2004
1

First published in Great Britain by
HarperCollins*Publishers* 2003

ISBN 978–0–00–788846–7

Typeset in Sabon by Palimpsest Book Production Limited,
Polmont, Stirlingshire
Printed and bound in Great Britain by
Clays Ltd, St Ives plc

I have many people to thank for making this book possible. First of all, there are my husband Denis, daughters Nikki, Bethany and Tamsin and son Simon, who are always supportive, and a special thanks to Simon for designing my website. My daughter-in-law Carol, son-in-law Steve and mother-in-law Nancy are encouraging too, and Nancy also helps me with the memories she has of the times I am writing about.

I would like to take this opportunity to thank my special friends Ruth Adshead, Judith Kendall and Judy Westwood for their immeasurable support, and my agent Judith Murdoch, editorial director Susan Opie and editor Maxine Hitchcock for their belief in me. I really appreciate their help, advice and constructive criticism.

Thanks must also go to Ann Temple of the Railway Restoration Society based in Donegal Town, whose help was invaluable, and to Carl Chinn in Birmingham. I really would find it difficult to write as accurately as I do without the marvellous books he writes of old Birmingham. Immense gratitude to you all.

I would like to dedicate this book to my eldest daughter, Nikki Wilkes, with all my love.

CHAPTER ONE

Both Bridie McCarthy and her cousin Rosalyn were lying across the straw bales on the upper floor of the barn, the place both girls made for when they needed a bit of peace. Rosalyn was reading the latest letter from Bridie's sister Mary, who was married and living in Birmingham and had written asking if Bridie could come and stay with her a wee while before school opened again in September.

Rosalyn handed the letter back to Bridie with a sigh. 'You're so lucky,' she said.

Bridie didn't contradict her cousin. Instead she said, 'Well, Mary did promise I could go on a visit when she had her own place. You mind they had to stay with Aunt Ellen first after their marriage last year?' She hugged her knees with delight. 'I can't wait.'

'I bet,' Rosalyn said. 'Anything would be better than this place day after day.' She crossed to the barn window and Bridie got to her feet and joined her. 'It's not to see Birmingham,' she told Rosalyn. 'It's to see Mary. I've missed her so much since she left. Before then – Mary leaving and all – I thought life would just go on the same way year in, year out.'

'For me it does.'

'No, even for you there's change,' Bridie reminded her. 'For a start you'll be working in the shirt factory in Donegal town in a few weeks, now that you're fourteen, instead of going back to school.'

'Aye, I'll work longer hours, give most of my pay to Mammy and still be at her beck and call when I'm home. "Rosalyn, do this, or that, wash the dishes, see to the weans, change the baby". God, it would sicken you.'

Bridie burst out laughing. 'Don't be such a grouch,' she said.

'Well, don't you ever want something to happen?' Rosalyn demanded. 'God, Bridie, there must be more to life than this.'

Bridie looked out at the farm and countryside she loved with all her heart, where the sun shone down from a cloudless sky giving everything a glow. In front of the squat whitewashed cottage the hens strutted about the yard, pecking the grain that had fallen between the cobbles, while the cows placidly chewed the cud in the lush fields and occasionally leaned their heads on the five-bar gate to watch the world go by. To the side of the house was the orchard, the trees heavy with fruit at that time of the year. Much of the fruit would be picked in another month or so, Bridie knew, and bottled or made into jam, except for the apples. They would be stored in straw-layered barrels in the barn.

Everywhere she looked there were trees and greenness and beauty and it always left her with deep satisfaction to look upon it. There were other cottages like their own dotted about, all on the same lines and most with a curl of smoke wafting from the chimneys. Some cottages seemed almost to nestle in the verdant green Donegal hills that were dotted with sheep who tugged relentlessly at the grass.

The lane to the road divided the cows' field from the tilled ground where Bridie could see her father and her brother Terry working. Just a little way along that road the lane meandered down to run alongside the rail bus tracks at the bottom of the farm.

The red and cream diesel-driven rail buses had been a feature of Bridie's life since as far back as she could remember. Her father had told her rail bus tracks were laid all over Donegal and ran on narrow rails because they had to climb and dip over unaccommodating hills, or negotiate other austere landscapes. He'd said they had opened up life for the people in the outlying farms and villages, which had been fairly isolated until then.

The one that ran past the bottom of the McCarthy farm came from the port of Killybegs in the west. In the cars and trucks pulled behind the rail bus would be fish from Killybegs, and cattle, sheep and produce from the surrounding farms. The rail bus would bring back vital foodstuffs, coal and Guinness from the north.

It also took fathers to work and mothers to shop. Bridie had been on it herself a few times with her mother, as far as Donegal Town, on the rare occasions when no one was taking the cart in. She'd never travelled on it the other way though; there had never been the need.

She well remembered the day Mary left, beside herself with excitement. She'd been mad to go with Aunt Ellen and Uncle Sam, who'd wanted to take her back for a wee holiday to their house in Birmingham, and she hadn't been at all sure that her mother would allow it. Bridie had been sorry to see her sister go and would have been worse still if she'd known she'd never come back to live at the farm again.

She wondered if her mother had had an inkling of the way it might turn out, for she'd not wanted Mary to go either and Bridie had overheard the conversation she had about it with her sister Ellen. 'What is the point of going to a place like Birmingham for a holiday?' Sarah had complained. 'Haven't you said it's fine and dirty and the air full of smoke and fumes from the factories? Hasn't Mary all she needs here for a holiday if she wants one?'

'Aye, and what does she see of it?' Ellen retorted. 'Cooped up all day in a shirt factory.'

'It was her choice to work there,' Sarah said, bridling at the implied criticism.

'I wasn't blaming you, Sarah,' Ellen said in a conciliatory tone. 'But let me take the girl for a wee change. Show her things and take her places you haven't here. I'd like to do it, Sarah. You know I think of your children almost as my own.'

Sarah could say nothing after that. The blight on Ellen's life was the fact that she and Sam had never had any children. Ellen, older than Sarah by five years, had lived with Sam's parents in Letterkenny for six years after her marriage and initially put the fact that she was childless down to the stress of living with in-laws she barely got on with, certain it would come right when she and Sam had a place of their own.

She'd seen and approved her sister's marriage to Jimmy McCarthy, and only had a slight twinge of envy at the birth of Seamus the following year and Johnnie the year after. Shortly after this, she followed her husband to Birmingham, where an uncle promised him a job in a new rubber factory set up by an Irishman named Byrne, later called Dunlop's.

Ellen had been glad to go, for Sam's father's farm made little enough money and Sam, being the second son, would never inherit it anyway. At first, all they could find to rent were two mean little rooms and Ellen was actually glad she hadn't weans to see to in the place and said as much to any who asked her.

She'd been married almost ten years when they got the house on Bell Barn Road and she settled down to life there. She was confident children would be part of their marriage and, please God, children she could rear, not like her poor sister Sarah, who'd lost three wee babies to consumption. But no children came. Ellen had a comfortable home – Sam earned good money, though he worked hard for it and came back home each evening as black as any miner and stinking from the rubber, and he was a good man, a good husband and provider and, Ellen thought, would have made a wonderful father. But it wasn't to be. 'What can't be cured must be endured,' she told Sarah, when she had eventually come to terms with her barren state. She visited her sister and her children at least once a year, sometimes twice, and all of them loved her and Sam dearly.

Sarah had never resented the love her children had for her sister and her husband, for didn't she love them herself and felt heartsore that they hadn't been blessed with children? She was quite willing to share hers. Ellen had never suggested taking any away before though and Sarah had serious misgivings. But then, she told herself, she had Mary all the time, and Terry and young Bridie too. Surely she couldn't be selfish enough to begrudge her sister a week or two of her daughter's company?

'Sure don't I know you love my weans?' she told her sister. 'And it's bad of me to deny you Mary's company. It isn't as if she's not due for a holiday from the shirt factory either. I'd say she was more than entitled. So you take her along with you and Sam and Godspeed to all of you.'

Bridie knew then that Mary would go and that she'd miss her desperately. As it was she'd hugged and kissed her that early morning as the family all assembled at the end of the farm where the rail bus would obligingly stop to take Ellen, Sam and Mary on their journey.

As it had pulled up beside them, Mary had peeled herself away from her weeping sister, who was wrapped around her, and had turned to embrace her parents. Ellen had taken Bridie in her arms. 'She'll be back before you know it,' she promised. Bridie had tried to swallow the sobs and nod to Ellen. She couldn't blame her aunt, she loved her too much and anyway she'd heard her mammy say often how hard it was not to have a chick or child belonging to her.

After the rail bus had left the farm and Bridie's parents and Terry returned to the farmhouse, Bridie had climbed up on the five-barred gate as she'd often done with Rosalyn and watched the rail bus chug its way to Derg Bridge Halt, the next station.

From this height, as long as the sun shone, and no mist shrouded the hills you could often see the glint of the tracks disappearing between the two towering peaks in the distance known as Barnes Gap.

Her uncle Francis, Rosalyn's father, would keep

them all entertained on winter evenings with tales of the highwaymen who used to lurk there in the past and prey on the unsuspecting people travelling along the road.

Francis was a gifted storyteller and he could paint a grand picture in words, and Bridie gave a smile at her own foolishness as she remembered how feared she used to be. Today Barnes Gap was a famous landmark where only sheep, not highwaymen, wandered at will.

The sun had turned the rivers running down the mountainsides into silver snakes and a tributary of one of those rivers ran beside the farm. Bridie could see it in the distance and she remembered playing in there as a child and how the boys had learned to swim where it ran deeper behind the rocky waterfall. She gave a sigh of pleasure at the memory as she turned to face her cousin. 'I'd never want to leave here, Rosalyn. I love it all. What more could you want? It's beautiful!'

'Aye. Beautiful and dull, deadly dull,' Rosalyn replied contemptuously. 'But you at least can get away from it. If Mary's place doesn't take your fancy, haven't you two fine brothers in New York?'

Bridie knew she had. They were shadowy figures she could barely remember, who sent weekly letters to her mother Sarah with dollars folded inside them.

'I can't remember either Seamus or Johnnie,' Bridie protested. 'I was only five when they left in 1919, and before that they'd been at the Great War for three years.'

Rosalyn, a year older than Bridie, remembered how happy everyone was that Bridie's older brothers had escaped injury in the Great War that had killed so many and arrived home, if not totally fit and well, at least in one piece.

Their happiness was short-lived though, for in the early spring of 1919, two weeks after the boys had come home, they'd both contracted Spanish flu.

Bridie had crept about the house of sickness on tiptoe, listening to the adults talk. She didn't understand much of it, but knew her brothers were very sick, and with the rest of her family she'd said prayers and attended Masses though she barely knew them.

The two boys had rallied and began on the long road to full recovery when, despite Sarah's efforts to isolate them during their illness, their young brother and sister, Robert and Nuala, then aged seven and nine, caught the flu too. Sarah was worried, but she told herself that the children had previously been fit and healthy, and they'd surely have more resistance than their brothers who'd spent years fighting a war from an open trench they'd shared with ice and mud and rats. However, Sarah had underestimated the speed with which the illness could take hold. Neither Sarah's stringent nursing care, the masses said, novenas begun nor rosaries recited in many neighbouring houses could save the young children who died just two weeks after the onset of the disease.

Bridie had been beside herself with grief, unable to understand how children fit and healthy one day could just up and die in no time at all. Robert and Nuala, the siblings nearest to Bridie's age, had been her playmates, together with Rosalyn and her brother Frank, and Bridie missed them dreadfully. Rosalyn had been almost as badly affected and they'd often crept away together to escape the grief.

It was usually Mary who found and comforted the two wee girls. Sarah and Jimmy were too racked with sadness, Johnnie and Seamus were riven with guilt from bringing the disease into the family, and Terry was busy trying to keep everything ticking over, although he was stunned with sorrow himself.

Then, with the family coming to terms with their loss, Seamus and Johnnie, unable to stand the guilt any longer, suggested going to their uncle Connor in New York in the autumn of 1919. Ireland was on the brink of civil war at the time and Bridie remembered her mother saying the boys had survived the war, as well as pulled round from the Spanish flu, and she didn't want a British Tommy gun to end their lives and so she'd made no objection to them going and trying their luck in America.

Although Bridie barely remembered the two brothers she still got that blood was thicker than water when all was said and done and a brother was a brother. 'I'm sure they'd be delighted if you were to join them,' Rosalyn told Bridie. 'They'd hardly refuse now, would they?'

'Probably not,' Bridie said, considering it. 'But I don't think I'd like America, not from what they say in their letters anyway. I'm not like you, Rosalyn, I'm happy here and Mammy and Daddy would hate me to leave.'

Rosalyn knew that was true. Bridie had been pampered all her life, being the baby of the family. After the deaths of Robert and Nuala, Sarah had taken even greater care of her youngest child. She was slight, very small, and Sarah thought she hadn't the constitution or physique of the children she had left to rear.

She appeared incredibly frail, yet Bridie never sickened for anything. After Robert and Nuala died, Sarah worried constantly about her. The choicest cuts of meat were hers and there was always a newly laid egg and fresh milk whenever she wanted it. She was expected to do little in the house: Sarah said she did enough at school and encouraged her to go out into the sunshine, or sit by the fire to rest herself.

Rosalyn often resented the way Bridie was treated. Apart from her elder brother Frank, there were also four much younger weans at home: her mother had suffered a series of miscarriages after her birth and so she'd been eight when Declan was born, followed by Nora, Connie and Martin. She seldom had a minute to call her own and yet Bridie could swan around the place, being petted by everyone because she looked so sweet.

And she did, that was the very devil of it. She was elfin-looking with large, expressive, deepbrown eyes, ringed with long black lashes, which showed up against her creamy-coloured skin, and just a hint of pink dusted across her cheeks. Her nose was like a little button, and her mouth a perfect rosebud above a slightly pointed chin that showed how stubborn she could be at times, not that she was thwarted in many things she wanted. Bridie's shining glory though was her hair. It was thick, the colour of deep mahogany, and hung in natural waves which were tied back with a ribbon, curling tendrils escaping and framing her pretty little face.

She was well loved, Bridie. Her parents were fair besotted by her and seemed to find it amazing that they had given life to this beautiful, fine-boned child and Mary and Terry petted and spoilt her too. She was also a favourite in Rosalyn's own home and even Frank was gentle with her.

Yes, Bridie had a fine life, Rosalyn thought. Why ever would she want to leave? Yet a restlessness had begun to stir in Rosalyn and she knew Barnes More, which was just three miles away from Donegal Town in neighbouring Northern Ireland, would not be able to hold her for long. 'Well,' she said, 'I intend to go as soon as the opportunity arises. Mammy's brother Aiden keeps talking about trying his luck in the States, but he hasn't done anything about it yet. He's sweet on Maria Flanagan and that's what holding him, Mammy says. I don't intend to get sweet on anyone over here. There are men galore in America. I'll chance my arm there.'

'It's not your arm they'll be looking at I'm thinking,' Bridie said with a broad grin.

'Bridie McCarthy,' Rosalyn shrieked in mock indignation. 'I'll . . .'

But Bridie never found out what Rosalyn was going to say because just at that moment they heard Aunt Delia's voice in the yard. 'Rosalyn! You, Rosalyn!'

'Oh, Dear God, now I'll catch it,' Rosalyn said with a groan, catching sight of her mother's angry stance from the barn window as she stood in the yard below them.

Bridie watched her cousin run across the yard to her mother, feeling sorry for her. She had hardly any time to herself. Once, Bridie had asked her mother whether she thought her aunt Delia was unfair on Rosalyn.

'Well, she has her hands full with four wee ones and all,' Sarah had said. 'And,' she'd added, 'Francis isn't always easy. 'Course, your father won't hear a word said against him.'

Bridie was familiar with the story of how her father Jimmy and his wee brother Francis were the only ones left after cholera had swept through their family. Female relations had arrived in droves to claim wee Francis who was but five. Jimmy had been twenty years old then and refused to let him go. Instead, he had farmed the land and reared the boy himself.

Jimmy had married Sarah when she was just seventeen and she helped in the rearing of Francis, who was by then twelve years old. Later, as a grown man, he had met and married Delia and Jimmy had helped him buy the farm beside them when it became vacant. Because of all this there was a special feeling between the brothers, though they were totally different both in looks and temperament, and the families saw a good deal of one another.

'What's wrong with Uncle Francis?' Bridie had asked, intrigued, for she thought her uncle grand, full of fun and wit and always ready for a wee game or a laugh.

Sarah had given a sniff and with that sniff and from the look she also threw her, Bridie knew she was wasting her time asking. 'Never you mind, Miss,' Sarah had snapped. 'Delia has her work cut out, that's all I'm saying.'

Doesn't need to take it all out on Rosalyn, Bridie thought now as she watched Rosalyn trailing behind her mother across the orchard that separated their house from her aunt and uncle's. Rosalyn had her head down and Bridie guessed she was crying.

She wondered if she should have written and asked Mary if Rosalyn could come with her to Birmingham. But she really wanted Mary to herself. She doubted that Rosalyn would be let come anyway. How would her mother manage without her? Then there was the job she was starting soon in the shirt factory in town. She would be beginning that before Bridie had to go back to school.

At one point it seemed that even Bridie wouldn't be able to go because Sarah didn't want her travelling alone. Normally, Ellen would have come over like a shot to take her back, but she was struck down in bed with a bad attack of rheumatics and couldn't make the trip.

But Bridie was desperate to go and when Terry offered to go with her as far as the boat and meet her from it on her return, Sarah reluctantly agreed. Bridie had grown very fond of Terry who'd been friendlier to her since Mary had left, knowing how much Bridie would miss her. Now the two got along well, even though Terry was seven years older than her.

Despite Bridie's spirited claim that she could look after herself, she was glad Terry was beside her to negotiate rail buses and trains, especially when she saw the big port of Belfast where the ferry was waiting. Bridie suddenly wished Terry was coming all the way with her. Terry wished that too when he saw Bridie hanging over the deck rail, the case hurriedly borrowed from their uncle Francis beside her nearly as big as she was.

For two pins he'd have hopped up there with her and hang the consequences. He was at any rate heartily sick of the farm. But he knew he couldn't do that to his father, not just leave him in the lurch that way. So he waved goodbye to his little sister as the boat set sail and hoped she'd remember what he'd said about changing trains at a place called Crewe.

However, Bridie had the vulnerable appearance of someone who needed looking after and, in a boat packed with Irish families, she was befriended by many a mothering soul. They were a great comfort when she felt a little sick and a true help when it was time to disembark. Someone eventually settled her onto a train bound for Crewe and, once on the train, Bridie again found that people were only too happy to assist a wee girl travelling alone and there was someone to carry her case and direct her to the right train for Birmingham. Bridie knew without all those kind people she would have been utterly lost.

Even with their help though when she finally alighted from the train at New Street Station, she felt exhausted and frightened, and stood on the windy, dirty platform, surrounded by bags, wishing she'd never come. She was scared witless of the noise around her. People shouted at each other above the din and there were sudden yells as people greeted others and sometimes gales of raucous laughter.

Porters rushed about with trolleys full of suit-cases. 'Out the way,' they'd cry, or more politely, 'Mind your backs.' But above it all was the noise of the trains: the hiss of the water on the tracks, the pants of steam, the ear-splitting screech of the whistles and the roar of trains approaching other platforms, arriving in a cloud of smoke.

Never had she been so glad to see anything as she was to see Mary's welcoming face, her warm, comfortable arms enveloping Bridie immediately and taking much of her fear away. 'Oh God, Mary, how do you live in such a place?' she cried. 'How d'you stand it?'

'Och, sure you get used to it,' Mary said dismissively. 'Come on away home. I've the house shining like a new pin and food fit for a king to cook for you.'

Bridie was terrified by the tram ride, far too frightened to take in the things of interest they passed which Mary pointed out to her. They alighted by the shops in a road called Bristol Street and she felt as if all her bones had been loosened. They turned up a little alleyway called Bristol Passage and came out into Bell Barn Road and Bridie stood for a moment and stared. There were row upon row of houses squashed up together, all grim and grey, matching the pavements and cobbled streets. But Mary didn't seem to notice her sister's horrified face. 'Come on,' she urged and, pointing down the road, added, 'Aunt Ellen's house is just down there. She's in Bell Barn Road, and we're just beside her in Grant Street. We'll go around later, I'm seeing to things while she's laid up.'

Mary's front door opened straight onto the street, with another door in the entry leading

17

down to the courtyard. Bridie was to find out during her stay that six houses opened on to that yard. The brewhouse was there too, where Mary, along with everyone else, did her washing on Mondays with the one shared tap. Mary told Bridie the tap often froze altogether in the winter, but added it was a grand place to hear all the gossip while you awaited your turn.

On fine Monday mornings, the washing lines crisscrossing the yard were filled with flapping washing, lifted into the sooty Birmingham air with the aid of tall props. The miskins were kept there too, where people tipped their ashes and where the communal dustbins often spilled rubbish on to the cobbles, and beside them, at the bottom of the yard, were lavatories which were shared by two families.

But that first day, looking around the inside of Mary's room, Bridie thought it was as small as it had looked from the road. Her head was reeling. She had no understanding of such places, of so many people, families, living together: it seemed there was no space, no air for them to breathe at all.

And yet Mary seemed ridiculously proud of her house and she had made an effort for Bridie's visit. A new rag rug was in front of the shining fender and the mantelshelf was dotted with plaster ornaments each side of the large wooden clock in the centre. Above the mantelpiece was the familiar picture of the Sacred Heart of Jesus, and to the side of the fire was an alcove, which housed the wireless. Bridie remembered how Mary had written home in such excitement about it.

> *We have to have something called an accumulator to get it to work and have it charged at the garage on Bristol Street. However, really it's no problem and grand altogether to have music on or even a play to listen to now and again.*

'We have a new gas cooker too now,' Mary said proudly. 'We used to cook on the fire when we first came here.'

Bridie had noticed the hooks on the chimney wall, reminiscent of her own home, and she now turned to look at the large, squat, gas cooker positioned between the table on one side and the door to the scullery on the other. There was also a press, which Mary called a sideboard, with more ornaments on it. 'I keep good plates and glasses and such in there,' Mary said as she tipped water from a lidded bucket into the kettle. 'I don't keep anything of importance in the scullery, the walls run with water in the winter.'

Bridie had a peep inside and could see, even on this summer's day, what Mary meant. There was little there, just three shelves, housing a variety of odd plates and cups, a stone sink and steps leading to the coal cellar. There was no tap, but Bridie had expected none as Mary had already told her family when she wrote to them that they got their water from a tap in the yard that often froze altogether in the winter. 'Shall I take my case up first and get settled in?' she asked.

Mary nodded. 'Aye, if you like. I'll have a cup of tea waiting for you when you come down. I'd best start the tea or Eddie will be in on top of us and not a bite ready.'

'Where am I to sleep?'

'In the attic, pet,' Mary said. 'We've borrowed a mattress for you, but the sheets and blankets are my own. The bed's made up for you, but you can put your things in the cupboard. There's a hook if you want to hang anything up, unless it's anything special like your clothes for Mass – I'll put those in my wardrobe. Leave them down on my bed and I'll see to them.'

In the attic another rag rug had been placed between the mattress laid on the floor and the cupboard, covering the bare boards. There was no other furniture and the room was dim with the only light coming from a dusty skylight.

Having put her belongings away, Bridie was glad to return to the living room. Mary had drawn the curtains and lit the gaslights which now popped and spluttered. She'd lit the fire too and it danced merrily in the hearth and Bridie was glad of it, for the evening had turned chilly. She had to admit that it all looked rather cosy. Mary handed her a cup of tea while she lit the gas beneath a pan of potatoes and another of cabbage.

'Now,' she said, 'I don't have to do the bacon for a while yet, so take the weight off your feet and tell me the news from home.'

What Bridie found particularly hardest to cope with in those early days in Birmingham was the noise. Inside the cottage in Ireland, it was often so quiet you could hear the peat settling into the grate, the ticking of the mantle clock, or her father puffing on his pipe.

Outside, she might hear the gentle lowing of the cows and the clucking of the hens, or the sweet singing of the birds. She'd hear the wind setting, the trees swaying and the soft swishing sound as the breeze rippled through the long grass, or the river rumbling as it ran across its stony bed.

There was nothing to prepare her for this crush of humanity, the walls so thin every sound the neighbours made could be heard. She hated the shrieking of the children in the street just outside the window and the cackling laughter and shouting of the women doing their washing in the brewhouse. She hated the tramp of hobnail boots on the cobbles as the men made their way to work and the factory hooters slicing into the quiet of early morning.

But most of all she hated the traffic: the clanking trams and rumbling omnibuses, the roar of petrol-drawn lorries and vans and cars. Even the dull clop of horses' hooves disturbed her. These city horses were as unlike those at home as it was possible to be. They were tired and sad-looking. And why wouldn't they be, Bridie thought, with hard roads beneath their feet day in, day out. She wondered where they were stabled because there was precious little grass to be found. She guessed the horses saw as little of it as the people.

And that was another thing, the people. They unnerved her. She supposed they were kind enough, but their voices grated on her and she could barely understand what they said anyway, their accents were so alien. She couldn't seem to get away anywhere to be alone, to have a bit of privacy, and she wondered if Rosalyn would have made a better fist of it than she was doing. Frowning, she admitted she probably would.

She couldn't say any of this to Mary though. How could she? Mary had chosen to make her home in this hateful place and so Bridie couldn't go around moaning and complaining. But she was incredibly homesick and eventually felt if she didn't tell someone how she felt she would burst and so, without mentioning a word to Mary, she poured her heart out to her mother in a letter, telling her everything that she hated about the city her sister lived in. She told her parents of something else too. She'd wondered when she'd arrived why there were so many idle men about. They lolled on street corners, hands usually in their pockets and flat caps on their head. Back home in Ireland, she'd seldom seen a man idle in the middle of the day, unless it was a Fair Day, and she'd asked

Mary about it, revealing all to her parents in a letter home:

Mary said the men have been that way since they were demobbed from the army. There is no work for them and many of the families are starving. I know she's right, for you only have to see the children, with pinched-in faces like old people's and so thin they're just skin and bone. They have arms like sticks and quite a few have running sores on their body. Most of them are clothed in rags and many are barefoot. Aunt Ellen said even in the dead of winter it's just the same.

Bridie was no stranger to running barefoot. In her mind, to cast off her shoes and run across the springy turf and leap the streams was linked to the freedom of summer – few children back home wore shoes then. However, in September, before she returned to school, along with the schoolbooks and jotters her parents bought her, there would be a pair of shoes. They mightn't be new, but they would be freshly soled and heeled, and there would be stockings too to keep her from freezing altogether.

She looked at the children around the streets and hanging around the Bull Ring when she went there with Mary and wondered if many of them had ever had shoes. She doubted that when the winter chill came they'd have thicker clothes to wear either, or a good, warm coat and hats, gloves and scarves to keep the life in them.

It's awful, Mammy, is surely is to see so many people living like this, she wrote.

There had been poverty at home in Ireland, of course there had, and people with large families they could barely feed used to get food vouchers from the St Vincent de Paul fund. The nuns there would find clothes for the children to wear, but here it was the sheer numbers of poor that overwhelmed her.

It bothered Sarah too when she read Bridie's letter. 'Fancy not having shoes for the winter,' she remarked. 'Although I shouldn't think it's pleasant running barefoot through city streets at any time.'

'It's the men out of work that I feel sorry for,' Jimmy said. 'God, what that would do to a man, not being able to provide for his family. Seems to me Ireland wasn't the only one betrayed by that damned war. "Land fit for heroes" and they can't earn a bite to put in their families' mouths.'

'Aye,' Sarah agreed with a sigh. 'It must be dreadful and Bridie doesn't seem to be enjoying it at all.'

'Ah well, she'll soon be home again,' Jimmy said, 'and then life will go back to normal. No danger of Bridie taking a liking to the place and wanting to live there anyway.' And that made Jimmy a happy man – it would make his world complete if, when

Bridie did decide to marry, it was to one of the local boys and she'd live not far from them.

'Aye,' Sarah said with feeling, for she'd missed her youngest daughter and longed to have her home again. When she'd been placed in Sarah's arms after her birth, Sarah thought she'd never rear her. She thought she'd go the way of the three she lost to TB after Johnnie. Then when Robert and Nuala had both died, she was convinced that Bridie would never reach adulthood. But here she was, on the threshold of it, and still fit and healthy, as beautiful and kindly as ever. 'Aye, she'll be home soon enough,' Sarah said with satisfaction. 'And, if you ask me, I think it will be a long time before she goes so far again.' She could have added, 'Unlike Mary.' She'd been so upset when Mary went on her wee holiday in the spring of 1926 and had fallen in love with a man called Eddie Coghlan. It had only helped slightly that Eddie was from Derry and a good Catholic into the bargain, because it still meant their daughter would be living and bringing up any grandchildren miles away from them.

Sarah had been inclined to blame her sister and wrote her a letter telling her so but, as Jimmy said, love is not a thing you can watch out for. Ellen couldn't have known that Mary would lose her heart to a man at the Easter dance they'd taken her to at their local Parish Church. At least, he'd said in Eddie's defence, he was in work, not everyone was as fortunate.

So Eddie was welcomed into the family and

Sarah never admitted how much she missed her eldest daughter. As long as she had Bridie, she told herself, she would be content, so Sarah was glad Bridie was disliking the place so much.

But, little by little, Bridie got used to the noise and bustle of the city and started to enjoy her stay at Mary's. Eddie went out of his way to make her welcome, but she most enjoyed the times she had alone with Mary. One day, when they were alone in the house, she asked her a question that had been playing on her mind since she arrived, for Mary looked far rounder than she remembered her. 'Mary, are you having a baby?'

'Aye. Didn't Mammy tell you?'

'No. Why didn't you? You never said in your letters.'

'It's silly to say the same thing twice,' Mary said. 'I write to you about different things, but I did think Mammy would say. I'm five months now. What did you think, that I'd just put on weight?' Without waiting for Bridie's reply, she asked, 'Would you like to feel it kick?'

Bridie flushed and looked at her as if she couldn't believe her ears. 'Don't you mind?'

'Not at all.'

Bridie put her hand out and felt the child move beneath her fingers and saw the material of the smock Mary had on ripple. She was awed by the thought of a living being inside her sister. And then, because it was her sister and she felt comfortable enough, she asked the question she'd puzzled over for an age: 'Mary, how did it get in there?'

Mary was surprised Bridie hadn't tumbled to it living on a farm. But then she remembered Bridie was always sent elsewhere when the bull or rams were due to service their cows and sheep. It was an effort to protect her, Mary supposed, but children could be protected too much.

She bit on her lip as she considered whether to divulge the whole matter of sex with her younger sister. She'd never get the information from their mother, she knew that, because she'd never discuss anything so intimate. Mary had got all her information from Aunt Ellen and she often thanked God she had.

So she told Bridie how the seed inside her had grown into a baby and watched Bridie's eyes open wider and wider in shock as she spoke. 'Something else occurs before a woman can have a baby,' Mary told her. 'They're called periods and they mean you bleed from your private parts every month. You need to know: I began mine at school and because I hadn't been warned, I thought I was dying. Sister Ambrose eventually found me in the toilets, limp from crying, and explained it to me and took me home.'

'Was Mammy cross?'

'No,' Mary said. 'But she was embarrassed. She told me she had linen pads in the press ready and I was to pin one to my liberty bodice. When they were soiled I was to put them in the bucket she'd leave ready and that respectable women didn't need to know any more than that, in fact they didn't need to talk of it at all.'

'And that bleeding happens to every woman every month?' Bridie asked, curling her mouth in distaste.

'Aye,' Mary said, smiling at her sister's discomfort. 'I'm afraid it does. It's a sort of preparation for motherhood and even people like Aunt Ellen, who've never had children, have periods.'

'So, when . . . How will I know when it will be?' Bridie asked.

'Your body will change first,' Mary told her. 'Your breasts will begin to grow and you'll get hair down below.'

Bridie let out a sigh of relief. She'd been horrified to see the little swellings around her nipples and even more so to see hair sprouting where it had never done before, certain that she was abnormal and too worried to even contemplate discussing it with Rosalyn.

Mary heard the sigh and saw the relief, but hid her smile. She was glad she'd told her. 'But,' she cautioned her, 'don't you be telling Mammy about this, d'you hear? She'll have my mouth washed out with carbolic.'

'I won't,' Bridie promised with a giggle, visualising her mother forcing a bar of soap into Mary's mouth. 'I'm glad you've told me. I've wondered, you know.'

'Of course you've wondered, it's natural,' Mary

said. 'And you needed to be told. But one thing I do agree with Mammy about is respecting yourself. It's all the advice she ever gave me, but for all that she was right. Boys will try to ... well, you know what I mean, and if you let them, they'll not respect you anymore. Wait for the ring like I did. Believe me, it's worth it.'

'I don't know if I want to get married,' Bridie said doubtfully. 'I don't think I want to be doing that sort of thing to make babies either.'

'Oh you will, little sister,' Mary said with a laugh. 'You will.'

CHAPTER TWO

Almost as soon as Terry picked Bridie up at the docks three weeks later, she knew there was something wrong with him. But she also knew to press him would only annoy and so she waited for him to tell her.

She hadn't long to wait: Terry was bursting to tell somebody his news and as soon as they were seated on the train, he couldn't contain himself. Bridie looked at him in astonishment. 'Leave the farm? But, Terry . . .'

'Hear me out first,' Terry said, 'and then judge if you want to, Bridie.'

Bridie nodded and Terry went on. 'Look at me – I'm twenty years old in a week's time, I never go out, I've never dated a girl in all my life and why? Because I never get a penny piece of my own, that's why. Oh, they point out, Mam and Dad, that this place will be mine one day – Seamus will hardly want it – and they remind me I have a warm house and plenty of food and clothes bought for me when I need them. Aye, I do, working clothes and a suit for Mass that I never even get to choose the colour and style of.

'I can't stand it, I tell you, Bridie. I don't like farming anyway, never have, and I won't grub around in this place for much longer, with Mammy doling out small amounts of money to me for the collection at Mass as if I was a wean.'

Bridie saw some of the injustices of Terry's predicament that she'd never realised before. 'Oh, Terry,' she said. 'Couldn't you tell Mammy and Daddy how you feel?'

'Do you think I haven't tried?' Terry snapped. 'It's like talking to a brick wall.'

'But where will you go?'

'New York,' Terry said. 'Seamus and Johnnie said they'd send me the fare.'

'But what about a job?' Bridie said, for she knew as well as any that unemployment was rife everywhere since the Great War and getting worse. 'It's as bad there as here. Worse, in fact. They have soup kitchens in America, Terry.'

'I know,' Terry said. 'That's the threat Mam and Dad use when I've mentioned it to them. Not that I've said that much, you know. I've just tested the ground as it were. I wrote to Johnnie and he said he can probably get me set on alongside him in time. There's nothing for now, but he's keeping an eye out and will send for me. I'm willing to work. I'll not go to America and live off him and

31

Seamus, never fear. All I'm waiting for is word and the money for the fare.'

Bridie knew then that eventually Terry would go. It might be weeks or even months, but he wouldn't stay.

However, the weeks rolled by and soon winter was upon them again and still no word came from America. Still and all, Bridie told herself, there might not be a place in America for Terry for a long while. She couldn't imagine Johnnie and Seamus to be the only Irish boys with relations clamouring to join them. The dole queues in America were as long as those anywhere else and why would they take another person into the country when it made more sense to employ one of their own?

That winter proved to be a severe one and both Jimmy and Francis were worried about their pregnant ewes. Rosalyn came over one day and complained how bad-tempered her father had become lately. Bridie expressed surprise – Francis usually had a smile on his face and had a far more relaxed attitude to life than his brother Jimmy.

They were, as usual, in the barn and Rosalyn peered out of the barn window as she said, 'Poor things to be born in this anyway.' She rubbed at the window with a mittened hand, clearing the ice. 'I mean just look at it,' she said. The landscape before them was covered in snow blown into drifts at the sides of the fields and gilding the trees and hedges.

Bridie shivered, despite her thick coat. 'Aye, you'd think they'd wait till spring is really here and the snow had at least disappeared,' she said. 'I think God slipped up there.'

Rosalyn gave her a push. 'Don't let the priest hear you say that, Bridie McCarthy,' she said in mock severity while her eyes twinkled. 'You'll spend the rest of your life on your knees repenting, you will.'

'Aye? Well, I'll say one for you when I'm down there,' Bridie promised with a smile.

But in all truth there was not much to smile about during those bitterly cold days and the only bright news at all that awful January was that Mary had given birth to a baby and named him Jamie after her father. Jimmy was ridiculously pleased by the gesture and that evening talked of Mary coming home when the baby was a bit older. 'Show me my namesake,' he said with a broad grin.

Bridie was glad to see that smile; for far too long her father had had a frown creasing his brow. It was a pity, then, that Terry had to spoil it. 'Aye, that's right. Get another one back here that you can chain to the bloody land.'

'I chain nobody, boy.'

'Yes you bloody do,' Terry said, leaping up and reaching for his coat.

'Where are you going? There's work to do.'

'Oh,' said Terry in mock surprise. 'You surprise me! Work, is there? Well, get some other silly bugger to do it. I'm away out.'

'Terry! Come back here!'

As the door slammed shut, Bridie looked fearfully at her father, but he made no effort to follow his wayward son. The peat in the fire settled and hissed and the clock's tick seemed very loud. Everyone seemed fearful of breaking the silence and Bridie picked up a sock from the mending basket by her mother's feet and began to darn the large hole in the heel.

By mid-March, the long months of the winter were behind them. The snow and ice were long gone, the lambs had all been born fine and healthy and spring planting was going on apace. The sun was shining in a bright blue sky and Bridie, having celebrated her fourteenth birthday in February, felt happy with her world.

She was, however, rather at a loose end. It was a Saturday and also a Fair Day in the town, where the farmers bought and sold their stock. Terry and her daddy had gone in early with some calves to sell. They'd offered her a lift into town, but she'd said she'd not felt like it that day but then, calling to see Rosalyn, she found she'd also gone into town with her own brother and father very early that morning. 'She thought you'd be gone in too,' said Delia.

'No,' Bridie said. 'Daddy offered, but I didn't fancy it today. Never mind, I'll see Rosalyn later.'

After helping her mother all morning, she'd been too fidgety to stay in and had gone out tramping the hills later that afternoon. Everyone seemed either to be indoors or in town because she met not a soul and so was pleased on her return to see her uncle Francis approaching her as she neared the outskirts of the farm. She waved to him.

It was as she got nearer that she noticed his strange gait, his slightly glazed eyes and slack mouth, and she realised that her uncle was drunk. She wasn't totally surprised. He'd been in the town for many hours and the bars, open all day, would be thronged with friends and acquaintances with nothing to do for hours but drink and reminisce. Many men, her father included, would probably be the worse for wear that day.

'And how's my favourite girl today?' Francis cried.

'Ah, then it must be me you're talking about since there's not another soul around for miles,' Bridie answered with a laugh.

In two strides, Francis was alongside his niece. 'God, Bridie, but you're a sight for sore eyes,' he said. His voice was husky and thick and the way he was looking at her was sending shivers of alarm down her spine. She told herself not to be stupid. This was Francis who she'd known all her life. Dear God! There was no need to be nervous of him. He'd got drunk and was acting oddly, that was all.

'Hush, Uncle Francis,' she said in a voice she forced to be steady. 'You'll have my head swelling and I'll not get in the door.'

Francis, his mind addled by the many pints

of ale he'd drank that day, was confused. Bridie was his niece and yet he wasn't seeing her as a niece, but as a desirable young lady and one he'd secretly lusted after for months. It was a fact he'd kept hidden from everyone and the guilt had made him short-tempered with them all at home.

But now here she was, all alone and not a soul about. He grabbed her around the waist and, stunned, she made no protest until he held her against him, his hand clamped against her back. Bridie remembered what Mary had told her about men and women just the previous summer and when she felt the hardness of her uncle she knew what it was that he was pressing against her. She was suddenly aware of every bit of him and she started to wriggle and protest.

Francis's thick lips descended on Bridie's, holding her so tight she was unable to get away. When she felt her uncle's hand trailing up her leg, she was filled with panic. Lifting her foot, she stamped on his toes with all her might and Francis, taken unawares, slackened his hold slightly and she was able to twist out of his grasp. She stood facing him, her eyes sparkling with anger, and her chest heaving. 'What d'you think you're doing, Uncle Francis?'

Francis was angry with himself. What had compelled him to grab Bridie like that? He'd fought the attraction this long while and now . . . now, to give in like this. But it would never do for her, for anyone, to guess his thoughts and so he answered angrily:

'What d'you mean, what am I doing? You could see what I was doing, giving you a kiss and cuddle, as I've done since you were a child. There was no need to make such a fuss and near lame me in the process.'

Doubts began to creep into Bridie's mind. Had she read too much into what Francis had done? True, the kiss was one he'd never given her before and she hadn't liked it much, but that could have been because he was drunk. It could all have been down to the drink. Maybe she'd exaggerated the whole thing. She must have done, she told herself, for her uncle Francis would never hurt her, she was sure of that.

She felt rather silly as she said softly, 'I'm sorry, Uncle Francis. I didn't mean to offend you.'

'Yes, well, we'll say no more about it,' Francis said. 'I might have surprised you a wee bit and I've been drinking all day.'

Relief flooded through Bridie. That was it then. She'd been foolish. 'You'll not tell them at home, sure you won't?' she asked her uncle.

'Not a bit of it,' Francis replied. 'Don't fresh yourself. This will be just between us two.'

But for all Bridie's relief, she tried to make sure after that that she was never alone with her uncle, especially when he'd taken a drink, for she saw his eyes on her, sometimes in a most disturbing way.

She never tramped the hills again either and, on Fair Days, she either stayed around the farmhouse with her mother, or went into the town with her father and stuck like glue to Rosalyn.

She finished school in June and Sarah told her to have a wee holiday before looking for a job. Bridie hadn't forgotten Terry's threat, but it had been so long now with never a word that she'd pushed it to the back of her mind. She told herself it might be years before Terry was able to go to America.

She really wanted a job in the shirt factory in town beside Rosalyn, but she knew if Terry did leave, a job off the farm would be out of the question. It was too big for her father to manage on his own and she'd be the only one of the family left then. She'd have to stay and help him. Because she was the youngest and so small, she'd been protected from much of the work. Now, she faced the fact that if she was to be of any help to her father and not a hindrance altogether, she would have to learn, and fast, for farms carried few passengers.

She began to tail Terry as he went about his jobs and Terry, admiring her guts and determination, took time to teach her, even though he worried that some of the work might be too much for her.

'Talk Daddy into getting someone in to help once I've gone,' he told her one day. 'I'm going to tell him you can't manage because I don't really think you'll be able to do all I do. And for God's sake, if you're determined to take on the farm, stick out for a proper wage. It's only fair and it's important to have money in your pocket.'

Bridie knew all Terry said was true, but she couldn't see her daddy hiring help. It went against his principles of it being a family farm. Maybe she'd grow a wee bit more yet before Terry was ready to leave and there was always Frank within calling distance. She was sure he'd give her a hand if she needed it. Rosalyn always said he had a soft spot for her. The point about a wage, however, was a good one. One reason for getting a job, as well as helping the family out, was to have money to spend as she wished.

One day in late July, when the warm sun shone in a sky of Wedgewood blue, Terry was working in the fields when he saw the postman, Abel Maloney, turn in the lane. It wasn't that unusual, so Terry took little notice, until Abel hailed him. Almost every week, Abel carried letters to the McCarthy house from their sons in America and he knew their writing well, so he said to Terry, 'Your brothers are after writing to you now too.'

Terry stared at the man for a second or two before the significance of what he said caused him to throw down his spade, leap the hedge and take the letter from his outstretched hand. He went to the privy – the only place he could think of where he wouldn't be disturbed – and ripped the envelope open.

Dollar bills were folded inside the letter and

Terry stuffed those into the pockets of his breeches and smoothed out the sheet of paper.

Okay kiddo,
I just might have a job for you at last. The factory are setting up new lines making waterproof mackintoshes and they'll be up and running in three weeks or so. I'll put your name forward, but there would be hundreds after each vacancy, so there is no way I can hold it for you and there will be a damned long wait for anything else if you let this one go. I presume you have primed Mammy and Daddy what you intended to do when the time was right so I advise you to waste no time in buying a ticket and getting your arse over here pronto. See you soon hopefully.
All the best
Johnnie

Excitement leapt inside Terry initially and then reality struck. It was about the very worst time to leave the farm with not even the hay gathered in. But then was there ever a good time to leave a farm? And as Johnnie said, if he passed this offer up, then he might as well say goodbye to his dreams of going to America altogether. Johnnie thought he must have discussed the possibility of him joining his brothers with their parents, but though they'd both sensed his dissatisfaction, the idea that he might leave the farm had never occurred to them and Terry wished now he'd given some hint of it. Well, he thought, that can soon be remedied. The sooner he told them the better for speed was of the essence, so he squared his shoulders and made his way to the farmhouse.

The resultant row was so fast and furious that Bridie fled to the bedroom and buried her head beneath the bedclothes. Sarah pleaded and cried and Jimmy thundered and roared while Terry shouted back. Francis and Delia were brought in to try to talk some sense into the boy and the following day Father O'Dwyer was called.

By then, Terry was barely speaking to his parents, but his determination to leave had not been altered at all though everyone had thought and said he was wrong, ungrateful, neglecting his filial duty. His parents, their farm and their welfare were, they said, his responsibility. Who was to help them now if he ran away like this? Surely to God he couldn't expect his wee sister to take up the reins?

Bridie tried to keep out of it. She wanted no one to see the tears she shed, for it would be just another stick to beat Terry with. She knew she'd miss him more than anyone – it had been just the two of them for so long and she knew she'd be lonely. It wouldn't have mattered so much if she'd been going into town to work; then there would have been Rosalyn and other girls to talk to through the day, but she knew it would be the loneliness as well as the workload that might wear her down now.

'Do you hate me, Bridie?' Terry asked, coming

across her in the barn in tears. He'd fought all the people that opposed him and pleaded with him and yet it was Bridie, who had said so little, who played on his mind.

Bridie raised her face, her eyes red and swollen from crying. She knew Terry had his ticket and would be leaving in the next few days and she wanted to bang her little fists on his chest and tell him he couldn't go. What was he thinking of to leave her like this?

But how could she let her brother go with only recriminations ringing in his ears? 'No,' she said. 'I don't hate you, but I'm sad – I'll miss you.'

'Oh God,' Terry said, feeling ashamed for his sister's sake. 'I'll send for you, Bridie, when I've . . .'

'You know I can't leave here,' Bridie said quietly, and she put her arms around Terry and kissed him on the cheek and left him, sobbing.

Terry left in August 1928 and, in the early weeks, Bridie often felt she couldn't go on. She saw the farm for the first time as Terry had seen it: one relentless round of work with never an hour, never mind a day, off to do with as she pleased.

At first, she sought her bed straight after the evening meal, so tired even her bones ached. However, bit by bit, her body became accustomed to the hard physical work and she had a wage to be picked up at the end of every week to look forward to, though her parents had balked at that initially.

'But why do you want a wage, Bridie?' Sarah had asked.

'Everyone has a wage, Mammy, if they do a job.'

'Yes, of course, if you work outside the home,' Sarah had conceded. 'Here you get your meals and clothes bought for you when you need them.'

'Ah, but d'you see, Mammy, that's it,' Bridie had said. 'You say I have clothes when I need them, but really you mean your choice of clothes when you think I need them. As for meals, wouldn't anyone working here be fed?'

'Well, yes,' Sarah had had to agree. 'But . . .'

'There isn't any but in this, Mammy,' Bridie had said, hardening her heart against her parents' confused faces. 'There has been no cost to you in working clothes, for I'm wearing Terry's.'

She was, too, although they had been refashioned. By taking in the crotch and chopping inches off the legs of the breeches and cutting down the work shirts, repositioning the buttons and chopping the sleeves to fit, she had her made them fit her just right.

'I'd like the same as Rosalyn earns in the shirt factory,' Bridie had said. 'Less what she pays in keep. I think that's fair.'

'Fair or not,' Jimmy had said, 'none of our other children have demanded a wage for working their own place.'

'It's not my place, it's yours,' Bridie had reminded him. 'And I know Terry asked for a wage because

43

he told me. Maybe if he'd been given one he'd have stayed longer.'

'Are you threatening me, Bridie? I'll not stand that,' Jimmy had blustered. 'Big as you are . . .'

'Daddy, I'm threatening no one,' Bridie had said gently. 'I'm just stating facts. I'll work as hard as I'm able, but I need money of my own.'

Jimmy had knocked his pipe against the hearth, filled it with infinite slowness and drew on it. He had no wish to alienate his darling daughter 'Well,' he had said at last, 'I think what Bridie has suggested is only fair.'

Sarah had looked at him, open-mouthed, while Bridie had reached up and kissed her father's stubbly chin. 'Thank you, Daddy,' she had said. 'I appreciate you listening to me.'

She had missed the look that passed between her parents, the one that said they'd raised a treasure, a daughter in a million, for that treasure, worn-out by hard work, had taken her weary bones to bed.

Francis wondered if Bridie had any idea of how fetching she looked as she worked the fields in her brother's cut-down clothes. She was like a wean dressing up, except no wean had a figure like the one she was developing. Her eyes were like pools of dark brown treacle and could flash fire, but mainly sparkled with laughter, and however her hair was tied back, curls would always escape. Sometimes just to look at her could stop the blood pulsing in his body. He knew he could do nothing about it but look, for the girl was his niece and yet but a child. But God, if things were different . . .

Francis was on his way to the McCarthy house for a rambling session with these thoughts churning in his head. In the late autumn and winter, with the harvest safely gathered in, rambling nights were popular in the country houses.

Word got around that a rambling was to be held at such a house and neighbours and friends would come from all over. The men often had an instrument with them and always a drink of some kind. It was usually poteen, which was brewed in stills in the hills of Donegal, as everyone knew but no one spoke of.

The women would bring slices of soda bread, or barn brack or similar, and sometimes a bottle of homemade wine, and in an instant a party would begin with the rag rugs rolled up for the dancing.

One of Bridie's earliest memories was of lying in her bed, her toes curling with excitement at the tantalising music and the rhythmic tap of the women's feet as they danced on the stone slabs of the cottage floor below. There'd be a break halfway through when they'd eat and drink deeply and talk. The murmur of voices would rise and fall, sometimes heated and raised in argument, sometimes quieter and gentler. But the music would always begin again and she'd go to sleep with the tunes running through her head.

Now, though, Bridie was allowed to stay up for the rambling. She had turned out of her work clothes and after a wash from the basin in her room, she had changed into her second-best dress and was ready with Sarah to greet the first arrivals.

Francis was one of the last guests to arrive and there was a whistle of approval as he drew a large bottle of poteen from beneath his coat. 'I hope you didn't get that from Tommy Flaherty?' one of the men said. 'I heard the Garda are after him.'

'Christ, haven't they been after him for years?' another put in. 'Haven't caught him yet?'

'He's too wily a fox for them,' said the first man.

'Anyway,' Francis said. 'They're only cross because he won't supply them. They like a drop the same as the rest of us.'

'The priests do at any rate, I know that,' said Jimmy. 'I passed on a bottle to Father O'Dwyer once and he was delighted with me so.'

'Aye,' Francis said. 'Did you hear the one about the young curate from England who came to help out a country priest in Ireland? He'd had a man in confession admitting to making poteen. As he'd never heard of such a thing before and wasn't sure of the penance to give him, he went to the older priest and said, "There's a man here making poteen. What shall I give him?"

'"Well, be careful now," said the older priest. "These men would fleece the likes of you. I never give more than three and six a bottle."'

There were gales of laughter at this. 'It's right enough too,' one said when the laughter had died down. 'Stingy buggers, priests.'

'Come on,' Jimmy cried. 'The night's running away with us and we've not played a tune yet.'

Bridie helped the women pile food onto plates on the big table, but surreptitiously watched the dancers. Mary had taught her some dances before she went away, but she'd not performed any since she'd left and was surprised how much she remembered. One of the women, seeing her watching, seized her hand and pulled her in to join them and she danced along with the rest.

She was glad when a halt was called for the food – the sweat was running from her – and she slipped outside for the night air to cool her down, walking a little way away from the house towards the orchard.

When she heard footsteps behind her she turned, expecting it to be one of the other women as hot as herself and taking the air, but it was her uncle Francis.

Bridie hadn't forgotten her earlier encounter with her uncle, but had passed it off as a one-off experience and not something to be too worried about. And yet she felt alarm as she remembered her uncle drinking deeply of the poteen that evening.

But, she told herself, she could come to no harm. She could see the light of the cottage, other people were no distance away. She was safe and so she relaxed a little. 'I think you're avoiding me, Bridie,' Francis said, wagging his finger in the exaggerated manner of the drunk.

'Not at all,' she said.

'Oh, I think so,' Francis said. He put his hands on her shoulders and turned her around to face him. 'Are you afraid of me?'

'No. No . . .'

'I don't think that's true,' Francis said. 'Have I ever hurt you?'

'No.'

'Am I likely to then?'

'I don't suppose so.'

'So you won't object to giving me a kiss?'

'No,' Bridie said. 'But only on your cheek.'

'Jesus, that's a wean's kiss,' Francis said and, before Bridie could respond further, clasped her tight against him again, but this time his other hand caressed her breasts and began fumbling at the fastenings of her dress before she managed to break free. Her dress hung half open, the bodice underneath exposed and the hair she'd spent hours putting up hanging in untidy strands around her face, which was red with shame.

'You mustn't do such things,' she said, turning her back on her uncle to fasten herself up and tidy her hair. 'What if I was to go to the house and say?'

'Say what?' Francis said. 'I'd say you led me on. You left the house first, remember. What if I say you'd arranged it all. No one will blame a man for taking what's on offer.'

'You wouldn't do that!' Bridie cried, swinging round to face Francis again. 'You wouldn't be so cruel!'

But as she looked into his face she knew he would and, what's more, she knew he'd be believed above her. Maybe her parents would believe her, but even then there would be doubt and suspicion. 'Why do you hate me so?' she cried in distress.

'Hate you!' Francis said incredulously. 'How can you say such a thing, Bridie? I love you. You are incredibly beautiful. It almost hurts to look at you, but you're a temptress. You tempt men with those big eyes, with those long eyelashes you flutter so seductively, your luscious figure, your young beautiful breasts, your . . .'

'Stop it! Stop it,' Bridie commanded. 'You mustn't talk this way, Uncle Francis. It's the drink talking.'

'Aye, maybe it is at that,' Francis said, but he knew this feeling he had for Bridie never went away, it was just when he was sober he could keep it in check.

'I'm going back to the house now,' Bridie said. 'Don't follow me, please . . .'

Francis said nothing as she walked away and once in the house, she pleaded a headache and said she was ready for her bed. 'I thought the air might clear it,' she said, explaining her previous absence. 'But it didn't.'

'I wondered where you'd disappeared to,' Jimmy said. 'Did you see Francis on your travels?'

'Yes,' Bridie said. 'He's over by the orchard,' and then she fled to her room, closing the door before she let the tears fall.

*　　*　　*

49

By the time Bridie was sixteen she was beginning to feel desperate about Francis, for try as she might to avoid him, he seemed to find many occasions when he would get her on her own. Even when he just ogled her, it made her feel sick, but sometimes, usually when he'd had a drink, he wasn't content with that alone.

Bridie didn't know what to do, where to go for help or advice. She was at her wit's end when she decided to write to Mary, though she knew it would be hard to commit such words to paper for even to think of them made her face flame with embarrassment.

> *Dear Mary,*
> *Please help me. I am having trouble with*
> *Uncle Francis and I don't know what to do. He*
> *looks at me funny and sometimes touches me*
> *and kisses me. I've told him to stop and that*
> *I don't like it, but it makes no difference. I've*
> *even said that I would tell Auntie Delia, but he*
> *just laughed. He knew I would never do that,*
> *but what should I do, Mary?*

She couldn't totally avoid her uncle because she couldn't physically manage some of the jobs on the farm. Frank had readily agreed to help her with the heavy stuff, but it was usually her uncle Francis who came to give her a hand, giving the excuse that Frank was busy with something or other.

Mary had become angry as she'd read the letter

50

and more by what her sister didn't say than the words she actually used. It brought back to her mind the time she was fourteen. 'Dirty bloody pervert!' she exclaimed, tossing the letter to Eddie. 'Read what our Bridie has written. God, it's almost unbelievable. Uncle Francis, for God's sake!'

Eddie jiggled his baby son in his arms as he scanned the page. 'She doesn't say much,' he said at last.

'Well, she wouldn't, would she?' Mary cried. 'What d'you want, that she explains it to you chapter and verse? What she says and hints at is quite enough to tell me what's going on.'

'Why doesn't she kick the man in the balls if she's so bothered about it and tell him to behave himself?' Eddie asked.

'It's not as easy as that,' Mary said, knowing full well the dilemma Bridie would have found herself in. 'I should have gone over to see her this summer, especially with Aunt Ellen's rheumatics starting up again and being unable to go herself.'

'You knew nothing about this in the summer,' Eddie reminded her. 'And then the money was an issue with Junior here taking such a lot of it. There was your aunt being laid up too. How could you have just upped and left for a week or two?'

Mary knew she couldn't have done, not really, but she felt guilty about her sister. She promised her she'd be home the following summer and until then advised Bridie to be very careful of her uncle and try to avoid situations where she might find herself alone with him and to make sure she never, ever encouraged him in any way.

At the end of the letter she suggested that she should perhaps broach the subject with her mother. But when Bridie received Mary's reply, she screwed it up in impatience.

What the Hell did Mary think? That she encouraged, even enjoyed, the advances of a man she thought of as a fatherly figure? And didn't she think she'd tried to avoid being alone with him? The fact that the farm was isolated in many areas made that almost impossible. And as for telling her mother . . . Well, that was a non-starter.

What had she expected, she asked herself, that Mary would come up with some plan to scupper her uncle? She didn't know, but she did know she viewed the future with dread and would continue to unless she could find some sort of solution. Each day now she woke up with a dead weight in her heart and a stomach turning somersaults in case she should have to ask for help in some area of the work. She wished someone could tell her how to deal with it.

By the late spring of 1930 the situation between herself and her uncle had got worse rather than better and she knew something had to be done, and so she decided to take Mary's advice and speak to her mother.

It was not a success. Sarah truly didn't see there

was a problem, or chose to misunderstand what Bridie was trying to say. Bridie, knowing of her mother's naïvety, chose to believe the former. Not that she was experienced herself, but every nerve in her body cried out that what her uncle was doing was wrong. Yet, unless she was able to describe in detail what her uncle said and, more importantly, where he touched her, which she couldn't begin to explain to her mother; she'd never understand. 'What do you mean, you don't like him kissing you and holding you?' Sarah demanded. 'Hasn't he done that since the day you were born?'

'Yes, but . . .'

'But nothing, Miss. God, Bridie, I hope you're not getting above yourself, I thought you had more sense.'

'I have, Mammy. It's just that . . .'

'I hope you haven't been bothering your father with this nonsense? You know what he thinks of Francis. God, I'd hate to be the person that came between them.'

No, she'd said nothing to her father, she wasn't a fool altogether. And she didn't want to be the one that would separate one brother from the other either as her revelations certainly would. She realised in that moment that she was on her own and not even Mary's promised visit in August of that year could lift her spirits.

However, Mary believed every word her anguished sister had written to her, and with reason, and was furiously angry on her behalf. She intended to seek her uncle Francis out at the first opportunity and put the fear of God into him.

But when Mary eventually arrived back home she was the feted daughter, welcomed home with Aunt Ellen, now semi-recovered from her rheumatics, and wee Jamie, an enchanting toddler turned two years old, who enthralled Jimmy and Sarah and even Bridie.

It was almost a week before Mary got her chance to see her uncle Francis without anyone else in earshot. She'd said nothing to Bridie of her intention and now she faced her uncle across the field of ripening hay he was surveying.

Her stomach churned as she looked at him. He seemed so harmless. But she hardened her heart against him for Bridie's sake. 'I believe you've been giving our Bridie a hard time recently?'

'Not at all. What's she been saying?'

'Never mind. She's said enough,' Mary snapped. 'We won't go into it now – you'd just deny everything, I imagine, and then I'd get angry, because I'd stake my life on Bridie telling the truth. All the years of her growing up, I've never known her lie.'

'I demand to know what she's complained of,' Francis said. 'How else can I protest against it?'

'Don't even think you can,' Mary answered scathingly. 'If you examine your conscience, you'll know what Bridie has complained of. And I'm telling you it has to stop, here and now. You think if she complains she won't be believed, she's even told me that. Well, let me tell you, if this doesn't stop, the letters she's sent to me, telling me what you try to do and what you say, will be given to prominent people in your life. Aunt Delia, for example, or Father O'Dwyer. Believe me, if you do not leave my sister alone she will not be the one painted black in this instance because I'll tell my tale too. Some people might then begin to wonder about Sally McCormack so think on, Uncle Francis.'

Francis began to bluster. 'Mary, for God's sake. You know there was no proof that I'd ever touched that gypsy brat. As for your sister . . . Well, let's just say she has a vivid imagination.'

'And me? Have I a vivid imagination too?'

'You misunderstood me.'

'Like Hell I did,' Mary spat out.

'Look, Mary, Bridie has got the whole thing wrong, out of proportion. That's all it was and that's all I'm prepared to say on the subject.'

'Well, it isn't all I'm prepared to say,' Mary barked out angrily. 'I don't care what label you put it under, or how you try to justify it, if she writes to me in the same vein again, you will have cooked your goose as far as your family, your wife and your standing in the community are concerned. I hope you understand that.'

Francis understood all right. He stood at the crossroads of his life and he knew if he was to go forward, Mary would ruin him. Somehow, he had to control the fascination Bridie held for him in order to keep the life he had and, though he made no reply, Mary knew she'd frightened him and dearly hoped it was enough to help her sister.

CHAPTER THREE

Mary never told Bridie of the conversation she had with their uncle Francis and the threat she'd issued, so Bridie didn't look for any significant change in his behaviour once Mary left for home.

But at the harvest, which the two families had always worked together, Uncle Francis was quite curt with her, when he spoke at all. She didn't see why he should seem so annoyed with her, but preferred that attitude to his previous one, so didn't bother worrying over it.

She still viewed the coming winter – the rambling season and Christmas – with apprehension, but she needn't have worried. Francis made no attempt to waylay her, or even say anything slightly suggestive, but rather seemed to avoid her if he could.

She was able to say this in a letter to Mary, who was glad she hadn't Bridie to worry about for that autumn she had discovered she was expecting again. The baby was due in April and she knew she'd have her hands full soon enough.

*   *   *

In the New Year 1931, Father Dwyer began a fortnightly social in the church hall for young Catholic boys and girls over the age of sixteen. There was to be no strong drink, but it was a place to meet and chat and dance to the records played on the old gramophone belonging to the priest.

It hardly headed the list of exciting places to be but, as Rosalyn said, it was better than nothing and might brighten up those bleak winter months. Nearly everyone in the place was known to them anyway – most of the girls they'd been at school with, while the boys were usually their brothers or cousins, or friends they'd known for years.

Bridie could have been in great demand and yet as the winter came to an end, she'd given none of the boys the slightest encouragement to take an interest in her. 'What's the matter with you?' Rosalyn asked, as they walked home together one night. 'It isn't as if you don't know the boys. You even know most of their families.'

'I know.'

'Don't you like any of them?'

'Not particularly. Not the way you mean.'

'Don't you want to be kissed and held and . . . well, you know?'

Oh how well Bridie knew and she also knew she'd had enough of that sort of carry-on with her uncle to last her a lifetime. There was anyway no point in it.

'You'll never get married the way you go on,' Rosalyn told her.

'I might not want to get married.'

'Oh God, Bridie, you can't want to be an old maid?'

'Look, Rosalyn,' Bridie said. 'Say I really liked one of those farmers' sons at the social tonight and we began walking out together. If we should decide in time to get married, where would I live? If I moved out of the farmhouse what would happen to Mammy and Daddy?'

'They'd get someone in to help them. Lots have to do that,' Rosalyn said. 'You can't stay with your parents all the days of your life, Bridie. It's not healthy.'

But Bridie knew her father would hate to get a stranger in to help him on the farm. He'd rather break his neck trying to do it all himself than that.

'Daddy said you're wasting yourself,' Rosalyn said.

'Oh, did he?' Bridie retorted. 'What does he know?'

'He was only concerned about you,' Rosalyn said. 'You know how fond he is of you.'

Fond, Bridie thought grimly, is that what they call it these days? 'Your father should mind his own business,' she cried angrily. 'He should look to his own life and keep his nose out of my affairs.'

'Look here, Bridie.'

'Leave it be, Rosalyn,' Bridie said. 'I'm away home.'

Rosalyn looked after her cousin's retreating figure

and couldn't for the life of her think what she'd done or said to upset her so much.

Bridie was ashamed of her outburst and glad that Rosalyn was not one to bear a grudge, for she couldn't wait to show her the latest letter from Mary telling her of the birth of another boy whom they'd called Mickey after Eddie's father. There was also one from Ellen saying her and Sam would be over for a wee holiday later than usual, maybe September time.

When they arrived, the hay was all safely gathered in as the summer had been glorious and Ellen came with tales of the hungry baby Mary could barely satisfy. 'She's feeding him every minute and he's so big, you'd never believe it,' Ellen said. 'I've told Mary that child doesn't need milk, he needs good roast meat and potatoes, that one. And as for Jamie, I tell you that child is one body's work. Dear Lord, Mary often doubts he'll ever grow up, he's in so many scrapes.'

'We're all longing to see them,' Sarah said.

'Maybe next year I'll come with her to give her a hand – Jamie will surely fall overboard the minute her back was turned.'

'He sounds a handful right enough.'

'He's full of life and fun, that's all,' Ellen said. 'They have only the streets to play in too, remember. You can't always be at the park.'

'There's more space here.'

'Aye, that's true,' Ellen said. 'But there's dangers too. Jamie might easily sink into the midden, or drown in the river, or fall down the hillside.'

Bridie laughed. She longed to see Jamie and the new baby and wondered as the work slowed down for the winter whether she'd be able to go over to see them. Even a week, or failing that a few days, would be better than nothing.

But the trip wasn't to be. Ellen and Sam had only been gone home a week when Sarah tipped a kettle of boiling water over her legs and feet as she attempted to fill the teapot on the hob. The scalds were bad enough and needed the services of a doctor, but a more longer-lasting concern was why it had happened in the first place. It appeared that Sarah's left arm had given way on her.

As the scalds healed, the arm got steadily weaker and the doctor was able to offer no reason for it, or treatment, or possibility of a cure. Gradually, Sarah was able to do less and less and Bridie had taken on more, until she knew even to take a day off now would be out of the question. Her mother's disability had tied her even more firmly to the farmhouse and yet Sarah could hardly be blamed. It was just the way of things.

Bridie lifted the burden of the house onto her narrow shoulders and found as time passed she had scarcely a minute to call her own. Even those winter months that usually weren't so frantically busy on the farm were not easy for her. There was still the washing to be done, the cooking and breadmaking and the dairy work, which her mother had always taken the brunt of previously.

Christmas and the New Year passed in a flurry of activity and even more cooking than usual and Bridie looked forward to 1932 with little enthusiasm, although she would be eighteen in February. This year she'd be able to go to the Harvest Dance. It was the highlight of the year – Rosalyn, being a year older, had already been there the once and had hardly stopped going on about it for weeks afterwards.

Some parents had allowed their daughters to go at sixteen, but Jimmy, Francis and Delia had been adamant that the girls were not to go till they were eighteen, for drink was served there, and that Frank should take them there and fetch them home again.

Bridie was more excited than she would normally be; since her mother had scalded herself, she'd not even been to any of the socials, though Rosalyn had urged her to. 'Come on,' she said. 'It's the only chance we'll have to do things like this. My aunt Maria said if she knew what she knows now, she'd have stayed single longer.'

'I don't blame her,' Bridie said. Delia's brother Aiden had married his Maria and now had two boys of three and two and a baby girl of six months old. He'd gone to America and got work with a gang of navvies in Central America, but so far had found nowhere suitable for his family to live so that they could join him. Rosalyn was fond of her young aunt and, feeling sorry for her, often went round to give her a hand.

'I told you I don't want to get married,' Bridie said. 'Didn't you tell me Maria has barely time to blow her nose?'

'God, Bridie, you're little better,' Rosalyn reminded her and Bridie knew she had a point. 'Ah, but it would be worse if I had weans to see to as well,' Bridie said. 'Weans are lovely when they're someone else's. I mean I love Mary's, but want none of my own yet a while.'

'Well, it wouldn't be sensible without a husband,' Rosalyn said with a giggle and Bridie gave her a push.

'You know what I mean.'

'Oh I know all right,' Rosalyn said with a nod and a wink, and the girls laughed together.

But for all that, Bridie was looking forward to seeing Mary and her two sons, who were coming over for the last three weeks in August with Ellen and Sam. She knew that there would be little extra work involved for her, apart from making up the beds, as both Mary and Ellen would give a hand in the house.

When they arrived, Mary and Ellen were astounded at Bridie's workload and Ellen gave out both to Jimmy and Sarah for allowing it. 'Get someone in to help on the farm,' she said sharply to her sister. 'And if your Jimmy is too stiffnecked to do that, at least get someone in to help in the house.'

But Sarah was no more inclined to have a stranger in her kitchen than Jimmy was in his farm, Bridie knew, and realised the situation was unlikely to change. Ellen felt sorry for Bridie, but also for her sister too. She knew how much of a burden Sarah felt already and didn't want to add to her problems by continually carping at her.

There was little Ellen could do long-term to ease the situation for the family, but she did tackle Bridie about the social evenings that she had stopped going to. 'I got out of the way of it when Mammy scalded herself,' Bridie said, and gave a shiver at the memory of it. 'God, it was a desperate time.'

'I'm sure it was,' Ellen said. 'But what about afterwards, when your mammy recovered a bit?'

'There is so much to do,' Bridie replied. 'And I'm always so tired by the evening. It hardly seems worth it.'

'Of course it's worth it,' Ellen retorted sharply. 'It's not helpful to be buried away in this place with two old folk and never seeing anyone else day in and day out.'

'I see Rosalyn.'

'Aye, but isn't she at work every day?' Ellen said. She knew too that soon Bridie would lose Rosalyn as well because Delia was after telling her just that day of the offer Rosalyn had received that she'd be mad to refuse. She guessed that Bridie hadn't a hint of it, or she'd certainly have mentioned it. She knew also how much Bridie would miss her cousin and had no intention of telling her, particularly as the details were not finalised yet. However, Ellen knew it was even more vital now that her niece meet other young people. 'You need to get out more,' she continued. 'Jimmy tells me you hardly ever go into the town, even on a Fair Day.'

'We can't both be away from the farm,' Bridie protested. 'Anyway, I'd hesitate to leave Mammy.'

'Well, you'll leave her tomorrow,' Ellen said determinedly, 'because you and I are going to town. Mary is here to see to things – we'll take the rail bus in, so we will.'

'But why are we going to town?'

'Why? Because, my girl, I see you for ever in breeches and shirt. I bet you've nearly forgotten you're a girl – a young lady. For your first Harvest Dance, I want you to be the belle of the ball. We're going to choose the dress of your dreams.'

'Oh,' said Bridie, and felt stirrings of excitement at the prospect of new pretty clothes. She went to bed that night dreaming of the next day.

'Right, Sam,' Ellen said as the three of them reached the town, 'here's the list Sarah and Jimmy gave me for things they need.'

Aye,' said Sam, taking it from her. 'Where will you be when I finish?'

'How would I know that?' Ellen asked. 'I don't know how long things are going to take. Wait for us in the hotel and we'll have our dinner there before heading for home.' She nudged Bridie as she spoke. 'Bit of a treat for you.'

It was a treat. The whole day out was just wonderful. Just to be there in the town, carefree and not with one eye on the clock all the time, worrying about her mother and knowing there would be a pile of jobs waiting for her back home, was sheer bliss. 'Oh, Aunt Ellen,' she said. 'It's tremendous, the whole thing. Thank you.'

'God, girl, you've got nothing to thank me for yet,' Ellen cried. 'Come on now, let's do some serious shopping.'

And with that, Ellen tucked her arm through Bridie's, gave a desultory wave to Sam and the two set off to conquer the town.

Ellen led the way to Dumphries, the elegant and pricey dress shop Bridie had never been through the door of before, where she had Bridie try on one dress after the other.

'What d'you think? Which one do you like?' she asked Bridie who could only shake her head in reply. She'd never seen such clothes – how could she choose? One was as beautiful as the next.

'Shall I tell you my choice then?' Ellen asked, and Bridie nodded her head eagerly. Ellen held up a dress of golden brown with a pattern of green and russet running through it. 'Put this one on again.'

Bridie took it from her aunt. It was beautiful: the bodice was of fine shimmering material over a skirt of satin and was worn just off the shoulders. It felt so good next to her skin. 'You don't think it too low?' she asked, anxiously tugging at it. It showed her figure to perfection with just a demure hint of cleavage.

'Not at all,' Ellen said firmly. 'It's a dance.

Everyone will wear similar things. Trust me.'

'But my shoulders are bare,' Bridie went on. She'd never had anything like this in her life. 'Isn't it . . . ? Maybe people will think it a little fast?'

'Bridie, you're eighteen,' Ellen said. 'The time for childish dresses is past – and you don't wear sensible clothes that you wear for Mass to a dance, especially your first.'

Bridie still looked doubtful and Ellen said, 'I'll buy you a stole to cover your shoulders if you're so worried. But once the dancing starts, you won't want a stole hampering you. Come on, take it off and we'll get them to wrap it up. Now for the underneath.'

'Underneath!'

'Bridie, you don't wear flannel bloomers under a dress like this,' Ellen said with a twinkle in her eye. 'We need lace bloomers and petticoats. No need for any sort of brassiere though, for the dress is fitted to show off your bust.'

Bridie felt her face flame with embarrassment at her aunt talking this way, and in the hearing of the shop assistants too. She knew full well the dress was fitted to show off her bust. That was what worried her most, especially the reaction of her mother when she saw just how much flesh the dress showed off.

She couldn't help, though, but be impressed by the soft bloomers with deep lace edging and the matching petticoats and before they left the shop, true to her word, Ellen bought a stole of soft brown wool shot through with threads of gold that went perfectly with the dress. Then she marched Bridie to the shoemaker's and bought her the softest, daintiest boots of tan leather.

'And now,' she said as they stood outside the shoemakers, 'I've made an appointment with the hairdresser.'

Bridie's hands immediately flew to her head. 'My hair! What's the matter with my hair?'

'Nothing,' Ellen said. 'Or at least nothing that can't be fixed.'

'What d'you mean?'

'Now don't fly off the handle,' Ellen said. 'I'm not talking of shaving your head, but it needs to be thinned a little. It's so thick it tangles easily. And then maybe a wee tadge off the length.'

Bridie had had little time to do anything with her hair but wash it for years, yet she was still apprehensive. But she needn't have worried. Submitting to the hairdresser's skill, she saw her natural waves again become apparent and the straggly locks cut off, reducing the length to just below her shoulders.

'Do you like it?' she asked Ellen, still doubtful herself.

'Like it? Girl, it's tremendous so it is,' Ellen said excitedly. 'And d'you like the length? You could wear it down to the Harvest Dance. All you'd need would be two Spanish combs to fasten at each side. God, Bridie, you're going to look the business!'

Bridie's head was reeling. She'd never had so much spent on her in the whole of her life. 'And

68

now we'll be away to the hotel for a big feed,' Ellen said. 'Come, girl, let's see you knock them dead in that place, even wearing those old clothes you have on. Their eyes will be out on stalks, so they will.'

'Oh, Aunt Ellen,' Bridie said, her face flushing with embarrassment. Ellen wondered if she didn't see the way the men looked at her. Was she as unaware as she seemed to be of her beauty, and not just beauty alone, a sort of allure that seemed to draw people to her?

However, while Bridie might have been unaware of the interest of those in the town, she was more than aware of the astonishment of her family as she and Ellen turned into the yard later that afternoon.

They were all there waiting for her: Jimmy and Sarah, Mary with Mickey in her arms, and Jamie standing at her feet. No one spoke because no one could think of words to say. Bridie's gleaming hair bounced on her shoulders, the only restraint two sparkling combs in either side. The effect was to make her eyes look larger, even clouded with apprehension as they were now. Her mouth was strained a little as she awaited their verdict on what she'd done, what she'd allowed Aunt Ellen to do.

Mary recovered first. She went forward, handed the baby to her father and put her arms around her sister. 'You look gorgeous,' she said. 'Your hair really suits you like that.'

'Wait till you see the dress,' Ellen said. 'She'll look even better with the whole rig-out on.'

Later, alone in her room, Bridie tried on her new things. When she had pulled the dress on and had fastened it up, and fitted her feet into the dainty little boots, she turned to look at herself and was astounded at the reflection that stared back. Bridie had always thought Mary was the beautiful one in the family with her raven black hair, flawless skin and vivid green eyes. Now, though, she saw she had something special herself and she was quite unnerved by it.

Mary came into the room and stood in open-mouthed admiration. 'God, Bridie,' she said, 'you look fantastic!'

'It's all Aunt Ellen's doing,' Bridie said proudly. 'She said she was fed up seeing me in breeches and shirt. But these clothes, Mary, I'm not really sure, and she's spent a small fortune.'

Mary could tell that: you didn't get clothes like that for pennies. Yet she didn't resent the money Ellen had spent on her sister; Ellen was a generous woman and she'd had plenty of help from her herself. 'Are you going to show Mammy and Daddy?'

'D'you think I should? I mean what if Mammy doesn't like it?'

'Why shouldn't she?'

'Well, you know,' Bridie said. 'It's so low. Won't she give out?'

Mary laughed. 'She won't dare. It was Aunt Ellen's choice, don't forget. Tell her you'll keep the stole wrapped around your shoulders all evening.'

Sarah was inclined to say plenty when she saw

her daughter come out of the room, but any mis-givings she had were forestalled by the cries of admiration from Jimmy. Because Bridie was so small and because her shape had been hidden for so long – for even the few dresses she had already did little to flatter her – he'd not believed she'd changed much from the wee girl who used to trail after him. Now, it was as if the caterpillar had turned into a butterfly before his eyes.

Jimmy wasn't usually given to much praise of how a person looked: he and Sarah always believed it led to a person thinking too much of themselves. But now Jimmy crossed the room and put his hands on Bridie's shoulders and said softly, 'Darling child, you look so lovely.' His gaze took in all around as he asked, 'Did you ever see anything so beautiful?'

'Thank you, Daddy,' Bridie said, relieved he wasn't shocked, disgusted even, at the cut of the dress. She stood on tiptoe to kiss his cheek and he put his arms around her. She met Ellen and Mary's eyes across the room and they all knew, with Jimmy's open approval, Sarah would say nothing detrimental about the outfit.

Bridie was sorry to see her sister and aunt leave, and not just because they had shared the burden of work, allowing her free time to get to know and play with her nephews, but also because of their cheerful company.

But she was too busy to miss them for long, as the hay was ready to be cut and stacked in the barns for the winter feed. Francis and Frank came to help as they did every year and Jimmy and Bridie would then help them in return at their farm, Delia keeping them well supplied with sandwiches and tea as Sarah wasn't able to.

As she toiled alongside the men, slicing through the hay with her scythe, Bridie couldn't help recollecting the harvest time when she was small. She remembered what fun Uncle Francis he'd been then. His good humour and stock of jokes seemed to take some of the ache from bent backs and threshing arms. He'd always seemed tireless himself. Even after a day's work, he would think nothing of tossing Bridie and Rosalyn up on top of the stacks.

Bridie remembered the smell of newly mown hay, the thrill of fear as they slid down the sides of the stack and the way the bits of hay went up her nose and in between her clothes, tickling her. She was often tired, hot and dusty, yet she'd enjoyed the harvest then and had to admit most of that enjoyment had come from her uncle Francis. Now, she kept as far from him as possible and knew she'd be glad when it was over and she wouldn't have to work near him at all.

After the harvest was safely in, they all visited the peat bog together. Again, Bridie remembered her trips as a child, with her and Rosalyn thrown into the back of the cart, with her father and Francis up in front, and Terry and Frank walking behind. Uncle Francis would sing rebel songs all the way there, his voice rising in the mist of an autumn morning.

Bridie had always loved the damp mossy smell of the bog and the way the spade slid so effortlessly into the peat. Usually black sludge would seep along it, squeezing between her bare toes and slapping up her legs. She liked the feel of it and never minded the icy coldness. She remembered how her mother would often give out when they arrived home and have her stand in a basin of warm water to be washed down before any of them were given a meal. It was part of her childhood; the time she thought would go on for ever with no change.

Now she walked alongside Frank and there wasn't the hint of a song from her often morose uncle. The fun had gone out of it as it had gone out of a lot of things. These were now just chores to be done in order to get by for another year.

However, at last, the day of the Harvest Dance arrived. Frank was to take them up to it and bring them home afterwards, but at the last minute he went down with flu and wasn't able to. 'We can go ourselves,' Bridie insisted. 'Haven't we often enough for the socials?'

'Not tonight,' Sarah said. 'Some of these young fellows will have the drink on them. Lord knows what they'll be up to once the night's over.'

'Well, sure I'll take them up,' Jimmy said, 'and go to collect them.'

'Aye, but you'll not know when it might be

finishing,' Sarah said. 'Ask Francis. He often goes up to the dance himself.'

Bridie wanted desperately to protest. She wanted to say she'd have anyone but Francis, but remained silent, afraid of what her uncle might say if she spoke aloud her fears. She resolved to stick to Rosalyn and her friends like glue.

Later, when her uncle Francis called for her, he stood speechless in the yard, wondering if Bridie had any idea how tempting she looked dressed in her finery as she stood framed in the doorway with the lamp behind her. Her eyes were sparkling and her face aglow with excitement at the thought of going to her first real dance and her dark brown hair, which she had rinsed in rain water earlier that day, shone as it bounced on her shoulders.

The blood coursed through Francis's veins as he stared at her. He caught a glimpse of one bare shoulder as she adjusted the beautiful stole about her and picked up her bag where she had put the soft kid boots, wrapped in paper. These boots were the loveliest footwear she'd ever owned and she had no desire to tramp across the bog and rocks of Ireland in them, her old working boots would do well enough for that.

Many must have had the same thought as Francis, for Bridie was in great demand all night at the dance and had such a good time that she barely noticed her uncle at the bar, drinking steadily and watching her broodingly.

Lots of the young girls had their eye on some

fellow or other and Bridie knew a lot of couples often began walking out from the Harvest Dance. 'Anyone you fancy?' said a girl in Bridie's ear. 'You have plenty of choice anyway, for you've seldom been off your feet all night. You must have danced with half the men in the room.'

But none of the men had stirred Bridie in any way. Quite a few had asked if they could see her again, begin walking out with her, and she'd immediately shied away. She had no wish to be unkind, and just said she was not ready for that level of commitment yet, but she saw the disappointment on all of their faces.

She refused to worry much about it though. She was here to enjoy herself and that's what she intended to do and she told Rosalyn the same as the two went arm in arm back to the dance floor after the Harvest Supper.

It was as they came back into the hall that a girl said to Rosalyn, 'Won't you miss all this?', the sweep of her arm taking in everything.

'I suppose,' Rosalyn muttered, her eyes avoiding those of her cousin.

'What did she mean?' Bridie asked when the girl was out of earshot.

It was obvious that Rosalyn was uncomfortable. Bridie saw her lick her lips nervously before she replied, 'Didn't your Aunt Ellen say? I saw her talking to Mammy when she came over and I thought . . .'

'What are you on about?'

'I'm . . . I'm leaving.'

'Leaving?'

'Leaving here. Leaving Ireland.'

'Leaving Ireland?' Bridie repeated. 'Why, in God's name? And don't you think if I'd had just one sniff of that, I'd have been around to your house straight off to ask you about it?'

Of course Rosalyn knew: telling Bridie was what she'd dreaded most about the whole affair. 'Why on earth are you leaving?' Bridie demanded. 'Do you mean really leaving, or just going away for a wee while?'

'No!' Rosalyn couldn't let her think that. 'You know my aunt Maria, well, Uncle Aiden has somewhere for them all in America now. But Maria can't face the journey alone and is afraid of something happening to the weans, so she's offered to pay my fare to go over with her.'

'To what?' Bridie cried. 'Here you have a job – a life. What would you get in America?'

'Experience,' Rosalyn said. 'Oh, I don't know.' She knew Bridie was hurt and upset and she wanted to explain it to her, make her see what a chance it was. Bridie knew, or she'd realise when the hurt had eased, that Rosalyn would never have been happy in rural Ireland all the days of her life. God! She'd made that plain enough from when they were in their early teens.

Now her young aunt had handed her the means to leave on a plate and her mother, far from opposing it, had urged her to go. She told Bridie this. 'Mammy's all for it. She says it's a chance that might never come again. 'Course, the weans are older now and able to help more. Nora's only a year behind Declan at ten. I was a fine hand in the house when I was ten and there's no babies to see to now either. Mammy says I must go. She said these are opportunities that you must take when you're single.

'As for a job, I'm sure I could get one over there soon enough if I wanted one. Maria doesn't want me to work, not at first anyway. Aiden earns good money and he wants me to stay with her too, for he says Maria is bound to feel strange at first. He thinks she'd settle better with someone of her own beside her.'

Bridie couldn't believe it. Neither Terry leaving, nor Mary moving to Birmingham, had affected like this. Rosalyn had been living next door to her since they'd both been babies and they'd been inseparable ever since. She couldn't visualise life without her. Even when Rosalyn began work and had been in town during the day, they'd still seen each other in the evenings and at the weekends. Unlike Rosalyn, who'd made other friends at work, Bridie had had no opportunity to do that. It had never bothered her. She'd never really needed anyone but Rosalyn.

Hurt and frightened of the loneliness she'd feel at her cousin's departure, she spat out sneeringly, 'Oh, that's it then, you'll be a skivvy for your sister-in-law. Fine job that will be.'

'Don't be like that, Bridie!' Rosalyn cried. 'I'm sorry I'm going, for your sake, and I'm going to miss you like crazy, but . . .' She shrugged. 'Maria can't go on her own, not with the three weans so small. If your Mary asked you for help, you'd break your neck to do it and you know you would.'

She might like to, Bridie thought, but knew she couldn't up sticks like Rosalyn could, no matter what fix Mary was in. The heavy cloak of duty and responsibility kept her successfully on the farm. A lump lodged in Bridie's throat and she was scared she was going to cry. She fought to control herself; she couldn't bear to make a holy show of herself like that. She swallowed the lump and suddenly she felt anger at the unfairness of life course all through her and turned once again on Rosalyn. 'Go to bloody America then,' she snapped. 'And I hope it stays fine for you.'

'Bridie . . .'

But Bridie turned away from her cousin. Tears had begun to seep from her eyes and trickle down her cheeks and she ran from the place lest anyone should see. She knew she had to move well away. Anyone could be about the hall outside: people out for a breath of air to cool off, courting couples – anyone. There was a little copse of trees not far from the hall so she made for there and leaned her head against a tree trunk. She could still see the twinkling lights of the hall and hear the laughter and tantalising music from inside and it cut into her very soul. It felt like a mockery, especially as she remembered how excited she'd been about the dance. At the thought of that, the tears came in earnest, almost bursting from her in a torrent.

She had nothing with her to wipe her eyes; she'd run in a panic, leaving behind her bag, her work boots and her stole. But she couldn't go back for them, she'd look a sight and she knew her eyes would be puffy and red from crying and everyone would know something was wrong.

But then what should she do? She couldn't go home yet; her parents might still be up and would wonder why she was back so early. They'd know she'd have been upset by something and wouldn't rest till they got it out of her.

She'd take a walk, she decided. Her kid boots would be ruined, but no matter. It was precious few dances she'd go to after this one.

One person, the one who'd watched Bridie all night, had seen the altercation between her and Rosalyn. He'd seen Bridie's flight and Rosalyn biting her bottom lip in consternation.

But he didn't approach his daughter. Instead, he'd slipped outside and stood by the side of the hall and then, hidden by the velvety darkness, had begun to move forward. He'd watched Bridie approach the edge of the copse and had heard her tears, but he had not moved closer until he seen her enter the small wood and then he began to follow in earnest.

CHAPTER FOUR

When Bridie heard the snap of twigs behind her, she told herself not to panic and stop imagining things. This was the wood not that far from her home that she'd walked in and played in as a child many a time. It was also the home of many small animals and birds and the rustling and cracklings around her were them going about their business, or settling down for the night.

She did stop once and looked around surreptitiously, but she saw nothing and chided herself for her foolishness. Even when she thought she heard breathing behind her, she thought she'd imagined it.

So when a hand shot out and grasped her bare shoulder, she jumped and opened her mouth to let out a scream, but the other hand, already clasped firmly over her mouth, effectively stifled it. 'Don't be frightened, Bridie,' a familiar voice said. 'It's me – Francis.'

That hardly made Bridie feel better and her heart

was hammering in her ribs. She told herself not to overreact, to act as normally as possible. Whatever had ailed Francis a couple of years before had effectively passed and so she said sharply, 'Uncle Francis, what are you doing? You could have given me a heart attack.'

'I was looking out for you,' Francis said. 'You shouldn't be walking home alone. I promised your mother . . .'

'I'm perfectly all right,' Bridie snapped. 'I'm a wean no longer. And if you wanted to walk me home, why didn't you call out? Why did you creep up on me like that?'

'If I'd have called out, you'd probably have run away,' Francis said. 'And break your neck likely as not because you're nervous of me, aren't you?'

'If I am, it's with reason.'

'Ah no,' Francis said, slipping an arm around Bridie's shoulder and beginning to caress it gently as he continued, 'I'd never hurt you, Bridie.'

'Don't,' Bridie said impatiently, trying and failing to dislodge her uncle's hand.

'Don't be mean to me,' Francis said. 'Sure aren't you the loveliest thing to walk the earth?'

'Stop it, Uncle Francis!' Bridie said. 'It's the beer talking.'

'Aye, the beer,' Francis agreed, shaking his head sagely. 'The beer unlocks the flood of words I've longed to speak to you. Words like "love" and "adore". Words like "bewitch", for that's what you do to me.'

'I won't listen to this,' Bridie declared. 'It's wrong. You're drunk and you'll regret all this tomorrow, if you remember it at all.' She glanced around furtively to see if she could break away from him. But even as she thought of it, she rejected it. Francis had been right about one thing: the wood was inky, pitch black. The harvest moon must have been covered by cloud, for no light from it penetrated through the canopy of leaves and she knew she'd probably fall headlong before she'd gone any distance. In fact, the only thing she could see in the dark was the strange light dancing in her uncle's eyes and then the flash of his teeth as he opened his mouth and said huskily, 'I'll regret nothing. I just want to remember you just as you are tonight.'

Oh God, Bridie thought in annoyance. The bloody man was a pest and the only thing to do was humour him. She wasn't exactly frightened, she was unnerved, but knew better than to show him that. 'Go home now, Uncle Francis,' Bridie pleaded with a sigh of impatience. 'Go and sleep it off, for God's sake.'

'Sleep off this madness I have for you?' Francis cried. 'The thing that gets between me and sleep, my work, my peace of mind? Dear Christ, Bridie, you don't know what you do to me.'

That's it! Bridie thought, angered at last. This sort of talk had to stop and if Francis wouldn't listen to reason, maybe he'd listen to fury. How dare he think he could just accost her whenever he had the notion and spout such rubbish? 'Now look here, Uncle Francis . . .' she began angrily.

She got no further for suddenly her mouth had been covered by his. But this kiss was different from the others, for she felt her uncle force open her lips and thrust his tongue into her mouth.

Revulsion filled her being and she fought him like a wild thing, lashing out until she felt her own arms firmly pinned her to her sides. She writhed, squirmed and wriggled, trying to free her feet to stamp on his toes, or release her knee so that she could thrust it into his groin. But Francis held her so fast to him that she could do none of these things. Suddenly, she realised with horror that her struggles to escape had excited her uncle further. She was crushed into him so tightly that she felt his penis rise and harden and heard him moan as if he were in pain. But Bridie knew it was no pain. Never in her whole life had she been so terrified.

Francis released her mouth and her arms to pull the dress down over her shoulders and expose her breasts. Bridie gave a yelp of terror and, pushing him with all her might, she twisted from his grasp.

As she attempted to run, Francis made a grab for her and she felt her bodice nearly ripped from the dress entirely as Francis used it to swing Bridie round to face him. He held her as she stood before him, her dress open to the waist, her breasts exposed. She wanted to die with shame. Bridie saw her uncle's eyes looked stranger than ever and his breath was coming in short gasps. 'Ah God, Bridie. You're lovely, so you are.'

Bridie trembled from head to foot. 'Please let me go Uncle Francis. I won't tell a soul, I promise it, on my mother's life.'

'Let you go?' Francis repeated, as if in surprise. 'You stand with your luscious breasts inches from my face and my manhood throbbing and ask me to let you go?' He grabbed her hands as he spoke and forced them down the front of his trousers. Bridie felt the nausea rising in her throat and she prayed silently for the ordeal to stop. *Oh Jesus Christ help me!*

'Please, Uncle Francis, stop this now!' she cried, somehow managing to pull her hands free. 'For pity's sake.'

'Ah, pity's sake,' Francis said. 'What about the pity of an uncle who cannot get you out of my mind?'

'No! No!' Bridie shrieked and tried to twist from Francis again. For a few moments, they swayed together as Francis fought to still Bridie's mouth with a kiss without losing his tight hold. Suddenly, Bridie gave an almighty heave, hoping to take Francis unawares and break free. But Francis held on as they both overbalanced and they went crashing down on to the leaf-strewn mossy ground.

For a few moments, Bridie lay stunned, and then she became aware of the twigs and tree roots sticking into her, pressed down as she was by Francis who lay on top of her, kneading her breasts and then rolling her nipples roughly between his fingers.

Her mouth was free and although she was screaming inside, she couldn't seem to form the sound. The kneading stopped and Francis fastened his mouth around one of Bridie's nipples, biting and nuzzling, while his hands went beneath her underskirts, pulling at her bloomers.

'Oh, Dear God, no,' she cried. 'Uncle Francis, please, please leave me alone.'

It was if she'd not spoken and as she wriggled and writhed and struggled beneath him, she felt his fingers inside her and let out a cry of agony. Immediately a hand was across her mouth. 'Shut up, you silly bitch,' her uncle said. 'You'll enjoy this if you let yourself and though I've no desire to hurt you, if you make any noise, I'll knock you senseless. Do you understand?'

Oh God, she understood all right. She lay transfixed with abject fear for she knew he meant every word. This man, with the wild eyes and slack lips, was a stranger, not the uncle she'd loved near all her life. Tears streamed from her eyes as terror engulfed her.

'After this you'll be begging for it,' Francis said.

Oh dear sweet Jesus, please don't let this happen to me, Bridie prayed silently, even as she saw Francis unzip his trousers. Let someone come. Let something happen to stop this.

But nobody came. There was only Francis's voice, telling her to lie back and enjoy it, for by

God he was going to, and assuring her he'd never hurt her, not in all the world. And then she knew he spoke lies for pain, such as she'd never felt in all her life, shot through her as Francis entered her and she groaned in sheer agony and despair.

It seemed to last for ever, an eternity, but eventually Francis stopped his panting and pulsating and let out a cry of triumph. He slumped across Bridie. She lay still, terrified to move in case she should rouse him in some way. Every part of her body ached and she wanted to die. For such a thing to happen to her . . . Oh dear God, what should she do? What could she do? She felt defiled and utterly dirty, filthy and so bitterly ashamed.

She didn't know how much longer it was before Francis came to. He stumbled to his feet, shaking his head in a bemused way as if he didn't know how he'd got to be there. In the moonlight dancing through the orange and brown leaves he saw Bridie, lying on the ground. The bodice of her dress was nearly ripped off, her underclothes pushed up to her waist and her lace bloomers to the side of her.

He zipped his trousers up and wondered why Bridie made no move to cover herself. 'You all right?' he asked.

Bridie wondered if she'd ever be all right again. She made no answer and Francis became uncomfortable. 'We'll say nothing about this,' he said. 'I wouldn't like your parents to know the little wanton you are. I wouldn't like them to hear how you left the dance early. When I came to find you, not wanting you to walk home alone, you waylaid me in the wood, wearing only that dress that doesn't leave much to the imagination. You made up to me and I had to be quite firm with you.'

'That wasn't how it was,' Bridie said. 'I shall tell the truth. What about my dress near torn in half?'

'That happened as I struggled to stop you stripping off,' Francis said. Bridie looked at him with anguished eyes. How could she go home and burden her parents with this? It would be her word against Francis's. Even if they believed her totally, it would split the families in half.

'Look,' Francis said, guessing some of the thoughts running through Bridie's mind. 'Best say nothing. After all, there was no harm done.'

No harm done, Bridie thought. Christ!

'Come on.' Francis held out his hand to help her to her feet but she barked out, 'Leave me alone. If you lay one hand on me ever again, by Christ I'll kill you even if I have to wait years to do it!'

Francis laughed a little nervously. 'Aren't you taking our bit of fun a little seriously?'

'Our bit of fun? Don't flatter yourself,' Bridie said with scorn. 'There was no pleasure or enjoyment for me in what you did, just shame and revulsion. Get out of my sight before I scream my head off and hang the bloody consequences.'

*   *   *

Much later, when Francis had skulked away into the night, she got onto her hands and knees and then to her feet, staggering slightly.

Everywhere seemed to ache or throb and she'd thought she'd probably have a mass of bruises in the morning, a fact she'd have to hide from her parents. She also found that blood had trickled from her and had stained the ground and some of her petticoats and dried onto her legs. She pulled on her bloomers and rearranged her clothes, and hoped she could reach the relative safety of her bedroom without her parents, or anyone else, catching sight of her. She had no idea of the time, no idea whether the dance had finished and no way of knowing. She made for home in a roundabout route. When she got to the head of the lane, unmolested and unseen, she gave a sigh of relief.

The cottage curtains were open slightly, but the Tilley lamp on the windowsill was lit, so Bridie knew then her parents had gone to bed. She hoped they'd be well asleep too, for their bed was in a curtained alcove in the room and if Sarah was awake, she'd be likely to get up to find out what Bridie had thought of her first dance.

Bridie lifted the latch of the cottage stealthily and stole in quietly. She could hear the snuffly snores of her parents and thanked God silently. But still she had to wash the blood from her legs. She lifted a small pan of water from the bucket by the door and took it into her room.

She took the lamp in the bedroom with her and

undressed, flinging the ruined dress to the back of the wardrobe along with the kid boots, now not fit to be worn. Then she tipped the water into the chamber pot and began to wash herself all over, dabbing gently at the bruises and abrasions that she could see with a handkerchief from her drawer and rubbing the blood from her legs.

She folded the soiled underclothes to hide the bloodstains and put them at the bottom of the drawer, intending to hide them until she had her period when she could pass the blood off as her monthly bleeding. She eased the window open and tipped the water away before putting on her nightdress and getting into bed. She didn't feel much cleaner. Even if she was immersed in water for hours and her skin rubbed raw, she'd never, ever feel clean again.

When Bridie woke the next morning, it was daylight and she lay for a moment and let the events of the previous night wash over her and felt her face, her whole body, grow hot with shame as she remembered what had happened.

She got out of bed and began to dress, but all she had for her feet was an old pair of boots of Terry's which were far too big for her. They'd have to do though. Maybe her parents wouldn't notice. She hoped Rosalyn would have taken her things home with her and prayed she'd bring them round later, for not even for a million pounds would she go to her house and risk meeting her uncle.

She found out that her father had already done the milking when she went into the kitchen where her mother was frying rashers at the fire for breakfast. 'We let you lie,' Sarah said. 'It's not often you have the chance to and you were powerfully late in last night.'

'Thank you,' Bridie said, but her tone was muted, her eyes downcast. Sarah was not surprised – Rosalyn must have told her the news.

'So Rosalyn told you then, about her going to America,' she said as she broke eggs into a pan.

'You knew?' Bridie said accusingly.

'No, no, not at all,' Sarah said. 'Not till last night anyway when Delia came to tell me. She apparently mentioned it to Ellen, but it was all up in the air then so Ellen said nothing. Pity, though, that Rosalyn chose to tell you last night. It would have spoilt the night, news like that.'

Aye, as if that was the only thing to spoil it, Bridie thought to herself.

'You'll miss her,' Sarah continued. 'God, the two of you have been thick since you were weans.'

'Aye, I'll miss her,' Bridie agreed. 'But I'll get used to it soon enough, no doubt.'

'Aye, surely. Life goes on.'

In a way, Bridie was glad to have the excuse of Rosalyn leaving to explain her dejected attitude, for she found she couldn't forget, even for a second, that revolting scene in the woods and she knew her parents were worried about her, for her mother said she looked as if the weight of the world was on her shoulders.

Later that day, Rosalyn came around with the things she'd left. Bridie had been on the lookout for her, not wanting her parents to discover she'd left the dance early, and she pulled her quickly into the barn where she exchanged Terry's boots for her own. 'Where did you disappear to, Bridie?' Rosalyn asked. 'Daddy was hours looking for you. Did you just head for home?'

'I might have,' Bridie snapped, the mention of Francis playing the part of a concerned uncle making her feel sick. 'You were hardly bothered and I don't think it's any of your business anyway.'

'Oh, Bridie, don't be like this!' Rosalyn said. 'I know you're upset I'm leaving, but . . .'

'God, don't you think a lot of yourself?' Bridie cried. 'Don't you pity me, Rosalyn McCarthy. Pity yourself or some other in need of it. I'm grand, so I am.'

Rosalyn went home, offended. Bridie didn't blame her and felt bad about upsetting her dearest friend, who would soon be gone, and probably for ever. Another thing to blame Francis for, she thought, spoiling the last weeks they'd have together.

An uneasy truce was formed between Bridie and Rosalyn, however, and Rosalyn was glad. She was leaving in just over a month's time and didn't want to go without making it up with her cousin.

As for Bridie, she was desperately unhappy. She

couldn't look at her uncle Francis, or speak to him unless forced to, but she could not afford to draw attention to this and invite awkward questions. She wished the two families didn't see so much of each other. There were days when she seemed so sunken in misery that nothing seemed to lift her. 'I didn't think she'd be as upset as all this at Rosalyn leaving,' Sarah remarked to Jimmy one day. 'For all they'd been bosom friends. She always seems to bounce back, our Bridie, but I can hardly reach her at the moment. I wish she was still small and I could cure any hurt with a kiss and a hug. I mean, it's even stopped her monthlies.'

Bridie had realised that herself one day when, searching for clean underwear, she came upon the soiled petticoats. Her heart seemed to stop beating as realisation dawned. She sat down on the bed because her legs had begun to tremble. Rosalyn was due to sail in two days' time, and it was a month since the dance – she should have started her period a week after it.

Oh dear God! Surely she couldn't be pregnant? The disgusting episode in the wood couldn't have resulted in a child?

The worry of it clouded Rosalyn's departure and haunted her every minute of the day. Should she write and tell Mary, she wondered? But how could she write something like that? And would Mary feel bound to tell her mother? Maybe she was panicking over nothing, she told herself. All sorts of things could stop periods. She heard it said often enough.

Rosalyn left on a drizzly, early November day and the two girls kissed and hugged and vowed they would write. Bridie watched her climb into the rail bus, carrying Maria's two-year-old while Maria held the baby in her arms and the older child by the hand, and she felt black desolation sweep over her at the loss of her friend.

A week later, Bridie realised that she had missed her second period and two weeks after that she was sick in the chamber pot as she got out of bed. The same happened the next morning and the next and almost every morning after it. She was whiter than ever and dark smudges had appeared beneath her eyes. 'That girl will sicken if she goes on like this,' she overheard her mother say to her father.

'She looks far from well indeed,' Jimmy agreed.

'I've heard her being sick a time or two as well,' Sarah said. 'God knows, she's thin enough already. I think I'll have the doctor look her over if she doesn't pick up. Maybe she needs a tonic.'

Jesus! Bridie knew what sort of a tonic the doctor would order and that news would tear the heart out of her parents. What was she to do? Eventually they would find out. Pregnancy was something no one could hide for ever.

She lay in bed, night after night, thinking what to do as one November day slid into another. But there was no solution. If she were to tell her parents now what had happened the night of the dance, doubt would linger. They'd wonder why she'd said nothing that night. Francis had his story ready too;

he'd already told her what he'd say if she accused him. Dear Lord, he might deny it altogether and lay the blame on one of the young lads at the dance.

He might say they'd been around her all night like bees around a honey pot and suggest she had been more than willing. And hadn't he told Rosalyn he'd searched the place for Bridie and not been able to find her? She knew with dread certainty that Francis would be believed before her.

When news of Bridie's pregnancy got out, her parents would be destroyed. Out would go their respectability, their standing in the community. The two families who'd helped each other and shared things for years would be rent apart. It would be particularly hard for her parents to cope; maybe they'd find it so hard they'd have to leave the farm, their life's work, perhaps even leave the town.

And the townsfolk would blame her. She must have asked for it, they would say, must have done something to provoke such a thing. God, she could almost hear them. 'Can you trust the young hussies these days, wearing less clothes than is decent and teasing and tormenting honest men? Jesus, it would take a man to watch himself.'

There would be little or no sympathy for her. She'd be the disgraced single parent and her parents dragged through the mud with her. And at the end of this, would be a bastard child that no one would want, a symbol of her loose behaviour, a child that would be held up to ridicule and scorn because he or she had no father.

She knew it would be better if she was well away from the place before the pregnancy should be discovered. Yet, she asked herself, how could she just up and leave? But she knew in her heart of hearts that she must. Though her parents could not manage without her on the farm, neither could they cope with what she carried in her belly and she had no right to shame them like that.

Other people had begun to notice that Bridie looked far from well. Father O'Dwyer had stopped her in the church porch and commented on how pale she was. 'Mind, I suppose everyone has poor colour at his time of the year,' he had continued. 'It doesn't do my old bones much good either. We'll all feel better in the spring, what d'you say?'

Bridie had said nothing and managed only a fleeting smile. If she stayed until the spring, the decision would be taken out of her hands and her life, and that of her parents, might as well be over.

All the next week she dithered. Her father had never seemed so old, so stiff, and her mother's one arm was more useless than ever. She was slow to do everything and, Bridie guessed, often in pain. How in God's name could she leave these good kind people to cope by themselves?

Then, one evening, her mother said, 'I'm making an appointment for you to see the doctor this week, Bridie.'

'What?' Bridie cried, startled and alarmed.

'Look at you, there's not a pick on you,' Sarah said. 'People are commenting on how thin you've got, and there are bags under your eyes too. You're not right and haven't been since Rosalyn left. You've got to eat more; you're not eating enough to keep a bird alive at the moment. Delia said that is probably what has stopped your monthlies. She says she's heard of it before, but whatever it is, I'm sure the doctor will sort it out.'

Oh by God he would sort it out right enough, Bridie thought. 'Mammy,' she pleaded, 'just leave it a wee while longer. You're right, I haven't been sleeping, and I will try to eat more, but don't go bothering the doctor yet?'

'I don't know,' Sarah said. 'Your father's worried.'

'Please, Mammy? Leave it just a bit and if I'm no better in a week or two, then I'll see the doctor.'

Sarah reluctantly agreed, but for a while only and Bridie knew that for her the die was cast. She'd have to leave her home and as speedily as possible. She knew she would be castigated by everyone about. Neighbours were well aware how much Bridie was thought of, for her parents said so often and also said how they relied on her, but Bridie could do nothing about people's opinion. Better they thought her the worst daughter in the world than stay and let them find out the truth.

Later in bed, sleep driven from her with worry, she thought of what she must do. There was only one place to go and that was Mary's; she would know what to do. But how to get to there without detection was a problem. She couldn't tell her parents that she was going away for a wee holiday and go along to Barnes More Halt and buy a ticket like any other body.

In fact, she couldn't go on the rail bus at all this side of the border; anyone could spot her. If she could make it to Strabane Station, which was in the English six counties, and catch the steam train from there to Derry, she'd have a chance of getting away. A girl travelling alone would also be less noticeable in a busier place, whereas she'd stand out like a sore thumb in a country station.

She also had to be well away from the farm before her father rose for the milking at five o'clock. She knew the first rail bus left Killybegs at five o'clock, as she'd often heard it chugging past the end of the farm while she was at the milking. According to the rail bus timetable it didn't reach Strabane until half past six. There the travellers would get out and board the steam train for Derry, she remembered that from her last visit.

But how was she to get to Strabane, about twenty miles away or more? She'd have to go in the middle of the night, but she'd never walk that distance in time for the five o'clock train. Her father once told her a person could walk four miles an hour at a steady pace. But his steady pace was a run for someone of Bridie's size and that was also on a good flat road in the daylight. It would be different up hill and down dale in the pitch black. She thought bleakly that it was one thing to decide to leave, but quite another for it to be achieved. She mulled the problem over and over in her head, without coming to any conclusion, until sleep finally overtook her.

The next day, as she was at the back of the barn searching for a sack or two to collect any tree branches brought down by the gales of the previous days, she uncovered Mary's old bike.

Her father was busy elsewhere and there was no one else about, so she hauled it out, dusted it off roughly and studied it. It was in a sorry state altogether: rusted up, missing some spokes and the tyres as flat as pancakes. It had once been Mary's pride and joy and the first thing she'd bought when she'd began at the shirt factory in the town. She'd used to go in and out of town on it most days then, unless the rain was lashing or the snow feet thick on the roads, for she said it kept her fit, as well as saving the rail bus fare.

Since she'd left, it had lain unused, forgotten about. Bridie could cycle – she'd learned from Mary when she was a child and carefree – and a germ of an idea began to grow in her mind. She didn't know if she could ride a long distance, she'd never tried, but it was the only way she could think of. Could she do the bike up until it was fit to carry her to Strabane and cycle all that way, in the dead of night, and make it in time to catch the steam train to Derry? She hadn't a clue, but she was determined to have a damned good try.

With her decision made, she wrote to Mary. It was 1st December and to delay any longer would be foolish. She was sure Mary would help her when she knew the truth, but she decided she'd not tell her too many details in a letter, too risky that. She'd tell her just enough to make sure she knew how serious the problem was.

> *Dear Mary*
> *I am in big, big trouble. It is not my fault, but I must leave here and quickly. Please don't let Mammy know any of this and write as quickly as you can and let me know when I can come.*
> *Love Bridie*

She tried not to think of the ordeal before her, lest the thought of what she had to do frightened her so much she wouldn't go at all. She busied herself instead with the task of getting the bike into some sort of working order, oiling it and cleaning it in her odd spare moments. The last thing she wanted was to be stranded on a road in the middle of the night. It was hard work, for she had to do it in bits, and she always had to remember to hide it well afterwards – it would never do for anyone to catch sight of it and start asking awkward questions

She waited anxiously for Mary's letter, which she wrote back by return.

Dear Bridie

I hope you don't really mean in trouble,
but I won't waste time with questions now. I
presume you're not telling Mammy and Daddy
what you're doing. I hope you've thought this
through, because they'll probably never forgive
you, but you must be desperate to consider this
course of action and you know you'll always
be welcome here. Make your arrangements and
send a letter, or if there's no time for that, a
telegram, and I'll be at the station to meet you.
Love Mary

Bridie had waited till she was in bed to read Mary's letter and turned onto her side and cried tears of pure relief as she read the welcome words. When she woke the next morning, her pillow was damp and the letter was still clutched firmly in her hand.

Bridie knew the time for wishing things were different was over and done. Now she had to think of more practical issues. She' been to Strabane just once in her life and that had been five years before and by rail bus, not bike.

How then did she think she could just set out for Strabane with no planning? She was in bed that night when she thought of it: she'd have to follow the rail bus tracks. They would take her there all right.

Bridie knew there was a rail bus timetable in

the drawer of the press and she stole out of bed. 'That you, Bridie?' Sarah shouted from behind the curtain.

As if, thought Bridie, it could be anyone else. 'Aye, Mammy.'

'Are you all right?'

'Grand, Mammy. I just have a thirst on me. I need a drink of water.'

'That will be the bacon. I thought it was over-salty myself.'

'Aye,' repeated Bridie. She prayed her mother wouldn't take a notion to peer out from behind the curtain. She'd find it very difficult to explain why she was easing the drawer of the press out gently and extracting the timetable from it.

But she didn't stir and when Bridie called out, 'Goodnight, Mammy,' the voice that answered her was slurred with tiredness. 'Night, child. See you in the morning.'

Back in bed, Bridie moved the lamp nearer and read the names of the stations under her breath. From the station nearest them, Barnes More, there were Derg Bridge Halt, Meerglas, Stranorlar, Killygordon, Liscooley, Castlefin, Clady, then across the Urney Bridge into the English-ruled county of Tyrone and Strabane Station. She knew that she would have to memorise them and went to sleep with the station names running through her head.

Her home and the farm had become dearer to Bridie as the time drew nearer to her departure and she often found herself looking around as if committing it all to memory, as if she might never be allowed to come back. She knew how hurt her parents would be when they found her gone. Yet that would be nothing to the shame she'd heap upon them if she stayed, she reminded herself. What if her mother had demanded her see the doctor in the meantime? She'd forced herself to eat more to allay her mother's fears, although she often felt sick and overfull. Of course, Sarah could have tumbled to the realisation of her daughter's pregnancy herself. Many a mother would have done by now, for she'd not had a period since mid-September and was sick nearly every morning, though she tried to hide that from her parents.

So resolutely, she made her plans. The McCarthys didn't possess a suitcase. When their children had left home, they'd bought whatever possessions they needed. All Bridie was able to find were two hessian bags and her meagre possessions were soon packed into them. They'd probably be easier to carry on the bike, one hanging from each handlebar, than trying to balance a case in front of her, Bridie reasoned.

Eventually, all was ready, the bike as good as she could make it. The last thing she'd done was pump up the tyres, praying that there were no punctures in the inner tubes, or that they hadn't perished away altogether, and had hid the bike back in the barn for the last time. With her heart as heavy as lead she lay on her bed, fully clothed, and waited.

CHAPTER FIVE

Bridie knew she would have to climb out of the window. She couldn't risk the cottage door and she must wait until she was as certain as she could be that her parents were asleep.

Oh, but she was so very tired; she'd been up since five and on the go all day, but she daren't close her eyes, for if she did, she'd probably sleep until morning. Yet her eyelids were so heavy they were closing on their own. She yawned and wriggled on the bed. Maybe she'd just rest them for a minute or two.

She suddenly woke with a jerk. Dear God, what had she done? What time was it? She fumbled for some matches and lit the lamp.

'One o'clock.' She must have dozed. What had she been thinking of?

She listened intently. The house was so hushed that the ticking of the kitchen clock could be heard. She eased herself from the bed, pulled her coat from the wardrobe, and put it on, tucking her scarf into her neck and pulling her hat over her hair. Then, she lifted up the money box where she'd put the wages she'd fought for, grateful that she had, opened it and tipped the money into the large man's handkerchief she'd taken in readiness from the laundry basket. She tied it with a knot and buried it at the bottom of one of the bags she'd had hidden in the wardrobe.

Her gloves she stuffed into her pocket and she took the letter she'd already written from beneath the mattress and smoothed it out.

> *Dear Mammy and Daddy*
> *I'm sorry I've had to leave this way, but I could stand the life no longer. I'm going to England, where I'm going to lodge with Mary for a wee while. I will write to you again to let you know how I am doing and I hope you will not be too upset or angry with me.*
> *Love Bridie*

She smiled grimly to herself as she re-read the last line. Upset! Angry! She knew her mother would be furious, raging, and doubted she'd ever truly forgive her. But it was too late for regrets.

She laid the letter on the chest, secured it with a candlestick, and then crossed to the window. It opened with a creak and whine that sounded terribly loud in the quiet house and for a while she stopped and listened, her heart in her mouth.

There was no stirring though, other than the

wind moaning as it buffeted the house and set the trees swaying and rustling. Bridie lifted the bags out of the window and then climbed out herself.

The raw and intense cold took her breath away and hurt her throat as she drew her breath in a gasp. The moon was full and hung like a golden globe in the clear night sky and the frost crackled underfoot on the cobbles as she made her way across them to the barn. She'd had the foresight to bring a slice of soda bread with her, which she shared between the two farm dogs, stilling the barks in their throat before they were able to rouse the house. She pulled the bike from the pile of sacks she had hidden it under, hung the bags on the handlebars and wheeled it up the lane to the main road.

There she stopped and looked down at the farmhouse. It looked so homely, so welcoming in the light of the moon. What if she could never go back? What if that door was closed to her for ever?

She pushed those thoughts away before she went scurrying back down the lane and into her bed. She mounted the bike and set off, glad of the warm clothes for the night was colder than she'd ever known it and the fields around were rimed in frost, which sparkled in the moonlight. She told herself to be stout-hearted. She was doing the only thing she could do and so she pedalled down the road towards Barnes More Halt and never looked back.

*   *   *

She was familiar with the route to the station at Barnes More and set off confidently alongside the river Lowerymore, the two dark mounds of Barnes Gap towering before her.

She was thankful to see that the rail tracks and the road ran side by side. The moonlight was helpful and it felt no distance to Derg Bridge Halt. It was as silent as the grave and Bridie rode past it quickly. The rail bus tracks then led over a single span bridge across the river known as the little red stream, or Sruthan Dearg, while Bridie took the road bridge further down, meeting again with the rail tracks as she began the route through Barnes Gap.

It seemed almost menacing to ride between those imposing craggy hills with the darkness thicker than ever. The wind channelling through the gap hit her at gale force and she had trouble controlling the bike. She rode on quickly, anxious to get away from the place, remembering suddenly the gruesome tales Uncle Francis used to tell her. And she didn't want to think of her uncle either. If the man had never existed, she'd not be scurrying from her home at the dead of night, pregnant, frightened and alone.

The darkness was no less dense when Bridie was through the Gap and she looked for the moon, but it was obscured with clouds and few stars twinkled. She wished she'd thought to bring a torch or lantern, something to light her way. She also knew that she had to skirt the edge of Lough

Mourne. It was a beautiful loch in daylight, but as she could see so little in the pitch black, she went on cautiously, afraid of going too close to the muddy banks and falling in.

The road and railway began to climb steeply up to Meerglas Halt built, people said, for the sake of Lord Lifford, the first chairman, who lived out that way. But before Bridie had gone halfway up, she was gasping for breath and her legs had begun to shake.

She could have taken an easier route lower down the hillside, but she'd have had to lose sight of the rail tracks then and, in such darkness, she was afraid that if she went too far away from the tracks, she'd never find them again.

She could ride no more so she got off the bike and pushed it up the road to the station, feeling the strain in the backs of her legs. The darkness was so intense, she felt she could reach out and touch it as she eventually mounted her bike again – the road didn't climb again for some time so she was able to ride more easily.

Suddenly the wind picked up and icy spears of rain began to stab at her and she groaned because she'd brought nothing to cover herself with.

The road began to dip at last and Bridie was glad to ease her legs. She freewheeled down while keeping the tracks in view as much as possible as they ran between shrubs and trees. The clouds shifted slightly and for a brief moment the moon shone down through the driving rain and she caught a glimpse of the steel girder bridge over the River Mourne.

She was nearing Stranorlar, the next halt along.

She redoubled her efforts until the stone viaduct spanning the River Finn came into view and she knew she was almost there. The road led downwards and over another bridge into the town of Stranorlar, but she skirted the town, riding around the outside of it before picking up the tracks again.

Her legs were tired, aching and cold, the rain was lashing at her and she longed to stop, to ease them for a moment or two, but didn't dare because she knew she had miles to travel yet. She forced herself on through the inky blackness, the sound of her wet wheels on the road covered by the noise of the buffeting, blustery wind, sending clusters of icy rain hammering against her.

She sighed as she passed Killygordon Station. As she left the bridge beyond it, she pulled in her bike, desperate to rest even if it were just for a moment or two. She could never remember feeling so cold or wet or miserable in her entire life. Her back ached, while the hands that gripped the handlebars were so cold, despite her gloves, now sodden with rain, that she wondered whether she'd ever be able to straighten them again. She was soaked through to the skin and had the greatest desire to put her head down and cry; in fact she did give in for a moment or two and laid her head on the handlebars.

She brought herself up sharply. She couldn't give in now. She was doing the only thing possible and was already halfway there. But it took every ounce of resolve inside her to set off again, every nerve in her crying out in protest.

She knew Cavan Halt was only a few miles away for she'd studied the timetable in detail and resolutely set off again. She said the rosary as she rode, the litany and familiarity comforting her for these were the prayers she'd been taught some many years before when the world was a safe and wonderful place. She implored God and the Virgin Mary to help her complete this hazardous but necessary journey

Liscooley Village was after Cavan Halt, but as she reached it, the rails deviated from the road, turning right in towards the station, while the road continued straight ahead to the centre of the village. Bridie was too wary of being seen, and possibly challenged, to ride through the main street so instead used the back roads and came upon the tracks again, just before the level crossing at the other side of the station.

She dismounted and tiptoed past the gatekeeper's cottage. It was doubtful if he would have heard the whoosh and swish of the wheels on the wet road, for the wind was hurling itself around the whitewashed dwelling and rattling the windows, while the rain was now coming down in sheets, but she could take no chances.

With a sigh, Bridie mounted her bike again, feeling low-spirited and unnerved by this long solitary ride in the rain and the cold as she toiled on towards

Castlefin Station. Suddenly Bridie realised the rails had disappeared away to the right, through dense tree and bushes that she couldn't follow.

She didn't know what to do other than continue on the roads and hope to catch up with them again. She shivered in fear at the thought of being lost in the dark cold night.

Maybe, she thought, that would be for the best, if she was to just let herself fall from the bike and curl up in a ditch somewhere to die. By the morning she would be stiff and though her parents might wonder what she was doing way out here on a strange road on her own, no one would say a word about it once she was dead. She'd once again be the sainted daughter and they would mourn her for the rest of their lives.

The tracks suddenly met the road again and Bridie drove these gloomy thoughts from her mind, sighing with relief. Castlefin Station loomed up before her a short while later and she dismounted, pushing her bike around the outside of it. Castlefin was the custom's post and she wasn't sure if it had a stationmaster's house or not.

Clady, the next station, wasn't far away, and though Bridie was just as wet and miserable as ever, and every push of the pedals was an effort now, the thought that she was nearly at her journey's end spurred her on. Added to that, the road was flat and the road and track ran side by side and so she didn't feel it was very long before she reached the station. Clady was the frontier post between the Irish Free

State and the British-ruled six counties and just after the station, Urney Bridge, crossed the River Finn into Tyrone. It was manned in the daytime, but fortunately not at night, so Bridie dismounted again and pushed her bike along the gravel beside the tracks, too weary to look for the road bridge.

When she reached Strabane Station, she could have wept with relief. It had been a harder, more gruelling ride that she had ever imagined and yet she had reached it and couldn't help feeling exhilarated.

That was until she tried to dismount and was so stiff and cold that she cried out as she tried to straighten up. Her legs shook from the unusual exertion and shooting pains ran through her fingers right up to her shoulders and she groaned aloud. She stood for a moment, not sure her legs could carry her further. Eventually, she moved off cautiously, staggering slightly as she clambered onto the station platform and looked about for a shelter of some kind.

There was a waiting room open, not a terribly welcoming place and with just basic benches around the walls, but it was out of the bad weather at least and she sank down onto a bench with a sigh of relief.

She had no idea of the time, but she was deathly tired. A sudden yawn overtook her and she leaned back and closed her eyes. Her stomach growled with emptiness and she wondered where she could get something to eat. She'd stupidly not thought to bring anything and had given the soda bread to the dogs back on the farm to quieten them. Now she'd get nothing before the morning but was almost too tired to care. She couldn't sleep deeply though. What if, after all the effort she'd gone to, she missed the train?

She kept nodding off, her head dropping forward rousing her and eventually, in absolute weariness, she unwound her wet scarf from her neck and, using that and her saturated hat as a pillow, lay down and fell into a deep, deep sleep.

Tom Cassidy entered the station a few minutes before the rail bus pulled in from Donegal. He was glad he was leaving his home but felt as guilty as Hell at that relief.

He had stepped into the waiting room to shelter from the weather and noticed the little girl – for that's all she looked – lying across the bench asleep. He wondered whether she was for the train to Derry like himself, or the rail bus back to Donegal, but whichever it was, if he didn't wake her she wouldn't catch either.

Bridie woke up bemused, cold and stiff and not sure where she was at first. She let out a cry of pain as she tried to straighten her legs that had gone into cramp while she'd slept.

'Are you all right?'

'My legs! I have cramp.'

Tom wanted to offer to rub them for her, but he could hardly do that. 'If you try to stand, hold on to me and walk a little. It might ease,' he said.

Even through her pain, Bridie thought Tom's voice was one of the gentlest she'd ever heard and somehow trustworthy. She wished she could see his face properly, but the darkness had not lifted and although there were lights in the station, the waiting area was very dim.

But, as Tom had suggested, she struggled to her feet, holding tight to him, and he realised just how saturated her clothes were. He was about to comment on it when she suddenly cried, 'I have no ticket. I have money, but I arrived too early to buy it.'

'I'll get your ticket,' Tom offered, and Bridie rooted in her bag, unearthed the handkerchief, exposing some coins and a fair few notes as she unknotted it. 'Where are you making for?'

'Derry,' Bridie told him.

'Single or return?'

'Oh, a single,' she said. 'I'm going on from there to Belfast and across on the ferry to England. I'm bound for Birmingham.' Bridie was surprised she'd told a stranger this; she was usually more cautious. But she felt instinctively drawn to this man.

Tom's face creased in anxiety. 'Look, you are all right, aren't you?' he asked, alarmed. 'You look very young and . . . well, you're not running away or anything, are you?'

Bridie ignored the last question. Instead, she said, 'I was eighteen last February, so I'm nearly nineteen. I'm going to my sister's for a wee while and I'm wet because I cycled here and set out far too early because I wasn't sure how long it would take me.'

'Sorry,' Tom said. 'You just don't look eighteen.'

'You can't see me any better than I can see you,' Bridie complained. 'You're going on my size alone, but I've told you the truth.'

That seemed to satisfy Tom and he took her money and went out to the booking office just as the rail bus pulled into the station. Bridie emerged from the shelter cautiously, worried that there might be someone on board that rail bus who might recognise her. But few passengers travelled at that early hour in the depths of winter and she knew no one and so, more confidently, she followed Tom to the other platform where the train to Derry stood waiting.

Tom helped Bridie on to the train, stowing her bags on the seat beside her before saying, 'Why don't you take your coat off, it's soaked through.'

'It's no good,' Bridie said. 'My things underneath are wet too. I've bought other things with me, but they'll probably be just as bad. The bags are sodden.'

'Even so,' Tom said, unbuttoning his coat, 'take it off and put this around you.'

Bridie did as Tom bade her and as he tucked his coat around her, he said, 'Maybe we should introduce ourselves?' and he extended his hand. 'I'm Tom, Tom Cassidy.'

Tom's hand was nearly twice the size of Bridie's. She'd thought of giving him a false name, but had rejected it. No harm in giving him her real name. It was a shame, but she doubted she'd ever set eyes on him again. 'I'm Bridie McCarthy,' she said and asked, 'Where are you bound for, Mr Cassidy?'

'Birmingham, the same as you,' Tom said. 'Now isn't that a fine coincidence? We can travel together if you'd like that, and the name's Tom. I've done this trip many a time. My parents have a farm that my sisters now look after. I was over because my father was ill. He had pneumonia and we thought it was the end. He had the last rites and all, you know. But he's rallied now and on the mend, so I thought it all right to leave him.'

Bridie hardly heard Tom, because as he spoke he'd glanced at his watch and she'd caught sight of the time: a quarter to seven. Her absence would have been noted by now. In fact, while she slept on the bench at Strabane Station, her father would have struggled from his bed for the milking.

Sarah would be surprised her daughter wasn't up. She would go into the room, maybe with a cup of tea to help rouse her, and she would see the bed not slept in and read the note. Oh God, how upset she would be. Angry yes, but first upset and confused, and her dear, kindly father too. She could hardly bear to think of what she'd done to them and she shut her eyes against the picture of them standing there, sadness and disappointment and shock seeping out of the very pores of their skin.

Tom knew he no longer had Bridie's attention, but he also knew that it wasn't mere inattentiveness or boredom with what he was saying that had distracted her, it was something much more. Maybe something he'd said or done had triggered a memory and a memory so painful that she'd shut her eyes against it. But before she'd done so, he'd seen the glint of tears there and the stricken look that had stripped every vestige of colour from her face.

He couldn't help himself. He leaned forward and asked gently, 'What is it?'

Bridie's eyes jerked open at his words and, looking at him, she had the greatest desire to tell him everything, to weep for her own unhappiness and that she'd bestowed on her parents for it seemed too heavy a burden to bear alone.

But she controlled herself. How could she tell her tale to a stranger? And however kind Tom Cassidy was, he was still a stranger. She gave herself a mental shake. 'I'm all right,' she said, and though Tom knew she was far from so, he felt he had no right to press her further.

He knew there was something badly wrong though. Surely no parents would let a girl set out on a filthy wet winter's morning on her own? He didn't know how far she'd come, but by the state of her clothes, it had been some distance. What sort of family had she to allow that? And she was troubled about something right enough.

She was obviously anxious to change the subject

as she said, 'I'm sorry, you were telling me about your family. What line of work do you do in Birmingham?'

'I work in the Mission hall,' Tom said. 'The poverty there is extreme. We take food out to those living on the streets, soup kitchens and the like, and to the families we also take food and clothes – some of the children have little more than rags to cover them and they never seem to have enough to eat.'

'I know,' Bridie said. 'I saw it myself when I was over before, though I was just a child of thirteen then. It must be terrible to be so hungry and cold.' As she spoke she realised how long it had been since she'd eaten and her stomach growled in protest.

'Are you hungry?' Tom said, hearing the rumble of Bridie's stomach. 'My mother and sisters have packed me food enough for half a dozen. Please help me eat it?'

Now he knew for certain there was something wrong, for surely to God a person wouldn't set off for such a journey without a bite with them. What manner of family did she come from at all? But again he felt unable to pry and instead began to open the various packages his mother and sisters had pressed on him.

Bridie watched Tom's broad hands unwrap the food, while her mouth watered in anticipation, noting that his hands were unblemished and smooth and his fingernails clean and well shaped. Then her attention was taken by the food and her interest in the man fled at such a feast before her.

There were four hard boiled eggs, slices of ham and others of cheese, and slices of thickly buttered soda bread, large pieces of barn brack and half a dozen scones. 'I have milk too,' Tom said, producing the bottle. 'My mother insisted on lacing it with whisky "to keep the cold from my bones" she said.'

Bridie had never drunk laced milk before; she'd never tasted whisky at all. But she found it was very pleasant indeed and considered Tom's mother a wise woman for thinking of it for it certainly warmed her up. The food also put new heart into her and made her more hopeful about the future, whatever it held.

When this was all over, she thought, maybe she could make it up to her mother and father for running away and certainly beg their forgiveness. Surely to God they wouldn't hate her for ever?

'I'm glad you have someone to lodge with,' Tom said suddenly, breaking in on her thoughts. 'Birmingham, like most cities, is a depressed place. The people back home seem to think you can peel the gold from the city's streets.'

'But how would they know how it is?' Bridie said. 'Many of our neighbours have travelled nowhere all the days of their life except into town on a Fair Day.'

'Yes, you're right,' Tom agreed. 'Still you have someone anyway. Where's your sister meeting you?'

'At New Street Station,' Bridie said. 'At least . . .

I must send her a telegram to tell her the times of the trains.'

'There'll be plenty of time when we get to Liverpool for that, I should think,' Tom said. 'I lived there for some time, so I know my way about.'

'Did you? Why did you leave?'

'Oh, there were reasons,' Tom said. That was his cue to tell Bridie all about himself, but he said nothing and instead changed the subject. Though Bridie chatted easily enough, she parried all his questions about her home or family, knowing it would never do for him to guess where she lived and how far she'd come. Instead, she asked Tom questions about himself and was particularly interested in anything he could tell her about Birmingham.

'But you know it already, surely?' Tom said. 'Didn't you tell me you were over before?'

'Aye, but I was a child just,' Bridie said, 'and my sister was expecting so we didn't stray far from the house. I went to the cinema a few times, though, to the Broadway near to where they live. That was truly amazing to me, and my cousin Rosalyn was green with envy when I described it. We went to a place called the Bull Ring a time or two as well, though never at night, although Mary said there was great entertainment to be had there on a Saturday. She used to get tired in the evenings, though, and she wasn't up to long jaunts.'

'Oh, you missed a treat all right,' Tom said. 'The

Bull Ring is like a fairyland lit up with gas flares and the place to be on a Saturday evening, if you can shut your eyes to the poverty all around. You must make sure you pay a visit this time and see it for yourself.'

'I will,' Bridie promised.

'There are cinemas too of course,' Tom said, 'like the Broadway picture house you mentioned, but I really like the music hall and that's what I spend my spare money on.'

'Music hall?'

'Now there's a treat if you like,' Tom said. 'The city centre is full of theatres and they put on variety shows and some do pantomimes. Have you ever seen a pantomime?'

Bridie shook her head.

'I didn't see one myself until I came to live in Birmingham,' Tom said. 'But they are very funny, well worth a visit. There was a moment's pause and then Tom suddenly asked, 'Do you dance, Bridie?'

'Dance?'

'Everywhere you go there are dances being held,' Tom told her. 'There are proper places of course, like Tony's Ballroom and the Locarno, but they're also held round and about the city centre in church halls and social clubs. There's often a dance hall above picture houses and even on wooden boards laid across empty swimming baths.'

'I can't dance at all,' Bridie said. 'Not like that. I know Irish dancing, I mean I can do a jig or reel or hornpipe with the best of them, but I don't know a thing about other types of dancing.'

'Well, if you have a mind to learn, there are schools about ready to teach you,' Tom told her. 'And sometimes only for coppers.'

'It sounds such an exciting place to live in, I saw less than half the place last time. I know nothing about these other things,' Bridie exclaimed.

'There's grinding poverty here too,' Tom reminded her. 'Sometimes the bravery and stoicism of the average Brummie astounds me. Some families we help are so poor, so downtrodden, and yet they soldier on, their spark of humour still alive. Those lucky enough to be in work fare better, but the hours of work are often long and the jobs are heavy and I can't blame them for seeking entertainment.'

'You seem so settled in city life,' Bridie said. 'Don't you miss Ireland?'

'Not so much now,' Tom said. 'I did of course, but I've been away from it so long. I miss the peace of it sometimes, the tranquillity that you'd never find in a city, but I feel needed there like I never was on the farm.'

'So you'd not ever go back to live there?' Bridie asked.

Tom was a while answering. Eventually he said, 'Ever is a long time, Bridie. Who knows what the future holds for any of us? But, for the moment at least, my place is there.'

And mine too, Bridie thought, but she didn't share her thoughts with Tom. She didn't know what the future held for her either and every time she thought of it, her stomach did a somersault.

Her silence went unnoticed, though, for the train was pulling into Derry and they began to collect their belongings together as they had to change to the normal gauge train for the short journey to Belfast and the ferries for England. Bridie tried to return Tom's coat, but he refused to have it back and insisted she wrap it around herself, carrying her own sodden one over his arm.

It was on the train that Bridie saw Tom properly for the first time and, now that the light was better, she realised he was a very handsome man. His hair was very dark and a little curly and he had the kindest brown eyes ringed by really long lashes. His nose was slightly long and his mouth wide and turned up and it gave the impression he was constantly amused by something. The whole effect was one of gentleness, kindness, though his chin seemed determined enough.

And then, as if aware of her scrutiny, Tom smiled. It transformed his whole face and Bridie's heart skipped a beat.

'I'm glad we're travelling together, aren't you?' Tom said.

Oh yes, Bridie was glad all right, but she thought it best not to say so and instead just smiled. She was not to know how expressive her eyes were, and that Tom was delighted she obviously liked his company, and they chatted together as if they'd known each other years as the train pounded its way towards Belfast.

'I don't remember being this sick last time I came,' Bridie said, wiping her mouth.

'Aye, but early December is not the ideal time to cross the Irish Sea,' Tom said, and Bridie looked out at the churning grey water, at the huge rolling breakers crashing against the sides of the side in a froth of white suds.

But, Bridie thought, the extreme sickness might have been due partly to her pregnancy, for she'd been nauseous enough at times without the help of the turbulent sea, but that was a secret she could share with no one and so she kept quiet and tried to control her lurching stomach.

It was too cold and altogether too wet to stay on deck any longer than necessary, but inside the smell was appalling, although the ferry wasn't so crowded. The place smelt of people and damp clothes and vomit from those who'd not made it outside in time. But prevailing it all was the stink of cigarette smoke that lay like a blue fog in the air and the smell of Guinness.

It gagged in Bridie's throat as Tom upended his case for her to sit on. 'Sit there,' he said. 'I'll get you something.'

'Brandy!' she said a few moments later. 'I've never tasted brandy.'

Tom sat on his other case beside Bridie and said,

'Then you've not lived. Get it down you. It will settle your stomach.'

'First laced milk, now brandy,' Bridie said with a smile. 'And at this hour of the morning. Dear God, this is terrible.'

'Aye,' said Tom, catching her mood. 'Here's the two of us turning into lushes. Now drink it down and you'll feel better.'

'Oh God!' Bridie cried with a shiver and a grimace at the first taste of it. 'It burns. It's horrible!'

'Think of it as medicine,' Tom said, and Bridie held her nose, for even the smell made her feel ill, and swallowed the brandy in one gulp, which left her coughing till her eyes streamed. 'Maybe the cure is worse than the disease,' she said eventually, when she had breath to do so.

Tom watched Bridie with a smile on his face, but his thoughts were churning. He'd never much bothered with girls before. In truth, maybe never allowed himself to be attracted to any. He knew all about girls though, hadn't he got three sisters? But this girl he'd just met was affecting him strangely. It wasn't her beauty alone, though that was startling enough, especially her enormous brown eyes with just a hint of sadness or worry behind them and her creamy skin. It was much more. She was small and fragile-looking for a start and had such an air of vulnerability.

Tom couldn't understand how she'd affected him so. Just looking at her, he'd felt a stirring in his loins that was so pleasurable, it was bound to be sinful and his heart thudded against his chest. He wanted to hold her close and protect her against anything that might possibly hurt her or upset her.

Bridie, with no inkling of Tom's thoughts about her, suddenly yawned in utter weariness. She'd had little sleep except for the bit she'd snatched in Strabane. Her smarting eyes felt very heavy and she closed them for a while to rest them.

But she swayed on the case as sleep almost overcame her and she jerked herself awake again. 'Are you tired?' Tom asked, and at Bridie's brief nod, he went on, 'Lean against me if you want, I won't let you fall.'

Bridie knew there was no way she should lean against some strange man, and though she liked Tom Cassidy, she had only known him a matter of hours. But she couldn't keep her eyes from closing; they seemed to have a mind of their own and for all she tried to force them open, it was no good.

Her drooping head fell on to Tom's chest and to prevent her falling off the case, he tentatively put his arms about her.

By the time the boat was ready to dock, Tom had an ache in his back from supporting his own weight and Bridie's. Yet it hardly mattered compared to the pleasure he had from holding Bridie in his arms that he'd wrapped so lovingly around her.

But, when Bridie awoke, she was overcome with humiliation for allowing herself to fall asleep lean-ing against a man in that compromising way. She remembered the last time she'd been held by a man – it had been her uncle Francis's arms around her and she stiffened at the memory of it.

Tom sensed her withdrawal, but he put it down to embarrassment and decided to make no comment about it.

Bridie realised when they docked in Liverpool and Tom helped her find a post office to send the telegram from before the train left that she'd never have managed without him beside her. 'I was lucky to have met you at Strabane,' Bridie said to him as they settled in the carriage. 'I'd have missed this train and would have had to have waited for the next one.'

'You'd probably have had a long wait,' Tom said. 'The trains are here to meet the ferries and there won't be one now for hours.'

'And you, the seasoned traveller, would know all about it,' Bridie said with a smile. 'Why did you go home so often? Were you very homesick?'

'In a way,' Tom said. While Bridie had slept on the boat he'd decided to himself that he would tell her what he'd been doing in Liverpool. It was not a fact he readily advertised, because he found people often treated him differently, but if he wished to see Bridie again, he felt she ought to know. 'I was a child just when I left the first time,' he said. 'I was in a seminary in Liverpool, training to be a priest.'

'A priest!' Bridie jumped away from Tom as if she'd been shot. The thought paramount in her head was to thank God she'd not poured out her sordid story to him as she'd longed to on the train. She'd have hated to see his lips curl in disgust and the scorn in his eyes had she given in to such a weakness. But if he was a priest, why had he held her that way in the boat? 'So you're a priest then?' she said.

'No, no, I've never been ordained,' Tom said. 'I was to be, but I began to have doubts. The Bishop sent me to Birmingham to work in the Mission with a Father Flynn, a good friend of his. He expects me to work off any reservations I have and go back for ordination.'

'And will you?'

Tom shook his head. 'No,' he said. 'I'm not cut out to be a priest, I know that now. My vocation was one planted and fuelled by the visiting missionaries. Once I'd actually given voice to this possible vocation, which was probably little more than a childish fancy, things were taken out of my hands. My mother had me up before the priest faster than the speed of light. He was delighted, feather in his cap, and he informed the Bishop.

'Events went so fast after that that I had no time to think. The priest told my mother she'd given up her only son to God, the ultimate sacrifice and one she'd be rewarded for in Heaven, and I was whisked away to a seminary in Liverpool.'

Bridie nodded, for she knew how it was. Catholic mothers were often told by the priests that their first son should belong to God. Mothers would often offer prayers and novenas that their eldest son, or failing that one of his male siblings, might have the vocation to become a priest.

Fathers usually didn't have the same yearning at all. They looked to their sons to take over the farm or family business, to give them a hand and ease their load. But even they found that if a child admitted to having a vocation to enter the priesthood, their standing in the community was raised. They would be set apart, a holy and devout family, and people would be behave differently, more respectfully before them.

She knew too that to decide to leave the seminary, to decide the priesthood was not the line a boy wanted to follow, was worse than not going in the first place. It would be disgrace on the family and so she enquired gently, 'Do your parents know about your doubts?'

'Yes . . . Well, I didn't tell them straightaway that I'd decided to leave, but I dropped broad hints. In the end I had to come out with it though; I thought it wasn't fair for them to harbour false hopes.'

'And?' goaded Bridie.

'They refuse to accept it,' Tom told her. 'My mother says she will have to hang her head in shame. She'll not be able to face the neighbours. Of course she was allowed to run up tick in the shop and my father a big bill in the pub on the strength of my becoming a priest.'

'I tried to explain it to them. I tried to say it

had not ever been a true vocation, but an idea fostered by the parish priest and the Brothers that taught at the school and magnified by the visiting missionaries, until it was easier to go along with it than not. And then of course I was just a boy. Obedience had been drummed into me. I couldn't defy a priest, a teaching Brother or a missionary Father.'

Bridie knew he could not, but she could also imagine Tom's parents' reaction, though she felt sorry for him and thought he was doing the right thing. 'I'm glad you're not going to be a priest if you feel that way.'

Tom smiled wryly. 'You're the only one then,' he said. 'I'm not flavour of the month at home. And then, after all the talk and explanation, my mother said to me this morning, "Don't let's be having any more of that sort of talk, so. Go on back now and do your duty, for it will break my heart now if you give it up." How d'you counter that?

'She can't see that my work with the Mission is as worthwhile as that of a priest. The people I work with are the unsung heroes in our society, not those dashing off to save the souls of the heathens in Africa, but those who toil tirelessly and usually for little or no reward to alleviate suffering and abject poverty in their own towns and cities. I respect them so much.'

Bridie heard the fervour in Tom's voice and the light of enthusiasm and purpose in his eyes and had great admiration for him. She knew it was not a weakness to admit he'd made a mistake, but a strength.

She'd love to see him again, but she could not. He was the first man she'd ever felt so drawn to and she sensed he would be kind and considerate, at least up to a point. She was sure that point would be reached if he had an inkling of what she was carrying, the trouble she was in. Dear God! She had a feeling she wouldn't see him for dust. Not that she would ever put it to the test. Anyway, she told herself firmly, what right had she allowing herself to be drawn to any man when she had this massive problem to overcome.

She knew he liked her; she wasn't stupid. Despite that, she decided after she left Tom at the station, she'd make absolutely sure she'd never see him again and she was surprised at the sharp stab of regret she felt at making that decision.

CHAPTER SIX

Mary was glad to see her young sister arrive safe and sound and thanked Tom Cassidy, whom Bridie introduced her to, for looking after her so well. She could tell that the man more than liked her young sister but that Bridie was giving him no encouragement. Quite right too, Mary thought. After all, she knew nothing about the man and if Bridie was in the condition that Mary suspected she was, a man was the last thing she needed.

Bridie, for all that she knew she couldn't see Tom again, was sorry to see him go and even sorrier when she realised that she'd hurt him. 'I thought you liked me?' Tom had said plaintively when he'd tried and failed to get Bridie to agree to meet him again.

'I did . . . I do.'

'But not enough to see me again?'

'Oh Tom, I hardly know you.'

'Well, isn't that the point? You'll get to know me. We'll get to know each other.'

'No, Tom.'

'But why?'

'I just . . . it's just . . . I'm not ready for anything like that.'

'It can be on your terms,' Tom had pleaded. 'We can meet just as friends if you want to?'

Oh, how Bridie had longed to say she'd love to get to know him better, to have a courtship like any girl her age would want. But she knew she couldn't. So regretfully, she'd shaken her head. 'Birmingham is new to me. I need to be on my own – to be free. I'm sorry, Tom, but that's how it is.'

'Is that your last word?'

'It is.'

'Then,' Tom had said, 'I suppose I must accept it.'

And he did accept it, though she could feel still his hurt and confusion. She'd introduced him to Mary and he'd been as polite as good manners dictated, but he couldn't hide his unhappiness. Mary, however, had no time to worry over it. She wanted to get Bridie home as soon as possible, to get to the root of the problem, and Bridie was not averse to this either. With a bass bag in each hand, they gave a last wave to Tom before making their way to the tram stop outside the station.

The short winter day had ended and night had fallen again, bringing with it sleety rain. Bridie gave a sigh. 'It rained nearly all the way to Strabane,' she said. 'Everything I wore and carried is probably ruined – my coat is still damp, even though I wore that Tom Cassidy's coat for most of the journey and we tried to spread mine out as much as we could to dry it out on the train.'

Mary stared at her. 'Strabane!' she repeated. 'How the Hell did you get to Strabane?'

'I cycled.'

'Cycled? All the way to Strabane?'

'Mary, I had to go so far,' Bridie said. 'What was the good of me sneaking away in the dead of night and then being recognised at the first station?'

'But still, Bridie, it was one Hell of a jaunt. God! It must be twenty miles – more even.'

'I know,' Bridie said ruefully. 'My bottom can testify to it. In fact my whole body can. I've never ached so much nor been so cold or miserable in all my life. And I used your bike, Mary, and I had to leave it at Strabane. I'm sorry, I could see no way of getting it back to the farm.'

'Well, it's hardly needed there now,' Mary said. 'I can't see Mammy and Daddy going out for a spin on it. Mind you, I'm surprised it wasn't rusted away to nothing, it was second-hand when I got it.'

'It was a bit,' Bridie said. 'I rubbed a lot off and pumped up the tyres, but I had to do it when I had a minute and no one else was about.'

'How did you know the way?'

'I didn't,' Bridie admitted. 'I hadn't a clue, I followed the rail bus tracks.'

'God, Bridie, that was clever,' Mary said admiringly. 'And brave. Coming all that way by yourself in the dead of night.'

'I wasn't brave,' Bridie said. 'I was scared stiff a lot of the time, but I was also desperate.'

Her voice sounded forlorn and Mary felt so much pity for her her heart ached. She knew, however, if she showed sympathy openly, Bridie would probably cry. And so she said, 'Never mind, pet, we'll soon be home.'

'Where are the weans?' Bridie asked as they settled themselves on the tram.

'Ellen was minding them till Eddie got home,' Mary said. 'I don't take them out in weather like this unless I have to. Mind you,' she said, 'Eddie will probably be home now and spoiling them to death. He's that soft with them, but then,' she added, 'I'd rather have him that way than the other way and the weans adore him.'

Bridie was pleased for Mary, even though she felt a stab of envy. It was obvious she still loved Eddie and that they were happy together. She couldn't imagine anything so wonderful happening to her, not now.

'I've left a stew ready to heat up,' Mary went on. 'You need something to stick to your ribs in this weather.'

Bridie was pleased at the mention of food. The breakfast she'd shared with Tom had done her little good as she'd deposited most of it in the Irish Sea and after her sleep on the ferry she'd woken up very hungry. At Crewe, where they'd had to change trains, Tom had bought them both tea and sandwiches, but that had been a while ago and her stomach was complaining again.

Once in the house, Bridie found it just as Mary said. Eddie was cavorting on the floor with his two wee sons and they were squealing with delight. 'Will you get up out of that, Eddie,' Mary said, though Bridie saw the twinkle in her eye. 'God knows, I don't know who has the least sense.'

Eddie got to his feet and grinned at her. 'We're only having a bit of a game,' he said. 'And I laid the table first and lit the gas under the stew. I knew you'd be back soon.' Then he looked past his wife to Bridie and smiled at her. 'Hello, Bridie,' he said. 'You're welcome.'

'Thanks, Eddie.'

Mickey hid behind his father, but Jamie remembered the young aunt who'd played with him in Ireland. 'I've been to your house, haven't I?' he said. 'Are you coming to stay in ours now?'

'For a wee while only. Do you mind?'

Jamie shook his head. 'Mammy said you're to go in the attic with me and Mickey,' he said, and he looked disparaging at his little brother before continuing, 'He's just a baby. He's scared of you.'

'Not scared, just a wee bit nervous,' Bridie said. 'You were probably the same at his age.'

'I was not!'

'Jamie, stop plaguing the life out of your aunt

Bridie and sit up to the table this minute,' Mary said from the cooker, and Bridie felt saliva in her mouth at the thought of food.

Later, with the children in bed and Eddie despatched to the pub, Mary handed Bridie a cup of tea and sat down opposite her near to the hearth. 'Well?'

And because there was no point in beating about the bush, Bridie said, 'I'm pregnant.'

It was what Mary had guessed from the cryptic letter Bridie sent, but she'd hoped and prayed she was wrong. It was the very worst news any unmarried girl could deliver and with a groan Mary replied, 'Oh God.'

'It wasn't my fault,' Bridie protested.

'It doesn't make a damned bit of difference whose fault it was,' Mary said. 'You know who'll take the blame for it.'

Bridie knew only too well. 'Why d'you think I ran away?' she said.

'Well,' Mary demanded again as Bridie continued staring into the fire and made no effort to speak further.

'What d'you mean – well?'

'You know damned well what I mean,' Mary said impatiently. 'Who was responsible for putting you in this condition?'

'I'm surprised you even have to ask,' Bridie said in a flat, dead voice. 'You know I didn't exactly have the life of Riley on that farm. I didn't have great occasion to meet men, let alone let them . . . well, you know.'

'Then who?' But even as Mary asked the question, she felt the hairs on the back of her neck stand up and an icy tremor run down her spine. A terrible, dreadful thought had just occurred to her, but she could hardly form the words. 'It wasn't . . . Oh dear God, please say it wasn't Francis?'

Bridie looked at her, her eyes glistening with tears, her face full of misery and despair as she answered, 'I'd like to be able to, but I'm afraid it was – my dear, sainted uncle did this to me.'

Although it was the news Mary had been expecting for Bridie to actually say those words shocked her to the core. 'Dear Christ!' she breathed. She covered her face with her hands for a moment and then she said, 'Why didn't you tell me it had all started again? By Christ, if you'd just given me a hint of it I'd have come over there and wiped the floor with the man.'

'It wasn't like that, 'Bridie protested. 'Don't you think if it had begun again, I would have done just that? He'd done nothing, or even said anything the slightly bit wrong for ages. This came out of the blue, the night of the Harvest Dance.'

Mary was puzzled. 'But Mammy said you went up to the dance with Rosalyn.' she said.

'Yes, and Frank was to leave us up, but in the end, he was ill and couldn't do it, so Francis took us.'

137

'Mammy said that in her letter,' Mary said with a nod. 'I must admit I was surprised when you barely mentioned the dance in your letter, I thought you'd be full of it.'

'I left early,' Bridie said. 'I'd just heard about Rosalyn leaving for America and I was upset so I went outside so no one would see me crying. I decided to go for a walk before making for home – the dance was still going on and I didn't want to go home too early.

'Uncle Francis followed me into that small copse by the hall and he raped me.' Bridie's eyes filled with the tears at the memory. 'After that, I didn't want to tell anyone of the Harvest Dance, I wanted to forget what happened. Then I missed a period. Mammy noticed, but put it down to my being upset at Rosalyn leaving. After I missed my second period, I started being sick and Mammy was talking of asking the doctor to look me over.'

'Does she suspect?'

'Oh no,' Bridie said. 'Such a thought would never occur to her. She thinks I'm working too hard and need a tonic. That's what I've let her believe too in the letter I left.'

'Well, that's one good thing at any rate,' Mary said. 'Now what are we to do?'

'I don't know,' Bridie said. 'I thought you'd have some idea.'

'What, Bridie?' Mary snapped. 'D'you think I'm some sort of bloody magician?'

Bridie felt crushed. Her one overriding thought

when she realised she was pregnant was of getting to Mary. She'd thought no further than that. Now she realised, with a sense of shock, that the problem still existed: she'd just moved it from Ireland to England. Mary couldn't work miracles, she had no magic solution, and she was as worried and pain stricken as Bridie.

'Oh God, Mary, help me,' Bridie pleaded. 'There is no one else and to nowhere else I can turn. What am I to do?'

Mary's heart constricted in pity for her young sister. She'd always had the solutions to Bridie's problems. Even when Bridie had written about Francis interfering with her, she'd gone over to Ireland and sorted it out. But there was no easy way out of this problem, no get-out clause, and it would do Bridie no good to let her think there was.

There was only one thing to do, though her mind recoiled from even voicing the thought and when she did, she said it in little more than a whisper. 'Bridie, have you considered the possibility of get-ting rid of it?'

'Get rid of it!' Bridie repeated in shock. 'Isn't that illegal?'

''Course it is,' Mary said. 'But I know people who've had it done. It can be dangerous though, not something to do unless you understand all the risks involved.'

'It's a mortal sin,' Bridie said quietly.

'Aye, there's that to think about too,' Mary

agreed. 'We'll discuss all the options and then decide. All right?'

Bridie nodded her head and Mary said, 'We must make our minds up quickly though. If you decide on abortion, we can't delay. The later you go, the more dangerous it will be.'

'How dangerous is it? What do they do?' Bridie asked.

'I don't know,' Mary admitted. 'I've never been near such a place to know what they do, but I've known desperate women who have and, God, you'd have to be desperate to do such a thing. I just know it's usually better to go to someone you know has done it before successfully.'

'Well, God knows I don't want to go through with it at all.'

'Aye, I know,' Mary said. 'I'd feel the same.'

'But I feel nothing at all for the child,' Bridie said, almost fiercely. 'I want nothing and no one belonging to Uncle Francis. That bloody man's near destroyed my life and that of our parents. I hate him and I'll go to my grave hating him and I know I'd hate the fruit of his loins too.'

'Don't cry, Bridie,' Mary said, dropping to her knees and cradling Bridie to her. 'I know how you feel about him and no one could ever blame you.'

'Everyone would blame me, Mary, that's the point,' Bridie said, pulling herself from her sister's arms. 'But abortion is against the law.'

'I know that.'

'What if it was found out and I was put in prison, Mary? I'd never be able to bear that.'

Mary's own stomach lurched at that thought.

'And there's the sin of it all,' Bridie said forlornly. 'There's nothing I can do to atone for this if I go through with it but if I don't . . .'

'If you don't, you'd be an object of derision and scorn to everyone and with the best will in the world I couldn't let you stay here.'

Bridie stared at her sister, horrified. 'Don't look like that,' Mary pleaded. 'Don't you see what would happen as soon as your condition was discovered? Ellen would have to be in the know and you never know how she would react to news like that, especially not being able to have children herself.'

'But it isn't just Ellen I'd worry about,' Mary went on. 'There are people around the doors from all over Ireland – Donegal even. There's a woman known as Peggy McKenna not far from here at all. You'd hardly remember her from home, but she was the eldest of five girls – Maguire was her name then – so you may remember her sisters. Her people lived near Barnes Gap – they'd all have been at Barnes More School with you.'

Bridie cast her mind back. 'There were Maguire girls I remember,' she said. 'They were all older than me and Rosalyn, not particularly friends or anything.'

'Aye, well, it would do you no good being friends with this Maguire or McKenna either, for she's a gossip and a troublemaker, a malicious old cow altogether. She'd love just to have a hint of something amiss. Oh, I tell you, Bridie, she'd make hay out of it, so she would.'

Mary saw the blood drain from Bridie's face at her words. 'Don't worry about her,' she told her sister. 'We'll have thought of something long before it becomes obvious. Peggy McKenna and her like will know nothing about any of this.'

Bridie knew, however, that it wasn't just Peggy McKenna she had to worry about. If she decided to have this baby here, somehow or other, her parents would get to hear of it. Ellen or Mary might easily let something slip in their letters home to make her mammy suspicious, or indeed the priest might say that Mammy had a right to know and take it upon himself to tell her. Bridie had seen coming to Birmingham as a partial solution to her problems, a safe haven where no one would know her. Now she saw quite plainly that it wasn't far enough away. She felt very frightened and alone as she looked at her sister, her eyes misted over again with tears. 'But where could I go, Mary, if not here?'

'Well, that's it, love,' Mary said. 'There are few places. There are these bloody awful homes run by the nuns where you can hide away till the baby's born and they take it from you and give it up for adoption. From what I heard from a girl who went in one of them, it was like a prison camp. They made them work hard, even while they were in labour, and were constantly reminding them of the sin they had committed and urging them to get on their knees and beg forgiveness.'

'Oh God,' Bridie said. 'Is that what I must do to save my immortal soul?'

'Bridie, love, it's just deciding what's best,' Mary said. 'Now, if you don't like the idea of abortion, then the home might be the only alternative.'

'It's not just that I don't like the idea of abortion,' Bridie said. 'I'm scared, and if I was to die, Mary, I'd go to Hell.'

Mary knew that too: the Church's teaching ingrained into them both was clear. Abortion was murder and the murder of an innocent child . . . God! It was a desperate thought altogether. Both women were silent for quite a while, each busy with their own thoughts while the fire settled in the grate and the gas lamps hissed. Eventually, Bridie asked, 'Does Eddie know?'

'Yes, Bridie,' Mary said. 'Or at least he knows what I suspected from your letter.'

'Aunt Ellen?'

Mary shook her head. 'If she knew the half of this, she'd take the first boat home and punch Francis on the jaw,' she said angrily. 'And while we might all want to do that, it wouldn't help at all.'

'No,' Bridie said dejectedly. 'Francis is going to get away scot-free.'

'Does he know you're pregnant?'

'God, no. And he'll never know either.'

'Didn't he think of the consequences? Didn't he talk to you afterwards?'

'Mary, if he'd have tried talking to me, I'd have killed him,' Bridie said grimly. 'I told him I would, if ever he touched me again, and I would have.' She shook her head and then went on, 'I think it was usually the amount he'd had to drink that caused him to attack me. It's nearly always happened when he was drunk.'

'Aye, many a man changes then, right enough,' Mary said. 'But still that's no excuse.'

'I've wondered since if it was my fault in any way,' Bridie said. 'I mean I was wearing that low-cut dress.'

'None of this is your fault,' Mary said firmly, holding Bridie in her arms again for she'd been rocking back and forth in great agitation.

'I'll tell you how it was,' Bridie said at last, her voice muffled against her sister's shoulder, 'and then you can judge.'

Mary listened to the tale of the young excited girl and the dance that, until she'd learned of Rosalyn's departure, had been everything she could have hoped for. She understood how upset her sister would be hearing about Rosalyn leaving and because, even as a wee child, she'd hidden away when she'd been upset, Mary wasn't at all surprised she'd run from the hall where no one would see her tears.

But this time she wasn't alone. Mary was shocked to the core when Bridie described the rape, and what Francis had said after it when Bridie had threatened to tell. She knew as well as Bridie that

Francis would be believed before her and everyone's lives would change if she'd spoken out.

'I'll show you what he did,' Bridie said suddenly, leaping to her feet.

While Mary had been washing the dishes, Bridie had opened the bass bags and hung all the damp clothes on the airer above the fire. Now she pulled the ruined dress out, which she'd brought with her to prevent her mother seeing it, and showed Mary the ripped bodice.

'D'you know what he's done?' Bridie said tearfully, holding the dress in her hands. 'He's spoilt everything that went before. I loved him, I would have trusted him with my life, I loved him like I love Daddy. Sometimes, if I'm honest, a little more than Daddy, because he was more fun and always seemed to have more time to play with me than Daddy had.

'Now that's ruined. I feel as if my life was a sham, my memories are tainted with what happened that night, and I'm so scared. I don't know what to do any more.'

'Oh Bridie.' Tears were running down Mary's face.

'What would you do in my place?' Bridie asked eventually and Mary shivered. She'd have hated to be in Bridie's position, and she had to admit, 'I don't know, Bridie, but in the end I think I'd risk an abortion and to Hell with my immortal soul. What do celibate priests know anyway and yet they sit in moral judgement on the rest of us.'

Blasphemous words surely. Bridie wasn't prepared to blame the clergy for her predicament – only one person was at fault and she knew who that was and she'd hate him as long as she had breath in her body.

'Can I think about it?' she asked Mary.

'Surely you can,' Mary assured her. 'This isn't something you can decide in a minute. D'you want another cup of tea?'

'No,' Bridie said. 'If you don't mind I'll go on up. I'm dead beat.'

It was a lie, but Bridie wanted to be out of the way when Eddie came in. She wanted to lay and think about the options open to her, limited though they were.

She lay on the mattress and listened to the children's even breathing and remembered her own secure and happy childhood, with the absolute love of her parents surrounding her like a warm cloak. She had believed as a child that, because of that love, nothing bad could ever happen to her. To Mary and Terry, she was the adored little sister, she had Rosalyn to play with and Frank to torment the pair of them, and Uncle Francis and Aunt Delia as surrogate parents, whose house was as familiar to Bridie as her own.

But then it had all changed . . . Stop thinking about it, she admonished herself sternly. Reliving it does no good. Solutions are what's needed.

She thought about the home that Mary had mentioned. She wasn't worried about the austere nature of it, or the work. God, had she ever balked at work? As for telling her she was sinful . . . Well, she'd keep her own counsel, but she wasn't the sinful one here.

But how could she keep the fact of where she was for months hidden from her mother? Wouldn't she think it strange if Bridie asked her letters to be sent to Mary? Wouldn't she ask what she was doing out in some obscure place that seemed to have no postal delivery?

Every way, the path was lined with thorns. She didn't feel she was having a baby, it was just like a leaden weight she carried in her stomach and she wished she could pluck it out and fling it far away from herself and her life.

Could she live with herself if she went through with an abortion though? But then could she live at all if she did nothing and had a bastard child, unloved, unwanted and stigmatised for ever?

She heard Eddie come in downstairs and Mary and Eddie talking together, the voices rising and falling too low for the words to be distinguishable, and lay, wide-eyed, in the bed, burning with shame at the imagined scene in the living room. She was no nearer sleep when she heard her sister and Eddie come up to bed, the rumble of voices continuing even then.

But they'd been stopped for some time when Bridie eventually fell into a fitful sleep. She dreamt that she was being prodded along a long dark corridor into a white-tiled room that was so bright, she had to shut her eyes for a moment against the brilliance of it.

When she opened them, she saw the bed: the only furniture in the room. A mighty push between the shoulder blades sent her sprawling across it and she turned and saw a priest standing beside her. He was dressed totally in black and had a baby in his arms, which he laid on the bed beside her, as he screamed, 'Wickedness! Wickedness! You'll burn in Hell's flames.'

He placed a dagger in Bridie's hand.

'Kill the child!' he commanded.

'No! No!'

'It's what you wanted to do. Hell's flames await you.'

Bridie let the dagger fall from her hand and it spiralled downwards and the blade pierced the baby's body. Blood spurted from the wound, a scarlet stream that soaked the sheet on which it lay. While Bridie looked at the child, horrified, the priest said in sombre tones, 'You are a grave sinner, Bridie McCarthy, and now you will burn in Hell's flames for ever.'

And then suddenly Bridie was on the edge of an abyss and a raging fire burned below, the flames licking the rim of the hole. She swayed slowly over the edge and as she was hurtling towards the flames, she let out a blood-curdling scream.

'Bridie, for God's sake.' She was aware of crying and then someone was shaking her. She opened her eyes blearily. Thank God, it had been a dream, a terrible, awful dream and the crying was from Mickey and Jamie who were staring at her in the light of the lamp Mary held, with eyes like saucers and tear trails on their cheeks. 'What's wrong with the weans?'

'You frightened them,' Mary said, lifting Mickey from his cot. 'That scream you gave was loud enough to rouse the dead.'

'Oh God, I'm sorry,' Bridie said, as Eddie came into the room to soothe Jamie. She was still shaking from fright and Mary asked sympathetically, 'Was it a nightmare?'

'Aye. Oh God, it was awful.'

'Little wonder,' Mary said, and Jamie looked accusingly across at Bridie. 'Why did you scream like that?' he demanded. 'You woke me up, you did.'

'I'm sorry.'

'Mickey was scared.'

'And so were you,' Mary said, but in a low voice for Mickey hadn't woken fully and was going drowsy again as she rocked him in her arms.

'I was not!'

'Keep your voice down,' Mary hissed. 'Mickey wants to go back to sleep.'

'I don't,' Jamie stated and he looked at his father full in the face. 'I'm not a bit tired anymore.'

Eddie gave a quiet chuckle. 'That's too bad, old man,' he said. 'Because I'm exhausted. I'm away to my bed now and you're to lie down in yours and go back to sleep.'

'But . . .'

'But nothing,' Mary interrupted with a sharp whisper as she laid Mickey down again. 'Lie down this minute and we'll have no more nonsense.'

Jamie, with a huge exaggerated sigh, threw himself down in the bed. 'I won't sleep,' he declared.

'Well, stay awake then,' Mary retorted. 'But be quiet about it for if you wake Mickey up again, I'll brain you.'

Bridie was still sitting up in her bed and Mary doubted that, while Jamie's claim that he'd never sleep was a false one, Bridie would close her eyes again that night. 'Come on downstairs,' she said to her. 'Give the wee ones time to get off. We'll have a drop of tea to settle you.'

'Oh no, Mary,' Bridie said. 'You must be tired out, I'll be fine. Go on down.'

'No, I'm grand so I am,' Mary said. 'Eddie needs his bed, he has work tomorrow, but I'm grand. Come on now.'

Bridie was glad to follow her sister, for she knew she'd be too afraid to sleep left alone.

The room downstairs was in darkness and like an icebox. Mary lit the gas lamps and poked up the fire, banked with slack for safety, and threw on some nuggets of coal before putting the kettle on to boil.

'Soon be warm,' she told her sister, who was still shivering from the cold as well as her bad dream. 'And a drop of tea puts new heart in a body.'

It did too, Bridie agreed just a little later, as she warmed her hands on the cup and let the heat from the fire, now blazing merrily, toast her cold tense body. She felt sufficiently calmer to tell Mary of the nightmare.

'Abortion is murder plain and simple,' Bridie said after she'd recounted the awful details to Mary, 'I didn't need a nightmare to show me that. But if I think about the other option, I know I could not go through with it. I was so ashamed when I knew you were telling Eddie. How could I cope with others watching me and judging me with my belly stuck out and no wedding ring on my finger?

'So, though I don't go against the Church's teachings lightly, or the law of the land, I've still decided on going for an abortion, Mary – it is the only way forward for me.'

Mary let her breath out slowly so that Bridie couldn't see her relief. After the horrific nightmare she'd described, Mary wasn't at all sure which way Bridie would jump. Abortion was known to be dangerous but, Mary thought, the only answer and she vowed she'd pray to Jesus and his Virgin Mother to keep Bridie safe.

CHAPTER SEVEN

Three days after Bridie had arrived in Birmingham, Aunt Ellen minded the boys for Mary. She thought Mary was taking Bridie to the Bull Ring, but instead they were making for a house in Varna Road, to see a woman called merely Mrs M, who'd promised to cure Bridie's 'little problem' with no trouble at all, if someone had ten pounds to pay her with.

Bridie insisted on paying. She had plenty of money still in the knotted handkerchief and she didn't want Mary to pay any more out for her. Eddie, while thankfully in work when so many weren't, wasn't paid much and she had no wish to be a financial drain on them. 'When this is all behind me, I'll get a job and pay for my keep,' she promised Mary as they alighted from the swaying tram.

Mary just smiled. After Bridie had told her of her decision, she'd contacted Ivy O'Farrel, three doors up, who'd found herself pregnant with her tenth child when she couldn't feed or clothe the nine she had. Her man had been out of work for five years, and to try and rear another child on the pittance she had to manage on each week had filled her with panic.

She'd said not a word to her husband but, pawning her wedding ring for the money, had stolen away one day to Mrs M when her husband had taken himself back to Ireland to bury his mother. Some neighbour women were the only ones she'd told. They'd looked after her, cared for her children, and kept their mouths shut about both. Mary had been one of these in the know and so Ivy was the one she confided in about Bridie's problem. Ivy had made all the arrangements.

'Best get rid of the old man for the night,' Ivy had said. 'She can hardly share the attic with the kids. And you'd best cover you mattress with summat – I bled like a stuck pig.'

God! What was she letting her little sister do? Mary thought. What if something went wrong? What if she should die? Oh God, she'd want to die herself.

'What's the matter?' Bridie said, bringing Mary's thoughts back to the present. Mary gave herself a mental shake. No way could she let Bridie have a hint of the doubts swarming through her mind. 'Nothing,' she said. 'I'm just a bit nervous.'

'You're a bit nervous,' Bridie cried incredulously. 'I'm bloody terrified, if you want the truth.'

Mary wasn't surprised, though she said nothing,

and she linked her arm with Bridie's and gave her a squeeze.

Mrs M was a tall, rather gaunt woman. Her grey hair, scraped back into a bun, made her face tight and strained, her eyes almost slanted, her nose pinched, her lips thin and hollows in each of the ruddy-coloured cheeks. Bridie smiled at her nervously while thinking she had a neck as wrinkled as a turkey cock and said, 'I'm . . . '

'I don't need to know who you are, where you live, or anything about you,' said Mrs M in a thin, sharp voice. 'Brought the money?'

Bridie nodded and held out the notes, which Mrs M held to the light before accepting them. 'Now,' she said, more amenably, 'how far on you are?'

'Two months,' Bridie said. 'At least I've missed two periods now, but my third would be due now any day.'

Mrs M nodded. 'Good,' she said. 'Should be a piece of cake. Some silly buggers leave it too late. Daren't risk it then, see?'

Bridie said nothing and Mrs M turned to Mary. 'You with her?'

'Yes, I'm her sister.'

'Don't need to know that. Don't need to know anything other than the facts. Safer that way, see?'

'Yes. I'm sorry.'

'Don't matter,' Mrs M said. 'I'm glad the poor bugger's got someone with her. Wait here,' she indicated the room she'd ushered them into, 'and I'll take your sister upstairs.'

Bridie followed behind the woman's tall figure as she led her from the room and mounted the stairs. With her heart in her mouth she entered the bedroom.

The woman pulled a screen towards her and said, 'Take your clothes off behind here from the waist down and lie on the bed. There's a blanket to cover yourself with.'

Bridie did as the woman told her, but as she lay on the rubber sheet on top of the bed, she began to tremble from head to foot.

'Scared?'

Bridie was startled; she hadn't heard the woman come back into the room. She nodded.

'No need,' Mrs M told her. 'Done this hundreds of times. And I'm clean. I've just been to scrub my hands. You get some dirty bitches in this business.'

Bridie watched her fearfully. She had her teeth clamped tight together to prevent them chattering and her insides were turning somersaults. 'Bring your knees up, darling,' Mrs M told Bridie. 'Relax now, 'cos I'm going to have a feel around inside you.'

Bridie's eyes widened in horror and shock. 'Don't look like that, duck,' Mrs M said, 'got to feel where to put the bleeding knitting needle.'

'Knitting needle?' Bridie repeated in a voice that trembled with fear.

'Where were you born?' Mrs M said scornfully. 'You want rid of a baby, right?' And at Bridie's brief nod, she said, 'Well, how the Hell did you think I was going to get rid of it – sing it a bleeding lullaby?'

'I don't know, I didn't think.'

'Well, don't think now either and let me get on,' Mrs M said impatiently and, afraid to do anything else, Bridie raised her knees and parted them and felt Mrs M's fingers slide inside her while she writhed and squirmed in embarrassment.

'Right,' Mrs M said at last, 'seems fairly straight-forward, any road. Now you'll feel a dull pain when I stick the needle in. Be obliged if you don't make much noise. Don't want the neighbours getting suspicious.'

'No,' Bridie said, wondering at the warning. She could cope with a dull ache, anyone could. But what she found hard to cope with was the sharp and agonising pain across her middle. It made her gasp and brought tears to her eyes but, mindful of Mrs M's warning, she uttered no sound, though she bit her lip till it bled. Mrs M was pleased, however. 'Good,' she said. 'All over now. Go home and rest, you'll bleed a bit but after that you'll be as right as rain again.'

'Thank you,' Bridie said, weakly wondering if she would be able to straighten up with the pains shooting through her. But she had a great desire to be away from this place and this woman who made money out of other's miscry.

She sat up slowly and, swinging her legs from the bed, she attempted to stand and reach her clothes hanging from the chair. But her head swam, her legs buckled under her and Mrs M pressed her onto the bed. 'Sit awhile,' she said. 'Take it steady.'

And Bridie took it steady after that. A few minutes later, she felt ready to move though when she descended the stairs, they swayed in front of her eyes. When Mary saw her white-faced, trembling sister almost stagger into the room, she turned on Mrs M fiercely. 'What have you done to her?'

'Got rid of her kid. It's what you wanted, ain't it?'

'She's ill.'

'She's in pain,' Mrs M retorted sharply. 'What the bleeding Hell did you expect? She'll recover. Take her home and see to her.'

Mary would have had more to say on the subject, but she saw that Bridie needed to be back home and tucked in the bed she had ready for her.

Bridie, in fact, remembered little of the journey back, except that every jerk of the tram sent pains shooting through her and that it seemed to take an eternity.

When they alighted at Bristol Passage, Mary cautioned, 'Now try and walk straight and upright, for God's sake. You're white enough to convince anyone interested enough that you were taken bad in the Bull Ring, but walking doubled over might be more difficult to explain.'

Bridie knew that Mary wasn't being unsympathetic, just practical, so she linked arms with her sister and with her support got inside the front door with no mishaps.

But once inside, Bridie leant back on the door with a sigh of sheer relief. 'Can I have any more linen pads?' she asked. 'The one you gave me was soaked through before we left the tram.'

'Right,' Mary said briskly. 'They're in the press in my room. Go on up. Bed is the best place for you anyway. I'll bring you up a cup of tea and a hot-water bottle for your stomach in a jiffy.'

'Am I In the attic?'

'No,' Mary said. 'In my bed. Eddie will stay at his mother's tonight. I'll put the word around that you were taken ill at the Bull Ring and that I'm looking after you. Eddie will tell his mother you're not well and lodge with her for the night.'

'Ah, Mary, I'd not want to put you all out.'

'Will you be quiet, Bridie. We've discussed it already and this was the easiest way. To get rid of the children would have to involve Aunt Ellen. Stop worrying yourself; Eddie knows all about it.'

Bridie felt too weak to argue further so she let herself be led upstairs. When she pulled back the sheets on the bed she noticed it was packed with towels. The hot tea was comforting, but the hot-water bottle was a godsend. Bridie had slept little the night before through nerves and suddenly felt incredibly weary and closed her eyes.

When Mary saw her sister sound asleep, she went around to relieve Ellen of her children. But when she heard that Bridie had been taken ill and had to be brought home, she insisted on keeping the children a little longer. 'You'll have your hands full enough,' she said. 'And if the girl doesn't soon rally, have the doctor in.'

'Yes, I will.'

'And while we're on, girl,' Ellen said, 'there're some questions I want answered.'

Mary saw the steel in her aunt's eyes so to give herself time to think, she said, 'I have to get back to Bridie.'

'You said she's asleep,' Ellen said. 'And best thing for her. You can bide for a few minutes and tell me why you lied to me.'

'Lied to you?'

'That's what I said,' Ellen told her grimly. 'You said young Bridie was coming across for a wee holiday. I wondered at it when in the summer she said she hadn't time to go to town, not even on Fair Day. But I thought now, in the wintertime, with the farm work not so heavy, maybe Francis and his son had stepped in to give the girl a break. That's what Bridie led me to believe when I spoke to her anyway.

'But now I know that's not the case at all, because I had a letter from Sarah this morning. She knew nothing about any holiday, nothing about anything, for Bridie left in the middle of the night. She only knew she was here because she said where she was making for in the letter she left her.

'Shabby trick that, girl, however fed up she was. And you must have been in on it too. And, from the tone of the letter, your mother thinks I knew as well. She seems to think I enticed the pair of you here, engineered the whole thing, and I'd like to know what's going on.'

'And I'd like to tell you,' Mary said earnestly, 'but it's Bridie's tale. Take it from me though, she had good reason to leave and in the manner she did. I hope she'll tell you all about it soon.'

'You tell me all about it now,' demanded Ellen.

Mary bit her lip anxiously. 'I can't,' she said. 'I'm really not being awkward, I just can't, but once Bridie is better, I'll encourage her to tell you everything.'

'Hmph, there's some mystery here and one thing I don't like is mysteries,' Ellen said. 'But we'll say no more about it for the moment. You'd best get back to your patient.'

Mary, glad to leave, hurried back home and went straight up to check on Bridie who she found still in a deep sleep. She put on the kettle to make herself a reviving cup of tea and toasted a couple of slices of bread in the hot coal embers for her lunch.

As the afternoon wore on, and there was still no movement from Bridie, Mary became worried. It was almost four and the daylight all but gone when she went upstairs. She lit the gas lamps first, feeling sure Bridie would feel disoriented awakening in the dark room, but as she touched her and attempted to rouse her she realised it was no ordinary sleep. Bridie was hot, burning up in fact, although her face was deathly pale. Terrified now, Mary threw the covers back and saw the blood pumping from Bridie's body in a scarlet stream. It had soaked through the towels she'd padded the bed with and was still coming. Quickly, she ran for more towels to pack around her, but she knew her sister was in peril and hadn't a clue what to do about it.

She ran for Ivy, who took one look at Bridie and readily agreed to fetch her aunt for her. 'Tell my aunt nothing about the situation,' she said. 'Just tell her I need her.'

'Yeah, no problem.'

'And, Ivy, she has the weans. Can you see to them for a wee while? I don't want them here.'

'No, by Christ, you don't,' Ivy said. 'They'll be all right with me.' She scurried away, glad to be away from the sight of the sick girl in the bed, with the life blood running from her and who she didn't think would be long for this world.

Peggy McKenna was a very nosy neighbour and one who lived just doors away from Ellen. She'd been intrigued that evening to see Ivy knocking frantically on Ellen's door. She was further interested to see that, after Ivy had been just minutes in the house, Ellen had rushed out and obviously in a hurry, for she ran past Peggy's window, fastening her coat, and hadn't taken time to remove her apron.

Peggy was all set to follow her when Ellen's door swung open again and Ivy left the house, holding Mary's elder lad by the hand and with the young one resting on her hip, following Ellen. It was easy to trail her without being seen in the murky gloom. Peggy slunk after Ivy and, seeing her go into her own house with the children, made her way to Mary's where she hid in a convenient entry.

Ellen thought the same as Ivy when she caught sight of Bridie. 'What in God's name . . . ?' But she knew what. She was no fool.

Mary looked up from where she was mopping Bridie's brow with tepid water and said, 'Yes, Bridie was pregnant, that's why she ran from home and came here.'

'Some butchering woman did this to her?' asked Ellen, and Mary nodded. 'We need to raise the end of the bed up,' Ellen said. 'She's lost more than enough blood already, I'll say.'

They used the fire bricks either side of the hearth and Eddie's books that stood in a shelf in the chimney alcove – Eddie was a great reader – and Mary heaved the bed up while Ellen slid the things underneath. The flow of blood slowed to a trickle and then virtually stopped, but Ellen still frowned. 'I don't like it,' she said. 'The girl is as white as a sheet and yet is burning up and she's lost far too much blood. I think she needs to go to hospital.'

Mary gaped at her. She couldn't believe she'd heard right. 'Ellen, she can't. What she did . . . Well, it's illegal. If she goes to hospital, she might get into trouble.'

'If she doesn't, she may die,' Ellen said bluntly, and Mary gave a gasp.

'Do you really think it's so serious?'

'I've no way of knowing,' Ellen replied. 'But the

girl's in a coma, with fever raging through her and that apart from the blood loss. I'll go for Doctor Casey, he's a good man, he'll know what to do.'

Peggy slunk back into the shadows when she saw Ellen leave the house again. She didn't make for any neighbour's house though, but went towards Bristol Passage. Suddenly, Peggy knew where she was heading for: the doctor's surgery was on Bristol Street that Bristol Passage led to. Sure enough, it wasn't long till Ellen was back with the doctor following behind her.

Doctor Casey was horrified when he saw the state of Bridie and immediately made arrangements to have her admitted to hospital. Bridie was unaware of what was happening to her. She never felt the ambulance men gently lift her from her bloodstained bed onto a stretcher, which they covered with a blanket. She didn't know of their struggle to get her down the stairs and into the ambulance, with a knot of neighbours gathered about the door and others standing on their own doorsteps.

From her hidden position, Peggy heard the ringing bell of an ambulance which drew up before Mary's door. She craned her neck to see better, but didn't move nearer, not wishing to be spotted. She saw enough though: the stretchered girl carried from the house, followed by the solemn figures of Mary and Ellen, while the doctor scurried past her to get in his car. And like every watching woman there, she knew what ailed Bridie McCarthy.

Few judged her though. She was Mary's Coghlan's wee sister and Mary was well thought of. A Catholic, but not one of the rowdy kind, and her husband was not in the pub knocking it back every night and then taking it out of her when he got in, unlike many men. They were decent and respectable people and so most thought some man had taken advantage of young Bridie.

'Ah, will you look at that,' one woman remarked as the ambulance began moving down the road. 'Some bloody sod's taken that girl down if you ask me and the poor bugger's tried to do away with it.'

'Be a bit of luck if she ain't done away with herself and all,' Ivy remarked. 'Christ, poor sod was still as death.'

Peggy thought it served Bridie right. Those bloody McCarthys always thought they were a cut above others. But she kept her thoughts to herself. Well, this was one in the eye for them. They'd bred a common little whore who couldn't wait to get her belly filled and, not content with that, had committed a greater sin in trying to get rid of it.

'Ah, God help her,' another said as the women began to disperse to their own houses. 'Sure she's little more than a child.'

Peggy wanted to scream that she was no child. It must have been five years since she was last over and she'd been thirteen then. The girl must be eighteen if she was a day. Peggy was the mother of two weans before she reached nineteen and she'd never lifted her skirts for anyone, even Michael, until the ring was on her finger. It wasn't always easy either, but she'd been taught right from wrong, not like that little trollop. But she said nothing to anyone and slid away down Grant Street, the darkness hiding the fact she'd ever been there.

Back in her own house, Peggy almost hugged herself in delight. She had a handle on Bridie McCarthy and intended to use it. For a start she would remind her that abortion, as well as being illegal, was a mortal sin. If she was to die without confessing and repenting of it, she would roast in the flames of Hell. Of course she might be dead already. She looked sick enough, but if she hadn't died, she'd make her wish she had before she was done with her.

Peggy McKenna was a sad and embittered young woman. She hadn't always been that way and certainly not at seventeen when she had married handsome Michael O'Connor who was twenty-two at the time.

Peggy's Michael worked the farm with her father Eamomn Maguire and was set to inherit it at the older man's death, what with Peggy having no brothers and being the eldest girl. Eamomn considered his son-in-law a fine fellow if he could just keep off the drink.

Peggy was happy, her life and future set. She knew in time they would build their own house on the farm, where they'd rear their family. However, unbeknownst to Peggy, Michael had become embroiled in the Troubles in Ireland, becoming active in the IRA cell operating from the hills of Donegal.

They'd been married less than a year when Michael had the tip-off to disappear if he didn't want to be shot. His name was known and the British Army intended to hunt him down. Peggy was pregnant and hated to have to leave her home, but would hate even more to lose her young husband. He was given papers taken from a dead comrade, Michael McKenna, and that's who he became when they travelled across the sea to the only relative he had outside the shores of Ireland, an uncle in Aston, Birmingham.

Peggy thought the house squalid, the area filthy and depressing, and the air fit to choke a body, filled as it was with putrid factory emissions.

She missed her home and her mammy and her gaggle of sisters though she tried, and failed, to like Michael's relations. Living with them was a form of purgatory.

It was in Bell Barn Road in the Horsefair area, far enough away from Michael's uncle and his family to suit Peggy, that her firstborn, Denis, was joined by a brother and three sisters over the next six years.

When Ellen Doherty had had her sister's child, Mary McCarthy over for a wee holiday, Peggy had taken an instant dislike to her. This was not for anything Mary did, but just jealousy eating at Peggy.

Mary was only three years younger than Peggy and, their parents being neighbours, they'd gone to the same school in rural Donegal. But now, while Mary was out and about enjoying herself, Peggy was tied to the house with babies amidst poverty, for Michael had lost the job his uncle had found for him.

When Mary met and married Eddie Coghlan, a fine upstanding man in steady employment, Peggy's jealousy grew, especially when her sisters wrote and told her how wonderful the wedding had been and of the spread put on for everyone after it.

Bridie came to see Mary in 1927, just after Peggy had had her fifth child, Patricia. Mary had told her Bridie was still small and thin and she was. It was hard to believe she was thirteen, but she was obviously well nourished, despite that. Her eyes were bright and clear, her skin glowed, and her deep rich chestnut-coloured hair shone.

Peggy couldn't remember what having a stomach full of food felt like anymore. Any food she could get hold of she gave to the weans, but they still often cried with hunger.

They often cried with cold as well in the winter. They went barefoot, for any boots they'd ever had had been pawned, and blankets for the beds went the same way. Now the children slept in the clothes they were wearing under a variety of coats. Their hair was lank, their grey faces pinched and thin, their arms and legs like sticks and their bellies distended.

Peggy told herself life was unfair. How she would have loved to have the money for one of her sisters to come on a visit, or for her to go home. She took an instant dislike to Bridie too.

Over the years, envy and jealousy turned to bitterness as her poverty grew deeper. Many neighbours bore the brunt of her verbal attacks till most left her well alone. And then Bridie McCarthy had arrived again. This time there had been no announcement and talk of it for days, even weeks, like there had been before and now she knew why.

She couldn't believe her good fortune. After all the years of envy, it was as if Bridie McCarthy had been handed to her on a plate. She would pay, and dearly, for killing an unborn baby was something she'd burn in Hell for. But long before that, provided the girl survived, Peggy would extract *her* payment.

Bridie opened her eyes four full days after she'd been admitted to hospital. She didn't know where she was and knew nothing of the battle that had gone on to save her life.

She lay still and cast her mind back. She remembered Mrs M and what she had done and the nightmare journey back home, being tucked up in Mary's bed and then . . . then nothing until now. She looked around her and knew she was in hospital and was frightened, for she knew she'd done an awful thing in trying to get rid of her child.

A nurse, bustling past the door at that moment,

caught the small sign of movement and went in. She seemed pleased that Bridie had her eyes open.

'What happened to me?' Bridie asked and saw the nurse's lips purse.

'Doctor will explain it all to you,' she said primly. 'He'll be along to see you directly.'

The doctor was a middle-aged man with warm grey-brown eyes which he turned on Bridie and said in a soft and gentle voice, 'You had an abortion, my dear, didn't you?'

It was useless to deny it, so Bridie nodded. 'Well, I'm afraid it caused you to haemorrhage,' the doctor explained. 'You were very ill when you were admitted.'

'Aye.'

'You know, my dear, that you were breaking the law?' the doctor said. 'If I was to inform the authorities . . .'

'Oh, please, please don't,' Bridie pleaded.

'Were you so desperate?'

'You've no idea,' Bridie sobbed.

'And the man? There was no way he could marry you?'

Bridie gave a dry, humourless laugh. 'There was no question of it, Doctor. The man was already married, well, married with a daughter my age, an older son and a clutch of younger ones too. He was also my uncle and he raped me.'

The doctor was silent. Bridie's eyes met his, and he knew this petite young woman spoke the truth because he saw the pain still there.

'No one would have believed me,' she went on. 'There would always have been doubt and it would have destroyed us all. Then I found I was having a child and I was in a panic. I ran away and came to my sister's. We talked about it for hours and I wrestled with it all night. It seemed the only way.'

'I see,' the doctor said. 'You realise you might have died?'

'I knew there was a risk,' Bridie admitted. 'And one I was prepared to take. Please don't tell the police.'

The doctor pondered for a while. The woman who carried the act out at least should be prosecuted for what she did, but that couldn't be done without involving the young girl, who he thought appeared to have gone through enough already. Anyway, it was doubtful they'd ever find the woman. They'd probably not even known her name and although they'd know where the house was, that probably wasn't hers. He'd heard such women often borrowed houses from friends.

Why should this young girl have to suffer the shame and humiliation of giving birth to a bastard child through no fault of her own? She'd taken the only course open to her and he wasn't going to shame her further. 'No, my dear,' he said at last. 'Set your mind at rest.'

Bridie's relief was transparently obvious and the doctor went on, 'Now, I want you to stay with us for a little while. You're far from recovered yet and really I'd like to see more flesh on your bones.'

'That's something my mother's been hoping to see for years,' Bridie said, and the doctor smiled at her before he left the room and Bridie closed her eyes again.

'Are you resting yourself?' asked an unfamiliar voice in Bridie's ear, jerking her awake. She opened her eyes to find herself looking into the watery blue, bloodshot ones of Peggy McKenna.

She was surprised, very surprised. She hardly knew the woman, and she'd expected no visits from neighbours. It wasn't their way to visit hospitals at all, and to visit Bridie would be acknowledging that they knew what she'd done. They did of course, although they'd keep quiet to protect their own, but because Bridie had broken the law and then had to be admitted to hospital, the authorities, maybe even the police, could be involved. No one wanted to get mixed up in that. They merely sent their good wishes for her recovery with Ellen and Mary.

But Peggy McKenna had a reason for visiting Bridie. She'd written to her sisters the day Bridie had been taken to hospital, telling them of Bridie's arrival at Mary's house, but mentioning nothing of the abortion. In their reply they told her of Bridie's flight from her home in the middle of the night and how she'd left her parents in the lurch. Few could understand why she'd done such a thing. It had, they said, been the talk of the place. Peggy had received their letter just that morning.

She knew full well why Bridie had done such a thing and now knew that her parents were unaware of any of it. This petted and pampered McCarthy girl had done a wicked, shameful thing with some boy or man who'd taken his fun and then couldn't, or wouldn't, marry her. She could bet that Bridie would pay dearly to keep her parents in ignorance of what she had done. Well, time would tell. Today, she'd just sow the seeds.

Despite Mary's warning, Bridie had no reason to be wary of a neighbour and so she said a little hesitantly, 'H . . . Hello, Mrs McKenna.'

Peggy seemed not a bit awkward as she settled herself on the chair beside the bed and leaned forward. 'How you feeling now?' she asked solicitously.

Bridie pulled away from the woman and her mouthful of foul-smelling, rotting teeth, and replied, 'I'm fine. Getting better, you know.'

'Ah yes. Glad you're feeling stronger. More able to face what you've done?'

'What?'

'It's common knowledge, Bridie,' Peggy said, and leaning closer she went on in a hissing whisper, 'abortion, wasn't it?'

Bridie looked around to the main ward she'd recently moved into to see if anyone had heard, but most people were either asleep or had visitors of their own. She didn't know how to answer

172

Peggy McKenna. Should she deny it? What good would it do? The woman had said it was common knowledge and she was probably right, so a denial would be useless.

Before she was able to say anything, Peggy said, 'Terrible thing that, to kill a baby.'

'You know nothing about it,' Bridie replied tight-lipped.

'Don't have to, do I?' Peggy said. 'I know enough. Thing is, I was wondering do your parents know? See, according to Mary, when we were at school, you were the golden girl, especially after the other two wee ones died. Mary said your mammy and daddy thought the sun shone out of your arse.' Peggy shook her head from side to side and regarded Bridie sorrowfully. 'If they could see you now, I think the pair of them would be destroyed, so they would.'

'You wouldn't tell them, sure you wouldn't?' Bridie said in panic. 'It would achieve nothing.'

'That's in your opinion,' Peggy said. 'But I'll bide my time for now.' She sat back in the chair, her hands by her side, and said, 'Intend to confess, do you?'

Bridie had no intention of confessing it. She'd told no priest anything about Francis's earlier encounters, never mind that one dreadful night, and she had no intention of doing so now.

'I mean they can't know, can they?' Peggy said. 'If they'd known you were sick in hospital, they'd visit you. Prayers would be said at church and Mary and Ellen would have Masses dedicated to you. I bet they've said nothing of this and that's wrong too. You can't just get away scot-free without confessing and asking God's forgiveness. If you were to die without atoning you'd tip straight into the fires of Hell.'

She watched the blood drain from Bridie's face as she leant back on the pillows. 'What do you want of me, Peggy?' she asked wearily.

'Well, first I want you to feel disgusted and ashamed of yourself,' Peggy told her.

'I did. I do.'

'Good,' Peggy said. 'You'll never forget what you've done, you know. Never. All the days of your life, it will haunt you. And God may have his revenge yet. Perhaps you'll never be able to bear another child. Think on that, Bridie McCarthy.'

Bridie thought of it. Peggy wasn't to know how low her self-esteem was anyway, nor as she began to recover, how guilt had begun to eat away at her. She had asked God's forgiveness over and over, but not through a priest, not in the confessional box. 'I've thought of all this myself, Mrs McKenna, so you're telling me nothing I haven't faced,' she said. 'And if I do as you say and confess all to a priest, will you give up this idea of writing to my parents?'

'I won't give up,' Peggy said. 'But I'll hold fire for a bit.'

'Please,' Bridie pleaded.

'Let's get this clear,' Peggy said briskly. 'You are not in a position to bargain with me. You go to confess when you're out of this place and then we'll see.'

When she'd gone, Bridie lay with her hands behind her head, staring at the ceiling and wondering why her life was so difficult. She'd have to go to confession, she knew that, to keep the wretched woman at bay for a little longer. She could not risk telling Mary or Ellen about Peggy McKenna's visit, or what she'd said to her. She knew they'd be incensed on her behalf, but if they upset Peggy McKenna, she might well carry out her threat and there was nothing anyone could do about that. After all she'd gone through to protect her parents, she didn't think she could bear that.

All this had come about because of her bloody uncle, she thought, and she didn't care how wicked it was, she prayed earnestly for the man to die.

CHAPTER EIGHT

The wards were being decorated for Christmas
when Bridie left hospital. It was just over a week
away and she was going to her aunt's home for she
had more room than Mary.

Ellen's house was exactly the same as Mary's.
The living room was small but warm and cosy.
The floor was covered with brown lino with beige
and yellow flowers on it and a soft deep brown
rug was pushed against the brass fender. A small
two-seater settee and an armchair in light brown
material and covered in gay handmade cushions
was pulled up before the fire. The mantelpiece had
few ornaments, but for the two silver candlesticks
to each side of it and the little red lamp that was
often lit in front of the picture of the Sacred Heart
of Jesus that hung above the fireplace.

Bridie was to have the attic, the only other available room, but while Bridie had been recovering
in hospital, Ellen had been busy. She'd taken up
the lino she'd had put down when Mary had first

come and replaced it with a nice pale blue one and on the floor bedside the bed was a bright rag rug. The wardrobe and dressing table had also been bought for Mary that time she'd come over with Ellen and Bridie was grateful for places to put her few things.

Every effort had been made to make her comfortable and welcome and normally Bridie would have been delighted with such a room, if she hadn't been burdened down with guilt and shame for what she had done.

There had been no Christmas cards from home for any of them that year: it appeared Sarah was cross with Ellen and Mary as well as Bridie. There was, however, a card from Francis and Delia. Bridie would have thrown it in the fire, but Mary intervened and said it would have been Delia who sent it and she was a victim of Francis too, in a way. Inside was a letter for Bridie, chiding her for her irresponsible behaviour.

> *Dear Bridie*
> *I can understand you wanting to leave the farm, but not why you did it in such an underhand way. I don't think your parents will ever get over it.*
> *Your father was killing himself on the farm, though Francis helped him as much as he could. But at last he's agreed to have a man called Willie Palmer in to help him and the man's wife, Beattie, offered to give your*

mother a hand around the house a few days a
week. She deals with the washing, ironing and
baking and some of the work in the dairy and
it seems to be working, though your mother
finds fault with everything she does.

Your mother is very bitter towards you all.
You most of all but Mary and Ellen for their
part in it too. I can only hope time will heal the
breach between you and I wish you a peaceful
Christmas and New Year.

Your loving Aunt Delia.

Delia knew nothing. She wasn't aware that the man she shared a bed with and who had sired six living children had also forcibly bedded his niece and that that child had been flushed away. She felt almost sorry for her, married to such a man, and she'd taken no account of her letter, which had been written in total ignorance of the circumstances.

But the letter had brought to mind again the deal she'd made with Peggy McKenna and which Peggy referred to again every few days when she visited Bridie. When Bridie told Mary she was going to take confession and tell the priest everything she was horrified.

'You don't have to. They know nothing about it. Leave it so, Bridie? Let them think you've just come over for a wee holiday over Christmas.'

'I can't.'

''Course you can.'

'I can't,' Bridie said. 'You don't know what this is doing to me.'

'And what d'you think will happen to me?' Mary asked.

'What do you mean?'

'They'll go for me too,' Mary said. 'They'll know I was in on it.'

Bridie knew her sister was right. 'All right,' she said at last. 'I see that it wouldn't be fair to bring the priests down about your head. But I feel I must confess, so I'll go into the city centre to St Chad's.'

Mary gave a small sigh of relief. If her sister was set on this course of action, then she was glad she was not going to St Catherine's. There were two priests at her parish church, Father Fearney and Father Shearer. Father Fearney was a tallish man with grey hair and wire-framed spectacles perched on a thin nose and behind them small blue eyes as cold and hard as pieces of flint. He had thin lips, a thin, rather scrawny neck, and a forbidding manner about him.

He saw his parishioners as full of sin and with no shame about them, no humility, no saving graces at all. He preached of it so often, no one was in any doubt about it. Few went to confession if they knew he was taking it. People said you'd only have to mention you'd forgot your morning prayers or let the odd bad word slip out of your mouth and he'd have you on your knees till the morning, begging forgiveness. God, what would he do to Bridie? Not that he'd be able to relate Bridie's confession, but then he wouldn't have to.

Father Shearer, the curate, was a different man entirely. He was younger and plumper, his face a reddish colour as was his head where his bald patch was growing more prominent every year. He had a benign, cheerful face with warm brown eyes, a wide nose and thick lips.

Father Shearer saw good in everyone. He was always the one to give a person another chance and seldom gave harsh penances to the penitents leaving his confessional box. But, in a way, Bridie would hate him to know more than Father Fearney. While the older priest would probably rip her to bits with his tongue, Father Shearer would just sound disappointed with her – scornful, disgusted – and she couldn't have borne that.

Bridie called at Peggy's house that evening and told her she was making for confession, but she was going to St Chad's in order to protect her sister. Though Peggy would have preferred her to confess to Father Fearney, she said nothing for she'd heard some of the priests at St Chad's were as bad as he was. Confessions were from seven to eight, and Bridie timed it to be in at the very end; she'd hate for the place to be full and all listening to what she had to say.

There was no one waiting in the old church that cold wintry night. Bridie knelt in the pew for a few minutes to pray and prepare herself and then, as there was no murmur of voices from the confessional box, she opened the door and knelt down on the hassock, her heart thumping against her ribs.

Father Robertson, on the other side, suppressed a sigh. He'd been preparing to leave when he heard the door open. He was cold, hungry and tired. His rheumatics were playing him up and particularly the leg he'd broken in his younger days. He shifted around to get more comfortable, but there was little room and he hoped fervently the confession wouldn't take more than a few minutes.

'Bless me, Father, for I have sinned. It's been three weeks since my last confession.'

'Yes, yes,' the priest said impatiently, and Bridie rattled through the usual litany of sins. Then came a pause. The priest suppressed a groan of annoyance. 'Go on, my child.'

'It's hard, Father.'

'God is forgiving, remember that. If you are truly repentant, he will forgive you anything.'

Bridie took heart at the priest's words. She had no wish to go on and wished she'd never come, but then she'd have had to face Peggy McKenna. Anyway, she told herself firmly, to come so far and not tell the whole of it would be a waste of time.

'Yes, Father,' she said. 'But to tell it all, I must go back a bit.'

Oh God, the priest thought, this will take all night. 'Go on,' he urged.

He listened to the story of Bridie's upbringing in rural Ireland, a seemingly idyllic childhood, surrounded by loving parents and siblings and beside her, her uncle, aunt and cousins. Bridie stressed the closeness between the families and the special bond between her father and her uncle.

Father Robertson wondered where this was all leading when suddenly Bridie's voice changed and, in little more than a whisper, she said, 'Then, Father, when I was fourteen, my uncle began touching me and kissing me.'

'Did you do anything to encourage this?' Father Robertson demanded sternly.

'No, Father.'

'Did you actively discourage it?'

'Yes, Father, I told him I didn't like it and he was to stop.'

'Did you confide in your parents at all?'

'I tried with my mother,' Bridie said, 'but she didn't seem to understand what I was talking about. She warned me to make no mention of this to my father, because my daddy reared my uncle when their parents died and there is special feeling between them.'

'But, despite all that, if you had confided in him, wouldn't he have believed you?' the priest asked.

'I'm not sure, Father. I loved my uncle too. At least I did then.'

The priest saw it all. The child grown to maturity, teasing and tormenting the man who'd always been like a second father to her, using her budding provocative ways until the mere man didn't know whether he was coming or going. That must have been the way of it, for if the girl had been completely blameless and been upset by the man's advances, she'd have found a way of telling her parents. And if she was a God-fearing and honest girl, wouldn't they have believed her before her uncle?

'Are you a truthful girl?'

'Mostly.'

'And are you a good girl? Do you attend Mass and the Sacraments?'

'Yes. Father,' Bridie said, and then in an attempt to explain went on, 'I was the only one left, the youngest, and I helped my daddy on the farm and my mammy in the house.'

'I see,' the priest said. 'Then I fail to see why you told no one of this happening between you and your uncle if you were as upset by it as you claim.'

'It did happen, Father,' Bridie protested. 'And I did tell someone in the end. I wrote to my sister. She lives here in Birmingham and she came over to Ireland in the summer two years ago and played war with Uncle Francis.'

'And did he stop?'

'Oh yes, Father, until the night I was at the Harvest Dance,' Bridie said.

The silence stretched between them and the priest said impatiently, 'Well? What happened?'

What happened? How could she say such words, describe such things to a man of God? Her mouth was so dry, she wondered if she'd be able to speak at all but then she began to stammer as she explained the row with Rosalyn causing her to flee and how Francis came upon her in the woods.

There was no doubting the girl's words as she described the rape and her uncle's reaction afterwards. The priest felt a stirring of sympathy for the girl. Whatever temptation was before the man, it was a dreadful thing he did to his own niece. 'Surely to God, if you'd gone home upset, confessed what he'd done . . .'

'And what then, Father? I would have ripped the two families apart and destroyed my parents' lives,' Bridie said. 'Then there would always be those that would wonder if I had led the man on. I told him if he ever touched me again I would kill him and I tried to put it from my mind.'

'That was very wise.'

'But not possible, Father, for I found I was pregnant,' Bridie said flatly. 'I was terrified, but felt the only one I could tell was my sister. She told me to come here. I couldn't just tell my parents that I wanted to leave. As I said, they relied on me. They'd have been upset and wanted to know why I was leaving them. I hadn't time for any delay, so one night, three weeks ago, I ran away in the middle of the night.'

Now the priest knew what the girl wanted, why she had come. She wouldn't be the first unmarried girl bearing an illegitimate child that had come to him, panic ridden and distraught. He had helped several of them, finding a place for them in the convent run by The Sisters of the Poor in Handsworth.

But Bridie was still talking, telling the priest how she talked for hours with her sister as they discussed alternatives. She looked at the priest earnestly through the grille. He must understand how frightened she was. She quaked at the thought of telling him what she'd done. 'I was at my wits end, Father. I didn't know which way to turn.'

'I do understand,' the priest said soothingly. 'You are not the only girl to feel this. I know of places for girls such as yourself where you could be cared for,' the priest went on. 'Run by nuns. I could put a word . . .'

'No, Father,' Bridie burst out. She was terrified now of telling the priest the whole of it. There was a sudden tension in the box that was almost tangible. Bridie lowered her head in shame and through the tears trickling down her cheeks, she muttered brokenly, 'Over two weeks ago I had an abortion.'

If the priest had been shot, he couldn't have reacted more violently. Any vestige of sympathy he might have felt for Bridie had been wiped out by her words. He jumped up, jarring his bad leg, and the pain intensified his anger as he spat out, his face almost pressed against the grille, 'An abortion? You sit there and calmly tell me you've killed your unborn child?'

Bridie was anything but calm, but she answered, 'Yes, Father.'

'Aren't you mortified by shame?' the priest

shouted. 'You've deprived an innocent child, who's never harmed anyone, not only of the gift of life, but of eternal life hereafter. Your baby will never be allowed to enter the Kingdom of Heaven. Did you think of that?'

Bridie hadn't and she wept harder as the priest railed on at her. She was glad of the emptiness of the church, that none would hear this torrent of venomous abuse poured down on her. 'You will go on your knees and beg God's forgiveness for this evil act you have done. You will remember to murder an innocent baby is the worst crime of all and you did murder it, make no mistake about it, just as if you killed a child, just as if you'd smothered one as he came from his mother's womb.'

'Oh God, I'm sorry, I'm sorry,' Bridie cried, the enormity of what she'd done suddenly brought home to her.

She didn't need the priest to tell her of her selfishness, that she'd only considered her own welfare, discounting that of the child she carried. She was as low as she could get as the priest went on about the home he could have got her into and her child being given to loving parents who could not have a baby of their own.

'A truly selfless act that,' the priest maintained. 'Allowing the child to live and helping a childless couple who'd love and cherish the baby you gave birth to, bringing he or she up as a good Catholic. Their souls would be saved.'

And of course Bridie could see that now. Why hadn't she thought that way? What matter that the word was the homes were like prisons? Surely she could have stood a few months of that to not only allow her child the chance to live, but to also help a childless couple.

All her life she had respected priests. She'd attended Mass every Sunday, taking Communion each time as the priest heard her confession weekly. She was a regular attendee at other church events, Benediction and Devotion, and always went to hear the missionary priests when they visited the town. She never really thought about her religion, it was just part of her. But at the centre of it was the priest, all-powerful and all knowing. They had a direct line to God and without absolution from them, you'd have to carry your sins about with you in a soul as black as pitch. Never had a priest spoken to Bridie in such a way and she stumbled from the church, filled with self-loathing. The penance was nothing. How in God's name could she ever atone for this despicable act?

She knew she was worthless and of no account, a bad taste in Jesus's mouth. She wondered for the first time whether it was worth going on. She could throw herself under a tram and everything would be over. Her parents would think her a grand girl if she did and none would ever know what she'd done. Everyone would be better off without her.

She'd taken a step forward, an eye on the tram clattering its way towards them, when a firm hand grasped her arm and pulled her clear. 'Careful!' a voice said. 'You don't want to stand so close.'

Bridie turned and found herself looking into the gentle eyes of Tom Cassidy.

'Bridie,' he said. Bridie was surprised he remembered her name. 'What are you doing here?'

'I was at confession.'

'Here? St Chad's isn't your parish church, is it?'

'No,' Bridie said, and gave a shrug. 'I was in town.'

Tom let that pass. 'It's lovely to see you again.'

'Is it?'

'Of course it is,' Tom cried.

Bridie thought of the things the priest had accused her of, the names he'd called her, and remembered that Tom had been in a seminary and, until recently, was destined for the priesthood. She knew he must never learn what she'd done. 'I'm not a fit person for you to know,' she said.

'Isn't that for me to decide?' Tom said with a laugh.

'No, believe me.'

Tom wondered what had happened to the girl he'd helped, the one he'd comforted on the boat and talked to for hours on the train just a few short weeks ago. She'd swept out of his life at New Street Station and he didn't know if he'd ever see her again, but his thoughts had been full of her ever since.

Now here she was saying she wasn't fit for him to know. He'd never heard anything so ridiculous.

And whatever she said, he had no intention of losing track of her again. 'Now come on,' he said, 'I know the type of person you are. We talked for hours, for God's sake,' he said. 'Would you consider going out with me one evening? We could go to the music hall, or the cinema?'

Bridie shook her head. 'You don't know me at all.'

'Bridie, stop it!' Tom said. 'If you think it's too forward going out with me one evening, bring your sister along too.'

'It's not that.'

'Then what is it?'

'It doesn't matter what it is,' Bridie cried. 'Leave me alone, Tom, for pity's sake!'

And at that, Bridie pulled her arm away that Tom still had hold of and ran. Tom almost took off after her, but people had begun to look at them and he had many glares thrown in his direction. Anyway, he was expected back at the Mission hall before nine, so he reluctantly averted his eyes from the running figure. He didn't know what was the matter with her; it was as if she carried the weight of the world on her shoulders and that somehow it was all her own fault. It was obvious, though, that she wanted no help from him. With a sigh, he turned away and made for the Mission hall, his heart as heavy as lead.

It was not only Tom that thought Bridie had the weight of the world on her shoulders. Ellen hadn't

189

known of Bridie's decision to confess about the abortion – Bridie had just told her aunt she was off to see Mary – but she knew it right enough when a tearful, distraught Bridie burst through the door that evening. 'What ails you, girl?' she asked, drawing her towards the fire, but Bridie was crying too much to answer.

She caught Sam's eye over the weeping girl she had clasped to her and he took the hint. 'I'm off for a pint then,' he said, taking his coat and cap from the nail behind the door. Ellen waited till the door closed behind him before she pushed Bridie gently into a chair and busied herself making a cup of tea for the two of them.

She said nothing till it was made. Bridie's tears were spent by then, but gasps still shook her body and her hands trembled as Ellen pressed the cup of steaming liquid between them. 'Don't try to speak till you've taken a few gulps of that to steady yourself,' she said. 'But then tell me what's upset you so.'

When Bridie did tell her about the priest's outburst, she was incensed. 'Bridie, love, you're not the sinner in this.'

'I killed a baby, Aunt Ellen.'

'No,' Ellen said. 'It wasn't a baby, Bridie. You stopped a baby being born, that's all. It's different entirely. And don't forget it was a baby you didn't want, forced on you by a man you should have been able to look to for protection. He's the one who should be before the priest this minute. He's

190

the sex-crazed pervert the priest should be wiping the floor with, not you.'

Mary said something similar when she was told, having been alerted to Bridie's despair by Sam. But Bridie couldn't get the priest's words out of her head. 'He said I could have had had the baby and given it away,' she said, raising her swollen face and red-rimmed eyes to Mary's. 'He knows of places I could have gone to. Then my baby would have lived – I could have given it away.'

'Bridie,' Mary said gently, 'something happens to a woman when she's pregnant, not just to her body, but to her mind too. When the baby's born and laid in your arms, it's, well, I can't explain, but the rush of love you feel . . . I couldn't have given either of my sons away, not for anything.'

'Yes, but I didn't love the baby. It wasn't like with you. You love Eddie, that's why.'

'No, I don't think it is just that,' Mary said. 'I think it's just nature's way of preparing you. All I'm saying is at the moment, you're full of remorse and guilt the priest has loaded on you, but if you'd had to give up a child you'd given birth to, you'd be feeling even worse, I think.'

It helped Bridie to know that Mary and Ellen were supportive, but the guilt didn't ease and it was compounded by Peggy McKenna. She'd seen the girl tear past her house that evening and, noting how distressed she was, she'd smiled. Later, passing her in the street, she'd muttered, 'Glad to see you did your duty,' before adding, 'I'll be along to see you one of these days.'

The blood in Bridie's veins seemed to turn to ice. 'Why?' she asked.

'Well, I could say just neighbourliness,' Peggy said. 'But you and I might have things to discuss.'

'I've done what you wanted.'

'You've done one thing, the thing you should have wanted to do yourself for the good of your immortal soul,' Peggy said.

'Leave me alone, can't you?'

'Oh, that's no way to talk to me,' Peggy said. 'In fact, if I were you, I'd be very careful of what I said and how I said it. There's still some in Donegal ignorant of your story that would love to hear of it.'

'Please, Mrs McKenna, don't destroy my parents lives. None of this is their fault.'

'Maybe, I will, and maybe I won't,' Peggy said. 'But you just be careful, that's all I'm saying.'

So Bridie, mindful of Peggy's threat, was very careful over what she said to Peggy and there was plenty of opportunity for she seemed to be for ever popping up. Both Ellen and Mary noticed and had expressed surprise that Bridie had any time for Peggy McKenna. 'Keep away from her,' Mary advised. 'She's a troublemaker, I've told you,' and Bridie thought if only she could.

Christmas passed in a blur and though for the children's sake Bridie tried to ease the load from

her shoulders, it wasn't a total success. She was glad
when it was over and things were back to normal.
She'd written an impassioned letter to her parents
before New Year, begging their understanding and
forgiveness, and Ellen and Mary had written too,
both keeping to the story that Bridie had felt stifled
on the farm. She'd fancied a change and knew the
winter was the right time to leave.

Bridie received no reply from her mother, but
in the New Year, she got a letter from Rosalyn,
whose mother had written to tell her what had
happened.

> *I don't blame you for leaving, Bridie. It's
> just the way you did it. I told Mammy you
> must have been desperate, but she said you
> never complained about it, but you'd been a
> bit odd, like depressed, before you left. I'm not
> surprised and I said so.*
>
> *America is wonderful, the people friendly
> and the house Aiden has is the cutest thing. I
> get on well with Maria too.*
>
> *Maria feels for you too. She said if you want
> to travel further afield, she could find you a
> place to live here and a job, no problem. You
> just have to say the word. There is plenty going
> on here: dances and movies, so many people
> have cars, you'd never believe it . . .*

Bridie was tempted to go to the States where no
one would know a thing about her. And then what,

said a little voice inside her – tell Rosalyn about her father?

Bridie knew she couldn't go. She didn't want to be near Rosalyn, or any of Francis's family anymore. Just as his behaviour had spoiled and tainted all the good times that had gone before, now it had spread to them all too – Frank and Rosalyn, Delia and even the younger ones. She wrote a brief note back to Rosalyn, thanking her for the offer, but saying she was settled in Birmingham and she'd got a job.

That wasn't a lie – she had got a job in the Woolworths store in the Bull Ring. She'd been determined to get employment as soon as possible, but Ellen wasn't terribly optimistic that she would. 'There's no rush anyway,' Ellen told her. 'Sure I like the company and we have more than enough money to do us.'

But Bridie wouldn't be dissuaded. 'I must do something,' she said. 'My savings won't last for ever.'

'Well, good luck to you,' Ellen said. 'There's many in this city that want and need a job. And yet it is often easier for a woman than a man. If you're determined enough, you'll find something.'

But as one weary day followed another and Bridie trudged fruitlessly from factory to factory, her optimism began to flag. Everywhere she went, groups of jobless men stood about and she always felt sorry for them.

Most had totally inadequate clothes for the winter chill and their boots were often dropping to bits. They'd stand around aimlessly, greasy caps pulled well down, hands shoved in pockets and a look of despair on their faces.

Bridie could well understand it. She wanted a job to pay her way. What if she had a child to provide for, rent to pay, food and clothes to buy? Not to be able to do these things for their families would make the men, any man, seem worthless. It struck her that Peggy McKenna was married to a man out of work and she almost understood why she was the way she was. But that was when she was away from her. When she was near – Peggy talking to her, threatening and goading her – it always made Bridie's skin crawl.

One evening as she eased her aching feet from her boots, Ellen asked, 'Have you thought about shop work? There's more women taken on in shops.'

'But I don't know anything about shop work.'

'You don't know anything about factory work either.'

'Well no, but I thought I could be shown.'

'And so you could,' Ellen said. 'But what's there to know in a shop? It's easy. Can you reckon up?'

'Oh aye,' Bridie said. 'I did all the book work for Daddy. I've always had a good head for figures.'

'Well then, worth a try I'd say.'

Anything was worth a try so Bridie tried the shops on Bristol Street, to no avail, before making for the city centre. Nearly everywhere she went people expressed doubt about her lack of experience and Bridie had become downhearted by the time she reached the Bull Ring.

There the story seemed to be the same until eventually she asked in Woolworths. Bridie had loved Woolworths when she been there as a child and stayed with Mary. Any trip to the city centre included going to the Bull Ring and looking around Woolworths. She'd loved the rush and bustle of the place, the girls in their smart green uniforms standing behind the dark wood counters, punching the prices into the tall brass cash registers with a confidence which Bridie could only admire.

They sold such an array of goods too, the counters often piled high with them. There were pots and pans and all manner of things for the kitchen, crockery and glassware and garden implements for those lucky enough to have a garden. There were books, large Bakelite records and a haberdashery counter and off to the side of that was everything for the hair: brushes and combs, and slides and ribbons and such like. But, best of all, was the counter with the toys and games and, of course, the one that sold the sweets. The great thing was that nothing cost more than sixpence.

That day, Woolworths was even more rushed than usual. Almost every counter had queues of impatient shoppers waiting to be served and shop assistants were scurrying around, trying to serve everyone as quickly as possible. For the first time, Bridie thought there was a good possibility of her getting employment. She was right: the manager was a worried man because many of his staff had been laid low with influenza. So when Bride asked about the possibility of a job, he decided to try her, despite her inexperience, but on a trial basis only. She was to start at eight o'clock the following morning.

Her family were delighted for her. 'It's on a trial basis only,' she reminded them.

'Och, away out of that,' Mary said. 'Once they see you in action they'll keep you on all right. One thing you've never been afraid of is hard work.'

The first morning she was put on the sweet counter, the very counter she used to hang around as a child, almost dazzled by the amount of sweets on offer and the variety. In fact so dazzled was she that when Mary had wanted to buy her some as a treat, she could scarcely make up her mind what to choose. She was working with another girl who introduced herself as Jean Tate. 'God, am I glad to see you,' she said. 'I've been on me tod since the New Year. It'll be nice to have another pair of hands.'

'Are there many off sick?' Bridie asked.

Jean nodded her head vigorously. 'You bet your life. Been going down like flies, they have.'

Bridie had to concentrate hard to understand all Jean said, she spoke so fast and the Birmingham accent was still tricky for her, but she was friendly enough and anyway listening to Jean was good practice for most of the customers spoke the same way. The Woolworths girls were quite interested in the pretty and petite Irish girl in their midst, but Bridie gave them little encouragement to find out any more about her. She didn't want them to know her past and anyway, didn't think she deserved to have friends.

Bridie was unaware that in trying not to give anything away, her answers were terse enough to be rude. When she'd been there a few days, Jean realised Bridie had told her little about herself and so in the canteen, she asked her directly, 'So where in Ireland you from then?'

'The north.'

'The British bit?'

'No, just outside that.'

'What you doing over here then?'

'My sister asked me over. She lives here.'

'Where's that then?'

'Edgbaston way,' Bridie said. She didn't say that she lodged with her aunt not her sister, nor offer any further information either. No one asked her because it was, as Jean said, like pulling teeth to get her to say anything at all. 'Maybe she has some dark secret in her murky past?' someone suggested.

'Oh give the kid a break,' said another. 'She's probably just shy. She might be a bit homesick too. Ask her out with us, why don't you.'

And Jean, feeling guilty because the other girl was probably right, did just that later that week. 'D'you want to come to the flicks with us Friday?' she asked.

'Flicks?' Bridie queried.

'Picture house, cinema, you know. There's a crowd of us go every Friday, it's a laugh.' Bridie couldn't imagine why anyone would want her in their company. She wouldn't go. 'I'm afraid I can't. Thank you for asking, but it's out of the question.'

She was unaware how formal and unfriendly her voice sounded, but Jean was not easily dashed 'Why,' she asked, 'summat else on?'

'Aye, yes.'

Bridie didn't say what and Jean didn't ask. She just went on, 'What about Saturday night then. We're going down the Alex to the variety show, then along to the Bull Ring after. What d'you say?'

Bridie wanted to say yes, she'd love to go, but she shook her head regretfully.

She reacted the same way when Jean asked her out the middle of the following week. 'It's Alice's big night, see,' Jean explained. 'She's been singing down this pub for flipping ages and she's just heard a bloke what gets jobs and that for singers has heard about her and is coming down this Thursday. We want to give her a bit of support, like.'

'I . . . I've never been in a pub in my life,' Bridie said.

'It ain't a rough place,' Jean assured her. 'It's a good night. They has this old Joanna – even when Alice ain't working we have fun there, singing around it and that.'

'I'm afraid I couldn't go to something like that,' Bridie declared stiffly.

'Say what you like about her being shy,' Jean said angrily in the canteen the following day, 'I know what she is all right, she's a bleeding snob, and thinks herself too good for the likes of us. She wouldn't even get off her bleeding high horse to cheer Alice on. Well, it will be a long time before I ask her out again.'

There was a murmur of agreement around the canteen; no one was going to rush to be friends with someone like that.

Another nail in her coffin, as far as the other girls were concerned, was that Bridie was a favourite with the supervisors and many considered she was sucking up to the bosses and making them look bad.

Bridie had been at Woolworths just over a fortnight when she jumped off the tram in a buoyant mood one Friday evening. She'd had to work a week in hand, but now she had her first pay packet in her pocket and she couldn't wait to show her aunt and begin to pay her way at last. Added to that, the boss was pleased with her diligence and hard work and said there was a good chance the job could be made permanent.

She was running up Bristol Passage and had reached the top of it when she came face to face with Peggy McKenna. 'Finished your week's work then?' she sneered. 'Your aunt was after telling me you had a fine job in Woolworths.'

'Yes, I have.'

'Money in your pocket then?'

Bridie, seeing the way the conversation was heading, felt sick. 'Not much,' she said. 'And I must give some of it to Aunt Ellen for my keep.'

'But you can spare a bob or two for me to put food before the weans, surely?' Peggy wheedled. 'I'm sure you'll see your way to do that when you remember what I know.'

With a sigh, Bridie opened her bag and extracted two shillings. 'I can give you no more,' she said, 'so don't ask me.'

'This will do for now,' Peggy said, and adjusted her shawl more tightly around her before hurrying away. Bridie followed, her earlier happiness wiped out as if it had never been.

When Bridie reached home, Ellen couldn't understand why she was so miserable. She thought that maybe she was missing her parents. Her first job, first wage packet, was something perhaps she'd want to share with them. 'Why don't you write to your parents and tell them all about your job?' she suggested later that evening.

'D'you think they'll answer if I do?' Bridie asked, and Ellen felt a lump in her throat at the wistful note in Bridie's voice. 'I don't know, pet,' she said. 'But you never will unless you write to them.'

Still Bridie's expression didn't alter so Ellen put her arms around her and held her tight.

CHAPTER NINE

On the face of it, Bridie had settled well into life in Birmingham, and was content with her job and family. But inside she was deeply unhappy. She knew she'd carry the guilt of what she'd done to that wee baby she'd been expecting all the days of her life. Peggy McKenna took two shillings or occasionally even a half a crown from her wages most weeks, which sometimes meant she had to walk to and from work and often did without her dinner in the canteen at lunchtime.

And yet she didn't mind the money as much as the things Peggy said to her. She told her she'd never find a man for she was bad through and through, anyone would see that, and she'd never have a family of her own and it served her right.

Bridie never contested any of the things she said, for she believed them and felt in a way it was right she should suffer like that – it was a form of penance. Ellen and Mary noted Bridie's despondency, but put it down to the fact that Sarah and Jimmy never wrote her the scribe of a letter in answer to the ones she sent them.

Sarah was as angry and hurt as ever and wrote to Ellen about Bridie's attempts at reconciliation:

If I'd had my way, I'd have thrown her letters away unread, but Jimmy said we had to hear what the child had to say. Child. By God, she's no child to do this to us, but then Jimmy was always soft with her.

And not the only one, Ellen thought. Maybe if she hadn't been so much the centre of their lives, they could eventually have got over her running away from them, but as it was she doubted it.

Bridie had also stopped writing to Rosalyn, primarily because she was the daughter of the man who still haunted her dreams. She explained it away to Ellen, however, by saying that she had little in common with Rosalyn anymore, that their lives had veered in different directions.

She didn't reply either to the slightly censorious letters that came from Seamus and Johnnie. Her mother had obviously written to them to put them in the picture. Bridie didn't much care what they had to say: they couldn't know about her life or their parents and so didn't even consider their opinions as valid.

Terry, who Sarah had also written to, didn't blame Bridie in the slightest.

*I'm surprised you stuck it so long, especially
after you wrote and told me about Mammy's
arm. No wonder you just upped and left one
day. It would have been better if you'd told
them, but I understand why you didn't. You
saw the pressure they brought down on me;
with you it would have been even worse and
you might have ended up staying. Mammy will
probably get over it soon enough and if she
doesn't, what odds? You have your own life to
live so stick to your guns, Bridie, and the best
of luck to you.*

Terry's letter reduced Bridie to tears, but she
brushed them away before Ellen spotted them.
She was glad that at least one of her brothers was
on her side and so she sat down and wrote Terry a
long letter about the job she had in Woolworths.

She told him about the Bull Ring and how
wonderful it was with the array of shops and
stalls that sold absolutely everything. She didn't
tell him of the old lags, usually blind or lame
veterans from the last war who sold matches or
razor blades or shoelaces from trays hung around
their necks and the old lady selling carrier bags.
She'd become inured to them now, as she had to be
to the ragged barefoot urchins who roamed around
the market, especially on Saturday when there was
no school.

She felt sorry for them, but when she said this
one day at work one of the other girls told her

not to waste her pity. 'Little tea leaves, the lot of them,' she said. 'Pinch anything not nailed down, them lot.'

Bridie said nothing. She knew the children were hungry: their large eyes and wasted bodies with stick thin arms and legs spoke for themselves and she often saw them fighting over the bruised fruit that had fallen from the barrows. The Bull Ring was where bargains could be bought and on a Saturday night a place of great excitement. Woolworths and the other shops would be closed, but the market was still operating and Bridie would see the shawl-clad, often barefoot women in the shadows of the gas flares. Many had a baby tucked inside the shawl and a clutch of children with them as they searched and begged for over-ripe vegetables and meat on the turn so that they could make a meal of sorts to feed their families.

Terry didn't want news like that, Bridie thought. In America, the land of plenty, he couldn't know how this place sometimes reeks of poverty.

But Terry could have told Bridie about the lines and lines of unemployed men there, and those who'd work a whole day for a loaf of bread. He could have told her of the beggars on the streets and the homeless who often froze to death in the sub-zero temperatures of a New York winter, and the soup kitchen and clothing banks set up to try and relieve the extreme suffering of the people.

But Terry told her none of this. He told her only

of his job, his apartment and his new girlfriend, a girl called Jo who was as Irish as himself.

Mary was worried about her young sister, particularly as she seemed to have made no friends. 'She seems to get on with the girls she works with well enough and is never away from the church with Benedictions and Devotion and all,' she told Ellen. 'She must meet young people like herself there and yet she never goes anywhere.'

Bridie went to everything the church had to offer, for God alone knew she needed all the prayers she could get. She wondered at first if Father Fearney looked at her in a funny way, or if she was just imagining it. Maybe that scornful, disapproving air was just the way he had of looking at everybody. Surely if he'd found out what she'd done, which he could have if Peggy McKenna had wished to be really vindictive, he'd have said. He wasn't the sort to keep quiet about such a thing, not him. God, he'd be more likely to publicly shame her from the pulpit.

Then she noticed he had the same expression the one time she'd been home when he'd called at Ellen's. Ellen offered him tea, of course, while the priest looked disdainfully at the armchair till you almost wanted to apologise that you were expecting him to sit in it. Did the priest want a wee sandwich, Ellen had asked, or a few biscuits? He accepted everything offered, though looked far from grateful and never said thank you. He asked

Bridie questions about her home in Ireland, her job at Woolworths, what she thought of Birmingham and how long she intended to stay, as if he was interrogating a suspect, and didn't seem greatly pleased with the answers either.

'What is it with that man?' Bridie asked when he'd gone. 'He's not exactly filled with Christian joy, is he?'

'He's not filled with much other than his own importance,' Ellen said angrily. 'D'you see the food he took off me? Well, I gave it to him to save some other poor beggar. I can afford it, but I've seen him accept hospitality from those not able to put food on the table. He's pompous and unfeeling and would take the bread from a baby's mouth and think the action quite justified.'

Bridie found out that Ellen's views were shared by most in those mean streets, though few were as open in saying so. Priests had influence and power and were well in with God and you can't afford to upset a person like that.

She continued to go to the church services, however, but she managed to slip in and out of the church without making contact with anyone, feeling sure that no one would want to know her if they had any idea of what she'd done.

Bridie's nineteenth birthday came and went without any acknowledgement from Ireland. Mary and Ellen tried to make the day a bit special and Bridie was tremendously touched by the card which arrived from Terry with ten dollars tucked inside.

That evening Ellen tackled Bridie over the meal. 'Did you tell them at work it was your birthday?'

'No,' Bridie said. She knew that the girls were cool with her, but also that it was her own fault and maybe only what she deserved.

'I thought you might have been going out somewhere? Have something planned?'

'No. No, nothing like that.'

'Oh,' Ellen said. 'Is there none you work with you'd like to make a friend of?'

'No, not really,' Bridie mumbled.

'She's got out of the way of making friends,' Mary said when Ellen recounted the conversation. 'Stuck away on that farm for years. The only one she saw besides Mammy and Daddy was Rosalyn.'

'I don't think it's that entirely,' Ellen said. 'It's more what she thinks of herself.'

Ellen was right. Bridie told herself a life of solitude was all she could expect. What if she'd become friends with someone and let slip what had happened? Dear God, it would be awful! At least this way she was tolerated. She didn't want friends, she didn't need them. As long as she had Ellen and Mary, letters from Terry and the church services she attended regularly, she told herself she was content.

She was in fact achingly lonely. She'd listen in to the girls' chatter in the morning, about their trips to the cinema, acts they'd seen in the music hall, or the dances they had been to. Some had boyfriends and the things they said about what they got up to often made Bridie's face go hot in embarrassment.

She longed to have someone to talk to, someone to sit at her table at lunchtime. Some of the girls would go out at lunchtime to pick out bargains or just for a look around the Bull Ring and she'd watch them enviously through the window. She'd see the girls in groups, often arm in arm, laughing together or picking over the bargains at a stall, exchanging banter with the costers, and she'd feel more miserable and alone than ever.

When March dawned as blustery and wet as the previous two months, few were surprised. Most people had become despondent about the continually grey clouds, so low and thick they turned afternoons into evening. That was the kind of day it was the Saturday Bridie finished work.

She groaned as she left the house when she saw the drizzling rain and turned up the collar of the good warm coat Ellen bought her. She had said Bridie needed good warm clothes if she had to go out in all weathers to get to work each day.

A crowd of people, late shoppers, were around Speaker's Corner where Ernie McCulloch was speaking. She'd been told about the man just after she began work, for he was a familiar face in the Bull Ring. He was described as the 'Prime Minister of the Bull Ring,' or the 'Prince of Beggars,' for the man raised much money for the poor and needy.

And God knows, thought Bridie, listening to him for a moment or two, he has plenty to choose from.

All around him were many like that, ill-clothed, pinched thin with hunger and most of the children barefoot. Bridie felt uncomfortable in her nice warm coat, the matching gloves, scarf and hat that Ellen had knitted for her and her stout winter shoes.

She'd been glad of the clothes Ellen had bought or made her and of the clothing club she paid into each week, for though Ellen let her keep half a crown for herself, some weeks Peggy had most of it off her. But still, when the collecting tin came around, she put the sixpence into it and wished it could be more. It was as she turned away that she heard her name called and saw Tom Cassidy detach himself from the crowd. 'I thought it was you,' he said. 'I wasn't sure. It was the coat and all. You look . . . You look lovely.'

In spite of herself, Tom's words brought a smile to Bridie's lips, though her face flamed in embarrassment. Her mouth was suddenly incredibly dry as she turned to face Tom.

'Hello, Tom.'

'Hello,' Tom said, and added with a laugh, 'God, but it's good to see you again.'

Bridie was almost mesmerised by the look in Tom's beautiful, brown eyes and they stood gazing at each other. There might have only been themselves in the world. The rest of the market, the resonant voice of Ernie McCulloch, the shouts and cheers of the crowd all ceased to exist for them. Tom Cassidy knew he loved Bridie McCarthy as he'd never loved anyone before and doubted he'd love anyone so much again.

He remembered the last time they'd spoken and how Bridie had gone on about not being a fit person for him. Replaying the conversation in his mind afterwards, he'd convinced himself she'd felt that way because he'd once been going in for the priesthood. So now, in an attempt to reassure her, he said, 'I've officially left the seminary now. They've accepted my final resignation and know I won't change my mind.'

Bridie didn't speak, but her head was in a whirl. This couldn't be happening to her, she couldn't let it happen. She must go.

'Speak to me? Say something?' Tom pleaded, and Bridie opened her mouth, but before she was able to say anything, the sleety drizzle turned into a downpour of stinging stair rods. The crowd around Ernie McCulloch's soapbox ran for cover and so did Tom, dragging Bridie after him.

They stood in the shelter of a shop overhang and Tom drew Bridie towards him, gently wiping her face with his snow-white hanky. She felt too weak to stop him, even when he slipped his arm around her shoulder and held her close she didn't protest. She didn't seem capable. It seemed so right, so good. Much more than contentment was filling her body now. She leant her tiny frame against Tom's and sighed, sensing the emotion running through his body and matching the tingling in her own. She felt warm, safe and secure, and the rain pounding the pavements and the icy wind seemed not to matter a jot.

'Can we go somewhere and have a drink, a cup of tea?' Tom said, his voice apprehensive, afraid that Bridie would reject him again.

His words brought Bridie back down to earth. How could she even consider going out with this good, kind man? It couldn't be. She shouldn't expect or look for happiness. But she hadn't looked for it, she told herself. It had come to find her.

'You will break my heart if you walk away again,' Tom said earnestly. 'Please, please don't do this to me.'

Bridie could hardly bear the look in his eyes, the painful pleading. That look would haunt her for ever if she was to walk away now and she found she had neither the heart nor the will to do it.

But something still stood between them, a secret. Bridie decided she must tell Tom. If, after that, he decided to have nothing more to do with her, at least it would be his choice. Her own feelings mattered little.

'I can't go for a drink with you now, Tom,' Bridie said, and at his protest held up her hand. 'Let me finish, please. I lodge with my aunt and she has a good dinner waiting for me every night. I couldn't just not turn up, she'd be upset and hurt. But I will meet you later.'

Tom's heart soared with joy. 'Will we go to the pictures, or to see a show?'

'No, Tom,' Bridie said. 'Somewhere where we can talk. I have something to tell you.'

'You're not married already?' Tom exclaimed in horror.

'No,' Bridie answered with a smile.

'You've decided to become a nun?' Tom persisted.

'No,' Bridie said again, giving Tom a slight push.

'Well, then nothing you can say will be of any importance.'

'I'll be the judge of that,' Bridie said.

'Yes Ma-am,' Tom said in a mock American accent with a salute that made Bridie laugh aloud, bringing the eyes of the people sharing the canopy with them upon her. Most smiled at the strikingly beautiful girl and the very handsome young man. They were so obviously in love with one another that it shone out of them. It was a bright moment in the dreary and dismal evening and many felt cheered because of it.

'Where shall we meet?' Bridie asked, oblivious of the people's interest in them.

'I'll pick you up from home,' Tom said. 'And I'm taking you there tonight.'

Bridie opened her mouth to say something, but closed it again. Tonight would determine everything. 'All right,' she agreed. 'And now that the rain's eased a little, we'd best make a move, or my name will be mud in the house.'

Bridie almost welcomed the cold and the blustery

rain because it encouraged Tom to hold her close against him and inwardly she hugged herself with delight.

'Seems nice enough,' Ellen said later to Mary when she popped around for a chat about Bridie's date. 'Said she met him at Strabane.'

'Aye,' Mary said. 'They travelled together. She told me all about it. I could tell he was interested at the station, but Bridie either wasn't, or wouldn't let herself be.'

'Well, she had a lot on her mind at the time,' Ellen remarked grimly. 'What's he do, this chap? Bridie was very vague.'

'He was training to be a priest, I believe,' Mary said. 'But he decided it wasn't for him and now works at some Mission place, helping the homeless, feeding and clothing the poor, that sort of thing.'

'Worthwhile sort of job,' Ellen remarked. 'And unless things change drastically, one that will keep him going for years yet.'

'Aye,' Mary agreed with feeling. The unemployment situation was getting worse. Every day you learned of more laid off and Mary worried about the same happening to Eddie. She and Ellen and the others with men in work did what they could for their unfortunate neighbours. Ellen would knit various odds and ends and Mary always passed on her children's clothes. They would both often make an extra big stew or broth to give to families near starvation and they often took in the children roaming in the street and fed them bread and jam.

But they could do little for the daily grind the families endured, and each winter the undernourished young and the elderly would fall prey to illness and disease. Now Mary understood her mother's worry over Bridie. She guarded her sons carefully, well able to understand Sarah's pain in losing five children. She was sure that she could not have borne it

Mary worried about Bridie too and so she was glad that her young sister had at last agreed to go out. 'She'll tell him all about it, this Tom Cassidy,' she told Ellen.

'Surely not? She won't load that on him tonight?'

'Oh aye, she will,' Mary insisted. 'She meets things head on, young Bridie. And she'll work on the assumption that it's best to get it into the open now at the beginning than to get fond of him and then tell him. That way, if he feels he can't take it, she'll be more hurt.'

'And what do you think he'll do?'

Mary shook her head. 'I don't know,' she said. 'It's a big thing for a man to take, any man. But most, if they care for you at all, would stand by you. After all, the rape was hardly her fault. It's the abortion that really bothers her – he was training for the priesthood and you know how they rant on about abortion.'

*   *   *

215

Bridie was glad that Tom was able to find a secluded table for them in the pub in the city centre he'd taken Bridie to. She'd hate to be overheard and was glad too of the dimness of the place – it suited her purpose.

She asked for orange juice, while Tom had a Guinness, and she didn't begin her tale until the drinks were before them.

All the time she spoke, Tom's eyes never left her face. He didn't speak or make a sound. But when she began to describe the rape, he took hold of her hands, which she was wringing in agitation, and squeezed them gently, his eyes clouding in sympathy as he heard of Bridie's pain and humiliation. He felt raw emotion running through her.

So much was now apparent to Tom. He understood why she was in such a bedraggled state at the station in Strabane, why she was alone, why she'd brought nothing to eat. He imagined her pain at being forced to leave her home in such a way, and the miles and miles of unlit roads that she'd traversed in the wind-driven rain and cold of a December night. He felt such tremendous admiration for her courage and determination and yet all she seemed to feel about herself was shame and degradation.

Bridie disengaged one of her hands to take a drink and, as she did, he used his handkerchief again to dab at the trails of tears running down her face. 'Go on,' he urged gently. And Bridie went on, glad of the strong hands that encircled hers so securely. She came at last to the end of her tale, her voice by then little above a whisper. When Bridie's eyes met his, her heart was pounding so violently she felt sure Tom could hear it and her mouth was so dry she could scarcely speak. She was afraid of what he thought, but suddenly he gently tilted her face upwards and all she saw in his beautiful, brown eyes was deep, deep sympathy. 'Are you not shocked?' she said. 'I feel such shame, such disgust at what I've done.'

'The abortion, you mean?'

'Of course.'

'Bridie, my poor dear,' he said. 'Listen to me. The abortion wasn't your fault any more than the rape was.'

'But . . .'

'But nothing,' Tom said. 'You asked me if I was shocked. I'll say I was. But not at you, my darling girl, but at what happened to you. A woman can seldom beat off a man intent on violating her. But for a woman as frail and small as you, there would be no way at all you could have prevented what happened. You kept quiet for the sake of the families and the life they'd have, not yourself. I know how it would be. None better.

'And the pregnancy caused you to run away, with condemnation coming from all sides. What else were you to do?'

'The priest said . . . The priest said . . .'

Bridie couldn't go on. She was afraid she would cry great, gulping sobs that couldn't be hidden. But

Tom knew what she was saying anyway. 'Celibacy brings its own pain and torment among priests,' he said. 'But one bad thing it does do is remove us from ordinary people, particularly women.

'I was revered in my home town because I was entering the priesthood. It was as if I'd become some sort of God overnight. I wasn't supposed to act, think or feel as ordinary mortals. The point is, though, that when these mortals come to you with problems they're having in their marriage or whatever, you have no experience to draw on.

'Many priests fail to understand women's feelings. Your uncle, for example: the priest said little of him in condemnation, according to what you told me. Your uncle forced you to have sex and left you with the consequences, yet you're thought of as the worst in the world, leaving your parents in the lurch that way. Then you had to make the decision to abort your own baby and yet his life carries on the same way. That can't be right.'

'But it was a mortal sin.'

'But if you're sorry you did it . . .'

'No,' Bridie put in, 'I'm sorry I was forced to do it nearly lost my life after it, but I think in the same circumstances I'd do it again.'

'Look, Bridie,' Tom said, 'such a thing will never happen to you again. Talk to God and he will give you peace. He understands what's in your heart more than any priest. And then put this behind you. Let me try and make you happy.'

'You're so good, so understanding,' Bridie said,

and added in amazement, 'I didn't think men like you existed, I never thought I'd find happiness and fulfilment again.'

'You can,' Tom said. He leant across the table and stroked Bridie's hands gently. 'You're very special to me, Bridie. I love you.'

Bridie drew her breath in sharply. She had imagined she'd never hear those words.

'Tell me how you feel about me,' Tom pleaded. 'Do you like me a little?'

'I like you more than I can say,' Bridie said. 'And . . . And yes, I love you with all my heart.'

Tom's eyes were dancing with happiness and he leaned across the table again and kissed Bridie gently on the lips.

CHAPTER TEN

After that first date with Tom, Bridie agonised over the story she had told him, despite his sympathetic reaction. She knew she'd had to tell him; no way could she have started any form of relationship with a man and not be totally honest, but she worried about his reaction. Oh, she knew what his initial response had been in front of her, especially when she'd been so distressed. But when he'd left her outside Ellen's front door and began the walk home, had he thought that he'd had a narrow escape? Had he been alarmed that he'd nearly allowed himself to be drawn to such a girl – one used and abused and turned murderer?

Bridie barely slept and when she rose for nine o'clock Mass, Ellen took one look at the girl with the lint-white face with blue smudges beneath the red-rimmed eyes and felt her heart contract with pity. She'd been in bed when Bridie had returned from her date with Tom Cassidy and so hadn't seen her. She presumed Bridie had done what Mary had thought she would and told Tom and it hadn't gone down at all well. That young man was not the man Mary imagined, she thought to herself.

She said nothing about the evening to Bridie and cautioned Mary, who she met later at Mass, to say nothing either. 'Least said, soonest mended, I always say,' and Mary agreed.

Bridie, who'd expected her aunt and sister to quiz her about the night before, was heartily glad they didn't, and she castigated herself for expecting any man to want anything to do with her.

She was totally unprepared for the knock that came on her aunt's door that day after dinner, as they sat together with a cup of tea and Sam dozed in the chair nearby.

Few people knocked on doors in that area; the priest maybe, or the doctor, and so Ellen looked at Bridie, her eyebrows raised in surprise, before pulling herself to her feet. She was surprised and not that pleased to see Tom outside, convinced he'd upset Bridie the previous evening. 'Yes!' she barked.

Tom was surprised at the woman's abrupt tone. 'Can I . . . May I see Bridie?'

Ellen was confused. She looked into the room and saw that Bridie was agitated and yet . . . yet there was a light dancing in her eyes. Her eyes slid to Tom's face and she saw the rapt attention there. Well, if that's the way the wind blew, she decided she'd do all she could to foster it. 'Come away in,' she said to Tom, and threw the door open wider.

Sam, roused by the noise, sat up in the chair when he realised they had a visitor.

'Sit down, Mr Cassidy,' Ellen said. She liked the look of this young man, she thought, studying him surreptitiously. She'd liked the look of him when he'd delivered Bridie home from work the previous evening and then later when he called to take her out, but neither time had she spoken to him above a greeting. She knew looks weren't everything but the man was fine and handsome and if he was keen on young Bridie then she needed to know more about him because despite her terrible experience with Francis, Bridie was naïve about the ways of the world and some men liked to play fast and loose with women.

However, within minutes of talking to Tom, Ellen knew that he wasn't like that. She liked the easy, yet respectful way in which he spoke to both her and Sam and the way he was so open and honest about everything. She learned about the small farm in the north of Ireland where he'd grown up which, being a boy born after three sisters, he was set to inherit. But then, as a child, he felt he had a vocation for the priesthood and was sent to a seminary in Liverpool.

'And what happened?' Ellen asked.

Tom told the tale of the young boy who'd tried to repress doubts that he'd made a mistake for years so that he wouldn't disappoint everyone until the doubts grew until they could be ignored no longer. He was sent to work with a friend of the Bishop, a

Father Flynn, who Tom said was such a fine man who did marvellous work with the poor and needy, in order to settle his mind.

'However,' Tom said. 'Within a few weeks of arriving in Birmingham, I knew that the priesthood wasn't for me and I'd been right not to go forward for ordination feeling like I did. I've officially left the seminary now and am a full-time lay worker at the Mission'.

He spread his hands. 'And there you have it,' he concluded. 'As for Bridie, I like her very, very much and if she's agreeable, I would love the opportunity to get to know her better.'

His eyes met Bridie's and Ellen plainly saw the spark between them. In that look, Ellen knew that Bridie had met her soulmate and her heart was eased, for she knew in Tom, Bridie had the chance of regaining happiness.

'He's a fine man,' she told Mary later when Tom and Bridie had gone out for a walk. 'Good, upright and honest, and Sam thought the same.'

'So why was Bridie looking like a ghost through Mass?' Mary asked.

'She was worried he'd have second thoughts,' Ellen said. 'I snatched a few words with her when she went upstairs to change her shoes and fetch her coat. I wanted to make sure she really did want to go out with him and hadn't just said yes for a quiet life. You were right, Mary. She told Tom everything that had happened to her when they met yesterday. She worried all night that he might think the worst of her because of it.'

'Bridie doesn't know her own worth,' Mary said. 'She is beautiful, so delicate-looking, that given the slightest encouragement lads would trample one another to the ground to look after her, yet she seems unaware of it. Still, if she's found a decent lad now to care for her, then I'm delighted.'

'At least he knows all now,' Ellen said. 'There will be nothing to jump out at him later.'

Bridie was glad of that too when she found Peggy waiting for her as she made her way home from work the following day. 'Fine man you have there,' she said sneeringly.

'Aye.'

'Catholic, is he?'

It was on the tip of Bridie's tongue to tell Peggy to mind her own business, but she didn't dare. 'Aye, a good Catholic.'

'And does he know, this good Catholic boy, what you did? That you murdered your baby?'

'Aye, he does,' Bridie was able to answer. 'I've told Tom everything.'

She knew she'd taken the wind out of Peggy's sails and she pushed past her and made for home.

And so Tom and Bridie's courtship began and what a wonderful courtship it was, especially for Bridie. Everything was new and exciting to her. Though Tom's salary was not great, he was generous with what he had and it mattered little to Bridie where they went. The nearby Broadway cinema was a treat as was the ABC further up Bristol Street. Sometimes they went into the town to a cinema there. But wherever they went, Bridie would be more than pleased. The cinema always seemed a magical place to her. Tom bought sweets for her as they went in and Bridie would love the feel of her feet sinking into the thick red carpet as they followed the usherette's dancing torch directing them to their seats.

The screen would be covered with thick velvet curtains and in front of it would be flimsy gauze, ruched and fastened at the sides, and she'd sit in breathless anticipation as the organist would pound out popular tunes on the piano. Then the lights would dim further, the curtains would pull back and they would hear the whirr of the projector start up and see the smoke of the beamed spotlight that came from the ceiling. Then the crowing cockerel advertising *Pathe News*, would resound around the cinema and Bridie would settle into her seat with a contented sigh.

She didn't really care what the film was. She wasn't that keen on the frightening ones like *Dracula* or *Frankenstein* but even those gave her the chance to grasp Tom's hand tight and hide her head in his jacket at the scary bits. She enjoyed *Tarzan the Ape Man* and laughed herself silly at Charlie Chaplin's antics in *City Lights*. She also saw Gracie Fields in *Sally in our Alley* and that meant especially a lot to her because just a few weeks later, she saw the lady in person at the Hippodrome.

They had to go up into the gods, where the stage was miles away and the seats hard, for Tom hadn't money for the better seats. Bridie certainly didn't care and she watched enthralled at the doughty woman, as small as herself, but with a powerful voice, belt out song after song until she held the audience in the palm of her hand.

Bridie thought she liked the music hall even more than the picture house because the people were real. There was George Formby and his ukulele, Max Miller, Tommy Trinder, Harry Lauder and countless more. She saw singers, dancers, acrobats, conjurers, comedians – such a variety of acts. And there was a vast array of theatres to choose from. If the programme at the Hippodrome didn't tempt, there was always the Alex or the Empire, or the Grand in nearby Corporation Street. Then there was the Theatre Royal in New Street, which showed musical comedies, or the Rep, which showed more serious plays.

But the most important treat Tom gave to Bridie was the idea that she was worthy of love, of friendship; she was a person he had chosen to get to know better. For the first time in a long, long while, she began to feel better about herself and she made tentative approaches to the girls she worked with. It was easier now that she had things to say, for she was able to discuss films and musical acts she'd seen and talk about the stars with the rest of them.

The girls didn't bear any grudges towards Bridie

for her initial reaction to them – most thought she'd been a little shy, unused to their ways and maybe terribly homesick. Whatever had ailed her in the beginning was over now. Bridie was glad of their friendship. They were all interested in hearing about Tom and Bridie was only too happy to talk about him.

'Takes you to the pictures a lot does he, this Tom?' a girl asked one day.

'Aye . . . Well, I suppose.'

'Want to watch him, I'd say.'

'Why?'

''Cos, they takes liberties,' another said with feeling. 'God, sometimes I think it's the only reason they go to the cinema. Went out with one chap and he had his bleeding hands all over me. Thought I was out with a bloody octopus.'

'Yeah,' said another. 'They buy you a packet of acid drops and a choc ice and think it's license to undress you in the back row.'

'Tom doesn't do anything like that,' Bridie said, shocked at the casual way such things were spoken of.

'What does he do?'

'He holds my hand.'

'Is that all?' the first girl asked. 'You mean he don't try 'owt on?'

'No!'

'Well, I'd say he's either a saint or a nancy boy,' the first girl declared.

'Or a gentleman,' the supervisor declared, seeing

Bridie's confusion and embarrassment and feeling sorry for her 'But whatever Bridie's boyfriend is or isn't doesn't matter to you. What does matter is getting back to the shop floor because your dinner hour is nearly up.'

A few of the girls made faces behind the supervisor's back, but they all followed her meekly enough. Bridie thought of the conversation all afternoon. She wasn't sure what a nancy boy was, but it didn't sound a nice thing to be. She knew it was mainly her fault that they only held hands. She enjoyed some forms of intimacy and could even tolerate his arm around her shoulders, unless he tried to press her against him, but the minute he tried to pull her into a tight embrace, she would stiffen and pull away. She tried to explain to Tom that every time he did that, it reminded her of Uncle Francis and also tried telling herself not to be so silly, but it was no good.

Then, one Saturday towards the end of April, as Tom met Bridie from work, he suggested they go to the Bull Ring that evening. It was dry and quite warm and Bridie readily agreed. The girls at work often talked about the fun to be had on a Saturday night at the Bull Ring and she remembered Tom describing it all to her in the train way back in December. She'd never seen the Bull Ring at night; the time she was over before, Mary used to be tired in the evenings and not really up to jaunts like that. She was filled with excitement to be going to such a place.

Most of the shops were shutting that Saturday evening as Bridie emerged and Tom ran across to Mountford's the butchers to buy a meat pie each to eat as they walked through the cobbled streets. Most of the barrow boys were still there, their wares lit by spluttering gas flares, and the place was almost as busy as daytime.

The Market Hall was still open and full of people so Tom took Bridie's hand and led her up the steps. Bridie was glad to see the steps cleared of the old lags who made her feel so sad. They wandered between the stalls as they ate their pies, looking at the array of goods for sale.

Some stalls sold food, fruit and vegetables, eggs, cheese and dairy produce, while several sold flowers. Others were festooned with clothes or bales of clothes and were alongside those selling pots and pans, crockery, toys and sweets, and there were also some junk stalls where you could pick up many interesting things.

The pet stalls always had a crowd around them, watching the boisterous puppies at play in their sawdust filled boxes, or the kittens mewing plaintively. There were chirpy budgies and twittering canaries, rabbits and hamsters in cages and fish swimming endlessly in glass aquariums.

'I've never seen the point of fish,' Bridie said. 'Just swimming round and round like that.'

'No, nor me,' Tom said. 'I wouldn't mind a dog though, but not here in the city centre. A dog needs space to run.'

Bridie remembered the dogs back home and agreed with Tom, but as they turned to leave, Tom touched her arm. 'It's nearly seven o'clock,' he said. 'Let's wait awhile.'

Moments later the clock began to strike. The noise dropped suddenly in the Market Hall and everyone turned their heads to watch. Four life-size figures appeared from the clock, three knights and a lady, and struck the bell with hammers seven times. It was a beautiful piece of craftsmanship. 'It's grand, isn't it,' Bridie said as the notes of the chimes died away.

'Aye,' Tom agreed. 'But a man was telling me the clock had a curse on it.'

'Why?' Bridie asked as they made their way down the steps again.

'Apparently the fellow that made it wasn't paid in full and he put a curse on it.'

'Don't seem to have worked, does it?'

'No,' Tom said. 'Probably just a tale. Heaven only knows who starts these rumours.'

Outside, it had got much darker. The little blind lady selling carrier bags had gone from her pitch outside Woolworths and her place had been taken by old Gypsy Boswell, who claimed she could tell fortunes.

'Jimmy Jesus is up on the soapbox,' Tom whispered, pointing to the man with white hair and a long white beard. He had a long brown coat, tied with string, and boots with the toes kicked out, but you forgot all that when you heard him speak, preaching the gospels in a soft, refined voice, urging you to repent of your sins and remember that God had given his only son to save mankind.

As usual, he was heckled. It was normally youths who began shouting at him and, as Tom and Bridie began walking towards Jimmy, one of them suddenly yelled, 'Put a sock in it why don't you, old timer. Nelson must be sick of listening to you,' referring to the large sculpture of Nelson in the middle of the Bull Ring.

Jimmy Jesus's rheumy eyes sought the young man's for a second before he said, 'He well might be, young man, but he at least is too much of a gentleman to say so.'

There was a ripple of laughter through the crowd and the youth coloured slightly, but could find no reply, and Tom smiled as he drew Bridie on.

There was so much to see: the man tied up in chains, who claimed he would get free when the money in his hat reached a pound, and around the corner from him a juggler and a man on stilts. Then there was a fire-eater and a man who lay on a bed of nails. 'Come on, duck,' he encouraged Bridie. 'Stand on my belly, why don't you? Promise you I won't look up your skirt like.'

Bridie shook her head, laughing, as Tom took her hand and like children they danced and pranced to the accordion and fiddle players assembled by the now closed Rag Market, singing the words to the old songs like everyone else around them.

'D'you like cockles and whelks?' Tom asked as

the strains of the Sally Army brass band, marching their way from the Citadel, were heard in the distance. 'I've developed a taste for them since living here.'

'I've never tried them,' Bridie admitted. Tom insisted she had a large dish, which he covered liberally in vinegar.

'Well d'you like them?' he demanded when Bridie had sampled just a few, and though she tried valiantly to cover her distaste by nodding vigorously, he wasn't fooled. 'Not everyone feels the way I do about these,' he said, taking Bridie's dish and tipping it into his own. ' "Waste not, want not," my mother used to say.'

'You don't mind me not liking them?' Bridie said.

'Why should I?' Tom asked. 'One man's meat and all that.' And then he bent down and whispered, 'Would you rather have a baked potato?'

'I think so,' Bridie whispered back, and grabbing her hand again, Tom dragged her over to the baked potato stand. The potato was at first too hot to handle and Bridie had to jiggle it from hand to hand. When she eventually bit through the soft, slightly smoky tasting skin into the creamy potato beneath, she knew she preferred it above seafood, and munched happily as the Sally Army band marched into the Bull Ring playing and singing 'Jerusalem' very loudly.

'They do marvellous work,' Tom said to Bridie. 'They're thought well of down at the Mission.'

Bridie often found Tom's views strange. She'd been brought up to believe that the Roman Catholic Church was the one true Church, founded by Peter, an apostle of Jesus Christ himself. Every other religion was false and the people worshipping them destined for Hell. Despite the McCarthys' relative proximity to the border separating the Free State from the six British-ruled counties, she'd met few people from the Protestant faith until she came to England. She knew though that she was forbidden to take part in any service conducted by them, or even enter a non-Catholic church.

Tom, however, despite his years in the Seminary, had a far more liberal outlook. He worked with many religious groups and often recounted the lively debates they had about their varied viewpoints and now here he was saying the Salvation Army did good work. 'Why the long face, sweetheart?' he asked as he finished the last of his whelks and licked his fingers.

'I haven't got a long face,' Bridie protested. 'I'm just confused about what you said about the Salvation Army, you being a Catholic and all.'

'Sweetheart, we're on the same side,' Tom said. 'The people we help have their own devil to fight. It's called extreme poverty and if we can help more people more effectively by banding together then why not? In the end, whichever way we chose to do it, we're worshipping the same God.'

It was a shocking statement, almost blasphemous. But as Bridie watched the earnest faces of the men and women of all ages from the Sally Army singing and playing their hearts out, she began to see what Tom meant.

They stayed to the end, singing the hymns they recognised and listening to those they didn't, and Bridie felt marvellous to be a part of it, all with solid, dependable, lovely Tom beside her. Eventually, the music drew to a close and Bridie saw a group of down-and-outs moving forward. 'What's happening?' she asked.

'They take the homeless over to the Citadel for soup and bread,' Tom replied. 'They run hostels too and will try and find a bed for the old or those they think are ill. Like I said, they do great work.'

Bridie watched the old, shuffling men and even women falling into line behind their smartly dressed benefactors. They were the sort of people most would cross the road to avoid. They were ragged and dirty and probably smelled, yet they were welcomed warmly.

Tom and Bridie walked home, hand in hand through the dark streets, and Tom was happier than he'd been in a long time because he knew he was at last making headway with Bridie. He'd known when he'd listened to what had happened to her that he'd have to have immense patience and he had. He'd never press her, but he felt that night their relationship had moved forward a pace or two.

He knew he wanted Bridie as part of his life and he knew too there would be no opposition from her aunt and uncle or her sister and her husband. They all liked him and whenever he called at Ellen's house for Bridie he was welcomed in and tea and a bite often almost forced upon him. In fact, it was difficult to leave sometimes. But he never showed impatience, partly because he'd become fond of Ellen and respectful of Sam, but also because he knew that if he wished to marry Bridie before her twenty-first birthday, Ellen might have great influence persuading Bridie's parents to agree.

Bridie hadn't let herself think that far ahead. All she knew was that she was walking on a balmy spring evening, holding hands with the loveliest man in the world and going back to a home where she was loved. She had a supportive sister just around the corner and a job she enjoyed where she'd begun eventually to make friends. What more could she want?

She knew though what she did want and that was a letter from her mother. Tom Cassidy was fast becoming the most important person in her life and she'd written to her parents telling them all about him. But, like all the other letters, there had been no reply.

Terry had replied when he'd received a similar letter from Bridie. He'd said if Tom Cassidy was a good man and they loved each other then she should hang on to him. He was marrying his Jo in May and hoped for a cluster of children before too long and wished Bridie all the best.

Ellen could see that though Bridie had been

cheered by her brother's letter, her mother's lack of response troubled her. So Ellen wrote her own letter, extolling Tom's virtues and said Bridie could look further and fare worse. But Sarah's reply stunned her, for she said Bridie was no longer their daughter and they had no interest in what she did or who she'd met.

'The woman's inhuman,' Ellen said to Mary when they were alone. 'I know Bridie running away would be hard to take, and thank God they never knew the real reason for it, but she can't disown her like this. Blood, after all, is thicker than water.'

Bridie was unaware of Ellen's intervention. Each Sunday, she wrote a letter to her parents but she had given up the idea of ever getting any kind of response. And so, that night walking back home with Tom, she was almost content.

Tom felt it too and also a softening in Bridie. That night for the first time, before her aunt's darkened house, he drew Bridie towards him and bent his head to give her a chaste kiss. He felt her stiffen in his arms, but he held her tighter and then, as his lips touched hers, she sprang back with a cry of alarm, threw her hand up and delivered a ringing slap across his left cheek.

When he'd held her tight against him, she'd imagined she was back in the little wood in Ireland, struggling with Uncle Francis and when Tom kissed her, she saw Francis's face and Francis's thick lips and she'd reacted in fright and panic.

But it wasn't Francis she'd hit, it was her dear,

darling Tom. In the dim light of the street lamp, she saw the crimson stain of a handprint across his face and was mortified by what she'd done. 'Oh God! Oh God, Tom, I'm sorry! So very, very sorry!' she cried as tears spurted from her eyes.

She stood up on tiptoes and traced gentle fingers around the mark. 'I . . . I don't know what came over me.'

Tom removed her hand gently from his face and kissed her fingers. 'I do,' he said. 'And I don't want you to worry about it.'

'But . . .'

'But nothing, Bridie. You need time to forget what happened to you and learn to trust me. You may need a lot of time, but it will come. I'm a very patient man. Don't worry.'

'You won't tire of me?'

'Tire of you, not at all,' Tom said. He held both her hands close to his face as he said. 'I don't know if you realise this, but I love you, Bridie McCarthy.'

'Do you?'

'I do truly,' Tom said. 'These are just words I know, but in time I'll show you how much I mean them. And now, Bridie here's four more important words. Will you marry me?'

Tom hadn't meant to ask Bridie to marry him so soon, but the moment had just seemed right.

He could see Bridie was stunned. She was just staring at him, as if she couldn't believe her ears. And she couldn't. 'D'you . . . D'you mean it?' she said at last.

'I do.'

'Oh. Then the answer is yes, Tom. Yes. Yes. Yes,' and Bridie's arms went voluntarily around his neck and this time when his lips met hers she didn't push him away.

But Tom knew Bridie still had a long way to go and so he didn't kiss her properly or for very long. And when he felt his own body stirring with desire for her, he moved away slightly, not wishing to frighten her to death altogether. 'There are practicalities to consider,' he said. 'Before anything else you will need permission from your parents for you're only nineteen.'

Bridie wondered how she'd get permission to do anything from parents who refused to acknowledge her, but said nothing. 'In the normal way of things I should ask your father's permission,' Tom said, a small frown appearing on his forehead. 'But in this case . . .'

'Ask Uncle Sam,' Bridie suggested. 'That's if you want to do it properly, but you know he won't say no. He likes you. They both do.'

Tom didn't forsee any problems there. 'And I'll have to tell my parents too,' he said.

And then a thought occurred to Bridie. 'Will they, your parents, expect you to go home and run the farm?' she asked. 'Now you're not to be a priest.'

'Would you mind being a farmer's wife?' Tom asked.

Bridie gave a shiver of distaste. How she would

hate living just a few miles from her parents. She knew she would feel more than uncomfortable. And then, there was Francis. How in God's name would she ever face him again?

But then she looked at the dear, dear man before her and knew if he left her, her life would have no meaning and so she said, 'Tom, I would go with you to the gates of Hell and back.'

'Oh my darling love,' Tom said and his kiss was spontaneous and very, very sweet. 'I know how hard it would be for you to move back, but that will be unnecessary.'

'Oh.'

'My sister is getting married,' he told Bridie. 'She's the eldest, Agnes, and well over thirty. No one thought of it at all. The chap she's marrying is a man called Tony Canley and the Canleys have a farm on the borders of Antrim. But they had three sons and a fair few girls too and Tony is the third son. He'd been brought up to farming and yet the chance of him ever running his own farm is slim. Agnes wrote and asked me if I had any intention of coming back ever. I told her no and her and Tony could have the place and welcome to it.'

'Wasn't that a wrench for you?'

'Och, not at all,' Tom assured her. 'I haven't really been on the farm since I was twelve. I don't know that I could take to it again. And the place . . . It's so dead. Remember, first I was in Liverpool and now Birmingham. I like the city life and my work at the Mission and I love you and want you in my life, by my side, bearing my children.'

'And I want it too,' Bridie said. 'Oh, Tom more than anything in the world I want that. I want to shout it from the rooftops that I love you so, but I can't even tell my aunt and uncle until tomorrow, because all the lights are out, so they must be in bed.'

'Never mind, my love,' Tom said. 'We have a lifetime before us. Now I must save to buy you an engagement ring.'

'I want no engagement ring,' Bridie said firmly, for she knew the price of them. 'Your word is better than any engagement ring. I'll be proud to wear your wedding ring. It's the only one I need or want.'

'Oh, Bridie, I love you so.'

'And I love you, Tom. I'm sure of it now,' Bridie said and she stood again on tiptoe and placed her lips on Tom's.

There was a near explosion in Tom at Bridie's nearness, the feel of her arms around him, their lips touching and though he longed to go further, it was neither the time nor the place and so he reluctantly pulled away and bade Bridie goodnight.

Bridie went inside, closed the door and leaned against it. Her whole face was aglow, her eyes sparkling and she felt as if she was walking on air. She was in love and with a wonderful, wonderful man and now they were to be married. After all that had happened, God had given her another chance.

And please God, she'd soon have a child conceived in love that she and Tom would take pleasure in rearing.

She didn't know how she reached the attic, for she had no recollection of mounting the stairs, but there she was. She told herself to try to sleep for then the morning would soon come and she could share her news with people who'd welcome it, but she lay for hours, wide-eyed, too excited and elated to sleep and went over every minute of that wonderful, wonderful evening.

CHAPTER ELEVEN

Jimmy McCarthy, with the milking and breakfast over, leaned over the farm gate and took a long drag on his glowing pipe. Mid-May, he thought, and the countryside had never looked better. He should have been a contented man: the spring planting was done and the lambs had all been born fine and healthy. There was plenty of grazing for the sheep and cattle in the green fields and hillside pastures and the hay for the winter feed was already ripening in the sun. Everywhere he looked he saw evidence of life, everything growing and new and even the hedgerows a riot of colour.

Life should have been good for Jimmy McCarthy. But there was an ache in his heart that had developed that December day he had come running to the house, having heard Sarah's anguished cry. He had seen her holding a letter in her trembling fingers, her face chalk-white. His little lass, the light of his life, his workmate, the one he'd thought would always be there, or at least close to ease his twilight years, had run away.

She'd not just left like the others had, having discussed it and made plans, she'd fled in the dead of night as if she couldn't bear to live with them a minute longer. He blamed himself; Sarah had been right, the child couldn't cope on her own, and he'd not listened. If only she'd told him, confided in him, he would have got help in.

He hadn't realised himself the amount of work she did. In the early days, if it hadn't been for Francis and his sons Frank and Declan, he'd never have got through at all. Now that he had Willie things were easier, especially as Sarah had at last agreed to have his wife Beattie in to help her in the house. Sarah had kicked up wicked about that at first. Jimmy knew it was hard on her, seeing another woman not even kith or kin to help her in the kitchen. It had caused a bitterness towards Bridie that had never eased, for though the woman did her best, she was still a stranger. Beattie could also talk the hind leg off a donkey, but in comparison, there was little conversation to be had from Willie at all. Jimmy gave a sigh. He missed the lively chatter of his daughter and wished he could at least find some way of healing the breach between her and her mother.

Every Tuesday, a letter came from her, as regular as clockwork, and that's what Jimmy was waiting for that morning, though Sarah would barely ever look at it and certainly wouldn't reply. Jimmy often thought of writing a wee note himself, but he hadn't much of a hand for writing. Sarah had always dealt with that kind of thing and anyway, he knew she'd fly into a fine temper if she'd found out about it.

Abel Maloney, the postman, knew all about Bridie McCarthy and what she'd done, indeed the whole of the town and most of the county had heard something of it. It wasn't that she'd left: few could say that her workload was easy, though there was something about duty to parents. Didn't the Bible itself charge children to honour their father and mother? No one could argue reasonably that sneaking away in the middle of the night was an honour to anyone.

And yet the child wrote home every week. Abel was quick to tell people that, just as the postmistress was just as speedy at telling those interested that the McCarthys never wrote back. They wrote many letters to America, to Seamus and Johnnie and Terry, and to Ellen and Mary in Birmingham, but she handled no letter addressed to Bridie McCarthy. Now, you could make what you like of that, but she knew what she knew.

Some townsfolk thought it served the girl right, that any girl who'd run out on her parents didn't deserve to be considered a daughter. Other more charitable souls thought it a shame that Bridie wasn't forgiven.

Abel was of the latter. He felt sorry delivering Bridie's letter every week, knowing there was little hope of it being answered and, as he handed the letter to Jimmy, he said, 'Here y'are then. Fine correspondent altogether, your Bridie is.'

'Aye,' Jimmy said sadly, taking the letter from Abel's hand. 'She is that all right.'

'All right, is she?'

'Aye. Aye. She's grand.'

'Good, good, glad to hear it.' Still Abel lingered, anxious to hear any gossip which could be speculated over for weeks. 'She's got a job there then?'

Without being rude, Jimmy couldn't refuse to reply to a question and run down the lane to rip open the envelope and read Bridie's letter as he longed to. He knew where Bridie worked, he had virtually memorised every word she wrote.

'Aye,' he told Abel. 'She has a grand job in a big store. A place called Woolworths. It sells everything for sixpence, so Bridie tells us.'

'Well, would you credit that?' Abel said. 'Sixpence, is it?'

Jimmy knew that that information would be all over town and county by the next morning. 'It's what she said,' he declared. 'And now I must be off. A farm doesn't run itself.'

'No indeed,' Abel said, pleased with the information he'd extracted.

But had he been in the farmhouse later, he'd have been far more interested in the information Bridie had to give her parents.

Dear Mammy and Daddy
I really wish I knew whether you read my

*letters or not, because I have something to ask
you. I have met a man called Tom Cassidy and
we've fallen in love and wish to marry. He is
a good Catholic man from Strabane, where
his family own a farm, and he works for the
Mission in Birmingham, which is a place that
helps the poor and needy.*

*If you were to meet him, I'm sure you would
like him, but I'm not asking that of you. I need
your permission to marry him though because
I'm underage. Do please say yes. Aunt Ellen
and Uncle Sam have both met him, and Mary
and Eddie, and they all like him.*

*Please, please say it will be all right to
marry Tom, because I love him dearly. Maybe
one day I could bring him home to see you
both. There's not a day that goes by when I
don't regret what I did that night nearly six
months ago, as I've told you in every letter
I've written. Can you find it in your heart to
forgive me and give me your blessing to marry
Tom? I hope so and look forward to hearing
from you.*

Love Bridie

'She wants to marry?' Jimmy said incredulously. It
was the last thing he expected. She was his baby, his
little girl. But he realised she wasn't any longer. She
was nineteen years old and old enough to marry,
but not old enough to do so without her parents'
permission.

'Aye,' Sarah said, and continued to poke at the fire as if her life depended on it.

'Have you no opinion on it?'

Sarah stood up and faced her husband. 'Why would I have an opinion on someone who is nothing to me?'

'She's our daughter!'

'She ceased to be that for me the night she left,' Sarah stated implacably.

'Och, Sarah! For God's sake . . .' Jimmy began, but he got no further for Sarah approached him with the poker raised above her head. 'One more word about it and I'll brain you,' she said fiercely.

Jimmy wasn't afraid of the poker or Sarah's threat of using it, but he was disturbed by her eyes glazed with pain, the deep lines scored in her face, and knew how she still suffered.

'Away out of that, woman,' he said, but gently. 'You strike me with that and it will be the last thing you ever do. I'm going out and maybe when you think on the letter, you may feel better able to reply to it.'

'That will be the day,' Sarah said grimly.

Jimmy said nothing further, there was nothing to say. He took his jacket from the hook behind the door and went out. When the door slammed shut behind him, Sarah sank to her knees, the poker dropping from her fingers as she covered her face with her hands, and cried as if her heart was broken.

* * *

Each day, the first question Bridie asked when she arrived home from work was whether there had been any post.

There had been a reply from Terry, in the throes of his own wedding plans, but nothing from her parents and as time went by, Bridie seemed to sink a little further down into despondency. It was putting a further strain on her relationship with Tom which was under enough pressure anyway. And that was Bridie's fault too, for their lovemaking had proceeded little further than that first kiss. Any attempt Tom made to go further, to touch her in any way intimately, caused her to fight and struggle as the concerned and kind face of Tom would turn into her uncle's, leering and lustful.

Tom understood, but Bridie began to feel things between them would never be right. What difference would a piece of paper make? Damn all, in her opinion.

It didn't help that Tom had received an angry letter from his parents. He'd told them he'd found a girl he loved very much and wanted to marry her. He had said they were just waiting for permission from her parents to allow them to marry and had waited anxiously for their reply.

He knew it wouldn't be something they could condone easily; they'd scarcely got to grips with the bombshell that he was leaving the priesthood. He knew his parents and it was the loss of face and standing in the parish that they'd regret most. They'd no consideration of his personal happiness.

But now, to tell them he wanted to marry . . . While he'd been single and working with and under the direction of a Catholic priest, there was always the chance he'd come to his senses and go back to the seminary. Now, if he married, that chance was gone.

The tone of the letter shouldn't, therefore, have come as a surprise. His mother said she was beside herself, her dreams for her son lay in tatters and now for him to heap such humiliation on them. Did he want them destroyed altogether? And what sort of a girl was she to attach herself to a man promised to God from when he was but a child? She must be a desperate sort of girl altogether and not one to be welcomed into the family. Tom shouldn't, for pity's sake, ask them to be pleased about any of it or give any marriage between them their blessing.

Tom was affected by the letter. Though he knew he'd made the correct decision by leaving the priesthood, he felt he'd let his parents down. Though he had no intention of losing Bridie, he couldn't help feeling guilty.

Bridie knew as soon as she saw him that day that there was something up with Tom. 'Did you hear anything from your mother?' Tom asked as they began walking along Bristol Street.

'No,' Bridie said. 'What about you?'

The evenings were light now until almost nine o'clock or even later and Bridie clearly saw the shadow pass across Tom's face before he replied, 'Aye, I had a letter this morning.'

'And did they blame me as I said they would?' Bride demanded.

Tom didn't know how expressive his face was, nor how bad he was at concealing the truth. While he protested that they didn't blame Bridie in the slightest, she knew differently.

'You're lying, Tom!' she said accusingly. 'Have you the letter with you? Let me see it.'

Tom did have the letter – it had come that morning as he was dashing out with some clothes they'd sorted out for some of the poorer families and he'd shoved it into his pocket so as to read it later on. He desperately didn't want Bridie to see it, but he was no match for her and when her hands dived into the pockets of his jacket, he knew he was done for.

Bridie read the letter and was completely silent as she scanned the words. Then she folded it carefully and gave it back to Tom. He saw her sad eyes and trembling mouth and said, 'They don't understand, they've never met you. You were nothing to do with my decision to leave the priesthood.'

'They'll never believe that.'

Tom had a sneaking suspicion that Bridie was right, but to agree would be madness. 'Yes, they will. Time heals most things.'

'Not in Irish towns and villages they don't,' Bridie protested. 'Things are passed on by word of mouth, with usually a bit added to it, and they live on for generations.'

'Bridie, it's not like that.'

'It is like that,' Bridie snapped. 'Just like that and I know who is to blame and that's me. I'm the one that is the worst in the world in my own village and now in yours, the wicked scarlet woman who went out to snare the priest. They think I'm not good enough for you and, by Christ, they're right. I allowed myself to be raped and then had an abortion to get rid of the evidence. My own parents think me so wicked they've disowned me and now yours are saying much the same thing.'

'Stop this, Bridie.'

'No, I'll not, because it's right. Don't get mixed up with me, Tom, I'm bad news.'

'Nonsense!'

'It isn't nonsense,' Bridie said. 'I've made a decision and I won't change it. You don't need me, Tom, I'm bad for you, bad for anyone I come into contact with. In time you will meet a good, wholesome, untainted girl who will be a fine wife to you.'

'I want you for a wife.'

'That wouldn't be a good choice, Tom – I love you too much to see you wreck your life and destroy the relationship you have with your parents.'

'No, I'll not let you do this,' Tom cried, grasping Bridie's arm tight.

'You must,' Bridie said in a flat voice. 'Take your hands off me, Tom, I want to go home.'

Tom saw there was no point in arguing further with Bridie in such a mood. 'I'll not let you do this,' he said again. 'Go home tonight if you must and talk it through with your aunt. I'll call for you tomorrow.'

'There's no point.'

'I'll be the judge of that,' Tom said.

Bridie shook her head, but said nothing further and, turning away from Tom, began making her way home.

Mary had left Eddie listening out for the children and had popped in to see Ellen. Sam had taken himself off to the pub and so the two women looked up at Bridie's entry.

They both took in the look on her face and Mary asked, 'What is it? What's wrong?'

Bridie swallowed the lump in her throat determinedly and willed her voice not to shake as she said, 'Tom is . . . We've split up. There will be no marriage.'

It was the last thing Ellen and Mary expected to hear and they both gaped at Bridie in shock. 'But why?' Mary demanded eventually.

'It's . . . it's a long story,' Bridie said. 'I don't want to talk about it. I'm going to bed.'

Neither woman said anything. They knew Bridie was controlling herself with difficulty and needed to be alone. As they heard her steps on the attic stairs, Ellen said quietly, 'I'll take her a cup of tea in a wee while. She'll have had a good cry then and maybe will be ready for a good chat.'

'Maybe,' Mary said doubtfully. 'This all boils down to Mammy, you know? Why don't they give her permission to marry Tom? I've told them what a lovely person he is.'

'And me,' agreed Ellen. 'I even said if she's so keen to put her out of her life, why is she blocking her chance of being happy with someone else?'

'I can't understand it,' Mary confessed. 'And the longer it goes on, the more depressed she gets. She feels she doesn't deserve happiness.'

'Does she?'

'Aye,' Mary said with feeling. 'I had a fair bit of that kind of talk after the abortion, but more after she confessed it to that damned priest at St Chad's.'

'Well,' said Ellen, 'that's decided me. The girl has had enough happen in her young life to withstand more heartache. I'll go over to Ireland as soon as I can and make Sarah, or possibly Jimmy, see sense if it's the last thing I do.'

'But what if the wedding's off as Bridie said?'

'It's not off,' Ellen said dismissively. 'Those two are made for each other, just like you and Eddie are. They've had a tiff and little wonder with all the pressure they're under. His parents won't be best pleased either, I shouldn't think. But the girl deserves a crack at happiness.'

Perhaps she did, but over the next week, while Ellen made arrangements to go to Ireland, Bridie became paler and more drawn than ever. She refused to see Tom if he called at the house, went to work, but never left the building at lunchtimes and dodged him on her way home in the evening, always leaving with a crowd of the girls.

She saw him of course. If he approached her counter she said she was too busy to talk and she ignored the dejected figure leaning on the wall, waiting for her to leave. She knew he'd not approach a giggling mass of shop girls, arms linked, marching through the Bull Ring. Most of the girls thought Bridie mad to throw up a boy as dishy as Tom Cassidy with those gorgeous 'come to bed eyes', as one girl was heard to say.

'Throw him my way, duck, if you can't stand the pace,' another put in. 'Christ! I'd give him a run for his bleeding money.'

But others were more sympathetic. 'You can't help it if you just don't fancy someone,' one of the nicer girls said. 'Give the kid a break. Don't matter any road what the problem is. If she doesn't want to see him, she don't have to.'

'Right, us girls have got to stick together,' said another and there was a chorus of agreement.

Peggy McKenna, who had a nose for scenting out trouble, soon realised things weren't right between Bridie and her young man. 'What did you expect?' she asked her one night as Bridie made her way home. 'No decent man would want anything to do with the likes of you.'

Peggy's words fed the unworthiness and low self-esteem that Bridie already felt anyway and she knew she'd been right to give Tom up.

But, as day followed day, she grew quieter and thinner. She found she couldn't eat and sadness seemed to seep inside her. But, she told herself, she had no right to happiness and if at any time she was to doubt that, Peggy McKenna would be at her elbow, heaping her with scorn.

Ellen told few people where she was heading. She hadn't told her sister Sarah to expect her, nor had she told Bridie where she was really going. Not wishing to raise the girl's hopes, she told her she was off to stay with a relative of Sam's down south who'd had a fall.

Mary, who knew of Ellen's plans and thought it highly unlikely that she'd succeed in changing her mother's mind, played along with the story.

Ellen wasn't so sure she'd succeed either when she alighted from the rail bus at the farm. Bone-weary and hungry, her spirits took a downturn. What was she doing, a woman of her age, running about between the countries trying to build bridges? And did she think she'd do any earthly good?

She didn't, not really. She knew her sister, none better, and once her mind was made up, that was usually it. 'Stop it,' she told herself sternly. 'A defeatist attitude is no good in a situation like this,' and she squared her shoulders and marched up the path alongside the meadow where the cows, placidly chewing the cud, turned their heads inquisitively to look at her. She went up towards the back of the cottage, wrinkling her nose at the stink rising from the midden. The hens, shut up for the night, started fluttering and clucking as they heard her approach and the young calves in the byre beside the house lowed gently.

Yet no one in the house heard her approach. Jimmy sat before the fire almost asleep, despite the early hour. He'd been up since dawn and tomorrow would be more of the same.

Sarah, too, was tired and had lifted the heavy pot from the hook above the fire and began to pour it into the squat brown teapot set beside the hearth when Ellen walked in the door.

Sarah stared across the room in shock at her older sister. She'd admired her for years, yet since Bridie had left home she'd felt differently about her. Sarah felt Ellen had let her down. She'd sworn she'd known nothing of Bridie's plans to run away and maybe that was the truth, but still the girl was staying with her. If she'd not been so keen to give her a bed, she might have come home, explained herself, told Sarah why she'd gone the way she had.

Ellen saw the hostility in Sarah's face and reminded herself that she didn't know and could never know Bridie's reasons for her flight. Once, Sarah would have flown across the room to hug her sister, bid her welcome and draw her to the fire, and she felt a pang of regret for that closeness lost. Oh, but how much worse for Bridie, she reminded herself. The petted and favoured child was now cast adrift for reasons not of her own making. If she was to have a future at all it lay with Tom Cassidy. Ellen discounted their quarrel; sure it could be mended with one word of consent from her parents.

Jimmy looked at Ellen. He'd been embarrassed at his wife's lack of warmth on seeing her sister. True, her appearance had been an unexpected shock, but she was family and a guest.

He pulled himself to his feet and went across the flagstones to Ellen in his stockinged feet, having removed his boots. He had his hand outstretched but, moved by the sadness he saw in her face, encircled her in a hug instead. 'This is a surprise, Ellen,' he said, releasing her at last, 'but a welcome one. What brings you out here?'

'Don't act daft, man,' Sarah snapped. 'You know why she's here and I'll tell you now it won't work. I have no child named Bridie, nor any interest in anything she does.'

'God, woman!' Jimmy cried. 'Ellen has just arrived and Bridie is our flesh and blood whether you like it or not. Give over now. Let Ellen come up to the fire and pour her a cup of tea at least.'

Almost grudgingly, Sarah welcomed her sister with a stiff embrace, but she did pour her a cup of tea. And since the Irish way was never to offer just tea, there were also slices of soda bread, home-cured bacon and tomatoes, and slabs of barn brack topped with thick creamy butter.

The food revived Ellen, but only slightly; she was still very tired. Jimmy saw that she was and was glad. He was in no state himself for an emotionally charged situation that evening. The following day was early enough for any sort of confrontation.

But he couldn't get himself ready for his bed with both women there, positioned as it was in a curtained alcove off the kitchen, and so he took his jacket from the door and whistled to the dogs. 'I'll take a look around before I turn in,' he said as explanation.

Sarah nodded. It was Jimmy's routine to check everything was safe and secure before going to bed. Then he'd come in, wind the clock, knock his pipe out in the grate and place the guard around the fire. So when the door closed behind him Sarah said to Ellen, 'Jimmy wants his bed. We'll away to the room. The beds are stripped, but I have sheets and blankets stored. You'll have to make up the bed, I can't with my arm, you know.'

'I'm no stranger to making beds,' Ellen said, and she went over to the chest her sister had opened and selected her bed linen for the night. She didn't think Sarah would follow her, but she did and she stood watching her making up the bed.

Suddenly she said, 'Why did she do it, Ellen? Why did our Bridie feel she had to run from us the way she did?'

It was the last thing Ellen had expected. She not only refused to answer her letters, but refused to talk about her at all in those she sent to Ellen and Mary and any reference they made about Bridie was studiously ignored. But glancing over at Sarah, Ellen was struck with pity for pain was etched on her face. Anger and bitterness was the armour assumed to help her cope with the hurt and Ellen could bet that she'd not have voiced the question if Jimmy had been in earshot.

But what could Ellen say? Oh, Bridie ran away because of years of sexual abuse from your brother-in-law, culminating eventually in rape? When Bridie found herself pregnant, she left to save the family from disgrace?

No, she couldn't tell her the truth. 'Och, you know these young ones, they take notions.'

'Did she tell you nothing? Surely you asked?'

'Aye. Aye,' Ellen said. 'But she said nothing definite, just that she was fed up of the farm and seeing no one, the daily grind, you know. I think she missed Rosalyn too.'

'Why didn't she say?' Sarah cried. 'We'd have got someone in to help. Oh, I know we weren't keen at the time, but we had to get someone in when she left. Francis got us a man who Jimmy gets on fine with. His wife Beattie helps me and while it's not the same as one of your own, it's not so bad when all's said and done.

'But as for missing Rosalyn, Ellen, I'm not so sure. Oh, she was upset at the time, no doubt of it, but now . . . Well, Delia says she never writes. Rosalyn writes to her, but she never writes back. If she missed her that much, wouldn't she send a wee letter now and then?'

Ellen, who knew that Bridie felt she couldn't write to Rosalyn because she was connected to Francis, said nothing to this, but she did try to defend her. 'She works hard, Sarah,' she said, 'and sometimes long hours. She doesn't get much free time.'

'Enough to get herself a boyfriend it seems.'

'Aye,' Ellen said. 'But that's natural enough, isn't it?'

'She's too young.'

'She's nineteen and Tom is a fine young man,' Ellen said. 'Oh Sarah, you know there's no law about this sort of thing.'

'And she needs our permission to marry him?'

'Aye.'

'Well, she can want,' Sarah stated flatly. 'We didn't want her to go, but she pleased herself. Well, I'll please myself and she can burn in Hell before I'd give my blessing to anything she does.'

'Sarah, this attitude doesn't help,' said Ellen with a sigh.

'It helps me, Ellen,' Sarah said tight-lipped. 'And what's more, that's my last word on the subject.' And with that parting shot, she swept from the room, slamming the door shut behind her.

Ellen knew to keep on about Bridie when Sarah was in this mood would only make her dig her heels in further, so she went in search of Jimmy the following day. She was glad he was in the lower field for then she couldn't be seen from the house – she'd told Sarah she was off for a walk.

She'd guessed Jimmy wouldn't be so rigidly

opposed to Bridie and she was proved right. He freely admitted he missed her and wished the situation could be put right between herself and Sarah.

'Have you told Sarah how you feel?'

'I haven't, well not in so many words, you know,' Jimmy said. 'I know the power of my wife's temper. Maybe in time she'll come round.'

'And what of Bridie and the young man she wishes to marry?'

'Och, sure, I don't want to get involved in that. Sarah is set against it.'

'I know that, but only as a way of punishing Bridie.'

'Not that alone. We don't know the man. We haven't seen him.'

'How can you see him when you've virtually disowned Bridie?' Ellen demanded. 'I've seen him, and Sam and Mary and Eddie have too, and we all like him and think he'll make Bridie a fine husband. You can even find out about the family he comes from if you've a mind. Strabane's not that far away.'

Jimmy was silent a moment or two and then he said, 'There's no reason for the hurry, I suppose?'

Ellen faced him levelly. 'No, Jimmy,' she said. 'None other than that they're in love.'

'And he has a decent job?'

'Aye.'

'Where would they live?'

'We'd search around as soon as you gave the

word. They could lodge with me for a time, but they'd need a place of their own eventually. Would you do it?'

'Not so fast,' Jimmy said. 'I'll have to look into it. Give me a day or two.'

'I can only stay a week at most,' Ellen warned. 'I came here on the spur of the moment.'

'You'll know well before then,' Jimmy said, and Ellen pressed him no more.

Ellen was worried about seeing Francis; not worried for herself, but afraid that by her manner, she'd show how disgusted she was with him. She thought it sinful that the man would get away scot-free and yet for Bridie's sake it had had to be that way.

She called in on Delia as it would have been regarded as odd if she hadn't, but she made sure it was a day when she knew Francis was in town. The wee ones were growing up now and Delia should have been less hardworked, but Ellen saw lines on Delia's face she didn't remember seeing before. It pulled her mouth down into a tight thin line. She knew she was looking at an unhappy woman and wondered if Delia had any idea of her husband's womanising.

She couldn't ask, however, and they talked of other things, only touching briefly about Bridie. Even then, Ellen didn't dwell on the reasons for Bridie's flight, but just spoke of her life now in the city, her job and her love for Tom Cassidy.

'Rosalyn shows no sign of settling down yet,'

Delia said. 'But God knows, there's time enough. She tells me of the great life she's living now and she knows marriage will put a stop to those high jinks.'

She sighed and said resignedly, 'Well, there you are. As my own dear mother used to say, "you make your bed and then you must lie on it".'

Ellen said nothing. Whatever ailed Delia's marriage she couldn't help her. She got up to go. 'Francis will be sorry he missed you,' Delia said at the door. 'Come again when he's home.'

Not likely, thought Ellen, but said, 'I don't think I'll be able to, Delia. This is just a flying visit. I don't want to leave Sam too long. The girls are good, but Bridie's at work all day and Mary has her hands full with the two wee ones, especially Jamie for he's one body's work, that wee scamp.'

And with that, Ellen was gone. Over the next few days, she stuck close to her sister and made quite sure that if she saw Francis, for it couldn't be totally avoided, it was always with others around her. She didn't trust herself – the first time she'd seen his open genial face, his hand extended in a welcome, she remembered what he'd done to Bridie and wanted to hit him with something heavy. She controlled herself with difficulty and shook Francis's hand, though the bile rose in her throat as she touched him.

She remembered how Bridie had told her she'd washed herself all over and wished she could have rubbed her skin raw after the rape. She understood that – after Francis had left, she went into the room and, pouring water from the ewer, she had washed and washed at her hands, eventually scrubbing at them with a nailbrush. She knew with a sudden realisation that while Francis lived, she could not come back again, not even for a visit.

One day while she was there, Jimmy made a trip with the horse and cart, leaving the taciturn Willie in charge. 'Said he's off to see some young calves,' Sarah replied to Ellen's question, but she was puzzled by his decision. 'I don't see that we need any more, but he wouldn't listen.'

But Jimmy didn't bring any calves back, saying they weren't worth having. Ellen wondered if the trip had anything to do with the talk she had with him, but didn't ask. Jimmy was not a man to be hurried – she would wait for him to come to her.

Jimmy sought her out the following day as she hung washing on the line in the orchard. 'I've been to Strabane as you suggested,' he said. 'I thought if some man was thinking of marrying my lass, I'd find out all I could. The lad was bound for the priesthood, I heard?'

'Aye, he was.'

'Did he give it up for Bridie?'

'No, months before,' Ellen said. 'He hadn't even met Bridie when he made that decision. She had nothing to do with it.'

'That's not the talk of the town.'

'It wouldn't be,' Ellen said. 'But it's the truth.'

'Fair enough,' Jimmy said. 'His people seem

respectable enough and the farm fairly prosperous. I didn't go to see them but I asked about.'

'I believe they're decent people, right enough.'

'Will he come back to the farm? Take it up again now he's not to be a priest?' Jimmy said. He hoped he would; he'd love to have his Bridie just a few miles away. He knew Sarah would soon come around, but Ellen shook her head.

'He has no interest in farming,' she said. 'His eldest sister is marrying a farmer and he's left it with her and his other two sisters. He said it's only fair. He was sent away to the seminary at twelve and now he's twenty-three and all those years they've worked alongside their father. He says they have more right to it than he has.'

Jimmy sighed. 'I suppose so.'

Ellen said gently, 'I don't think Bridie will ever come back here to live, but she has the chance of a decent life in Birmingham. She just needs your permission.'

'She'll never get Sarah's,' Jimmy said. 'But I spoke to the parish priest in the village and he said just the one of us could do it.'

'And will you?'

'Aye,' Jimmy said. 'I want my girl to be happy.'

CHAPTER TWELVE

Bridie couldn't believe that Ellen had gone over to Ireland and succeeded in getting her father's permission for her to marry Tom Cassidy. But still she shook her head glumly. 'Wasted journey for you, Aunt Ellen, for I'm not for marrying the man now.'

'Away out of that!' Ellen said sharply. 'It's me you're talking to, not some dumb chuck. I know you're eating your heart out for him.'

'I am not!'

'Oh yes you are,' Ellen said emphatically. 'And if you toss Tom Cassidy aside with your heart crying out for him, you will have played right into Francis's hands. Why are you so stiffnecked?'

'You don't know it all.'

'I know of the letter his parents sent that you were so upset about,' Ellen said. 'Mary told me you'd mentioned it. But tell me honestly, Bridie, did you expect them to be any different?'

'I suppose not.'

'You're not marrying *them*.'

'I know that,' Bridie cried. 'It's just . . . Oh God, Aunt Ellen, Tom, could find himself some nice girl, one who hasn't been through what I have.' She looked up at her aunt and said, 'I think he deserves better.'

'He deserves to have his wishes attended to,' Ellen snapped back. 'He deserves to have you take him seriously when he says he loves you and wants to marry you. Tell me, was his decision changed by the letter?'

'He . . . he was upset by it,' Bridie said at last. 'But no, his opinion hadn't changed.'

'No, and it wouldn't be,' Ellen said. 'Listen to me, Bridie. When you're a child, you need your parents' approval for things you do, but, as an adult, your life is your own and what you do with it is your business. It's nice if your parents are pleased with the way you live it, but just as you can't change their way of life and opinions, they have no authority over yours either. Sometimes you have to go against them for the sake of your own happiness.'

Ellen's words made an impression on Bridie. She thought of her life with Tom and then imagined life without him and knew which one she preferred. Mary, when Bridie asked her opinion, certainly agreed with Ellen. But she went further. 'Did you throw Tom over totally because of the letter his parents sent, or was it about something else?' she asked.

'Well, I suppose it was about Mammy and Daddy not giving permission as well.'

'Anything else?'

'What d'you mean?'

'I'll tell you what I mean,' Mary said. 'What Francis did to you that time in the wood, does it . . . did it . . . Look, what I'm trying to say is when you and Tom get intimate does it bring it back? Did you break it off with him because you're afraid of remembering?'

'No!' Bridie cried fiercely. 'I'm not just afraid of remembering, I'm afraid I won't be able to let Tom touch me. What sort of marriage is that, Mary? As for being intimate, well, that's a laugh, we just don't get intimate. And I don't see how I'll feel better because a priest mumbles some words over me and Tom puts a ring on my finger.'

'Oh, my love,' Mary said sympathetically. She wrapped her arms around her sister and thought if she had Francis before her this minute, she'd chop him into pieces and take joy in it. 'Have you talked this over with Tom?' she asked at last.

Bridie gave a sniff. 'Aye.'

'And?'

'He just says there's plenty of time.'

'Well, he's right.'

'I know, but . . . Well, what if it doesn't come right?'

'If it doesn't, then you've let Francis destroy your life totally,' Mary told her sister. 'Are you prepared to let him do that?'

Mary, watching her young sister's hurt and confused face, made a sudden decision to share her secret with Bridie. 'Look, Bridie, I never doubted a word you said when you wrote to me about Francis. I didn't want to believe what you were telling me,' Mary said, 'but, inside, I knew it was true.'

'Why?'

'Because of what happened to me too, when I was fourteen.'

'You mean . . . ?'

'Yes, Bridie,' Mary said. 'And not a soul has ever been told about it until now. I wasn't raped, nothing as awful as that, but what he did was bad enough.'

'What did he do?'

'He . . . It was the summer of 1919. I was fourteen and crying because of the wee ones dying. You mind how it was then.'

Bridie nodded. Oh yes, she remembered all right. She'd only been five, but she remembered that dreadful time. Grief had enveloped the house. The keening of the women seemed constant and was echoed in many houses throughout the north of Ireland at that time. It was no wonder Mary cried. God! Everyone cried.

'I'd stolen away from the house,' Mary said, 'not wanting to upset Mammy further, and I'd climbed up the brae to that hollow in the hills by Doolan's farm. I was lying on the grass crying when Francis came upon me. He said he'd been walking the hills, but afterwards I didn't believe that. The hill couldn't be seen from our house, but from his you would have a good view of me toiling there on my own, though the hollow would be hidden. I think he saw me and followed me. He'd know where I'd be making for, I'd done it many a time. 'Course, I didn't think that at the time. I was too sad to think anything at all. I just turned to him and said something like, "Isn't it awful?"

'He agreed it was and knelt on the grass beside me and started to stroke my arm. It was nice, comforting just to know someone cared about me and how I was feeling. For so long, with Seamus and Johnnie ill, then Robert and Nuala and Mammy so worried about you getting sick she'd hardly let the wind blow on you, I'd felt neglected. I never said a word, nor would I – to tell the truth, I felt awful even thinking about myself and I loved Uncle Francis for making me feel better.

'Then he started stroking my leg with his other hand and I didn't like that so much, but didn't want to make a fuss with him being so nice and all. He started asking me how I was feeling and did I like what he was doing and said that he could make me feel a lot better if he had the mind to.

'It was like a litany. He just went on and on, saying the same things and it became quite soothing. I was tired, for I hadn't had a full night's sleep for some time, and had a muzzy head from crying for hours, the sun was hot and with Francis's hands caressing me gently and his soft voice, I'd fallen into a semi-sleep.

'And then suddenly, one hand was underneath me, fondling my breasts, fumbling at the buttons of my dress, while the other had snaked up my leg and was inside my bloomers. God, I woke up quick, I can tell you.'

'What did you do?'

'I slapped his hands away and shot to my feet, doing up my buttons, and told him to get away.'

'Did he tell you it was your fault, like he did me?'

'In a way,' Mary said. 'He said I was enjoying it, or I would have complained earlier and he was only offering me what all girls wanted.'

'It's horrible, isn't it, especially afterwards when they say things like that? You begin to doubt yourself,' Bridie said.

'Aye,' Mary agreed. 'After that one time, he was always at me. But I had one weapon you hadn't.'

'What?'

'Sally McCormack.'

'Who's she?'

'The daughter of a gypsy that used to camp in the meadow by the stream in the town. Sally had long, raven-black hair and dark flashing eyes that could cloud with anger or scorn, but usually sparkled with good humour. She was very beautiful and wore long flowing clothes, jangly necklaces and bracelets, and was often barefoot.

'The gypsies used to stay all summer. They did every year, but that particular year, Daddy noticed

Francis seemed to have a lot of business in the town which kept him going in, night after night. Auntie Delia used to complain about it. She was getting over a miscarriage at the time and Francis told Daddy it was his way of coping. He said he'd been broken up by Robert and Nuala's death and then Delia's miscarriage and he drank to ease the pain. No one connected him to the gypsies. They were just a feature of the summer and tended to keep themselves to themselves unless they were hawking around the doors.

'That's how we got to know Sally of course. They'd drive up in a cart and the women would be selling clothes pegs and woven baskets, while the men offered to sharpen up scythes and sickles before they'd be needed in the autumn. Sally always came with the women and she often went round in the late summer to help pick the crops. She was usually full of fun and she seemed to have such freedom. The rest of us girls about the same age often envied her.

'With the nip in the air of late September, the gypsies were gone,' Mary said. 'And we young ones were sad, because they were a colourful addition to our rather mundane lives. But then one bleak November day, a caravan rolled up before Francis's farm. It was Sally's family. Her father got out, mad as anything, and said Francis had taken his daughter down and she was having his baby and what was he going to do about it.

'Francis denied it, of course, and because she

was a gypsy girl he was believed. A gypsy word couldn't be trusted – why wouldn't they sell their own mother for the price of a drink? some people said. Others claimed Sally had been free with her favours with all and sundry and was picking on Francis to provide for her bastard.'

'Didn't she protest?'

'Didn't have time. They were run out of town before she had a chance to defend herself.'

'So you never heard how it went?'

'I heard how it went for Sally all right,' Mary said. 'It was the talk of the place. She drowned herself in the river just a few miles away from the town the day after they were told to go. None of the gypsies were ever seen in the place after.'

'I'm not surprised,' Bridie said fiercely. 'How sad.'

'Aye, sad right enough,' Mary agreed. 'But I threw Sally's name at Francis, because I believed the girl. I told him maybe the townsfolk wouldn't have believed a gypsy girl on her own, but if I had told people what he'd tried to do to me, on the heels of Sally McCormack committing suicide, at the very least doubts would have been raised. And I told Francis the whole family was talking about the way he was out nearly every night in the weeks while the gypsies were camped.'

'Was he mad?'

'Mad? Aye, he was surely. He went puce. I thought he would hit me and I think he wanted to, but how would he have explained it?'

'And was that it then, he left you alone?'

'Aye,' Mary said. 'He had to really. He couldn't risk me spilling the beans about him. Not that I ever would, and for the same reason you couldn't for it would have destroyed us all and split the family in two, but he couldn't risk that.

'I never thought you were in danger when I left Ireland though. You were just a wean and anyway Francis had done nothing to me for years. But the point is, when I met Eddie and knew he was the one for me, I wouldn't let that filthy pervert spoil things for me. And don't you either,' she said, and she hugged Bridie tight.

Bridie felt new strength flood through her. She wouldn't be able to erase Francis totally out of her life, she thought, but he hadn't got to be at the forefront of her mind all the time either.

'I'll try,' Bridie said. 'And now I had better see Tom. I have some apologising and explaining to do.'

'Aye,' Mary said. 'For God's sake put the man out of his misery. He can't be held accountable for his parents, remember that, just as you aren't for yours.

'It's only just turned half nine,' Mary said. 'I'd be away now if I were you.'

Bridie arrived at the Mission house out of breath, both from hurrying and from the emotion pounding through her entire body, and she knocked at the door quickly before she lost her nerve.

'Bridie? What on earth . . . ? Is something wrong?'

How glad Bridie was that it was Tom himself who came to the door. 'Nothing's wrong, Tom,' she said. 'I mean everyone is okay, but I . . . I need to speak to you.'

Tom's heart plummeted. Has Bridie come to say it was finally over between them? That he was to stop trying to waylay her at work, stop hanging about the shop when she was leaving? He took his jacket from the hook behind the door and stepped out into the night.

Bridie being Bridie came straight to the point as she stood before him, wringing her hands together in agitation. 'Tom, I'm sorry for those things I said to you,' she said. 'I was wrong, but if you don't want me after I behaved as I did, I will understand.'

'Want you?' Tom cried, elated by Bridie's words.

He took her hands in his and kissed her fingers as he said, 'There's only ever been you, you silly girl. I thought you knew that. Bridie, I love you, I've loved you from the moment I saw you curled up on the bench at Strabane Station. Tell me, though, what's brought about this change of heart?'

'Mainly Ellen and Mary talking some sense into me,' Bridie said. 'It was all mixed up with not being worthy for you because of what happened.'

'None of that was your fault,' Tom said, dropping Bridie's hands and enfolding her whole body in a hug as he whispered into her ear, 'My darling, darling girl.'

'I knew that really,' Bridie said, 'but my parents aren't even speaking to me and then with the letter from yours . . . Oh, it's what I expected if I'm honest, but I just felt as if we were having to fight the whole world to be together and that it was my fault somehow and that you'd be better off without me.'

'And now?'

'Now I know I love you with all my heart and soul,' Bridie said simply. 'I can't imagine life without you. What's helped of course,' she added, 'is that dear Aunt Ellen went over to Ireland and, by whatever means, got my father to give his permission for our wedding.'

Tom gave a whoop of joy and, lifting Bridie from her feet, spun her around. 'Tom, hush. The people in the Mission will think murder's been done.'

Tom set her down, his whole face alight, and said in mock severity, 'And it will be, madam, if you don't marry me with all speed.'

'There is a little matter of where we are to live?'

'A minor matter, Miss McCarthy, a minor matter,' Tom said. 'What I want to know this instant is will you marry me?'

'Oh yes, Tom. Yes, yes, yes,' Bridie replied. 'And just as soon as you like.'

Tom bent and kissed Bridie gently and he felt her body stir against his and his kiss became more ardent. Bridie never thought of Francis once. She thought of the man she loved and was to marry and felt her body yearn for him, the tingle generated by the kiss reaching to her very toes.

Peggy McKenna couldn't believe that that young scut Bridie was getting married and to that fine handsome man Tom Cassidy. She needn't think she'd get away with anything either because she was married. The wee bit Peggy was wheedling out of her most weeks could be increased now she was marrying a man in work.

Tom and Bridie were married in September 1933 in St Catherine's Church with Mary as matron of honour. Bridie wore her sister's wedding dress, although it needed so much alteration to fit her slender frame that Ellen said it would have probably been quicker to sew a new dress from scratch.

But at least this way it saved money; they knew they'd need every penny when they had a place of their own. Not that that seemed likely and, as the wedding grew nearer, Bridie and Tom knew they had no option but to start married life at Ellen's.

Bridie was apprehensive. She loved Ellen and Sam, but the thought of her and Tom making love in the creaky attic with her uncle and aunt just below, listening to every noise and knowing full well what they were up to, well, it made her blush to think about.

She wondered if Tom felt the same. Possibly not. The girls at work said most men had sex on the brain and would be at it morning, noon and night if you weren't firm from the beginning and they never seemed to have a whit of shame about it either.

In the end Bridie needn't have worried, for her wedding day was wonderful from start to finish. The beautiful Nuptial Mass was said by Father Shearer with Tom's Father Flynn to assist him.

Unbeknown to Bridie, Father Flynn had taken a great interest in the courtship between her and Tom. When Tom had first come to the Mission, he'd been a confused and worried man. His arrival was followed by an impassioned letter from the Bishop, putting Father Flynn in the picture in case Tom hadn't told him everything.

However, Tom had. The words had spilled from him and Father Flynn knew almost immediately that, though Tom was a devout and ardent Catholic, he would not make a good priest. He didn't tell Tom this, but let him come to that realisation himself. He did, however, write to the Bishop. Although the Bishop had given no instructions to Father Flynn, he knew that he really wanted him to quell any doubts Tom might have and set him on the right path again. Father Flynn knew that could never be and he was doing his friend no favours allowing him to think it might.

When Tom returned in December after his father's illness, he was subdued, and Father Flynn knew something had happened to him in Ireland. He bided his time and eventually Tom told him of the girl he'd been attracted to on the journey home, but she had refused to see him again once they'd reached Birmingham. 'Is the girl a Catholic, Tom?'

'Oh yes, Father.'

'And did you tell her you were once destined for the priesthood?'

'Aye, Father.'

'Maybe that was it, Tom,' the priest said. 'Maybe she was unnerved by that knowledge.'

'What should I do?'

'About this girl, nothing,' Father Flynn said. 'If she's disappeared into the city, and all you know is her first name, you have little hope of tracing her. The thing to do is decide your own future first.'

'I don't want to be a priest, Father.'

Father Flynn smiled. 'I must say that's come as no great surprise,' he said. 'And I'm glad to hear it, I must say, if you are being attracted to young ladies.'

'Only one young lady, Father,' Tom protested.

'One so far,' the priest countered, and then went on, 'but joking apart, Tom, you should write directly to the Bishop and resign your place at the seminary if you feel that the priesthood is not for you.'

'I intend to do that, Father,' Tom said. 'I'm just sorry I didn't do it before I met Bridie.'

Father Flynn thought Tom had little chance of seeing Bridie again but when he had found her and she had agreed to walk out with him he'd been astounded. Tom brought her to the Mission to meet him and he'd known straightaway why

Tom had been so drawn to her. She was beautiful, it was true, but it was more than just that: she had an air of fragility and vulnerability that would make most men want to look after her.

It was belied by her voice though. Melodious as it was, you knew behind it was a woman of strong principles and determination. There was something else too hiding behind her eyes, something in her past maybe. He had mentioned it to Father Shearer, but he knew of nothing that could have caused it.

They wouldn't ever know either because, by tacit consent, both Tom and Bridie had agreed to say nothing to the clergy about the abortion.

'Well, whatever it was that upset her, it's over now, thank God,' Father Flynn said to Father Shearer. 'Let's hope it'll fade from her mind totally now she is married to Tom, for it's obvious they are made for each other.'

'Aye,' Father Shearer agreed. 'Though Mary told me their parents were none too keen on Bridie's marriage.'

'Oh?'

'It seems they thought they'd have her beside them for some years yet, if not for ever,' Father Shearer said. 'She's the second daughter to come to Birmingham and find a husband and she was the youngest. They feel the loss of her keenly.'

'Well, Tom's parents were, understandably, not too enthusiastic either.'

'Aye,' Father Shearer said, 'I can see they wouldn't

be and yet when you see Tom and Bridie together, you know they are very much in love.'

'Aye, yes indeed,' Father Flynn said, and they looked across the room to the couple surrounded by friends and neighbours. Bridie had been stunned by the numbers in the streets around waiting to see her leave her aunt's house earlier that day. She'd been reduced to tears by those who'd rushed forward and pressed presents into her hands when she knew they had so little themselves.

And now there was this wonderful reception that her aunt had insisted on paying for. Bridie held tight to her young husband's hands as if she couldn't bear to let him go. She was happy, so wonderfully, gloriously happy, she didn't know how you could feel this elated and not explode from it.

Her eyes suddenly caught those of the priests watching her and she raised her free hand to wave to them. The smile she gave was so radiant and so beautiful that Father Flynn gave a short gasp and understood fully why Tom loved Bridie McCarthy so much. He sent up a silent prayer asking God to care for them and give them happiness and maybe, in time, a fine family.

Ellen and Sam had bought the couple a double bed, for Ellen said they could hardly share the single one Bridie had, and Mary gave them two complete sets of sheets and an eiderdown. Terry had already sent a card with a twenty-dollar bill inside. It made up in a way for the lack of response from Tom's parents and Bridie's own after they had written and given them the date of their wedding. Hurt, Bridie still refused to let their silence mar their day.

And at the end of it, Tom and Bridie had the house to themselves – Ellen and Sam had taken themselves off to Mary's, where they would bide for the next two nights to give the newlyweds some privacy.

Bridie could have kissed them for their sensitivity; she was apprehensive enough of what would happen in the marriage bed, and how she'd react to it, without worrying about embarrassing Ellen and Sam by making a noise. But it turned out that she was worrying over nothing, for Tom did little that first night but hold her tight and stroke her body gently. He wanted more and knew in time Bridie would trust him enough to allow him to go further, but he was no brute and knew he must proceed slowly and eventually, not only would Bridie submit to him, but hopefully enjoy the act herself.

Bridie didn't know what was in Tom's mind: his talk of their exploring one another's bodies the following night was an alien one to her, but she did what he asked because she wanted to please him.

Ellen and Sam returned and took up residence again in their bedroom and Bridie found herself looking forward to the nights and the kissing and the fondling between her and Tom in the large double bed. She was enjoying the closeness of sleeping curled up with a loved one, of waking in the morning to find Tom's head on the pillow beside her.

It was weeks into their marriage before Tom was able to unlock Bridie's sexual urges, for so long held in check, but when they were released they took Bridie by surprise. Now she moaned in ecstasy, but softly as she was ever mindful of Ellen and Sam, and she wriggled and writhed beneath Tom as his hands caressed her gently and then more firmly, fondling her breasts, and stroking her belly, his lips following his fingers, until she cried out, her fist in her mouth to muffle the sound.

When Tom eventually entered her, she was more than ready and the pleasure, the joy and sheer exhilaration of it burst out of her as she let out a triumphant cry. Tom smiled for he knew he'd pleased his beautiful wife and in the room below Ellen smiled too, happy that Bridie was at last able to enjoy being with Tom. But more importantly, Bridie realised in that moment that what had happened between her and Francis bore no resemblance to the wonderful experience it could be between two people who loved each other so much.

By the middle of December, Bridie was almost certain she was pregnant. In contrast to the last time she found herself in this condition, she was absolutely overjoyed.

She could barely contain her excitement, but she'd missed just one period and by less than a fortnight, so it was too early to be sure. Not even a doctor would know yet and so she said nothing, not even to Tom.

It was February before she saw Doctor Casey and he smiled at her across the table as he confirmed her pregnancy. He remembered how she'd nearly died after going for an illegal abortion and he was glad that at least she hadn't been rendered sterile, unlike so many others. He hoped too that this child she was carrying would be a comfort to her; so many women felt guilty after an abortion. She'd never told him who the father of the first baby was and why he couldn't marry her and he'd never asked, feeling it wasn't his business.

But whatever the ins and outs of that last pregnancy were, there was no doubt about her delight over this pregnancy. The doctor was worried about Bridie's build though. From a cursory glance, he could tell that her hips were very slim – too slim to give birth naturally without great risk to herself.

He decided not to tell her that yet. He didn't want to be a prophet of doom and take the light of excitement from the young girl's eyes.

Everyone redoubled their efforts to find a house for Tom and Bridie once it was announced that a baby Cassidy was on the way. 'It shouldn't be too long,' Ellen said, thinking she was consoling Bridie. 'Half the people in these places can't afford the rent. They only leave it so long and then the bums come in and put them out. We just have to have our ear cocked to listen out.'

'Oh, Aunt Ellen, I hate to think of people on the street and me walking over them into their house.'

'If it's not you, pet, it will be someone else,' Ellen said. 'And they'll be out whether you take the house or not.'

'But where do they go?'

'They move into a couple of rooms, maybe, where the rent is cheaper, more manageable,' Ellen said. 'The lucky ones have family to take them in, some of the others live on the streets.'

'It's scandalous.'

'It's life,' said Ellen. 'For some poor beggars at any rate.'

Bridie felt sorry for anyone in that boat and yet she longed to have a place of her own. She loved Ellen dearly, but as she'd been forced to leave Woolworths the minute her pregnancy had been confirmed she found time often hung heavy on her hands.

Ellen had her own way of doing things and her own routine so there was little for Bridie to do in the house. Ellen encouraged her to take a wee walk every day, but Bridie was wary of leaving the house in case she should meet up with Peggy. The woman lived only yards from her aunt and if she saw her leaving the house, she would often follow. She seemed furious that Bridie was pregnant. Malice seemed to spark out of her at the news and she was more vitriolic than ever. For all Bridie's contentment in marriage and pregnancy, she'd begun to get jumpy again.

It was late June before Mary came into Ellen's in a rush one day. 'What is it?' Bridie asked in alarm, rising to her feet ponderously for she was seven and half months pregnant and each movement was slow and laboured.

'Nothing,' Mary said. 'Well, at least nothing bad. There's a house up our way, number nineteen, just four doors up from me, a good place, opens onto the street like mine and Ellen's.'

'Isn't that the Latimers'?' Ellen asked.

'Aye,' Mary said. 'Bert Latimer has had no work for four years or more. They owe six weeks' rent and the bums go in next week. They're doing a flit tonight and taking up in some rooms in a house off the Belgrave Road.' She faced Bridie and said, 'I know how you feel about this, our Bridie, and God knows it's a bugger. I feel for the family, especially as poor Dolly's on her time, but we can't help them and if you don't take the house someone else will.'

'I know,' Bridie said resignedly. 'What do I do?'

'You be up the landlord's offices tomorrow. They're on Bennett's Hill and make sure you're there early before anyone else gets wind of it.'

'You're sure they'll be gone?'

'Oh aye,' Mary said. 'Heard it from Dolly herself. They're moving out in the early hours with all they can carry and stopping the night at his mother's before going to the new place.'

And so, the next morning, Bridie, with Ellen in tow, was outside the landlord's offices. With her she had her marriage lines and two of Tom's wage slips to prove they could afford the place. By the end of the day, the agent had ascertained the house was vacant as Bridie had said and fairly well stripped of anything that could be useful. He grimaced to himself. The chances of getting the money owed to his employers was not high and the more time the house stood empty the more money he lost. By the end of that day, Bridie had the keys to number 19 Grant Street.

Bridie felt much more like a married woman with her own house and she took such pride in it and had great pleasure in furnishing it. They had enough money for lino for the living room and bedroom and Bridie lost no time in making rag rugs to brighten the place up. They'd also bought a second-hand table and a few odd chairs from the Bull Ring, together with two dull brown armchairs that Bridie promised herself she'd make cushions for from remnants at the market.

There was no need to buy anything much for the baby because Mary had kept all the things from Jamie and his brother. Bridie was glad of that because it gave her the money to buy material at the market to make some bright curtains to hang at the windows. Three days after their first wedding anniversary, she had them finished.

Tom said she wasn't to hang them; he'd do them when he came from work, but Bridie made a face at him. 'Expecting a baby is not an illness, Tom.'

'Maybe not, but stretching up like that can't be good for you.'

''Course, you know all about it.'

'I know enough.'

But when Tom had gone to work, Bridie finished off the last hem and got to her feet. She wanted to see them up and if she stood on one of the wooden dining chairs, she wouldn't need to stretch much. The chairs were a little rickety, but she was sure they'd bear her weight.

She was on a chair, curtain wire in her hand, when she heard the entry door open and gave a groan as she turned, certain it would be Mary who'd give out to her for trying to hang the curtains herself. But it wasn't Mary. Peggy McKenna watched the blood drain from Bridie's face with satisfaction.

'What d'you want, Peggy?' Bridie asked. 'You've had every penny I can spare this week.'

'That's a pity, I'm two bob short for the rent.'

Immediately Bridie's eyes slid to the mantelpiece where her purse was. Peggy, tracking her, crossed the room and picked it up. 'Help myself, shall I?' she said, snapping it open.

'Peggy, please, I only have three shillings to last me the week,' Bridie pleaded. 'Tom isn't well paid.'

'My old man's not paid at all,' Peggy sneered. 'Your old man will have to live on fresh air like we've been doing for years. I'm leaving you a shilling. Do a lot with that if you're careful.'

Bridie was filled with panic. How the Hell was she to survive the week on twelve pennies? 'Please leave me alone, Peggy.'

'I will, duck, well alone,' Peggy said. 'I'll go home now and write a wee letter to your mother, shall I?'

'No!' Bridie cried. 'Please don't do that. Dear God, what d'you want of me. I give you every penny I can spare.'

'Worth it, isn't it, to avoid upsetting your parents?'

'If that's what it takes.'

'Yes it is,' Peggy snapped. 'And no better than you deserve. I should look after that babby you're expecting well if I were you. God might have his revenge and take that one from you.'

'Get out!' Bridie screamed. 'You've got your money. Now leave me alone.'

When the door closed behind Peggy, Bridie held on to the window to steady herself. Her heart hammered against her ribs and she had difficulty breathing. She felt a wave of blackness envelop her and, frightened she was going to faint, tried to get off the chair quickly. It wobbled beneath her on the uneven floor and she fell, landing heavily on her side, and groaned as a dull ache began in her back and then moved around in a band across her stomach.

She tried to roll on her side, knowing she needed help, but she was in too much pain to move. She called out, but the people next door were out and no one heard her cries.

Mary found her some two hours later, barely

lucid from the throbbing spasms attacking her body. Gwen Andrews, the woman who acted midwife to most of the women in the area, would have nothing to do with Bridie when she was summoned. 'You're for hospital, I'm thinking,' she said. ''Tis a doctor you need.'

Doctor Casey was dismayed at the state he found Bridie in. It was worse than he feared; the child was not due to be born for weeks and yet both mother and baby were showing signs of distress and so he summoned an ambulance. Ellen went with Bridie as Mary had the children to see to and someone also needed to break the news to Tom when he came home from work. He was stunned. It was much too soon and she must have been very bad to be taken to hospital. 'Where is she?' he asked.

'The General. It was the closest.'

'I'll go straight up.'

'Ellen's there. They'll not let you see her.'

'Even so . . .'

'At least have a bite to eat,' Mary said. 'I have it ready.'

'I'm sorry, Mary, I know you mean well, but food would choke me,' Tom said. 'I must go to Bridie.'

Ellen sat on a hard bench in a dismal corridor. 'How is she?' Tom asked anxiously.

'She's in theatre,' Ellen said. 'No news yet.'

'Oh God!' Tom groaned. 'Ellen, if I should lose her . . .'

'Hush. Don't say such things,' Ellen said. 'I've been praying for her. She'll be fine.'

Tom opened his mouth to reply when he spotted the white-coated doctor approaching them. 'How is she?' he demanded. 'Bridie Cassidy, how is she?'

'And you are?'

'Her husband.'

'Well, your wife is through the operation and sleeping peacefully,' he said. 'The baby . . .'

Tom, who'd so desperately wanted the baby Bridie carried, no longer cared that much about it. Bridie was of more importance. They could have other children. 'Is it dead?' he asked.

'No, alive. Small, but alive and putting up a fight. She is in the baby unit. You can't go in, but can see her through the glass if you wish.'

Later, when Tom stood at the window and gazed at the bundled infant in the cot, he was astounded that such a tiny mite could survive and said as much to Ellen.

'Hush, lad,' she said. 'Where there's life, there's hope, and the doctor said she's a fighter. You've to be positive and strong for that wee mite and if she shouldn't survive, you must be there for Bridie because she'll need you more than ever.'

Bridie, recovering from her ordeal, wondered if Peggy McKenna had put a curse on their child, or if it was really God extracting his revenge, but none of these fears could she share with anyone and she lay in her hospital bed, desperately praying for a miracle.

The baby was to be christened. Father Shearer came immediately and his concern and consideration helped Bridie a good deal. 'This is just a precaution,' he assured her. Bridie remembered the other wee baby who'd not had the benefit of any sort of blessing and she felt sadness engulf her. She doubted she'd ever be able to take the child home and that would be judgement on her. From her wheelchair in the hospital chapel she watched the small bundle in Father Shearer's hands as he dribbled water over her tiny head covered with brown down. He christened her Catherine Rose.

Katie Cassidy, as she quickly became known, was a fighter, however, and two weeks later left hospital with Bridie weighing four and a half pounds. Ellen and Mary had been busy while Bridie had been in hospital, knitting and sewing tiny garments to fit the little mite who was too small to fit newborn baby clothes.

That first night they had Katie home, Tom put his arms around Bridie and together they looked down at their sleeping daughter. Tom felt he would explode with joy and he pulled Bridie closer, kissing her gently. 'There's only good times ahead of us now, darling,' he promised. 'Only good times.'

Bridie smiled at Tom. She trusted him totally and if he said they would be good times ahead then there would be. Maybe it was a good thing that neither of them saw what the next few years would bring.

CHAPTER THIRTEEN

Little Katie Cassidy continued to thrive, though she didn't grow much. For the first time, Bridie realised and understood her mother's anxiety over her when she was younger.

Tom, though, was delighted by his baby daughter and laughed gently at his wife's fears. 'Don't be fretting over her size, my darling,' he said. 'Isn't it said good things come in small parcels? And isn't she fine and healthy? That's what matters, surely?'

But Bridie couldn't help worrying: those damp, unsanitary houses were a breeding ground for disease and squashed together as they were, anything remotely infectious spread like wildfire.

Mary understood, for she felt the same over her two wee boys, though they were far more robust than their cousin Katie, who they were both enchanted with. Ellen and Sam, too, were captivated by the wee baby and both stood in as surrogate grandparents. But still the silence from

Ireland continued, even though Bridie had written to her parents and told them all about Katie.

When she suggested Tom do the same and write to his parents, he'd refused. Unbeknown to Bridie, Tom, had received an acknowledgement of his marriage, which his mother had addressed to the Mission hall. It was venomous and abusive and much of the abuse was directed at Bridie. They didn't know her, they said, and had no intention of knowing her, but they were aware of the type of girl she was. Did the two of them know, Tom's mother asked, or did they even care that they could hold their heads up no more? The whole family was a laughing stock. They were bowed down with shame.

Tom threw the letter away in disgust and knew he'd never damage Bridie's fragile confidence by showing it to her. He had no intention of writing again to his parents, who appeared to care more for their standing in the community than his happiness, and he would not allow them to taint Katie's birth with more malicious rubbish. He thought Bridie was wasting her time writing to hers as well, but in her heart of hearts, Bridie hoped the letter might just melt her mother.

Bridie desperately wanted her daughter to be accepted into the family, to be made welcome in her mother's home. But then would she ever let her go there, as young as she was, with Francis on the doorstep? No, by God, she wouldn't. She hated that man with a passion and she knew only through his death would she be free of him. While he lived, he corrupted everything.

Rosalyn had stopped writing to Bridie now, but her letters before she had stopped had been confused and unhappy, asking what she'd done to offend or upset Bridie so much that she could dismiss the years of friendship they'd shared. Her comments hurt Bridie, but not enough to pick up a pen and write back. She knew she was being unfair, but Rosalyn's father was Francis and while she couldn't help that, Bridie couldn't stop her skin crawling when she thought of him, or any member of his family. She couldn't write to Rosalyn as if nothing had happened and they were girls together again.

But, despite her mother's silence and Rosalyn's reproach, Bridie was so pleased to be a wife and mother that it shone out of her. She was determined to do the best she could. Tom felt it was a joy to come home to such a happy wife and smiling baby and would play each evening with wee Katie while Bridie put the finishing touches to his dinner.

The guilt Bridie felt was still there, and she knew would probably never leave her, but it was lodged deeper within her now, and she promised herself she would make sure neither Tom or Katie would ever suffer because of it.

Not only was she a happy and contented mother, she was a passionate and responsive lover. She never spurned Tom, or claimed she was tired, or had a headache, in fact she seemed to enjoy their lovemaking as much as he did. He knew this wasn't the case with a lot of women and he counted himself a lucky man.

'The *Evening Mail* claim there are two million unemployed now,' Tom said one night, shaking the paper in impatience. '1935, and things are getting worse. Many of the people are starving and no one seems to care. The Mission can only do so much.'

'I know,' Bridie said. 'And any weans dressed respectable at all are often wearing *Evening Mail* outfits. Now Mary's Jamie has started St Catherine's, he said a man comes around and looks at their shoes and clothes. If he thinks a child needs it, he comes back with boots and stockings.'

'They'd pawn them for the price of a decent meal,' Tom said dejectedly. 'I often think that's what happens to some of the families we try to help with warmer clothes. And then I think would I act any differently if I was as hungry as many of them are?'

Bridie gave Tom a kiss. 'You do your best, love,' she said, for she knew he took his work seriously. 'And maybe some of the stuff you give out is pawned, but the *Birmingham Mail* boots and stockings can't be because they're stamped. Pawnbrokers wouldn't take them. They'd get into terrible trouble if they were found out. Jamie said some children get jumpers and skirts or trousers as well and not everyone is grateful for it either.'

'Aye. Pride, you see.'

'Pride,' Bridie said scornfully. 'I'd rather have less pride than let my children freeze to death.'

'Easy to say when we're not in that position,' Tom reminded her gently. 'We're the lucky ones, Bridie.'

Bridie knew they were. Tom didn't earn much at this job, but it was better than the dole and if it wasn't for Peggy McKenna popping in whenever she took the notion, she'd be able to manage their money better.

Nobody was surprised, though, that in those mean little streets with the gangs of unemployed man in clusters about them, little fuss was made of the Silver Jubilee on 6th May. 'When you're living hand-to-mouth and never sure where the next bite is coming from, where's the money for party fare, or any form of jollification at all?' Ellen declared one evening when she popped around with Sam.

Sam, usually such a quiet man, agreed with his wife, but went further: 'If you ask me, this government would be better if they'd spent more time studying Germany and what's happening there, and less on a celebration to benefit just a few.'

There were disturbing tales coming out of Germany over the way the Jews were being treated: some of them had escaped to Britain and what they said was shocking, too shocking, many believed, to be true.

'Do you think these things we're hearing from

Germany are facts then, Sam?' Tom asked. 'You don't think it's just scaremongering?'

'No, I don't,' Sam said. 'I don't like this chap Hitler. He's not building up his armies for the fun of it.'

'But *is* he? Isn't it just propaganda?'

'No, I'm pretty certain it isn't.'

'Well,' Tom said. 'I just hope you're wrong.'

But Bridie knew Tom respected Sam's grasp of the situation. Ellen and Sam now had a wireless and could listen to the news as well as read about it in the papers. Bridie knew Tom would love a wireless, but he said first Bridie had to have a gas cooker which he was saving up to buy her. Bridie didn't mind cooking over the fire; it was what she was used to anyway, but Tom insisted she have one of the new stoves. 'When that's bought and installed,' he told her, 'then we can start putting money away for a wireless. We can only afford to save for one thing at a time.'

Bridie knew that it was sensible of Tom to think this way. She too had a horror of debt and God knows she had enough to shell out, trying to placate Peggy McKenna, as well as to save some money herself. Sometimes the money to buy a new pair of shoes for Katie, or a coat, or even just to survive, had to be borrowed from Mary. This money would be paid back as soon as Bridie could manage it and without Tom being aware of it at all. He'd not like that way of going on any more than Bridie did herself and it might cause him to ask awkward questions she'd be unable to answer.

She would hate to upset Tom; he was such a good husband and a wonderful father. It wasn't too hard to enjoy fatherhood, however, for Katie was proving to be a dream of a child, with a sunny disposition. Ellen said it was not to be wondered at. 'A happy mother means a happy child,' she declared, delighted to see Bridie so content after all she'd been through.

If it hadn't been for Peggy McKenna, Bridie would have been happier still. But though Peggy still frightened her, she refused to let her destroy her life totally. She knew this was what the woman wanted: to strip away the contentment and love she had for Tom and Katie and reduce her to a blubbering wreck.

Bridie would never let her do that. She was too secure with Tom and her delightful child for Peggy to get a foothold in there. But, despite this, she felt a fluttering of alarm when she missed a period around Christmas time, suspecting there might be another baby on the way and dreading Peggy finding out.

She was thrilled at the prospect of another child, however. Katie, now eighteen months old and both walking and talking, needed a playmate. She kept the news to herself till she could be more certain but hoped it would be a boy for Tom. He always said he didn't care what sex a child was and he had been over the moon when Katie was born, but she knew most men wanted a son and heir.

In January 1936, the King died and his son Edward VII succeeded him. 'I don't see what difference a new king will make to people like us anyway,' Ellen said. 'I mean will it give people jobs so that ordinary folk can feed and clothe their families and provide a roof over their head?'

Bridie agreed with Ellen's sentiments, although she was so contented and happy in her own life that she felt almost guilty when she knew for many families there was only poverty and misery.

Though they hadn't a lot of money, it didn't seem to matter that much. They had simple, inexpensive tastes and when Bridie told Tom in early February that she was pregnant again, far from being worried about the added expense, he was ecstatic.

Bridie was over four months gone when Peggy spotted her coming out of the doctor's one day and, although there was nothing physical which revealed Bridie's pregnancy, her suspicions were aroused. A few discreet questions asked of the neighbours, who didn't realise there was any secrecy about it, proved her suspicions to be true. She was furious that Bridie should seemingly go unpunished and be able to have more children after the heinous thing she had done in getting rid of a baby. Determinedly, she set off for the house.

Bridie had been expecting her for days and yet she jumped when the entry door opened. She hadn't seen Peggy approach and no one, except those on official business, ever knocked. Bridie turned and saw the smirk on Peggy's face and felt her heart sink.

She didn't ask what Peggy wanted; she'd know soon enough. She never knew when she would turn up. Sometimes she would leave her alone for a week or two and other times she seemed to be never off the doorstep.

'So you're sticking your fingers up at God again,' Peggy spat out. 'Dear Christ, the brazen cheek of you is amazing.'

'What's up with you?' Bridie said, though she knew full well. 'I'm having a baby, that's all.'

'"That's all" she says,' Peggy mocked. 'Well, God will not be cheated. One day, he'll take those children from you, just see if he doesn't. He'll take his vengeance on you for the child you murdered.'

Bridie opened her mouth to tell Peggy she was wrong, and that her God wasn't like that, just as she had a horrifying mental picture. It was of God descending from Heaven in the shape of a large bird and snatching up Katie and the blanket-clad new baby in powerful vicious talons and flying away with them.

Peggy, watching her face, knew that she'd hit home and she went on, 'Stands to reason. God will not stand by and see you rear two more children decently after murdering your first.'

'Peggy, what sort of malicious pleasure do you get out of hounding me like this?' Bridie snapped.

'No pleasure,' Peggy said, 'and I'm not hounding you. It's more in the nature of warning you.'

'Well, you've warned me,' Bridie said wearily. 'Now get out and leave me alone.'

'You mind your manners,' Peggy said menacingly 'or your parents might find a letter on the mat one of these fine days and don't you ever forget it. I'll go when I am good and ready and after you've given me three shillings to take with me.'

'Three shillings! God in Heaven, Peggy, why do you think I can give you money like this? I gave you four shillings only last week.'

'Then be thankful I've only asked for three this week,' Peggy said with an evil smile. 'Come on, cough up.'

Bridie paid up, knowing she had no choice, and also knowing that to last the week herself, she'd have to borrow from her sister again which would mean another lecture on managing her money better.

But while Bridie worried about the money Peggy extracted from her, far more upsetting was the way Peggy spoke about harm befalling her child. During the day, if Bridie kept herself busy – easy enough to do with a small child in the house – she could push such threats to the back of her mind.

At night, however, Peggy's words would hammer in her brain and conjure up images of the children being separated from her. If her threshing about the bed in the throes of a nightmare didn't disturb

Tom, then her sudden shriek or scream would jerk him awake quick enough.

He would hold Bridie's trembling body tight against him while he stroked her hair until she was calmer, assuring her over and over that it was just a dream.

He was worried about the dreams, though he didn't show his concern in front of Bridie, and instead confided in her sister. 'Do you think it could be the pregnancy causing it?' he asked.

Mary shrugged. 'Could be. Pregnant women get funny notions right enough. But if it goes on, I'd talk Bridie into telling the doctor.'

'Aye, I'll do that.'

Mary talked to Ellen about it, for they'd both decided to keep a weather eye on Bridie this time so that she did nothing to bring the birth on early like she did before.

'I don't think Tom could stand another do like last time either,' Ellen said to Mary. 'God, they nearly had him in the next bed, I tell you.'

'And didn't you say that the doctor said she would need that caesarean operation every time?' Mary said.

'Aye. He didn't tell me exactly,' Ellen said. 'Well, they don't tell you anything, do they? I overheard him saying it to a nurse. It's something to do with her hips being small and God knows they are that right enough, every bit of her is small.'

'Tom couldn't have known that,' Mary said. 'If

he'd have known I'm sure he would have mentioned it to me. I bet the doctor told Bridie and she decided not to tell him.'

'Could be,' Ellen said. 'Told me she doesn't like hospitals.'

'Well, it isn't a place I'd choose to spend a holiday,' Mary commented dryly. 'But if our Bridie needs this operation then she'll have it and no nonsense and if she doesn't tell Tom, then I will.'

But Bridie had already told Tom. She knew how worried he'd been last time and she didn't want to put him through that again. Then there was Katie to consider. She couldn't afford to put herself out of action for any longer than necessary.

So she went for the check-ups at the doctor's and at the hospital, but though Tom urged her to tell the doctors about the nightmares, she said nothing. She knew what caused them and knew all the pills and potions in the world would not help her. But despite the disturbed nights, this was a pregnancy Bridie sailed through, without even a hint of morning sickness and if it hadn't been for the excessive tiredness she'd have been glowing with health.

Ellen had taught Bridie to knit and she would spend many a happy evening making clothes for the new baby, or turning out little jumpers and cardigans for Katie, while Tom read pieces to her from the paper.

'Two thousand British men have joined the International Brigade to fight in the Spanish Civil War,' he told her one evening in August.

'Why would anyone fight for another country like that?' Bridie asked, perplexed.

Tom shrugged. 'An ideal,' he said. 'Something they believe in. And it might affect us eventually if rogue governments are in charge of countries that are not too far from us really.'

'Like Hitler in Germany?'

'Exactly like that and now you see the Germans are offering to send support to Franco in Spain. You see how the thing can escalate?' Tom said, and then he went on, 'And yet I can't help feeling that perhaps some men have joined up to fight to give them something worthwhile to do – men who've been out of work for years and all that's facing them is dull, useless days and hunger, cold and despair.'

'But they could be killed.'

'Ah yes, but some of the men I see here in Birmingham are so near the edge it's frightening. Their spirit is being killed and not just by idleness, but by eroding self-respect. When people say that a man and his wife need six pounds a week to keep above the poverty line, it would make me laugh if it wasn't so tragic. A man out of work in the same circumstances gets twenty-six shillings. How does that compare with six pounds?'

'Not many ordinary workers get six pounds though,' Bridie reminded him.

'Look at the railway workers you were telling me about just the other week who were earning just over two pounds a week.'

'That's right,' Tom said. 'And that's about average. God knows, I get little more than that myself. I tell you the country is going to the dogs.'

'Uncle Sam says it will take another war to sort it out.'

'Heaven forbid,' Tom said fervently. 'I hope he's wrong.'

Bridie shivered. She rolled up her ball of wool and stuck her needles through it. 'Don't let's talk about it any more,' she said. 'It scares me all this talk of war and it's not as if talking from now till doomsday will do any good. Added to that, this child of yours is kicking the life out of me. I need my bed because that other one, sleeping now like a little angel, thinks five o'clock in the morning a grand time to get up.'

Tom smiled at Bridie. She had a point. They were roused early each morning by the dulcet tones of their small daughter, singing her version of nursery rhymes. She didn't know or care about time. All she knew was that she was fine and rested and ready for the day to begin and so Tom found it hard to get cross when she greeted him each morning with a smile that lit up her whole face. Tom would lift her from the cot and hold her close. The love he had for this child, who he would willingly lay down his life for, often overwhelmed him.

Bridie was another one he loved to distraction and now, as he looked at her weary face, he said, 'Go on up, love. I'll see to everything down here and follow you.'

Bridie climbed the stairs wearily, her gait ungainly. She hated these last weeks when everything was such an effort and she was incredibly tired. When Tom came up just minutes later, Bridie was already fast asleep. She seldom slept deeply, however, or for long, and so he got in beside her cautiously, so as not to wake her.

Liam Thomas Cassidy was born on 2nd September, full-term and weighing in at eight and a half pounds. Tom was able to hold him straightaway and was amazed at the size of the child, used as he was to dainty little Katie.

He had a shock of dark hair, much more than Katie had had, and a little button nose and though his eyes were blue, they were the milky blue of a newborn which he suspected would probably turn brown later. He parted the blanket to examine his son, marvelling at the little hands and feet, the minute nails and his soft, unblemished skin. He'd not thought he could love another child as much as Katie, but he knew that he would love this little mite he held in his arms just as much and felt blessed.

'The world's gone mad altogether,' Ellen declared to Bridie as she popped in one day toward the end of November. She rocked Liam in her arms as she said, 'I mean those poor sods trailed all the way from Jarrow to present a petition to the Prime Minister and the bloody man wouldn't even agree to see them, let alone speak to them. It's scandalous! They say unemployment there is sixty-eight per cent.'

'I know,' Bridie said. 'I heard it too.' When she'd arrived home from hospital with Liam, Tom had presented her with a wireless. 'Oh Tom,' she'd cried in delight. 'Have we saved enough?'

'Not quite,' Tom had said. 'It's not something I agree with, but I got it on the hire purchase scheme.'

'What's that?'

'You pay so much in a week,' Tom said. 'As I say, it's not something I really believe in, but I wanted to give you a wee treat.'

'Oh Tom, you shouldn't have,' Bridie had cried. 'I would have waited.'

And then Tom took the pleasure of it away by saying, 'The way things are shaping up I thought we ought to have one.'

Bridie didn't want to know about the war clouds gathering all around them, but even she was disturbed when she heard of rioting in a mainly Jewish area of London, the Jews running for their lives as their shops and houses were looted and burned. Any that protested were beaten to the ground.

'Why pick on the Jews?' she asked Tom. 'Who are these people who do these dreadful things?'

'This was led by a man called Moseley,' Tom told her. 'He's formed the British Fascist Party.'

Bridie frowned. 'Fascist,' she said. 'Isn't that who we were fighting in Spain?'

'The very same,' Tom told her. 'You couldn't

see then why people were worried and incensed enough about Spain to fight and try and put down Franco. We can't all stand back, the evil is spreading.'

'It's horrible, isn't it?' Bridie said. She removed Liam from one breast and put him to the other and went on, 'It's the children I worry over. I mean it's enough of a daily fight to feed and clothe them decently and try and keep them clean and free from disease. These other things you hear about, well it's another sort of threat.'

Tom knew exactly what Bridie meant. The Mission ran a daily fight against poverty and disease. Life was enough of a struggle for many without further problems and yet the whole world was in turmoil: the rumours coming out of Germany were disturbing, as were Stalin's purges in Russia. Added to that, there was the civil war in Spain that Hitler had promised military aid for.

In the middle of this unrest, Edward VII abdicated the throne in favour of his brother Albert who would be known as George. There had been rumblings for some time about Edward, who was often seen in the company of an American divorcee, Wallis Simpson. He couldn't marry her and still remain monarch and, on 11ᵗʰ December 1936, Bridie and Tom listened to the broadcast from Windsor Castle, when Edward declared that he was:

'unable to discharge my duties as King as I'd

wish to do without the help and support of the woman I love.'

'Stuff and bloody nonsense,' Ellen declared the next day. 'Where's the man's sense of duty and responsibility?'

'Maybe it's a good thing the man did step down,' Sam put in. 'Great friend of the krauts, I believe. He was always dining at the German Embassy, not really a sensible thing to do these times. If anything does blow up, it wouldn't do to have a spy in the camp, one so powerful and so close to the seat of government.'

'I hate this miserable war talk,' Ellen said. 'For God's sake, there have always been wars and fighting. Doesn't mean we have to get mixed up in it.'

But really she said that for Bridie's sake who was looking from her husband to her uncle with apprehension. Ellen knew as well as any that Britain could hardly fail to be caught up in it. 'If you want to know,' she went on, 'I'll be glad to see the back of 1936. 1937 can't be worse and may easily be a tad better.'

CHAPTER FOURTEEN

But 1937 was no better for anyone and as 1938 dawned, the world seemed a more turbulent place than ever. Hitler and Germany were on everyone's lips. When Bridie let herself think of a possible war, she would tremble. However, she seldom thought about it too deeply. 'I mean it's not as if I could do anything to prevent it,' she said to Mary one day. 'Tom works hard and takes his work seriously and he's always tired when he comes in. I don't want to start him off worrying about a war that might never happen. There'll be time and enough to worry about it if anything does blow up.'

Tom was often worn down by the grinding poverty he saw daily that the Mission was only able to ease for a few, and then not with any sort of permanency, and was glad Bridie thought this way. His home was like an oasis of calm in a world gone mad, for even if Peggy McKenna had called that day, Bridie would not let the fear and distaste she always evoked in her invade into the time she spent with Tom. She'd push memories of her to one side and wrap her arms lovingly around her husband.

Liam had shed his babyhood and was now a boisterous toddler and had begun to demand attention from his father when he came in at night. He and Katie were often in pyjamas and nearly ready for bed by that time and Tom would roll around the floor with the pair of them in some rough and tumble game before snuggling down in the chair, one either side of him, while he read or told them a story.

Bridie was usually at the stove and she'd smile as she'd hear them playing together. Much as the children loved her, she never got a look in when Tom was home.

After the story, when Tom would roar like the giants or monsters he read about, or squeak like the wee mouse or pant like the train, he would carry the children to bed. 'Up the wooden hill to Bedfordshire,' he would cry and the children would giggle.

After they were tucked up with many hugs and kisses, Bridie would go up to give them both a kiss and help Katie say her prayers and feel a wave of contentment wash over her. Her eyes would often meet Tom's and she knew he felt the same. Many times she had blessed the day she met Tom at Strabane.

And then suddenly they could relax: war had been averted. Bridie was at Ellen's when Sam came in with the *Evening Mail* in the October of that year. She looked at the picture on the first page of Neville Chamberlain waving a piece of paper in the air. He was home from Munich after a meeting with Hitler and was declaring:

'I believe we will have peace in our time.'

'There,' Bridie said with a sigh of relief. 'All this talk of war and now it's come to nothing.' Ellen and Sam looked at each other, but neither said anything and Bridie was too preoccupied in getting the children home and starting the dinner for Tom to notice the silence.

Tom, however, said plenty, but not until the children were in bed and then Bridie looked at him aghast. 'Why don't you believe it?'

'Bridie, no one in their right mind would believe anything that man said, or give any credence to a piece of paper with his name on.'

'Well, what's the point of it?'

'Maybe Chamberlain is cuter than we give him credit for,' Tom said. 'Germany have been stockpiling armaments for years. When we eventually stand against them, and it is when not if, we need to be ready and we're not nearly that yet. Since the beginning of the year, things have been happening. Many of the families we help now have their husbands in work. You must have noticed there have been fewer men on the street corners over the last few weeks and months.'

Bridie nodded. No one could have failed to notice. She'd heard again the tramp of men's boots sparking on the cobbles as they made their way to work, and the factory hooters slicing into the early morning, signalling the start of the shifts. She'd also seen the women settling their tick in the shops and redeeming things from the pawnshops. It had been heartening to see their lives getting better. But at what cost? she thought now and felt bile rise in her throat.

'And now it will be stepped up, you'll see,' Tom went on. 'Everyone that wants it will have work. That's one good thing about war, possibly the only good thing.'

Bridie thought that if Tom was right and there was work for all, maybe Peggy McKenna's husband would benefit too and then the woman wouldn't need to come begging from her. Sometimes lately, to avoid Mary's wrath towards her for her inability to manage on Tom's pay, she'd been reduced to pawning the odd thing to put food on the table.

'I'm leaving the Mission,' Tom said suddenly, breaking in on her thoughts.

'But why?'

'Well, with the men going back to work, I'll hardly be needed – Father Flynn and the few volunteer helpers will be able to cope, I think. Anyway, if this Hitler and the German army is to be kept from invading here, every man jack will be needed to manufacture the means to stop him. I'll go into munitions.'

'You've never worked in a factory.'

'No, and there'll be hundreds like me,' he said.

He put his arm around Bridie and added, 'You may as well know too, pet, that when war is declared, I intend to enlist and so does Eddie.'

Bridie felt as if the breath had been knocked from her body. 'Enlist,' she repeated in a horrified whisper.

Tom covered her trembling hands with his own. He knew Bridie loved him, more than loved him, she depended on him, needed him.

But it was to protect her and the children that he was prepared to take this step. He'd seen and heard enough of Hitler's butchering methods amongst the Jews in his own country and could imagine with dread how he'd treat the occupants of a country he'd invaded and conquered. He knew too that if he didn't enlist it would only be a matter of time until he was called up.

All this passed through Tom's mind now as he saw the blood drain from Bridie's face and her eyes widen in shock. 'Bridie,' he said urgently, 'you must realise that is what I must do. Remember, Tyrone isn't part of the Free State. I'd be conscripted anyway in the end. Eddie doesn't have to enlist, but he said he's coming along with me.'

Bridie nodded, but her mind was in a whirl. She loved Tom so much, even more than when she'd married him. He was her rock when she needed one, the one who kept her steady, so that when Peggy listed any number of accidents that could befall her wee ones, engineered possibly by a revengeful God, Bridie would assure herself that

Tom wouldn't let anyone or anything hurt his children. But Bridie knew it would soon be down to her and her alone to protect her children.

The woman had the ability to frighten her witless at times, not for herself, but the news she held over her like a time bomb that could destroy so many lives, lives she'd struggled for years to protect. And then there were her children? What if something bad was to befall them? God, she wouldn't be able to live with herself.

She was so terrified that something would happen to them after Tom told her that he intended to enlist that she'd scarcely let them out of her sight. She wouldn't even countenance an evening out without them, even if it was only to the local picture house, leaving Mary to listen out.

Much as Tom loved the children, he loved Bridie more and it had annoyed him at first that he felt he had to confide in Mary. 'She never mentions the abortion, so of course I don't either, but do you think it could be preying on her mind? I only think that because she's so frantic about the children, petrified something might happen to them.'

Mary felt sorry for Tom and tried to reassure him. 'I don't think it's the abortion after all this time,' she said. 'If it was, wouldn't she have talked it over with me or Ellen? As for the children, well, some mothers worry more than others do. Our own mother nearly fretted herself into an early grave over Bridie, certain a puff of wind would blow her over.'

'This is more than natural concern,' Tom insisted. 'Shall I have a word with her about it?'

'No, I've tried that, but she says no,' Tom said. 'Leave it so. I just wondered if she'd mentioned anything to you, that's all.'

When the German armies, helped by the Austrian ones, marched into Sudetenland in October 1938 no one was surprised. 'Bloody Hitler,' Ellen remarked. 'He'll have the whole of Europe before he's finished.'

'That's his aim,' Sam said. 'He's been a problem for years. Don't know what the people were thinking of electing him and his damned party in the first place. He's a madman and you can't keep giving in to madmen. The day will come and, mark my words, it won't be long away, when Britain at least will have to stand up against Hitler.'

The day following Hitler's invasion into Sudetenland, Tom, having given the Mission notice, got himself a job at Fisher and Ludlow's making wings and bomb tails for Lancaster airplanes and where overtime was less of an option and more of a duty.

Tom didn't mind though. His ordinary salary was much more than he'd been paid at the Mission and with the overtime, it made a sizeable sum. Most weeks, money could be put in the post office saving account he took such a pride in. It was all in Bridie's name. 'You never know when you might have need of money,' he'd said in explanation when Bridie had asked.

'Oh,' Bridie said with a smile. 'I know that right

enough. When I run away with my fancy man, we'll need a bit behind us.'

Tom suddenly grabbed Bridie to him. 'Don't even joke about that,' he said. 'If I lost you, Bridie, I'd no longer want to live – I love you so much it hurts.'

'It was a joke, Tom. Why in God's name would I leave someone so good and kind, especially when I love that person with a passion too?' Bridie said. 'Tom, I'll never, ever leave you.'

'No matter what?'

'No matter what,' Bridie said in assurance, wrapping her arms around Tom and kissing him ardently in case he should have any doubt about her words.

The following month, Bridie and Tom listened to the wireless with horror as it described the pogrom issued against the German Jews living in Berlin. It was known as *Kristallnacht*, or the Night of the Crystals, because so much glass was broken – more glass it was said than was in the whole of Germany if they were to try and repair the damage.

But the storm troopers were not interested in repair, but in beating, maiming and often killing the occupants of the shops and houses that they had looted or smashed to bits and the synagogues they had set ablaze.

That cold night, Tom looked at his family grouped around the table – his beautiful Bridie, her eyes dark pools in her pale face; Katie, a carbon copy of her mother, looking from one parent to another, sensing the tension, but not understanding it. And then his more robust son Liam, just two years old and only interested in the food before him. An icy band of fear settled around Tom, not fear for himself, but for his family. He wondered how the Jewish fathers had felt seeing their wives and young children thrown out into that bleak winter's night, beaten, or even killed if they tried to resist.

Did the women cower in fear for themselves, for their children? Did they watch their houses looted, their furniture reduced to matchwood, or carried away to grace someone else's home, and see the flaming synagogues setting the winter sky aglow?

'How can we just stand by and see them do such things to people?' Bridie asked tearfully. The broadcaster reporting on the persecution of the German Jews had been moved by the news coming in. It had been apparent in his voice and his words had reduced Bridie to tears.

'What should we do, Bridie?' Tom asked. 'I'm appalled as you, but we're helpless. Ask yourself though how long can Britain go on pretending this isn't happening?'

Bridie knew what Britain must do, and that was declare war on Germany. She shivered in fear.

'Hitler wants to rule the world,' Tom went on. 'For years we've stood by and let the man stock pile arms and build up his army, navy and air force. He believes in the master race, blond-haired, blue-eyed people – true Germans, he says. Jews have no place in his plan. He thinks they taint the blood lines.'

'So we stand by while atrocities go on,' Bridie said. 'And just shrug our shoulders.'

'That seems to be the way of it,' Tom agreed. 'But maybe we won't be doing that for ever.'

Bridie felt as she was on a spiral, spinning inexorably to the war she dreaded, but that desire for justice would make inevitable. Each day the news was worse for the 'Night of Crystals' had had a domino affect across the whole of Germany and Jews were afraid, and with reason, for in towns and cities there were reports of the looting and burning of their property, and people being beaten, tortured, mutilated and killed.

'It's beyond human understanding,' Ellen said. 'God Almighty, what have the poor sods done to deserve what's happening to them?'

No one had had an answer to that. And then, in early December, there came news of another kind. Ellen came into Bridie's house, closely followed by Mary who she'd collected on the way, with a telegram in her hand. Soon the sight of a telegram would strike terror in people's hearts, but even then, a telegram seldom meant good news.

FRANCIS DEAD. JIMMY DEVASTATED.
FUNERAL FRIDAY. WANTS YOU ALL
HERE. SARAH.

'Francis dead!' Bridie repeated and she felt as if a huge weight had been lifted from between her shoulders. 'Francis dead. Oh thank God! Thank God!'

No one chided Bridie for her heartfelt cry, but when she said, 'I can't go. You can't expect me to mourn a man like that,' they all disagreed.

'Bridie, you must,' Mary said.

'Why must I? You can't ask that I go, it's inhuman.'

'You're not going for Francis, for God's sake. You're going for Daddy.'

'No!'

'If you don't go, this rift between you and Mammy and Daddy will never be repaired,' Mary said. 'Daddy gave you permission to marry, remember. He loves you and misses you. Whatever Francis was to you, to Daddy he was almost like a son, the child he raised to adulthood. He will be destroyed. Go – for his sake? Francis cannot hurt you any more.'

Bridie stared at Mary in horror. 'Not hurt me any more,' she repeated. 'Have you, either of you, any idea how I feel about that man? Just to think of him, or any belonging to him, makes my skin crawl. You don't know what you're asking me to do.'

'We do,' Ellen said soothingly. 'It's just that . . .'

'There isn't a "just" in any of this,' Bridie said and her voice rose in distress. Until then, the women had spoken in low, controlled voices, mindful of Bridie's children building some complicated construction with bricks on the rag rug before the fire. Now

Katie, alerted to her mother's tone, glanced up at them all.

None of them noticed her and Bridie went on, 'Doesn't it matter to either of you that it's his fault I'm here, his fault my mother won't bid me the time of day, his fault that I can never go home like any other body and be the beloved daughter, feted and made much of as you always were, Mary, when you came home, and your children such a delight to our parents as mine can never be?'

Mary knew that every word her sister spoke was true, but she also knew that if she didn't go back home, the rift between her and their parents would be wider than ever. So she spoke impatiently. 'I know that – God, aren't we all well aware of it? But, for Christ's sake, I'm not asking you to go home and honour the man. And while we're on, remember you're not the only victim in this. Mammy and Daddy suffered too at Francis's hand when you fled. But now Daddy is asking for your help. Are you going to turn your back on him, Bridie?'

For one brief moment, Bridie toyed with the idea of easing her parents' torment and confessing everything. But she swiftly rejected it. Whatever sort of a bugger a man was in life, in death he was a saint no less, and none would believe her now. But, more important than that, though the telegram was brief, it told Bridie enough to know how distracted with grief her father would be at Francis's death.

Could she then strip away the man's character, expose him for the filthy, bullying pervert he was and tell her father all he'd done to her? She'd be afraid for the state of her father's mind if she was to do such a thing.

She felt tears sting her eyes at the thought that they would probably go to their graves believing the worst of her. This, though, was one thing she could do for her father. For his sake, could she swallow the distaste and apprehension and go home to mourn Francis openly?

'Well,' Mary demanded, and Bridie realised how long the silence had stretched out between them. She looked around at the concerned faces of her sister and her aunt and then her eyes slid to the children and she saw Katie sitting up straight, staring at her. When Katie saw the glistening tear trails on her mother's face, she leapt to her feet. 'Why are you crying?'

Liam's head shot up at Katie's words and his own bottom lip began to tremble when he saw the tears on Bridie's cheeks. 'Hush,' she said, holding him close and taking comfort from it and then, for Katie's sake, she forced her stiff lips into a smile and said, 'I'm not crying, Katie, I have a cold and it's making my eyes water.'

Liam was comforted, but Katie wasn't fooled. She knew Bridie hadn't given her a real smile either, because it hadn't reached her eyes, and she crossed the room to stand by her side. She hadn't the whole gist of what had upset her mother, but she knew that her aunties had wanted her to go somewhere and she hadn't wanted to go and they'd upset her and so she glared at them.

Bridie shifted Liam to one hip and put the other hand on Katie's silken head and said, 'There's the weans and Tom. How can I just go and leave them all?'

'I can see to the weans,' Ellen said. 'I can't go myself, Sam's too sick to leave.'

Neither girl argued with Ellen. With the onset of the winter weather, the cold Sam had caught had turned to bronchitis and Ellen was constantly plastering his chest with camphorated oil and hot flannels which she had heating on the fireguard.

'You'll have your hands full already,' Bridie protested.

'Not at all,' Ellen said. 'It will only be for a few days and Mary's are at school all day. There's just your two and sure they're no trouble at all.

Liam smiled at the aunt he loved almost as much as his mammy. But Katie scowled at her. Ellen couldn't fathom why she should view staying with her for just a few days in such a bad light, when she'd always regarded it as a treat before, but then she saw her glance up at her mother and understood perfectly.

The child was altogether too bright and she vowed to try to explain things to her when she was at her house, not the whole truth of course, but something to satisfy a wee but feisty girl.

'Tom and Eddie will be there in the evenings too,'

Mary put in. 'And it won't hurt our Jamie to do his bit. Might put some sense on him.'

Bridie laughed. 'I hardly think so,' she said, for Jamie, who'd be eleven in January, was in some ways as silly as he'd been at three. Three times recently, he'd been brought home by a policeman: once for hitching a ride on the back of a cart and then another time for hanging onto a tram. He was thrown off as the tram went around a corner and nearly went under the wheels of a delivery van.

The policeman told Mary sternly that the van driver might never be the same man after it. That time, Jamie felt the sting of his father's belt on his backside. The last time he was brought home it was for climbing onto the roof of the laundry in Bell Barn Road, half of which was made of glass and anything but safe.

He'd been serving on the altar since he'd been nine, but even then there was a problem, as he'd been caught filling his water pistol with holy water and taking a sip of the priest's Communion wine. Bridie loved young Jamie, but had to admit Mary had her work cut out with him. Fortunately, Mickey was a much quieter child; though he admired his big brother, he'd inherited his dad's love of books and spent a lot of his free time reading. Eddie, delighted at his interest, had introduced him to the public lending library in town and Mickey had been astounded that two books could be taken out for nothing and kept for a fortnight.

'Aye, maybe you're right,' Mary said with a sigh.

'Nothing would put any sense in Jamie's head, but he can still do his bit. If we leave on Thursday and come back Monday – or Sunday if we can – the children will be left for the least possible time with Ellen and Sam – Eddie will be home for the weekend, or from Saturday lunchtime anyway.'

And so it was arranged and Bridie set out with grave misgivings that bitterly cold December day. Both women were sick on the boat, though it wasn't to be wondered at when white-fringed rollers, whipped by ferocious, icy winds, were constantly hurling themselves against the ferry's sides, causing it to pitch and list from side to side.

It was a bleak, cold and depressing time to travel, and too early yet for émigrés to be returning home for Christmas. Bridie and Mary were glad the carriages of both the train and rail bus were almost deserted though, for they talked a lot of Francis – the kind of man he'd been – and speculated about how he'd died. Bridie said fiercely that she wished she'd had a hand in it and while Mary understood precisely why she'd said that, it wouldn't have done for anyone else to overhear it.

As they neared their old home, Bridie began to feel even more nervous. They'd sent their mother and father a telegram detailing their arrival and she couldn't help wondering how she'd be received.

The short winter's day was nearly at an end when the rail bus drew up at the bottom of McCarthy's farm and there, in the gloom, Bridie spotted her father waiting for them. Gone were her nerves and apprehensions. She almost threw herself from the rail bus at her father and tasted the salt tears as she kissed his cheeks, lined with age and sorrow. She felt a terrific sense of homecoming and realised how much she'd missed her home, her parents, her former life.

But this trip was not for her, nor Mary: it wasn't even to bury the man who'd done his best to wreck her life. It was to bring some measure of comfort to her daddy who was truly bowed down with grief at losing his brother. His loss was compounded by the way Francis died, but this they didn't find out until later that evening as they sat around the fire.

Sarah had been rather stiff with both her daughters at first. If she'd have had a say in it at all, she'd have asked just Mary and Ellen, but the intensity of Jimmy's grief had frightened her and when he had said he wanted Bridie to come over as well, she had felt compelled to agree – she was afraid Jimmy might have gone to pieces altogether if she had opposed him. And yet, she couldn't fully welcome the girl who'd broken their hearts apart. Sarah fervently wished Ellen had been able to come to ease the tension between them all.

Bridie was tired and hungry and so was more upset by her mother's attitude than she would have normally been, for she knew her mother and had guessed how she would react. A meal restored Bridie's spirits, but though Sarah thawed towards Mary, her resentment at Bridie was still openly on display.

Later, as they sat around the fire, Mary produced photographs of all the children which Ellen had taken with the camera she'd bought for Jamie's First Communion. Although Jimmy was pleased to see how his namesake Jamie and his brother Mickey had grown, when he saw Katie and Liam for the first time, tears streamed from his eyes.

Looking at Katie was like looking at her mother at the same age, while Liam was more like his cousins, but with the podginess of babyhood still clinging to him. 'Daddy, don't cry,' Bridie pleaded, patting his hand.

'I'm grand, child,' he said, pushing a gnarled weather-beaten hand across his face. 'It was just seeing your weans like that for the first time. Look after them well and you too, Mary – guard your sons, for the world's a wicked place.'

That cryptic remark was later explained when Sarah told them how Francis had been found beaten up in a ditch. 'It wasn't the beating that killed him,' she said, 'it was the weather too. If it had been warmer, he'd have probably survived it.'

'But who beat him up?' Mary asked.

'No one knows,' Sarah said. 'Nor does anyone know where Francis had been that night, or where he was returning from. I don't know if it had anything to do with it, but gypsies were seen in the area some days before and you know they haven't been here for many a year. They were blamed, of course, especially as they suddenly disappeared the next day.'

'That's their way though,' Jimmy put in. 'Sometimes I think the gypsies are blamed for things they haven't done because it's easy. I'm not saying they're angels or anything, the gypsies, it's just . . . Well, let's say I don't think Francis's killer, or at least the one who beat him up, will ever be caught. People think it was a gypsy and it will be left there. Whoever it was, I hope at least he'll rot in Hell when his time comes.'

Bridie and Mary exchanged glances and later in bed, Bridie asked, 'D'you think it could have been Sally McCormack's family after all this time?'

'Maybe,' Mary replied. 'But then again, like Daddy said, it might have nothing to do with them. Let's just say if I ever found out who it was, I'd shake him by the hand. After what happened to you and young Sally, I'd think he or she has done the world a service.'

The next day though, for their parents sake, Bridie and Mary put their grieving face on along with their black mourning clothes and followed the coffin to the church for Requiem Mass. Later, at the wake, while the beer, whiskey and illicit poteen flowed freely, Bridie heard constantly what a grand man her uncle had been.

He'd been the kindest and most generous man you could ever wish to meet. Nothing was too much trouble; for God's sake, the man would give you the shirt off his back if he thought you had need of it. And then wasn't he full of fun? Never a dull moment with Francis. He didn't take life seriously, always ready with a joke and a laugh. He liked a drink, they said, there was no denying that, but no harm in that at all, and though he could drink many a man under the table, he was a good provider, a wonderful father and husband. His family would miss him sorely and so would his friends. God, but it was a terrible tragedy! A great loss! An awful great loss!

'God, next they'll apply to have him canonised,' Bridie hissed to Mary. 'It makes me feel sick. How soon can we get rid of people?'

'Not for hours yet,' Mary whispered back. 'And it would reflect badly on the family if you were to disappear, so don't think of it. He's six foot under and can hurt you no more, so hang on.'

So Bridie gritted her teeth. She commiserated with Frank and Delia and the little ones who were little no longer. Rosalyn was now married to a man called Todd Fleming but couldn't be there because she'd been unable to get a flight out in time for the funeral. She was sure her mammy would understand.

Delia understood only too well and Bridie was relieved: she'd been worried about meeting Rosalyn again and was glad their first meeting wouldn't take place on this occasion, when she was fraught enough, especially as she guessed Rosalyn, who had thought the world of her father, would be incredibly upset and might think Bridie's behaviour odd.

Bridie and Mary left early Monday morning, exhausted, having had to act as though sorry for

Francis's death when really they would have preferred to dance a jig on his grave. Bridie had got no closer to her mother either and, still not able to explain fully why she'd upped and left in the way she had, Sarah couldn't begin to understand her actions.

Bridie didn't know if she'd done her father much good either by coming until he enveloped her in a bear hug just before she was about to mount the rail bus. 'Thank you for coming, my bonny lass,' he said. 'I've missed you sorely.'

'And I you, Daddy,' Bridie replied sincerely. 'And I'm sorry for everything.'

'Nay, lass. Don't let our parting words be ones of apology,' Jimmy said. 'I only wish I could see more of you and my grandchildren too. If there's war in England, I want you to come here and bring the two wee ones with you,' he added suddenly, full of concern. 'And,' he said, reaching out to Mary. 'That goes for you too. Now don't forget.'

Bridie and Mary were moved by their father's concern. Both felt too that though it would take him some time to really get over Francis's death, their presence and the danger of war that hung over them had shifted the emphasis a little and might help take his mind off it.

'Not that we'd take him up on it, of course,' Mary said as the rail bus chugged its way towards Strabane.

'Aye,' Bridie said, catching her sister's mood.

'We can just be glad that we live close enough to be a support to one another.'

'Amen to that,' Mary said. 'You hold me up and I'll hold you up.'

Bridie was glad to reach home. The low clouds that had hung about all day had made the day dark and now with evening upon them, it was nearly pitch black. The streets' gas lights made little impression in the murky gloom with wisps of fog swirling through it and Bridie shivered. They'd sent a telegram to Ellen telling her of their arrival time and she'd been up to both houses and lit the fires, leaving them banked up with slack for safety.

Bridie crossed to the hearth and poked life into the fire and it was as she raised her head to lift the coalscuttle that she saw the figure pass the window. She groaned; the shambling gait of the shawl-clad person meant there was no mistaking who it was and a few minutes later she faced Peggy McKenna who'd come in the entry door.

'I came to sympathise with you on your loss,' she said.

'My loss!' Bridie said blankly. She almost told Peggy that it was no loss, but a blessing, but she didn't: for Peggy didn't know who the father of the child she had aborted was and she'd never know, it would only be more ammunition for her. So she quickly collected herself and said, 'Aye, my father was very cut up.'

'Invited you back to the fold and all,' Peggy said

sneeringly. 'Wonder if they'd be so pleased with you if they knew what I know?'

Bridie knew they'd be horrified. It would be no good telling them about Francis now. He'd turned into a demi-god after his death. Never speak ill of the dead, people said, and that certainly applied to Francis. If the news of her pregnancy and subsequent abortion got out now, she'd be castigated more than ever if she tried to tell the truth. Francis was more powerful from the grave than if he'd still been alive.

'Peggy, what do you want?' she cried. 'Your husband is in work now.'

'Aye, he is,' Peggy agreed. 'But the man has a terrible thirst on him. Sure, there's little left for the rest of us. Your man must get a good screw, all the overtime he does, and isn't he a fine and sober man. You can spare a few coppers, I'm sure.'

'I gave you three shillings before I went to the funeral,' Bridie protested.

'Three shillings – what good is that?' Peggy said. 'I want at least ten bob a week now.'

Bridie gasped. 'Peggy, I could never manage that. I only have housekeeping. I couldn't lose ten shillings a week . . . Maybe I could stretch to five,' she said weakly.

'Ten,' Peggy said. 'Or those people of yours will be getting a letter from me.'

Bridie suddenly heard her children approaching. Mary had offered to collect them from Ellen's and

Bridie could hear the high-pitched voice of her daughter and the shouts of Mary's boys.

'The weans,' she said to Peggy.

'I hear them,' Peggy said. 'I'm away, but I'll look in tomorrow. Ten bob – have it ready!'

Mary and Peggy passed each other in the doorway. 'What did she want?' Mary asked, almost as soon as she was in the door.

'To say she was sorry about Francis. Sorry for me, I mean,' Bridie said. 'I nearly told her what I really thought but managed to stop myself.'

'What was that, Auntie Bridie?' Jamie asked, and Mary gave her eldest son a cuff.

'My fault,' Bridie said with a wry smile. 'I forgot about little pigs having big ears,' and to her young nephew, she added, 'and as for you, you can mind you own business and not worry a jot about mine.'

'Don't encourage Peggy McKenna,' Mary warned.

'I don't.'

'Well, she's never away from the place,' Mary said. 'People tell me. They wonder at it because no one else has much time for her.'

'God, you can't blow your nose in this place before someone has you dead and buried,' Bridie snapped angrily, the stress of the fraught funeral, the insidious blackmailing of Peggy McKenna and the difficulty of getting her hands on ten shillings before the morning getting to her. 'I wish everyone would mind their own bloody business!'

'Oh well, if that's your attitude,' Mary said huffily.

Bridie immediately felt contrite. 'Oh God, I'm sorry, Mary,' she said. 'It's just the funeral and all. Stay for a wee bit.'

'I can't,' Mary said, still a little annoyed with her sister. 'Eddie will be in and no meal ready. Come on, boys.'

When she'd gone, Bridie sat on the chair and pulled her children onto her lap. 'Did you miss me, Mammy?' Katie asked.

'I did indeed,' Bridie said.

'And me?'

'And you, Liam,' Bridie assured him, and though she sat and talked to the children, hugging them and telling them about the cottage and the farm and their grandparents and cousins, the problem of getting ten shillings prayed on her mind. She only had a few shillings to last her until Friday, pay day, and the only other money she had was in the post office book that Tom set such store by. She'd thanked God he'd put it in her name, for she miserably conceded that she'd have to take money out of there, this week certainly. Maybe she'd have to take some out of it every week and she hoped and prayed Tom didn't look too closely at the book when he paid money in. She wondered bleakly if she'd be paying for Peggy McKenna's silence till one of them died.

CHAPTER FIFTEEN

Peggy McKenna continued to blackmail Bridie as 1939 dawned, coming almost every week for the ten shillings that Bridie often had to draw some, or all of, from the post office account. She thanked God that since Tom was working such long hours at the factory, he'd readily agreed with her suggestion that she put the money in every week. It would never occur to him to check it either and she thanked God for that too, for she often went hot and cold at the thought of Tom finding out how little savings they actually had.

Elsewhere too, the world was in total disarray. By the spring, Chamberlain authorised a doubling of strength of the Territorial Army and conscription was introduced. 'That's it then,' Tom said, turning off the wireless one evening. 'War can't be avoided much longer.'

They were all crowded into Bridie's house: Ellen, Sam, for he'd thankfully rallied with the warmer weather, Mary, Eddie and the boys, and no one disagreed with Tom. Half the world seemed ranged against Britain and despite America calling back its ambassador from Prague in protest after Hitler's invasion, they'd been remarkably quiet about other concerns.

'At least France is joining in with us,' Eddie said.

'Aye, if the bloody maniac attacks Poland,' Sam said. 'And he will.'

No one spoke; there was nothing to say. Each one was busy with their own thoughts, wondering what the uncertain future held.

Worried though Bridie was about her children's safety if war should break out, their general good humour and laughter lifted her spirits when depression at the turn of world events threatened to overwhelm her. Each day was increasingly precious to her as she sensed time was running out for them and Tom would soon have to leave his family to help the war effort.

Tom was only too aware of that as well and knew he would miss the harmony of his home, but that he had to fight to defend his family's right to liberty and freedom from oppression. He was glad though that when the time came, Bridie would have Ellen and Mary beside her.

Bridie was glad too, for both women were very important to her and at the beginning of the summer that year, Bridie said to Mary, 'I'm pushing all this war talk to the back of my mind as far as I can. I know Katie only looks about three, but she was five in June and will be at school in September – God knows I'll miss the chatter and company of her.'

Mary caught her sister's mood. 'I agree with you,' she said. 'Let's make this a summer for the children and make the most of every day.'

The weather was kind to them too, for while July was wet and miserable, from early August it was warm and sunny day after day. Bridie and Mary spent many days in Cannon Hill or Calthorpe Park with the smaller children. Jamie wouldn't come with them though: he considered himself far too old at eleven to be going about with women and kids. He'd also told his astounded mother that Jamie was a babyish name. From now on, he informed them all, his name was Jay.

'Thinks he's the bee's knees, that one,' Mary remarked to Bridie as they made their way towards Cannon Hill Park one afternoon in mid-August. Liam was kicking his legs in the pushchair while Mary held Katie and Mickey's hands. 'Says if his dad enlists, he'll be man of the house and not to even think of sending him away anywhere.'

'Evacuation?' Bridie said, and she shivered in sudden fear. 'I've never even given it a thought. I could never send my children to live with strangers – anything could happen to them. Were you seriously thinking of it?'

'Eddie and I have talked of it,' Mary admitted. She knew the way Bridie felt about her children. She seldom let them out of her sight. Even going to the funeral she'd fretted leaving them with Ellen, and that was with Tom on hand a lot of the time. She knew evacuation wouldn't be on the cards as far as Bridie was concerned. Still, Mary thought, she was no better – she couldn't imagine how empty the house would seem without her boys. 'Mine won't be going either', she said. 'Well, Jamie, or bloody Jay as he calls himself now, won't go and I'd not have Mickey go without him. To tell you the truth, I wasn't that keen anyway – sending your children across the country to perfect strangers, I'd be worried stiff about them.'

'I know,' Bridie agreed. 'God knows I'd be lost without mine and I'd never know a minute's peace if they were away from me.'

Air raid shelters were being delivered to those who had gardens to put them in and public shelters had been erected too. Local children, fortunately still on holiday from school, had been drafted in to help and fill sandbags to pile around the outside of them. Jay was amongst those helping. It was hot and heavy work, but he did it day after day, pleased that he was doing his bit for the war effort.

Mary, Ellen and Bridie went to the Bull Ring together to buy blackout material for the curtains and shutters to shield the windows, ensuring no light was visible to aid any enemy bombers. It was a big job and they were all grateful of the treadle sewing machine that Ellen had got a loan of from a neighbour.

'They look horrible,' Katie announced, as Bridie stood back to examine the curtains she'd just hung. 'Take them down.'

'I can't do that,' Bridie said. 'I'd be in real trouble. The ARP warden would be after me if I did.'

And they would. Many thought they were worse than police, parading around in their uniforms and throwing their weight about. Bridie, however, thought people might be glad of those wardens before too long. She'd seen the trenches dug in the parks and the wardens running classes in Calthorpe Park helping people practise first aid on volunteer patients, potential victims of the bombs everyone said would soon fall from the sky. It looked like some game weans would play together, until you remembered grimly why they were doing it.

Everyone was instructed to collect gas masks, which they would carry in a box around their neck at all times once war was declared. On the wireless, the normal sound of the air raid siren was demonstrated, and the whistle if it was suspected that poison gas had been used, but the information did little to reassure Bridie, but rather chilled her to the marrow.

For the first time, she wondered if she were selfish in keeping her children beside her, for her own sake, when they could live relatively safely in the country. Tom understood her concern, but he was as worried for his wife as the children.

One evening with the children in bed, he sat

on the chair and pulled Bridie onto his knee. All evening he'd known she had something on her mind but he also knew she'd say nothing until the children were out of earshot. 'What is it, love? What's bothering you?'

Bridie told him of her fears, especially those she had for her children. 'God, but I'd hate to put one of these contraptions on the children,' she said, dangling a gas mask in front of him by its strap. 'But then not to do it and have them poisoned to death . . . It doesn't bear thinking about. What if they're blown to smithereens by a bomb or crushed to death or trapped? Oh Tom, do you think I should send them away?'

'Yes,' Tom said firmly. 'And you should go with them.'

'Me?'

'Yes, love,' Tom said. 'You know I won't be here and I'll worry myself silly over you if you stay here – Birmingham is bound to be a target being such a large city and one that contributes so much for the war effort.'

'How could I run away to safety somewhere and leave Aunt Ellen and Mary to manage on their own?' Bridie demanded. 'And anyway, how could I just up and leave the house? It might not be much, but it's ours. You know yourself with the housing shortage here, if I was to leave, someone else would be in it before I reached Bristol Passage.'

Tom knew all Bridie said was right, but fear for

her safety overrode all practical concerns. 'You'd not even consider it?'

'No, Tom.'

'Well, I think the children would fret without you,' Tom said. 'Liam is not yet three years old and Katie is just five.' They knew no life beyond those narrow streets, where there might be many deprivations, but where most of the neighbours were decent people who were always there if help of any sort was needed. Maybe it would be better to stay where they were for the time being, Tom finally conceded, especially if Bridie was so determined to stay.

'Aye,' Bridie said with a sigh. 'They're both little more than babies. They'll bide with me like so many more and we'll face whatever comes together.'

The evacuation of women and younger children had begun in London in late August and plans were in force to evacuate the school-aged ones from other major cities on Friday 1st September.

Mary and Bridie went up to St Catherine's school that Friday morning to wave off the children whose parents had allowed them to be evacuated. There were about thirty of them assembled in the yard. Their clothes – two changes of everything – were in various containers, little cases, or haversacks; a couple even had their things in brown carrier bags. But every child had their gas mask in a case hung around their neck.

Bridie saw some of the mothers of the children

wipe tears from their eyes surreptitiously. Their children were nervous and apprehensive enough without crying in front of them Bridie thought, although she knew their hearts must be breaking, and she hoped no one would break down completely. Mr Steele, the headmaster, must have thought the same and he started the children singing 'Run Rabbit, Run Rabbit' as they marched out of the school and began to mount the bus that was to take them to Moor Street Station.

'Poor little things,' Bridie said to Mary as they made their way back. 'Some of the younger ones looked frightened to death and no wonder: even adults wouldn't like to be taken away and not told where they were going, to live with people they'd never met in their lives before.'

'It's hard, right enough,' Mary agreed. 'But what about the bombs? We all saw those pictures from Spain.'

'There are shelters,' Bridie said. 'That one just off Bristol Passage is only a few minutes away. But we're luckier, for we can hide out in our own cellars. We'll all be as safe as houses in there.'

''Course we will,' Mary said, and wondered who she was trying to reassure, herself or her sister.

And reassurance was needed even quicker than they expected, for they heard on the wireless that evening that Germany had invaded Poland.

* * *

Neville Chamberlain was to speak on the wireless the following Sunday morning. Everyone knew what he would say.

St Catherine's was packed for the children's Mass at nine o'clock and the same applied to many churches that day. Some, who'd rarely gone across the threshold of a church the whole of their lives, felt the need of spiritual guidance and comfort that morning.

Later, they all gathered in Bridie's house, feeling the need to be together as they readied themselves for the inevitable. Many neighbours who hadn't a wireless themselves wanted to hear the broadcast and crammed into Bridie's, far too many for the little house to hold, and so the door was left open to the street. Katie took one look at the mass of people and scuttled under the table, pulling her little brother after her.

There was a hush over everything: no baby cried, no dog barked, no squealing children played outside. The pavements and streets were empty. No trams clattered along Bristol Street, neither was there a light rumble of other traffic, or clip-clop of horses' hooves. It was as if the world held its breath. Everyone was waiting for the dreaded news from the Prime Minister. It finally came at 11.15.

'I am speaking to you from the cabinet
room of 10 Downing Street. This morning,
the British Ambassador in Berlin handed
the German government a final note

*stating that unless we heard from them
by eleven o'clock that they were prepared
at once to withdraw their troops from
Poland, a state of war would exist between
us. I have to tell you now, no such
undertaking has been received, and that
consequently, this country is at war with
Germany.'*

Bridie could hear the keening of women all around
her and she felt her own throat tighten and tears
sting her eyes, but she wouldn't let them fall.
She knew it was harder for the older ones, who
remembered the carnage of the last war, but if they
were to prevail, the women had to be as brave as
their husbands, many of whom would be facing
the enemy before too long. There was no time for
giving way to emotion like that.

She caught Tom's eye and reached for his hand,
but they'd barely touched when someone shouted,
'Look!' They were pointing at the window and
Bridie crossed to the door as people spilled into
the street. Against the backdrop of a beautiful
early autumn day where the sun, like a golden orb,
shone down from a Wedgwood blue sky, steel grey
barrage balloons were suspended, swaying gently
from side to side.

They looked ugly and out of place and struck
a chill into many a person's heart. Maybe they
were meant to be reassuring, a deterrent to enemy
aircraft, but in reality they looked menacing. 'Oh

Tom!' Bridie cried plaintively, her resolve to keep control evaporating immediately.

'I know, love,' Tom said. 'But now it's official, Eddie and I will be seeing about enlisting straight-away.'

Bridie always knew what he'd do when war was declared, so why did her body shake and feel as if it were comprised of ice? She wanted to plead with Tom, implore him to think of his family, beg him to wait until he was called up and not to volunteer today. She did neither of these things, for she knew Tom was doing what he felt he must. She drew on all the reserves of courage she had, willed her voice not to shake, and even forced her reluctant lips in the semblance of a smile as she said, 'Yes, Tom, I know.'

Tom was filled with admiration for Bridie's stoicism and he held her close for a moment, despite all those looking on, and said, 'You're a grand girl, Bridie Cassidy, that's what you are, a grand girl.'

'Are you going to be a soldier, Daddy?' Katie asked two mornings later, as she watched Tom pack his clothes into a suitcase.

'Aye,' Tom said. 'Uncle Eddie too, if they'll have us both. Will you like me being a soldier, Katie?'

'I don't know,' Katie said. 'What does a soldier do?'

'Well, many things,' Tom explained. 'I'll have a nice smart uniform that you'll probably like, but what I really have to go and do is try and stop a nasty man doing bad things and that means I'll probably have to go away.'

Katie looked hard at her daddy's kind face with the deep, brown eyes that often sparkled with laughter, and then her eyes moved to the sad face of her mother. She knew she didn't want her daddy to go away and leave them all, not even for a short time, so she told him, 'I don't want you to be a soldier, Daddy. I want you to stay here with us.'

'I'd like that too, pet,' Tom said. 'But I have to go.'

'Is it to do with those horrible curtains Mammy has on the windows?' Katie said, glaring at them. 'Mammy said she had to put them up.'

'Aye, my darling girl,' Tom admitted. 'It's all to do with this war everyone's talking about.'

'Then I hate war!' Katie declared.

'So do most sane thinking people, pet,' Tom said, getting to his feet. 'But now I must be away for your Uncle Eddie,' and he kissed Katie on the top of her head, then Liam, and lastly he took Bridie in his arms. She willed herself not to cry for the children's sake, but she wanted to hold back time, to keep this moment in Tom's arms, their children beside them, for ever. 'I'll be back before you know it,' Tom reassured her. 'I'll only be in training at Cannock Chase.'

But what was he training for, Bridie thought. To kill people and to avoid getting killed. Oh God, if anything should happen to her Tom . . . But she said none of this and instead gave a brief nod of her head. 'I know,' she said, her voice husky with the effort of not crying.

'I have to be away,' Tom said, glancing at the door. 'They're picking me up at Thorpe Street Barracks at eight.'

'Go on then,' Bridie said, pulling herself reluctantly out of his embrace. 'Wouldn't do to be late your first day in the army and I have to get Katie ready for school.'

But Bridie watched Tom through the window until he was out of sight. Already his step was firmer, his back straighter, and she knew he'd make a fine soldier.

Bridie missed Tom more than she ever thought and she wondered how she'd manage weeks and weeks, months and months, before he'd come home again. She was grateful for the photographs Ellen had taken of Tom and Eddie in their uniform because she was afraid Liam would forget his daddy altogether. Each night she propped the photograph up as she helped the children say their prayers and when she wrote to him, as she did every week, she'd tell him about the children, little snippets she'd remembered that they'd done or said. She'd help Liam write kisses on the bottom of the letter, though Katie could do hers unaided. They'd await his reply eagerly – Tom always included a little note for them and asked for a photograph of them, which Ellen and Bridie sent.

He told Bridie the training in Cannock Chase

was gruelling and his muscles ached in places he didn't know he even had them. He hadn't realised he was so unfit. Mind, he'd said, army issue boots were not made for running in, not made for much else but crippling the feet, and might be Hitler's secret weapon.

While he was quite keen on the training and the practise with weapons, as he felt it had some purpose, he was bored rigid with constant drill and the emphasis on neatness and presentation. He complained about it to Bridie:

You'd be very impressed if you could see the way I can make a bed now, square corners and so spick and span. I'd be the envy of many a nurse, I bet. It's amazing what you can do when the threat of a boot up your arse hangs before you.

And your boots and buttons must shine so that the bullying, sadistic Sergeant in charge of us can see his face in them. And what a face, Bridie! God, there's me, a devout Christian man, and yet I have never wanted to punch a man's face as I have that man's.

If I could see the point of it all, I'd feel better, but I can't. I mean, are the Germans supposed to be terrified of our bed-making skills, or maybe dazzled by our buttons, or awed by our marching hour upon hour, hoisting guns upon shoulders, and never firing a shot? I hardly think so.

I'm glad I have Eddie beside me. At least we can laugh it all off together. The men here are a grand bunch and we get along with them fine, and we'll make a good team when the time comes.

Bridie hoped Tom was right about the good team. She imagined if she'd been in the same position she'd value someone she could trust beside her. But despite that, she hoped Tom had weeks, maybe months, of training ahead of him before he would be considered capable to face the German forces who'd so far conquered all before them.

In late October, a mere seven weeks after Tom had left, he came home on a week's leave. He thought it was embarkation leave; he'd heard the rumours flying about the camp and been told by the old hands that the army always gave you leave before sending you overseas. He didn't tell Bridie this initially. She was so pleased to see him, she was almost speechless and he had no wish to take that look from her eyes when it would serve no purpose.

Liam had passed his third birthday and was as enormously proud of his soldier father as Katie was. She, though, was less dazzled by the uniform than her brother and wanted her daddy home again. 'Have you finished all the war now, Daddy?' she asked.

Tom laughed. 'I've barely started, pet.'

'Then what have you been doing?'

'Training?'

'Oh.' Katie wasn't sure what training was, but it sounded important and anyway she didn't want to spoil her daddy's leave, so she didn't say any more about him coming home.

Tom treasured every moment of that leave. He knew he would soon be facing the enemy and all the training he had, basic though it was, would come into play. He wondered if he'd ever have the nerve to kill another human being, or the courage to face danger and possibly death.

He shared these doubts with nobody and to anyone watching, he appeared not to have a care in the world. He devoted his time to his family, taking Katie to school and Liam for walks or to one of the local parks, swinging the little boy up on his shoulders when his legs were tired.

He gave himself up to the children until they went to bed: playing games, reading books, telling stories and tossing them about effortlessly until they squealed with laughter.

But when the children were in bed, it was time for him and Bridie. Though he loved Ellen and Sam and Mary, and would see them in the day, those precious hours in the evening belonged to him and Bridie alone. He wanted to hold her close as he'd longed to do many a night lying alone on an army bunk. He wanted to take her to bed and tell her and show her how much he loved her. And he wanted to commit every detail of his children and his beautiful, wonderful wife to memory. That last evening, he'd wished he could stop time, and when Bridie, seeing something was troubling Tom, enquired, he told her why.

'Overseas,' she repeated in a horrified whisper. 'So soon?'

'Sooner the better,' Tom said almost flippantly to hide his own anxiety. 'Hitler waits for no one.'

'Where?'

'I don't know,' Tom said. 'I don't even know if it's definite – we're not told until we go, you see. It's just a feeling, the hint of a rumour, no more than that.'

But Bridie knew with a dread certainty that Tom would soon be among the fighting ranks on foreign soil and later, as he slept, she wept in abject fear, muffling her tears into her pillow, lest she awake Tom.

CHAPTER SIXTEEN

Letters from Tom came regularly, but of course they said little. Bridie understood and in the same way did not moan about the blackout, although she could have done. It was universally hated and it was unnerving to go out in such complete and utter blackness. It reminded her of walking home from the socials with Rosalyn so very long ago. Sometimes they'd walked home in intense darkness, but often stars would twinkle in the sky and a helpful moon would light the way for them.

In the smoky Birmingham skies, where factory chimneys belched fumes and smoke into the air, few stars were visible and even the moon didn't seem so bright. In time, the residents of Birmingham would learn to fear clear moonlit nights, but no one knew that then. The blackout was dangerous too. In fact, before Christmas 1939, so many people had been killed and injured because of it, that vehicles were allowed shaded headlamps and people could carry shielded torches.

Christmas 1939 was a dreary enough time. There was no point in going into a city centre with no Christmas lights strung across the streets and no bright displays in the shop windows. Not that there was much in the shops to be bought: nothing in the way of gifts, no toys at all and even food, which was in increasingly short supply. If you complained at all, the shopkeeper would remind you that there was a war on, as if you needed reminding.

One thing that hadn't materialised though was the bombing that everyone had been prophesying would start straight after war was declared. Bridie was able to reassure Tom that they hadn't even had a hint of an air raid and were as safe as houses. Most of the children evacuated to 'a place of safety' had come back. In fact, so safe was it that people were dubbing it 'The Bore War.'

In January, another restriction came into force: rationing. Four ounces of butter or lard, twelve ounces of sugar, four ounces of raw bacon, three and a half ounces of cooked bacon or ham and two eggs a week were the staple rations. The egg allowance was a joke: because so many hens had been slaughtered to save on feeding them, eggs were in very short supply and you didn't necessarily get them.

But people struggled through and though they were often worried how to feed their families, most were fairly good-humoured about it. 'At least rationing is fairer than first come, first serve, or those who have the money stocking up and causing shortages, which was what happened in the Great War,' Ellen said as meat and tea were added to the ration list in March.

What wasn't fair for Bridie was the demands Peggy McKenna was still making on her. Tom wasn't earning the same money as he did on munitions, Bridie had told Peggy that, but it didn't move the woman a jot. Tom sent Bridie as much as he could and always told her to put so much in the post office each week to set aside for a rainy day.

It seldom reached the post office, though, for with Peggy's ten shillings to take out, there was very little left. If ever Tom had examined the book he'd have been alarmed at how little was in it and she trembled at the thought of him ever finding out.

She viewed the future with little optimism and it was hard to write cheerful letters to Tom feeling this way, though she tried. At least, she told herself, she was able to tell him with the utmost sincerity that she loved him and missed him.

And then, in late May, just six months after the men had left, Bridie read of the breaching of the supposedly impregnable Maginot Line stretching across France and of the British soldiers in retreat. She and Mary took themselves off to Ellen's, feeling the need to be together, for both their men were 'Somewhere in France'.

'You don't know they're involved,' Ellen said briskly to Mary and Bridie. 'No good looking on the black side. No news is good news, they say.'

That was the point; there was no news. Both women longed for a letter to say that their husbands were safe, but they received none and as the days passed, they devoured newspapers from cover to cover and listened to every news broadcast. The Allies seemed to be making for a place called Dunkirk, just across the border from Belgium. Jay found it on the map his father had hung on his bedroom wall before he'd left. He'd plotted the advance with coloured pins and found Dunkirk, but couldn't see how anyone was going to escape from there. 'It's just sand,' he said. 'Or it looks like that on the map.'

'Oh God, Mary, what chance have they?' Bridie cried, scrutinising the map with her nephew.

'That's defeatist talk,' Mary said defiantly, but really she understood Bridie's concern. Virtually the whole of Europe was under Nazi control, ruled by brutality and evilness. Britain stood as the one bright flame of freedom in an increasingly hostile world and now it appeared British soldiers were retreating to the beaches. Before them was the massed German army and behind them the sea. Some choice, some chance of survival!

There was a call to join up in the newly formed Home Guard – their brief to protect vital work places, railways, canals and other strategic sites and to deal with parachute invaders and emergencies. 'God, if I was a few years younger,' Sam said when he heard, 'I'd give them a run for their money.'

'Well, you're not and you won't,' Ellen said

emphatically. 'God, man, you'd be one of their first casualties.'

Sam was too old and infirm to be of much use, but many weren't and not averse to pitching in to the fight, though the only thing they had in abundance was enthusiasm. The *Evening Mail* reported that within a few days, 30,000 men had joined up from Birmingham alone. They paraded in civilian clothes, with just an armband to show people who they were, and trained with broomsticks because rifles were so scarce.

Some were scathing about the Home Guard, including Ellen. 'I can see the highly disciplined German army, who've ridden roughshod over every other country in Europe, being scared of this motley crew of the old, very young and infirm when they attack them with their broom handles,' she complained. 'What we want is our boys back home here, protecting our shores and skies.'

Unknown to anyone at that time, the evacuation of troops from Dunkirk had begun. It was a race against time, because by 25th May, the German Panzer division was only twenty miles away. However, because there was no harbour at Dunkirk, the big ships couldn't get close enough to reach the men and although the Royal Navy had gathered six coasters, sixteen barges and forty Dutch schooners to help, it wasn't nearly enough.

Since mid-May, people living on the south coast and owners of self-propelled craft measuring thirty to a hundred foot long and capable of crossing the

Channel, had been required to register them with the Admiralty. By 26th May, getting the men off the beaches as soon as possible was paramount and no one objected to their boats being commandeered, and in one day forty motor boats and launches had assembled at Sheerness. Once the veil of secrecy had been lifted on 31st May, many other civilian boat owners set off for Dunkirk on their own.

The papers had photographs of the little boats, of all shapes and sizes, sailing off across the Channel, as if going to some jolly regatta. No one watching them doubted the courage of those skippers who, unarmed and unprotected, were sailing defiantly to the hellhole of Dunkirk to rescue servicemen. They knew a bomb could blow them and their boat to kingdom come any moment, or a hail of machine-gun fire end their life, but they never once hesitated.

Most, the papers reported, ferried the men back and forth to the large naval ships anchored in deeper water. When the ships were full, many would then load their own boat to capacity and take the men back to Ramsgate, Eastbourne, or Sheerness, before returning to Dunkirk to begin all over again.

Now Mary and Bridie knew why there were no letters. They knew there'd be no telegrams either, for until the rescue was complete, no one would know for certain who was alive or who was dead.

At home, for the first time, the British people faced the possibility of defeat. People were urged to disable cars not in use, and lock up or immobilise bicycles and hide maps. Road signposts were removed and railway station signs painted over to confuse any potential invader, but all it did was bewilder the honest Brummies trying to get about their daily business.

There were more 'aliens' interned. Since 1939, any Germans or Austrians classified as 'Category A', or high risk, had been sent to internment camps while those in Category B had been granted restricted movement and those in Category C freed. This was now extended to Italians as Mussolini had entered the war. Many Italians in Birmingham had lived peacefully alongside their neighbours for years and most people were dismayed when Martiella's Bakery in Bristol Street had a closed sign plastered across it.

'Interned, I ask you,' Ellen said to any who'd listen. 'For making bread.'

'No, woman, for being possibly enemy aliens,' Sam put in.

'Enemy aliens, my foot,' Ellen said angrily. 'They've been here years, their two daughters work in the shop and their two sons are in the Forces fighting for our freedom, for Christ's sake!'

'It's war. We can't take chances.'

But someone must have taken a chance because the Martiellas were released, like many other Italian people, although they weren't allowed to own a wireless, had to abide by a curfew and could have their homes searched at any time.

Posters began appearing on hoardings. 'Be Vigilant – the Enemy is Near.' 'Careless Talk Costs Lives.' 'Is Your Journey Really Necessary?' People were also advised to clear their loft of anything inflammable in case of an incendiary attack. 'I haven't got a loft,' Bridie complained to Mary. 'Just an attic the kids sleep in, like most people around here.'

'Well, we can't lug everything down the coal cellar,' Mary said. 'We'll have to take our chance like every other body. If an incendiary raid does come, we'll have notice and we'll get ourselves out of here and keep ourselves safe, that's the main thing after all. The house can burn to the ground, for my money, as long as people are safe and sound.'

But uppermost in Bridie and Mary's minds was what might have happened to their husbands. The evacuation was reputed to be over by 4th June, but still they had no news. Churchill gave a speech on the wireless to inspire the disheartened people of Britain.

We shall fight on the beaches, we shall fight on the landing grounds, we shall never surrender.

It was stirring stuff and whether Tom and Eddie had survived or not, the evacuation had been a terrific achievement for two hundred thousand British men, along with one-hundred and forty thousand French and Belgium soldiers, had been rescued. But much equipment was lost and firms were asked to produce more and more guns, tanks, aeroplanes, anything at all for the war effort. Bridie felt she hadn't been pulling her weight in this war and wanted to be doing something, but she wasn't sure what.

The next day, Ellen came to see her. 'Have you heard the latest?' she said and, without waiting for a reply, went straight on, 'It's that McKenna family.'

Immediately, Bridie froze. Just the name had the power to petrify her. Without noticing, Ellen ploughed on, bursting to tell her the gossip. 'Peggy's old man has done a runner.'

'A runner?'

'Aye, raided an off-licence and went off with all the takings. Police were at the door asking for him, but Peggy said he wasn't in. 'Course they didn't believe her and went in to search the house. She was screeching at them; you could hear her the length of the street. Said she'd seen no sign of him or any takings and would she be living the way she does if she had money about the place. The police left but I doubt she'll ever clap eyes on him again and not much loss either.'

'Oh, Aunt Ellen!'

'It's true, dear,' Ellen said. 'The two deserve each other, but even I felt sorry for her afterwards, for the two policemen would hardly have been back in Steelhouse Lane when she had a telegram about her eldest, Denis, being killed at Dunkirk. Shame, he was the best of the bunch in my opinion.'

After Ellen left, Bridie expected a visit from Peggy, but she didn't come. She supposed she should go and commiserate with her for her loss, but she couldn't face it. As a parting shot, Ellen had said, 'See bad news travels faster than good. You'll hear from your man soon, see if you don't,' and Bridie hoped and prayed she was right.

The next day a letter popped through Bridie's letterbox as she was giving the children their breakfast. She snatched it up eagerly for she had few letters. She barely noticed the Ramsgate postmark on the envelope before tearing it open.

The children watched her, wide-eyed. Both had picked up on the agitation and anxiety in both their mother and aunt and knew it was to do with their daddy and Uncle Eddie being away, though nothing had ever been said. For a long time, there'd been little laughter or joy in their home and so they looked in amazement at their mother.

Her whole face shone as if someone had lit a light behind it, her dancing eyes were bright, and her mouth was split in a great smile as she turned to them and cried. 'Your daddy is alive. He's been injured and is in a hospital in a place called Ramsgate, but he's all right.'

Katie looked at Liam. Never had either of them considered that their daddy might be dead. But now they learned he was injured and in hospital. 'What's up with him?' Katie asked worriedly.

'He has been shot,' Bridie said. 'And he has wounds from something called shrapnel.'

'Who shot him?' Liam demanded indignantly but before Bridie could reply, Katie cast her little brother a withering glance and said, 'That's what soldiers do, silly, shoot each other.'

'Oh.' Liam said. 'Why do they?'

Katie had no idea, it seemed a crazy thing for anyone to want to do, but she wasn't admitting that to her brother and their mammy was paying them no mind. 'Daddy had to go away, didn't he,' she reminded Liam. 'That was to learn how to shoot bad people.'

Liam was very interested in this. 'And did he kill any bad people?' he asked.

'I don't know, I suppose so.'

Liam was trying to get it all straight in his mind. 'But someone shot our daddy and he isn't bad.'

'No, silly. It was the bad people did that to him.'

Liam considered this but still wasn't satisfied. 'Why didn't he duck?' he asked.

'Don't be stupid,' Katie said crushingly. 'You don't know nothing about soldiers. They can't just duck.' Then she turned to her mother who, having scanned the letter a few more times, desperate for more information, was now holding it to her chest while blessed, wonderful relief poured through her. 'When's Daddy coming home?' Katie asked, and her voice seemed to bring Bridie back to earth.

'A few weeks yet, he thinks,' Bridie told her.

'He says he's looking forward to seeing us all again.'

Katie and Liam were both pleased, for they loved their father dearly, and while Katie couldn't wait to get to school and tell her teacher and friends the good news, Bridie was just as eager to run and tell Mary and Ellen and the rest of the neighbours.

Everyone had been delighted at Bridie's news, even Mary, though Bridie saw her reading Tom's letter wistfully and immediately felt guilty. 'One from Eddie will come any day,' she told her gently, and Mary cast her a watery smile which Bridie saw was taking a great effort and said, 'Sure, don't I know that?'

Bridie had been back in the house just half an hour when, going over to the window to check on Liam who was playing in the street with other little boys, she spotted Peggy McKenna heading her way.

She groaned and when a black-shrouded Peggy opened the entry door and stepped into the room, she forced herself to say calmly, 'I was sorry to hear about Denis.'

'Aye,' Peggy said heavily. 'It was a blow. My eldest, my first-born. Always a special bond with your first-born. 'Course you'd hardly know that, seeing as how you killed yours.'

Bridie gasped. 'It . . . it wasn't like that, Peggy. You know that.'

'No, I don't. You killed that babby, just as if you smashed its head in with a brick.'

'I didn't. It wasn't . . .'

'Where d'you think its soul is now?' Peggy taunted. 'Not in Heaven, tainted with original sin. Poor little thing will be in Limbo. That's your fault. Does the baby's daddy know what you did? Who *was* the baby's daddy anyway?'

Bridie wondered why Peggy hadn't asked before, but she wasn't going to tell her. In her hands that knowledge would be explosive. 'Just a boy.'

'What boy? My family know everyone about that way.'

'He wasn't a local boy,' Bridie said. 'I used to meet him on a Fair Day. He came from Killybegs way.'

'So you lay and opened your legs for a boy you hardly knew?' Peggy sneered with a curl of her lip.

Better she believe that, Bridie thought, than guess at the truth so she gave a brief nod.

'So a trollop as well as a killer,' Peggy said. 'God, if your parents had any idea of the sort of girl they'd raised.' She had the satisfaction of seeing a shudder pass right through Bridie. 'You think God won't punish you for this?' she said. 'One day, when you're least expecting it, he'll strike.'

Bridie wished she could tell the woman to shut up, order her from her door, forbid her to come near her or hers ever again. Instead, she sighed and went across to fetch the ten-shilling note behind the clock.

'Ah, ten bob,' said Peggy, pocketing it. 'Have

to be a bit more now. Say a pound a week. That should cover it.'

'I can't give you any more,' Bridie said. 'It takes me all my time . . .'

Peggy continued as if she hadn't spoke. 'Good boy, my Denis. Always tipped his pay up. Even when he joined the army, he sent his ma something. But he's gone now and his da too – I suppose you heard what that silly sod did. Not that he ever gave me much, stingy bugger he was, and too fond of the beer. Still, he gave me something and now that's gone – and we can't live on thin air, Bridie.'

'Neither can I!' Bridie cried. 'You should have plenty coming in: you have Polly and Luke working at Dunlop's, and Theresa at Cadbury's, and Patricia is leaving school next year.' She could have gone on to say Peggy could get a job herself, for the government were crying out for people in all kinds of jobs, but thought better of it. She appealed to Peggy. 'Where the Hell am I to get a pound a week?'

'That's not my problem.'

'God, Peggy, I haven't got it. There's no way I could spare a pound a week.'

'Well, you'd better find a way,' Peggy said, 'for I'll be back next week and if I don't leave with a pound note in my hand, I'll write a nice wee letter to your parents.'

Peggy had no intention of writing to Bridie's parents – the money she extracted from her was too useful – but she enjoyed watching her squirm and she knew Bridie couldn't take the chance that she wouldn't write. She left Bridie's with a smile on her face. One of the neighbours, catching sight of it, remarked to another with a slight shiver, 'God, some poor sod must have got it in the neck – the only reason that woman smiles is when she's made someone else bloody miserable.'

All night Bridie wrestled with the problem of finding a spare pound a week to still Peggy's tongue. She could only imagine the letter she'd write. She went hot and cold just thinking about it. She pictured the shock and disbelief on her parents' faces, the hurt and disappointment that they would carry to the grave.

Eventually, she realised what she must do. Hadn't she begun to feel that she should do more to help the war effort anyway? Well, this was her chance and the only way to get enough cash to supplement the McKenna household. She decided to seek Mary's opinion in the morning.

But Mary had other things on her mind. That morning a letter had arrived from Eddie. He was in the same hospital as Tom, but in a different section. Neither had any idea the other was even alive as they'd got split up during the rescue.

'We must write to tell them,' Mary said, her face aglow, though her eyes streamed tears. 'Oh Bridie, I really thought he was dead after all this time.'

'Well, he isn't,' Bridie said, hugging her sister in

delight. 'We'll go and tell Ellen in a minute, but now, if you can think straight for just a minute, I'd like to know what you think of my idea.'

'What's that?'

'I'm planning on getting a job in a munitions factory.'

'Munitions!' Mary cried. 'Why on earth would you be wanting a job there?'

'Well, army pay doesn't go far.'

'Not with you, it doesn't seem to,' Mary snapped. 'I've never known such a one for wasting money. You can never make Tom's pay stretch. I get the same as you now, don't forget, and I'm able to manage.'

Ah, but would you manage so well if you had to put ten shillings a week aside for a blackmailer, Bridie longed to say, but she couldn't and took the rebuke from Mary silently.

Instead, she tried another tack. 'It's not just money though, is it?' she said. 'All men between eighteen and forty-one are being called up and many of them were previously making things for the war. Well, it's no good having soldiers if they have no ammunition. Look how much was left behind on the beaches at Dunkirk. We can't fight a war without armaments and lots of women work in such places.'

Mary knew Bridie had a point there, but Liam was still so wee. 'What about Liam?' she asked. 'Surely you're not expecting Ellen . . .'

'Of course not,' Bridie said. 'I know he'd be too

much for Ellen. She's not getting any younger, I know that as well as you.'

'Then who?'

'No one,' Bridie said. 'I was thinking of a nursery. They have one in Rea Street and people say the mothers who work in war-related industries get priority.'

'A nursery?' Mary said. 'I'm not sure . . .'

'I am,' Bridie said. 'It would do Liam good. There would be children to play with and it would get him away from the dirty streets and courtyards. Your Jay could leave him down in the morning and then take Katie on to school. It could be done, Mary, and if you see to them after school . . .'

'I might be going with you,' Mary said. 'A little extra money wouldn't go amiss and I'd feel as if I were pulling my weight. But I'd like to talk it over with Eddie first and you should discuss it with Tom.'

There wasn't time for that, but Mary wasn't aware of Bridie's urgency for money. 'I don't want to bother Tom with this,' she said. 'He's still recovering and I don't want him worrying about me. I'll tell him, certainly, but I want it all signed and sealed by then. I'm going up now to see about it. Really, Tom won't mind.'

Mary knew that; he didn't mind anything if it pleased Bridie. The man would get the moon from the sky for her if she so desired it. Mary wondered if her sister realised how loving and kind Tom was. Eddie was a good husband and father and she had no complaints, but Tom seemed to adore Bridie. But she decided to go along with her sister that day and find out about the nursery and all. She found it just as Bridie said. The nursery was prepared to offer a place to Liam if any work Bridie took up was related to the war effort.

They both noticed how little Liam's face had lit up at the large array of toys, but he made no effort to play with anything, or speak to any of the children, but just watched them shyly, as he held tight to his mother's hand, while she talked to the teacher, Mrs Walton.

Liam's large eyes grew even larger as they were shown around the brightly-painted rooms, the walls covered with children's artwork. Noticing Liam's interest, Mrs Walton asked, 'Do you like to paint, Liam?'

Liam nodded his head. He supposed he did, though he'd done precious little of it, but he'd like to have a go and he looked joyfully at the children doing just that at the easels. They were covered with apron things around them and yet they still had paint all over their hands and one girl even had a smear of blue across her face. Liam waited for Mrs Walton to tell the children off for making such a mess, but nobody did.

Mrs Walton, passing by the easels as she led the way to the playground, stopped by the painting done by the little girl with the blue-smeared face and said, 'What a lovely blue sky you have done, Margaret.'

'I like blue,' Margaret said. 'It's my favourite colour. What's yours?' she demanded of Liam.

He shrugged. No one had ever asked him such a thing before. 'Dunno.'

'You going to come here and play?'

'Dunno.'

'Dunno much do you?' the little girl said scornfully, and then added, 'If you come here, you can be my friend if you like. D'you want to?'

Liam shrugged again and was about to say 'Dunno' when he remembered the little girl making fun of him the last time he'd done that. 'Don't care,' he said and then as the little girl pouted at his words, he added, 'If you like,' and they smiled at each other before Liam hurried after his mother and Mrs Walton, who had made their way outside.

When he saw all the tricycles and the trucks in the playground and the grassed area with the slide and swings, he felt excitement tingle all the way down to his toes. He wished he could leap after the other children who seemed to be enjoying themselves so much. 'Can you just play with them?' he asked Mrs Walton.

'Of course.'

But Liam had to be sure. 'For nowt like?'

'Yes, Liam, for nothing,' Mrs Walton said with a smile, and Liam gave a sigh of contentment.

After that, Bridie hardly even had to ask Liam as they made their way home. 'Would you like to go there?'

He nodded eagerly. 'Every day?'

'Aye. Well, except Saturday and Sunday.'

'Can I play with all the toys and things?'

'Of course you can.'

'Can I paint and that, even if I get it all over me, like?'

'There are aprons to wear.'

Liam thought of the little girl Margaret and how she had paint everywhere, despite the apron, and said doubtfully, 'Yeah, but if I got paint on me, they wouldn't tell me off, would they?'

Bridie gave a little laugh. 'No,' she said and Mary added, 'I shouldn't think you could paint much without making a mess, Liam.'

'And those other kids, there, they won't bash me if I join in?'

'No, not at all. They'll play with you.'

'Oh,' Liam said, and he thought about Margaret who said she would be his friend and smiled as he said, 'All right then, I think I'll go.'

Mary and Bridie laughed. 'First hurdle over,' Mary said. 'Now we just have to get a job.'

But that was even easier for two women who didn't care what they did and the next day Bridie and Mary got a job making shell cases at Wainwright's Guns, a small factory in Cregoe Street, starting on Monday. This was what Bridie told Peggy when she came around the next week. 'I can't raise a pound this week,' she said. 'I can't give you what I haven't got. But when I get paid next week, I'll have the money for you.'

Peggy knew she'd get the money. Bridie was too

frightened not to pay her so she said, 'All right, I'll do with ten bob for now and I'll give you one more week. If you haven't the money for me next week . . . Well, let's just say I warned you.'

'I will,' Bridie promised desperately. 'I'll put it up as soon as I have my wages.'

Bridie wrote to Tom, as Mary had insisted, telling him of her decision to work in a munitions factory. She told him Liam's reaction to going to nursery and how, with Jay's help and Ellen's offer to see to them in the evening till she came home, it could be achieved easily.

Tom didn't mind Bridie taking a job, but really he would have preferred her, Mary and the children out of it altogether. But he knew it was no good asking her to reconsider, she'd only refuse.

He understood her decision to want to work towards the war effort. Things were so dire, it helped somehow to be doing your bit, and so he told her he was proud of her doing war work as long as she didn't wear herself out. He said too that he'd been delighted to learn that Eddie was alive and well and had gone over to see him. He also said they'd both be home before too long and sent his love to her and the children.

Three days after Tom wrote his letter, bombs fell in West Bromwich. They caused structural damage, although no loss of life, but it put paid to the people who thought Birmingham was safe being two hundred miles inland. Birmingham braced itself for a bombing campaign, for the city made so much for the war effort from Dunlop's making tyres in the north to Cadbury's in the south where cordite was put into rockets rather than soft centres into chocolates. The jewellery quarter was another area where the deft hands that set diamonds had been adapted to the fine and delicate work of making radar. The car factories hid shadow factories making military vehicles and, in the case of Vickers, Wellingtons and Spitfires. Birmingham guns were famous the world over. And then there were the small factories everywhere, churning out all manner of materials – Birmingham was a prime target.

'Hitler's intent on invasion, all right,' Sam said one evening, when Bridie and Mary had called in for the children. 'But our navy is stronger than theirs, he'll try to demoralise the people first, see. He's got a lot to learn, Hitler. When the British have their backs to the wall, they fight harder than ever.'

'And he won't get it all his own way either,' Ellen put in. 'Our air force will stop him.'

Bridie hoped Ellen was right. So far, nothing had stopped the madman.

Bridie found it was a mad rush each morning to get herself and the children up and dressed and fed in time for her to get to the factory on time. She didn't know how she'd have managed without Mary and Ellen, for often they would pop in to give her a hand. Then they'd leave Katie in with Jay and Mickey until it was time to take her to school, and drop Liam at the nursery on their way to work.

The children settled well into the new routine. Katie did not object to staying with her cousins for a wee while before school and they were seldom averse to playing a game to amuse her.

After school, Jay, Mickey and Katie would go back to Ellen's until their mothers came home and she would always have a little snack for them when they came in: a few scones she'd made, or bread and a smear of precious jam, or dripping toast. Ellen would even make time to lift Katie onto her knee and help her learn the words she'd been sent home with, or listen to her stumble her way through a reading book.

Liam's nursery opened longer hours to fit in with factory times, but he didn't seem to mind being away from his mother for so long, and when Mary and Bridie collected him in the evening, he was usually clutching pictures he'd painted, or models he'd made, which Bridie would display proudly around the room.

It was a good job the children were fine about everything, for Bridie felt the factory was very trying at first. She hated the green overalls she had to wear and the big thick boots, and the way she had to roll her hair up under a turban.

She found the place dirty, noisy and smelly and everything she touched seemed to be covered in oil. The work was boring too and the hours long, and the noise far too great for there to be much chit-chat between the women. Bridie was unnerved by some of the women, who seemed to shout a lot, and swear and smoke like any man and often wore lipstick so red, it was like a scarlet slash across their faces.

But when she said this one night to Mary as they made their way home, she told her off. 'Don't be such a little snob,' she said.

'I'm not!' Bridie said indignantly.

'Yes, you are, judging people.'

'I wasn't. I just said . . .'

'I know what you just said and let me tell you those women work as hard as anyone and that's all that matters in this damned war,' Mary retorted sharply. 'If it helps them cope to shout, or swear or smoke, then so be it. As for the lipstick, it's possibly to remind themselves they are women.'

Bridie thought Mary was probably right. After all, they hardly looked very desirable in their sexless overalls and boots with their hair coiled beneath a scarf in an effort to keep it clean as well as for safety reasons. But then Mary suddenly squeezed her sister's arm. 'Don't mind me,' she said. 'I snapped at you like a weasel. It's not you, it's me. I'm tired out and that's a fact.'

'Don't worry about it. I'm the same,' Bridie replied.

It was true. In the first fortnight at the factory, Bridie nearly followed her children when they went to bed, she'd been so worn-out. It reminded her of the early days on the farm when she'd been so exhausted. She knew, like before, it would pass, her body would get used to it, and now, though she was still tired coming home, she would revive after a meal. In those early days she had come home in a sort of stupor, so weary she was barely able to put one foot before the other.

In an effort to ease the boredom, *Workers' Playtime* from the wireless was broadcast to the various workshops and it belted out the popular songs of the day, loud enough to drown out some of the noise of the machinery, especially when the women's voices singing along raised the decibel level.

Liam, largely influenced by his days at the nursery, loved singing too and often entertained Bridie and Katie before bedtime, belting out the nursery rhymes and other songs he'd learned at school.

Now he and Katie interspersed these with 'Run Rabbit Run', 'Hey Little Hen' or 'Mairzy Doats', and other songs from the war like 'Kiss Me Goodnight, Sergeant Major' which they'd learned from Jay and Mickey.

But despite *Workers' Playtime* the work was often heavy and very tedious. There was often overtime, which Mary and Bridie would do if they were able and not for the money alone either, but to make as much as possible to fight this blessed war. It used to wear both Mary and Bridie down, but what depressed Bridie most was seeing a pound of her hard-earned money going out to Peggy every week.

The woman was well able to find a job herself and with all her youngsters working now, she had no need to squeeze the money out of Bridie. But Bridie never bothered saying this, she just paid her, so that she'd leave quickly.

She could just about cope with seeing that much of Peggy and didn't want to give her any excuse to hang about and prophesy dire accidents that could befall her children when God took his revenge. That always made Bridie feel sick. She loved her children with a passion and protecting her children through the war was enough of a worry without Peggy adding to it.

But, even with the pound given to Peggy, Bridie was well paid and by careful husbanding of the money, she knew she would be able to replenish most of the money she'd taken from the post office account. This was made easier with the children having their main meal at nursery and school, enabling her to make the rations she was allowed go further.

But there was no sign of frugality when the men wrote to say they were being discharged. When the hospital authorities found out they were related, they'd found them beds in the same ward and arranged to have them released on the same day.

They'd been in hospital for six weeks when they came home that bright summer's day in mid-July, far longer than Bridie and Mary had thought. Tom was pleased, however, for though his physical injuries had healed, his mental scars had taken longer and he'd been in no fit state to be released earlier for his nightmares frightened him. He had dreaded going home until he was fully better because the sight of him screaming and thrashing in the bed, sometimes muttering and shouting or laughing hysterically, would seriously affect Bridie. That was all behind him now, thankfully, and he and Eddie had three clear days to spend with their family before they rejoined their unit.

When Bridie first saw Tom, she realised with a pang that the young man she had fallen in love with had gone for ever. There were drawn lines on his face and greying hair at his temples.

But his smile was still the same and she sped across the room, enfolding him in her arms, feeling the tension seep from him, as he said huskily, 'Oh God, Bridie, how I've longed for this, to hold you tight and to cuddle my children. Nothing matters to me but you three. You must know that.'

Bridie did know. But Tom had seen things he could never tell her about that made his family all the more precious to him, like the town of Tournou they were making for as they'd been ordered to retreat. Before they reached it, they came upon lines of refugees – women, old men and children – machine-gunned as they had tried to escape the bombing. Some had been gunned down in the road and they lay there, spread-eagled in puddles of blood; others had cowered in ditches, but it hadn't saved them. Some had prams or barrows piled high with their possessions, the richer ones had donkeys or ponies pulling carts or had been leading their horses out of the town when the bombers came.

They heard the screams and cries of the animals before they got there. The scene would stay with him always, the dead bodies with the stench of death mixed with the smell of blood, their pathetic belongings spread along the road, their pet dogs dead or dying beside them, carts overturned and horses trapped beneath them, riddled with bullets and often with broken legs. They screamed in pain and the dogs whimpered and Tom and his friends put many out of their misery before going on, unable to do little else.

Tournou itself was pulverised by the bombing. Everywhere they looked, they saw shattered buildings reduced to a pile of rubble. Other buildings were split asunder, leaning drunkenly against their neighbour, their contents spilled out before them. The dead lay in rows on the streets and pavements and rescue workers tore at the piles of rubble with bloodied, blistered hands in the hope of finding more survivors, while dust swirled in the air, stinging eyes and lodging in noses and throats.

Tom was devastated. He'd heard of *Blitzkrieg*, the lightning bombing the Germans had practiced in Spain which had killed a thousand people in one attack. But a grainy photograph in a newspaper, or a broadcast on the wireless, did not begin to touch on the horror of it all.

He was appalled that what had happened in that Belgium town might happen in Birmingham, that Bridie and the children might be mercilessly gunned down trying to escape. He was desperate to get out of it, back to England where they could regroup and have another go at the madman and his brutal, butchering army.

None of this, though, could he share with Bridie. No way was he going to frighten her to death with the things he'd seen. Things that no human being should ever see.

Nor could he speak of the days they'd spent getting to Dunkirk with no food, drinking water from streams along the way, surviving on little sleep. When they stumbled onto the sands of Dunkirk beach, they were light-headed and extremely weak. The carnage around them and the noise was unbelievable.

The Stukas were circling the beaches, their machine guns relentless, and the Heinkels and Messerschmitts were bombing the small boats in the water, as well as the larger ships out at sea and the men diving into the water to escape or burrowing into the sand dunes. They lit up the sky in flashes as bright as day and answering them were the anti-aircraft guns set up along the beach and the RAF in their Spitfires, wheeling and diving around below and over the planes, the guns barking into the night.

Eventually, Tom and Eddie were pushed along

a makeshift pier head made from debris on the beach and loaded onto a small pleasure cruiser. They'd gone no distance when the skipper was hit by machine-gun fire and, as he fell to the cabin floor, a bomb blasted the boat out of the water. Tom found himself floundering in the dark, in the grey scummy water littered with bodies, with no idea where his comrades, including Eddie were. He was eventually picked up by another cruising boat and had been ferried to the Winchelsea.

Eddie, he found out later, had also been picked up by a private motor boat and the skipper, finding the Navy ships full to capacity, took his load straight across the channel to the south coast. Both men had gunshot and shrapnel wounds when they arrived in England and Eddie had also damaged his arm and leg too, but fortunately not badly.

Tom wanted to protect Bridie from the debacle of Dunkirk, the humiliating and harrowing retreat and the horrors he'd witnessed, not least the bodies littering the beaches. But Bridie, like her sister Mary, had read all the papers and listened to every news report and surmised much from what Tom didn't tell her and by the haunted look that often came over his face.

The dangers Tom faced daily invaded Bridie's sleep, especially after he returned to his unit, until Ellen and Mary took her severely to task about it. She had to buck up and be strong and brave, for the children's sake if not her own, they told her. Did she think she was the only woman in the world to be going through it?

Bridie took to heart what they said. She went to work with a will, and talked to the children often about Tom, lest they forget their father, and prayed for him diligently every night. She could do no more.

CHAPTER SEVENTEEN

The school holidays began and though Liam's nursery didn't close, it still left Katie on Ellen's hands all day, helped by the rather dubious attentions of Mary's sons. Mary had cautioned them, particularly Jay, about looking after Katie if they took her out.

She needn't have worried, for Jay had been enchanted by the frail-looking child since the day she'd been born. He thought she was like a perfect little doll and he'd no more risk any harm come to her than stick his own hand in the fire.

A change had come over him too since his father's return from Dunkirk; he'd realised that war was no game and that the time for childish tricks was over. He was twelve now and man of the house, for no one knew when his father would be home again. He would like to do something for the war effort himself, but he was too young to be considered in any professional capacity, but if looking after Katie meant his auntie Bridie could make more shell cases, then that was what he would do and, what's more, he'd do it well. 'Do you know where we went today, Mammy?' Katie said at the tea table that evening and, without giving anyone a chance to say anything, went on, 'Jay and Mickey took me to Cannon Hill Park and Jay let me plodge in the stream, but he kept hold of my hand so I couldn't fall in. I had to tuck my dress in the legs of my knickers so it wouldn't get wet. Jay said it was all right.'

Bridie felt little fissions of alarm run down her spine. Cannon Hill Park was a distance away and there were busy roads to cross. 'I hope you were a good girl for them,' she said.

''Course I was, Mammy.' Katie said, indignant that her mother could have considered the poss-ibility of anything else.

'Did you hold their hands?'

'Going I did, not coming back though.'

'And why not?' Bridie snapped.

'Because Jay carried me on his back because my legs were tired,' Katie replied. Bridie gave a sigh of relief.

Every night it seemed there was something else to tell about Jay. Jay had taken her to feed the swans and ducks that swam in the lake with stale bread and another day to fish for tiddlers with some little nets that Mary had. Katie was very disappointed her mother wasn't as excited as she was about the little squirmy things swimming aimlessly around in a jam jar.

'You should see how fast Jay can push the roundabout in Calthorpe Park, Mammy,' Katie told her one evening. 'It was the fastest ever and the swings went so high I thought I was going to come over the bar.'

Bridie was thoroughly alarmed by this and mentioned it to Ellen. 'Jay would not do anything to harm the child,' she said firmly. 'I must say I'm surprised at the turnout those boys are making, particularly Jay. He has mates around the door calling for him at every turn and yet he tells them he can't play about, that he has a job to do looking after his little cousin. I tell you, those boys have lifted nearly the whole load of looking after Katie from me.'

She didn't go on to say that she could have given the child scant attention without the help of the boys and outings would be out of the question with Sam to see to, because she didn't want Bridie to start feeling guilty. She knew the work her and Mary were doing, the work all the women were doing, was necessary if they were to win this damned war and defeat couldn't be considered.

Bridie, though comforted, asked Jay about the trip to Calthorpe Park when Katie claimed she nearly went over the bar. Jay laughed. 'Don't worry, Auntie Bridie,' he said soothingly, 'I'd never risk hurting Katie – I did push the roundabout fast, all the kids wanted me to, but I got on with Katie to make sure she wouldn't fall off or anything.'

The boy was so sincere that Bridie believed

him and felt much better about leaving Katie in his care after that and was immensely glad that the boys took her out so often away from the dirty streets and dingy, disease-ridden courtyards. Even when the days were dull and cold, or the rain washed the dust from the streets, the boys would amuse Katie. They played games: Snakes and Ladders or Ludo and they taught her how to play dominoes and draughts. Sometimes, they'd listen to the Ovaltiney's show on the wireless and help her crack the code they gave out at the end, or sing along with the war songs from 'Whistle While You Work'.

Mickey came into his own one cold windswept day when he introduced Katie to the public library. 'Did you know you can borrow books for nothing?' Katie asked her mother that night.

'I heard something about it.'

'It's great, Mammy. There are loads of books, shelves and shelves of them, and you have to be real quiet and talk in whispers. Mickey said if you sign the form I can get books out of my own. He said I can have a picture book for myself and another one that he will read to me. You'll sign it won't you, Mammy?'

Bridie signed the form with pleasure, glad to see her small daughter so entertained, but the culmination of it all was the trip to the Lickey Hills, where they'd gone all the way to the terminus on the tram and played hide and seek in the woods and ate the picnic Ellen had made for them in the green fields. Jay had once again carried tired Katie on his back to the tram on their return.

But while Katie was enjoying her holiday from school and the attention of her cousins, the first bomb fell in Erdington.

'Thought we were supposed to have sirens when enemy planes are coming our way,' Ellen said.

'This was only one,' Sam told her. 'Must have slipped through. They said they thought he was on his way to the Dunlop, but couldn't find it and dropped his load in Erdington.'

'Nice of him,' Mary remarked. 'I suppose now the canals are boarded over every night, it is harder to find.'

'Aye,' Sam said. 'Good idea that was, with all those factories on the Lichfield and Tyburn Road backing onto the canal, not to mention the one running alongside the Dunlop place and on up to the Vicker's factory on the Chester Road. God, any bomber seeing the glint in his lights could have had a field day and wiped out a lot of factories making things to win this war with no trouble at all.'

'I suppose we should be grateful there was only the one man killed and five injured,' Ellen said. 'But you can't help feeling that that man is someone's son, and he was but a teenager with his life before him yet.'

'And all those shattered houses,' Bridie put in, looking at the pictures in the *Evening Mail*. The houses stood glassless and sometimes roofless, the windows and doors blown out and the stuff inside the sagging walls a heap of rubble. 'Where will they live now?' Bridie asked. 'How will they manage?'

'The authorities will have it organised,' Sam said. 'And although it's sad for those people, we should think ourselves lucky – the south coast has been pounded for weeks: Ramsgate, where Eddie and Tom were until just a short while ago, and Southsea, Portsmouth and Dover, of course. Trying to smash the coastal defences, you see, and destroy shipping – Hitler's intent on invasion.'

A shiver of apprehension ran through the three women and then Bridie said, 'If the raids are to happen, you can all come in to me. It'll be better being together and the cellar should be quite safe.' Mary was agreeable but Ellen said nothing. She knew Sam would probably not survive another winter: the doctor had confided in her that his heart and lungs were both in poor shape and she knew that for he could barely walk a few paces now without becoming breathless. She doubted it would do him any good to get out of a warm bed and traipse downstairs to their own cellar, let alone roam the streets to someone else's. But she didn't want to load this on Mary and Bridie's shoulders, nor give Sam any inkling of how sick he was so she kept these thoughts to herself.

On 13th August the bombers returned, the Vickers factory making the Lancasters and Spitfires in Castle Bromwich their target. Five workers were killed there and two in houses nearby. Two days later, bombs fell in Hay Mills, Small Heath and Bordesly Green.

'Where are the bloody sirens for those places?' Sam declared furiously. 'I thought they had watchers out who'd warn people to take cover. A policeman pedalling a bike and blowing a whistle doesn't have the same effect.'

Most thought the same and the raids continued every night, lasting an average of five hours. As all industry was now mostly war-related and small factories were often cheek by jowl amongst and between the back-to-back housing, civilian casualties were rising. Everyone now had a tale to tell about dreadful tragedies, or miraculous escapes.

Not used to sirens sounding, when they did wail out on 25th August, they nearly lifted Bridie out of her chair in which she was dozing. She was tired; for although no raids had happened in that area, the crashes and explosions had been near enough to drive sleep from her, near enough some nights for her to rouse the children and creep down into the cellar.

The children thought it was a great game altogether and when eventually it grew quiet and Bridie deemed it safe to return to bed, they were loath to do so and were difficult to settle. Talking with the women at work, Bridie found most mothers with young children were having the same problem.

'It's as if Hitler's playing cat and mouse with us anyway,' another put in. 'Targeting a small area at a time, like.'

'Aye, but you don't know when it's going to be your area,' Bridie said, 'so you take shelter anyway.'

'Too right, you do,' another said. 'I don't want any of those buggers landing on me or mine.'

When the siren went off, it was just after they'd eaten tea so the children were ready for, but not in, bed and so Bridie ran upstairs and pulled blankets off her bed before hustling them down to the cellar, remembering first to pick up her shelter bag, which she always left ready by the door. All women had a shelter bag and in Bridie's there were ration books and identity cards, the post office book, insurance policies and treasured photographs. As she went down the stairs, Mary and her two boys came in the entry door. Bridie thanked God she'd have company, but asked anxiously, 'Are Ellen and Sam coming in too?'

'Don't think so,' Mary told her sister. 'Sam's wheezing a fair bit these last few days and although the days are still nice and warm, the nights can be chilly.'

Mary was right, but Bridie wasn't sure if it was the cold that was making her shiver so. At first the crashes and explosions were in the distance and then Katie and Liam, lulled to sleep on Bridie's and Mary's laps, were laid on the cushions Jay had run up and taken from the armchairs.

But they hadn't been long asleep when the pattern of explosions changed and they heard the drone of the approaching bombers coming their way and the barking ack-ack guns trying to bring them down. The first explosions made them jump and Mary and Bridie clutched at each other, the boys between them.

The children stirred on their makeshift beds and eventually Katie opened her eyes. Liam's were still tight shut, but he'd begun to whimper and so Bridie knew he was awake. So did Katie. 'Liam's crying, Mammy. He's scared,' she said, her own voice wobbly with fear.

She didn't have to say she was scared; her wide staring eyes spoke for her. Then a bomb fell extremely close and Katie gave a yelp of terror and leapt towards her mother. Liam began to sob in earnest.

Bridie lifted both of the children onto her knee and held them tight. 'When will it stop?' Katie asked.

Bridie shook her head hopelessly. 'I don't know, love.'

'I don't like it,' Liam complained.

'No one likes it, Liam,' Bridie replied. 'The thing to remember is that it's just a big noise. We're as safe as houses here in the cellar.'

It wasn't true, but it satisfied Katie and Liam and, besides, she had to tell them something. They were too young to deal with this. Mickey and even Jay were only weans too and she read the fear on their faces as well.

The clamour went on around them and Bridie felt her children jump at any close explosion and Liam had put his fingers in his ears more than once.

By the time the all clear had sounded, the children had dropped off, despite the noise, cuddled up to her. She hadn't been able to sleep herself during the raid, so she'd sat tense and awake, seeing the cellar walls shake and the mortar dribble out from the bricks, thinking each moment might be her last.

She smiled tentatively at her sister now. 'Bit too close for comfort, that lot.'

'Aye,' Mary replied. 'There will be some damage, I'm thinking.' She glanced across at her boys, their faces white with weariness and fear. 'I'd best get these home, but I'll give you a hand with the weans first.'

Bridie was glad of the offer of help. Mary gently lifted Liam from her sister's knee and carried him in her arms while Bridie readjusted her hold on Katie and followed her sister up the cellar steps.

It was as they entered the room that both women were attacked by a fit of coughing, caused by the dust swirling in the air that caught in their throats. They crossed to the window and saw the orange skyline. 'Something's on fire,' Mary said and Bridie nodded, unable to speak. 'And not too far away.'

It was the Market Hall in the Bull Ring, they found out the next day. The raid had removed the roof, reducing the building to a shell and destroying the magnificent clock, made of solid oak, to ashes. Bridie thought of the day Tom had told her the tale of the clock and the curse put upon it by the one who made it. Well, Hitler helped to make the curse come true, she thought. But however sorry she was for the clock's demise, people were more important and she felt heartsore for those injured or killed so far into the war.

That night there was another raid, but it had been too far away for Bridie and Mary to take to the cellar at first. It had begun just after midnight and Bridie had been in a deep sleep when the sirens woke her. The drone of approaching planes alarmed her and she realised they were much nearer, almost overhead. She jumped from her bed and, pulling a coat over her nightdress, roused the children in the attic, pulling blankets from the bed to wrap around them as the bombs landed nearby. Fear lent speed to the children who were very sleepy.

The time was half past three and Bridie wasn't surprised that her sister didn't join her. The raid was too loud and close for anyone to sleep and the children whimpered in fear while Bridie held them close, one on each side of her, in the rolled-up blanket. She crooned and sang to them, trying to take their minds away from what was happening above and praying earnestly that they might get out alive.

The next day, at work, she heard the main thrust of the raid had been around Snow Hill Station, taking in Summer Row, Edmund Street, Livery Street and St Paul's Square, so small wonder it had appeared close. This information was printed on notices spread about the city. Birmingham wasn't usually referred to by name in the national papers, but just known as a Midlands town, so as to not give the enemy any information on where they had struck and caused extensive damage, though the Birmingham papers – the *Birmingham Post*, the *Evening Mail*, the *Gazette* and *Evening Despatch* – mentioned it occasionally.

'Why don't they say what's happening to us in those other papers?' Ellen demanded irritably on the evening of 28th August. 'Other towns and cities are mentioned.'

'Don't be daft, woman,' Sam snapped. 'What d'you think it is, some kind of competition? They don't want Jerry to know that they've actually hit their target, that's why.'

But mentioned or not, every night there was a raid. The effect of those terrifying raids was apparent in the morning light. People had to get used to walking to work because the tram lines were lifted, and to seeing rubble-filled holes where there'd once been shops, offices and houses. The dust and the cordite smell lingered and pavements were often running with water. Sodden sandbags leaked sand onto pavements strewn with bricks, charred beams and snaking hose pipes and shards of glass splintered beneath people's feet.

But while Birmingham and other towns and cities throughout Britain were enduring nightly raids, devastation and death, Hitler had massed his invasion fleet on the other side of the English Channel. The RAF, to prevent the invasion taking place, took on the might of the Luftwaffe in a series of air battles that later became known as 'The Battle of Britain'.

On 7th September, London was attacked for the first time when three hundred bombers headed for the docks. This was seen as part of the build-up to invasion.

Everyone was on alert, the Home Guard mustering its members together, but by the end of the day there was no movement of German ships towards Britain. High alert stayed in force all the next day and night whilst the RAF continued to dispel the enemy.

One of the workers who worked alongside Bridie and Mary came to work in great excitement one day having witnessed a dog-fight between a German Stuka plane and a Spitfire above her house. 'Seen nothing so exciting in my whole life,' she said. 'There was a crowd of us cheering our bloke on.'

'He won, I suppose?' one woman asked.

''Course he bleeding well won. Didn't let up on the other one. Rat-a-tat, rat-a-tat – on and on it went. And then they both wheeled and dodged.

One minute the Spitfire was above the other and before the German plane had time to turn around, he'd dived below him and when he tried to follow, the Spitfire was up and to the one side of him and then the other. The German plane hadn't a chance. Eventually, it began to lose height, smoke spiralling out the back of it and the plane spun round, and hit the ground and exploded. I cheered and shouted till my bleeding throat was sore, I'll tell you.'

'Wish I'd seen it,' another said.

Bridie could understand, well understand their attitude, and yet she couldn't get the idea out of her head that the pilot was somebody's son, maybe a favoured brother, or a beloved daddy. But she knew such views would be unpopular and possibly misunderstood and therefore kept them to herself.

On 15th September, the RAF defeated the Luftwaffe in a large aerial battle. Hitler had failed to knock out the airfields or the anti-aircraft weapons, or destroy ports on the south coast, and now his famed Luftwaffe had been vanquished by the British. He put his invasion plans on hold, at least for that year.

But the people in Birmingham weren't able to breathe a sigh of relief. Almost nightly the sirens would wail and they would stumble from their bed and take shelter in some place they considered moderately safe.

Occasionally, there was a night without a raid, without blaring sirens, and on those nights, Bridie, like many more, would lie wide awake waiting for them. Any sleep she eventually, through sheer exhaustion, succumbed to was shallow and fitful. She was feeling the strain. She was constantly tired: coping with a full-time job and caring for children, as well as dealing with the blackout and juggling the ration books to provide meals and writing cheerful letters to Tom, was enough for anyone. But added to that was the parasitical Peggy McKenna, taking a pound a week from her and prophesying doom and gloom to her and her family.

The point was potential doom and gloom visited them almost nightly, not from any vengeful God in some pious retribution ritual, but from a nation of people very like themselves.

The first daylight raid came on 27th September at the Dunlop factory. The single bomb caused little damage and no loss of life, but it wasn't for the want of trying because after dropping the bomb, the pilot opened up fire on the people waiting at the bus stop.

There were other instances reported in the paper. There was talk of a Midland Red bus being machine-gunned and other men, seeking shelter from a raid, were trapped in an entry, unable to move because Germans were shooting indiscriminately. More shocking was the tale of a mother, baby in her arms and two children hanging to her skirts, who ran into a nearby park after a bomb landed on their home, only to be strafed with machine-gun fire.

Bridie wondered if their own soldiers would behave the same towards unarmed and defenceless civilians and sincerely hoped they wouldn't. She couldn't see her Tom doing that sort of thing anyway. She worried about him constantly. He could tell little in his letters, but she knew the dangers he faced daily.

She'd read enough about Dunkirk when it was actually happening and then when there was no news of Tom or Eddie. But when the men came home, their eyes told how much they had really suffered. Bridie remembered the night Tom's threshing in the bed had woken her. She's found him drenched with sweat and the next night his screams had nearly woken the street. There had been times when he'd stare into space for hours, his eyes bleak and haunted, often not hearing people when they spoke to him.

That was why most women didn't worry their husbands in the forces with domestic issues and just got on with life as best they could. They couldn't afford to consider defeat and hoped and prayed earnestly that their husbands would return to them in one piece at the end of it all.

A trip to the city centre now was very different to one before the war. The city itself had changed. Corporation Street had been very badly hit. C&A Modes and many other shops were gone, with gaping holes and piles of rubble in their places. Snow Hill had suffered badly from fire and many of the shops and offices on Colmore Road and out as far as St Paul's Square in the Jewellery Quarter had been burned to the ground.

Then there was the Bull Ring, but the main damage there was to the Market Hall. When Bridie first saw it after the August raid she wondered what had happened to the animals. Had they been wiped out with a bomb blast, or burnt to a crisp in the resultant fire, or had someone had time to open the cages and free them? And would they fare any better left running mad around the Bull Ring?

The Market Hall itself was just a shell and a barrier had been erected around it to prevent people getting too close, though a hole blasted in one of the walls enabled anyone to see in. Charred roof beams lay across the rubble, broken bricks, lumps of plaster, buckled iron stands and battered utensils of every description were piled inside. People had stuck Union Jack flags in amongst the rubble and one had a slogan beside it saying 'Burnt, but not broken.'

It was that defiance which brought the tears to Bridie's eyes and she turned to Mary, who'd accompanied her that Saturday morning, and said, 'Isn't it sad?'

'Aye,' Mary said with a sigh. 'It's like ripping out the heart of the city really. Do you mind how it used to be on Saturday evenings?'

Bridie did, oh yes. But now everyone scurried home early, scared of the dark, still more scared of moonlit nights. There was nothing to stay for, no gas flares now could light up the Bull Ring. Stall-holders too were anxious to pack up early and go home.

'D'you think we've had our lot now?' Bridie asked, for it was the first week in October and there had been no raids that week at all.

'I shouldn't think so,' Mary said. 'After all, Londoners are catching it every night and the south coast and Liverpool have also taken a hammering. Why should we be different?'

Bridie didn't know, she just hoped they were. But their ordeal was only just beginning, though they weren't aware of it.

On 14th October, Clementine Churchill – Winston Churchill's wife – visited the city. She went to two factories and an area particularly affected by bombing and Bridie and her fellow workers were allowed an hour off to wave to her as she passed along Bristol Street.

A Mrs Hurtle, whose house was in ruins, was reported in the *Evening Mail* as saying: 'Our house is down, but our spirits are still up.' Mrs Churchill was impressed by her unflinching courage, a facet she said she saw often amongst the working classes everywhere.

The Brummies had need of their courage, for once more the raids continued their nightly pattern. The attacks often went on for hours and incendiaries, parachute mines and landmines were being dropped as well as ordinary bombs.

A further worry was bothering Bridie though. Bridie's new gas cooker had been put in an alcove just off the cellar and since the middle of September, she'd been bringing food down to the cellar for the children and themselves. She'd also been making tea for her and Mary and cocoa for Mary's boys and her own two. Then she saw the article in the *Evening Mail* in mid-October. George Inman was a Home Guard Officer and had been called to a bombed-out house to help people who'd been trapped in the cellar after a raid, and which was filling with gas from a fractured gas pipe. George went in to rescue them and got two out before collapsing and dying from the gas poisoning himself.

Ever since, Bridie had tortured herself with the thought of them all, but especially her precious children, being choked to death with gas fumes. This fear had been fuelled by Peggy McKenna who'd saved the piece from the paper and brought it round to Bridie's when she collected her weekly pound note.

With Bridie so worn down with tiredness and worry for the children's safety, it wasn't hard to turn her view of the cellar being a sanctuary for them all to it being a grave. In fact she was so jumpy she declared she wouldn't spend another night there.

'Be reasonable, Bridie,' Mary said. 'The weans are only young. It's coming on to winter and the nights are chilly. Do you really want to take them down Grant Street and along Bristol Passage to a public shelter?'

'No, of course I don't,' Bridie declared. 'But neither do I want them to choke to death.'

'This is silly. It was one instance.'

'One instance reported,' Bridie said. 'There could be hundreds more. How many gas pipes do you know that could stand up to a bomb blast?'

'Oh Bridie,' said Mary in exasperation. Once Bridie had an idea fixed in her head, there was little chance of changing it, especially if it was connected with the safety of her children.

'I shan't use the cellar again,' Bridie said. 'You of course must do as you see fit.'

'I'll come with you, you silly bugger,' Mary said. 'If you're determined on doing this, you'll need a hand with the weans.'

'I think Bridie's clean barmy,' Mary said to Ellen later. 'Taking the kids from their warm bed and traipsing them through the streets to a public shelter.'

'Aye, well she has her reasons.'

'What will you do, Ellen?'

'Nothing,' Ellen said. 'Sam's not fit to leave his bed and my place is beside him.'

Mary said nothing. There was no hiding the fact that Sam was failing and she and Bridie were saddened by it, for the man had been kindness itself to them and they knew they would miss him.

*   *   *

The sirens screamed out just before seven o'clock on 19th November and Bridie groaned. They'd had raids all through November, almost every night and sometimes accompanied by a daylight raid too.

She didn't regret her decision to go to the public shelter, feeling sure it would be safer. But she did regret having to get the children up and out into the night and trailing them through the unwelcoming black night. Bridie had a flickering and shaded torch to light their way; she'd been lucky enough to find a shop that had some batteries left just a few days before. Batteries were like gold dust and she was glad of even that shaded pencil of light in the inky blackness.

She was so weary too, dead beat, and so were the children and had been already dressed for bed. At least she hadn't had to wake them she thought and she put their shoes and socks back on, pulled a jumper over their pyjamas and then helped them on with their siren suits. She pulled her own coat from the hook behind the door, slung her bag over her shoulder and held out her hands to Liam and Katie. 'Come on,' she said. 'Auntie Mary will be in on us in a minute and we won't be ready,' and they stepped out and Bridie closed the door behind them.

Mary was just coming for her holding Mickey by the hand, but there was no sign of Jay. 'Where's the big fellow?' Bridie asked with a grin as they began hurrying down the road, but the face Mary turned to her was far from happy.

'You tell me,' she said grimly.

'What is it?'

'Silly sod took himself off to Thorpe Street Barracks today so Mickey here tells me. Told him he was going to offer himself as a messenger for the Home Guard. I'll kill him when I catch hold of him.'

Bridie understood her sister's concern, but she said soothingly, 'He'll take shelter somewhere, Mary. He'll be all right.'

'But will he, Bridie? God knows, he's as big as a lad of fifteen,' Mary said, as they turned into the shelter door. 'By God, if they've taken him on without checking his age, I'll wipe the floor with them.'

Bridie said nothing, but she thought in the raids they'd had just lately, the authorities would be glad of anyone to pass messages or run errands and could easily turn a blind eye to technicalities like someone's age.

But to say this wouldn't help her sister so she patted her hand reassuringly. 'Jay isn't stupid,' she said. 'He'll be fine.'

'Aye,' Mary said with a sigh. 'He seems to have shed his childhood since Dunkirk. Wants to do his bit.'

Bridie had noticed the change in her nephew, who wouldn't be thirteen until the New Year, but many had had their childhood ripped from them as war stripped them of loved ones and their homes. 'Come on,' she said to Mary. 'Let's get in, Hitler's in a hurry tonight. And try not to worry about Jay. Like I said before, he'll be in a shelter somewhere worrying about you, no doubt.'

As the shelter door closed behind her, Bridie hoped and prayed that what she said was right.

The shelter was crowded. After the raid on Coventry five days before, Brummies were nervous. They'd suffered a fairly substantial raid the same night themselves, but Coventry had been nearly annihilated. Within a square mile, eighty percent of the buildings were destroyed, five hundred and sixty-eight people lay dead and hundreds more were gravely injured.

Bridie claimed one of the bunks up at the far end and Mary got the one beside her. People continued to stream in as the siren screamed out. Despite the raid, people were laughing and joking together. Irish Johnny had brought his gramophone. He probably had sweets too because he worked at Cadbury's. He didn't always come to the shelter because he did fire watching and a bit of Home Guard duty, being too old for the forces, but, if he'd got hold of any misshapes from Cadbury's he'd come down to the shelter the first chance he had.

He'd play all the Irish jigs and reels and catch up the children's hands and dance around the room in an effort to try and get them to ignore the thumps and crashes around them. And then, when they stopped for a breather, he'd produce the chocolates, which he'd share out amongst them.

Bridie watched the man wind up his gramophone and said, 'He's a kind man, that Johnny.'

'He is right enough,' Mary agreed. 'Let's hope this little lot's over and we can go back home soon before many reels are played, because to tell you the truth, I'm jiggered.'

The people in the shelters were unaware then that they were going to suffer a pounding similar to Coventry. They were used to the Germans' strategies though and when they heard few explosions and the distinctive whistle of the incendiaries, one man remarked, 'There y'are, Jerry does it all the bloody time, drops incendiaries to light up the targets like it's bleeding daylight and we risk breaking our necks in the blackout – it's madness.'

The bombers followed. The whistle as the arrows of death and destruction hurled downwards was almost as terrifying as the booming explosions when they landed. The ack-ack guns had started up their tattoo into the night, but nothing seemed to stop the bombs falling that night, one after the other, with barely a space between them.

Some shook the walls of the shelter and Bridie looked at them fearfully, wondering if the whole structure was going to collapse on top of them all. Two hours into the raid and Irish Johnny had put his gramophone aside and was leading the children in songs and hymns they knew. Many looked scared to death and with reason. Bridie felt as if every nerve ending was exposed and raw and primeval fear, such as she'd never felt in her life, was affecting her limbs, making her shake all over.

A woman gave a sudden shriek and sank to her knees and began to howl in distress, while another beside her began the rosary, playing the beads between her hands, saying the prayers like a litany.

Bridie's terrified eyes met those of her sister. 'Oh God, I . . . I'm so s . . . scared,' Bridie could barely speak, her teeth chattered so.

'We're all scared,' Mary said. Her thoughts were with her eldest son, no more than a boy, out in the teeth of the longest and worst raid Birmingham had ever endured so far.

'What . . . what right have I got to put them through this?' Bridie said, indicating the children. Both were sitting on the bunk, dropping with fatigue, yet too afraid to sleep. 'Why didn't I send them away when I had the chance?'

'Hush, Bridie. This isn't your fault,' Mary said. 'You made the same decision as me. We wouldn't send them to strangers.'

'Not strangers no,' Bridie said. 'But, maybe Mammy would have them. Didn't Daddy say they would?'

'Aye, he did,' Mary said, and she drew Bridie to her and put her arms around her. 'But remember Mammy didn't. Come on we'll talk about it later,' she said, frightened of Bridie's wild eyes and trembling body.

'If we survive you mean,' Bridie cried. 'And if we

don't, if anything happens to my children, it will be my fault, a judgement on me.'

'Bridie, that simply isn't true,' Mary said. 'Here, sit on the bunk. I'll pour you a nice cup of tea from the vacuum flask.'

Bridie's hands shook so much Mary had to cover them with her own to stop her spilling the tea all over her. She wished she'd had a drop of brandy to put into it, for the trauma of the last few weeks had seemed to have eventually got to her sister. Katie and Liam looked on with wide terrified eyes and her own Mickey was in little better shape.

She took the cup from Bridie's shaking hands, but held her arms so that they faced each other. 'Listen, Bridie,' she said, but quietly so the children didn't hear. 'You must pull yourself together for the children's sake. Do you hear me? If you're scared, think how they're feeling.'

The children, Bridie thought. How could I let myself go to pieces like that and frighten my children further? She forced a tentative smile to her lips and held out her arms to the children huddled on the other side of the bunk. Relieved, they scuttled across to her and, enfolded in her arms, buried their heads in Bridie's breasts. 'There now, there now,' she said, and began to rock them gently as they lay quiet. They knew their mother couldn't stop the noise, but somehow it was easier to bear when she cuddled them close.

Bridie sat like that for hours, unheeding of the ache in her arms, only aware that by not letting these children go, by being selfish, she could bring harm, even death to them, and she couldn't bear that thought. Whatever Mary said, she knew it would be judgement on her if that happened. She had to get them away before harm befell them, if it wasn't already too late.

Bridie knew it would be a great wrench to send her children away, but better for them than spending their nights cooped up like this and in constant fear of being buried alive, gassed to death, or blown to pieces. She should never have inflicted this on them. She should have taken them away when Tom suggested it.

She thought of the peace and tranquillity of her home on the farm and the marvellous childhood she'd had before Francis so terribly intervened. She wished she could say her children would enjoy the same. But, she couldn't, because at the centre of it was her mother and the hatred she still bore her.

She had analysed her behaviour at the funeral many a time since and knew what her mother had wanted was an explanation of why she had run away from them. When Bridie had been unable to give her that, her bitterness seemed to grow even worse.

But Bridie asked herself, would she care for her children? A sudden explosion made her jump and the children in her arms shuddered in fear and Bridie thought fiercely, *I'll have to make her see how bad it is. I must go over there and make her realise and beg her to make a home where my children can be safe*. With the decision made, she rocked her children backwards and forwards and crooned to them.

She'd gone past fear now. She felt she'd been sitting there for ever with the noises of Hell going on around her: the whistles of the descending bombs and the thump and crash of them exploding seemed not to touch her. It was like a background noise that had always been there. The shelter walls shook so hard that some of the unoccupied bunks at the far side became dislodged and fell to the ground with a clatter. Women jumped and squealed at the sudden noise, but Bridie barely raised her head to look through the blue fug of cigarette smoke to see what had happened.

There was little attempt at conversation now, and those who tried it murmured low. Mary lay on her bunk, holding Mickey. Her eyes were closed, but she was not asleep. Who could sleep in that noise?

Bridie wouldn't lie down. She couldn't; she felt she had to be ready. At one stage, she had the feeling that that night they would all die; no one could live through this carnage that was going on relentlessly. She and her children would be casualties of this war. God would have his revenge on them all right, but they would at least die in her arms – together.

The next moment, it seemed as if Bridie's predictions were right. A bomb landing close by sucked the doors from the shelter, even lagged as they were with sandbags, and plunged the whole place into darkness, taking, it seemed, the very air from the room.

And yet, it was not complete darkness, for through the door space a reddish-orange glow lit up the shelter. There was smoke circling around them and dust. Bridie could hear coughing and spluttering all around her, mingled with the crying and screaming.

'Are you and the children all right?' Mary gasped at last.

Bridie's eyes were streaming with the effects of the smoke and yet she said, 'Aye, are you?'

'I'm fine,' Mary said. 'And so is Mickey.'

'What happens now?'

'I don't know. This place isn't safe any more,' Mary said. 'Maybe we'll be directed to another shelter.'

It seemed that way. The shelter warden was moving around, assessing the injuries of any hurt in the blast and telling people to keep calm, but to collect their belongings up and gather their children together.

'I'm not traipsing the city in this,' Bridie said. 'I'll take my chance in my own cellar for the rest of the night.'

'Aye,' Mary said. 'You're right. I'll come along with you.'

They left the shelter together, Bridie almost staggering because she'd stayed in one position for so long. No one tried to stop them; the shelter warden had her hands too full to even notice. But once on the pavement, despite the raid, they stood for a moment, transfixed, with the children beside them. It was as light as day from the fires, which raged all around and through the city centre. Great orange-red flames licked the black sky and smaller pockets of fire were everywhere they looked. The smoke swirled about them and the air was thick with the smell of heat and smoke and cordite.

The noise was incredible. The assault was still going on, bombs still toppling from the droning planes ahead, then pointing downwards, speeding towards the ground and the resultant explosion. The resounding barrage of ack-ack guns went on unceasingly and emergency services rang their bells as they went speeding through the city streets. Mary and Bridie stepped over the burst sandbags which had bled on to the pavements and to each side and in front of the shelter were piles of rubble where once buildings had stood.

But there was only further danger in standing watching and so Bridie hung her bag over her shoulder and, taking hold of the children's hands, walked up Bristol Passage towards home.

But there was no home. Grant Street was just a sea of rubble, Bridie and Mary stood stock still and looked wide-eyed at one another. 'What is it?' Katie's shrill voice carried over the cacophony of sound. 'Where's our house?'

'It's gone,' Bridie shouted back. 'Flattened.'

'Ellen's,' Mary mouthed, and Bridie gave a brief nod.

Ellen drew them all inside. How welcoming were her arms that came around them, Bridie thought, and tears ran down her cheeks.

It seemed that in minutes, Ellen had them all down in her cellar, packed about with quilts and blankets, eating fish paste sandwiches and drinking tea.

The raid didn't finish until half past four in the morning and when the all clear sounded over the city, Bridie and Mary looked at each other shocked they had survived the night. Incredibly, the children had eventually fallen asleep, but Bridie didn't even feel tired anymore. 'Shall we go and see what we can salvage?' Bridie asked Mary. 'Ellen's here if the children should wake.'

'You go,' Mary said. 'I'm off to find young Jay.'

Bridie understood that well enough and so she went up the remains of Grant Street , while Mary went off towards Thorpe Street.

It was hard, under that sea of bricks and plaster roof beams and glass and the mangled contents of houses, to know where Bridie's house would be. But eventually she identified it, incredibly by the toy bunny rabbit Tom had sent Liam for his fourth birthday. Where he'd got it, God alone knew, but probably because his daddy had sent it, Liam had loved it and she spotted it squashed and battered and full of dust, trapped amongst the furniture broken to matchsticks.

She stood winding the rabbit's ears between her fingers and cried. It wasn't for the bricks and mortar, it was for the home she and Tom had built up, the things they'd saved for, the fun and laughter they'd had there, the memories, all wiped out by German bombs.

'Kept your weans safe this time, ducks,' said the hated voice of Peggy McKenna beside her. 'Though they've no place to lay their head this night. Mark my words, God will not be mocked.'

'Get away from me, you hateful woman,' Bridie screamed. 'Trading on the misery of others. Get your horrible venomous face away from me or I'll not be responsible for my actions.'

'Have you forgotten what I know?'

'As if I could,' Bridie said. 'But, you know, after last night it matters less.'

She was bluffing; it mattered just as much as ever, but she had to get Peggy away from her before she leapt on her and squeezed the life blood from her. And she could have done, she was angry enough.

She watched the woman shamble away and told herself enough was enough. As soon as she could, she'd go home to Ireland and beg her mother to take her children in before harm came to them and then she'd sort out Peggy McKenna once and for all.

CHAPTER EIGHTEEN

The way was blocked to Thorpe Street, with whole streets around it blown up with a parachute mine and a team of rescue workers trying to reach survivors. As there was no one to tell her anything, Mary stood stock still on the pavement not knowing what to do. Maybe at this moment Jay, having sat the raid out in a shelter somewhere, was at Ellen's and, knowing him, filling his face, while she stood in that freezing morning worrying about him.

She'd be better off waiting at Ellen's she thought and had actually turned away, when a warden stopped her. 'You Mary Coghlan? Jay's mother?'

Oh God. The blood ran like ice in Mary's veins. 'What is it? Is he hurt?'

'Yes, but not bad,' the warden said. 'I mean bad enough, like, but he'll live. Wall collapsed on him and another boy.' He didn't go on to tell Mary the other boy died, or that the two had lain trapped buried for three hours and he was one of the team who had dug them out.

'Where is he?'

'He was taken to the General,' the man said. ''Course, if they were full there, he might have ended up anywhere.' Mary knew that well enough, but still decided to try the General Hospital first.

It was no easy walk and several times she had to climb over mounds of rubble and glass, or step into the road to avoid them. Some of the people she passed looked bemused and stunned and stood aimlessly on the pavements, staring as if in disbelief at what had once been their home. Later, Mary knew she would mourn that loss too, but for now all that mattered was Jay.

In the distance, the town still burned fiercely, and as she drew nearer, she could even feel the heat of the flames. It seemed as if the whole city was ablaze. Much damage had been done in the raids earlier in the year, the October attacks being particularly severe, but this one topped them all in its ferocity and seemed intent on burning or bombing to the ground anything they'd left standing.

But anxiety for Jay nagged at her and she held on to the fact that he was alive, hurt the man said, but not bad. She knew until she saw him, though, had made sure herself that he was all right, that she'd not rest.

It was not at all like the early hours of the morning at the General Hospital. Most of the doctors and nurses, who should have finished their shift hours ago, had stayed and others who should have been off-duty had come in. They were all needed; the numbers already in casualty were being added to every few minutes. Mary wondered if in the mayhem around her, the mass of misery and human suffering, whether anyone would know or care about the whereabouts of one young boy.

But he was there and no one commented on her arrival at the ungodly hour or talked at all about visiting times. These were not usual days at all and rules had to be changed accordingly. A young and sympathetic nurse took in Mary's bedraggled, dusty clothes and her worried eyes and directed her to the ward Jay was in.

Her heart nearly stopped when she saw him. Bloodshot and scared eyes stood out in a face as white as the bandage enveloping his head, his left arm was in plaster and so was his right leg, which was raised by a contraption above the bed.

Later, much later, after stumbling back to Ellen's, her tears were finally released for she had been determined not to cry in front of her son. She accepted the tea Ellen pressed into her trembling hands and gulped at it gratefully. 'The doctor told me he was lucky,' she cried. 'Lucky, my God! He's a mass of bruises, black and blue all over his back and right side. He has a deep gash on his head and they had to shave his head to stitch it and his leg was twisted under him and is broken in three different places. Lucky! And yet the other boy's parents would change places with me this night – he was killed.'

'Ah God!'

'God's no help in this war,' Mary said bitterly. 'I think we've got to help ourselves. And this has decided me. My boy could be on the mortuary slab – he just missed it by a hair's whisker. As soon as he's out of that place and able to hobble about, I want him to go home to Mammy and Daddy and safety.'

'Good,' said Ellen. 'Even Jay is a child yet. And they'll all give Jimmy a hand, if he shows them how.'

Bridie smiled. 'One thing Daddy always had was patience,' she said. 'I'll make arrangements as soon as the ticket office opens for all of the children to go. The children won't be going in to school today; they couldn't cope with it after hardly any sleep last night and anyway they have nothing to wear. You'll have to explain to them at work too.'

'God, Bridie, will you listen to me? There is no more work for me, you or any other bloody body. The factories have gone up in smoke like the rest of the bloody city.' And then Mary covered her face with her hands and cried as if her heart would break.

'You need some sleep,' Ellen said, helping Mary to her feet. 'Go on up to the attic. I've made it as comfy as I can with the rugs and eiderdowns to lie on and there's plenty of blankets.'

Mary allowed herself to be led to the door to the stairs, but Bridie, though her smarting eyes were gritty with fatigue, refused to go. 'I need to get things done before I sleep,' she said, and Ellen didn't argue.

'I'll take Sam some breakfast later,' she told Bridie. 'It's early yet.' It was early, not quite half past seven, though it felt much later and Ellen went on, 'There'll be nowhere open yet. Why don't we have a wee bit of breakfast before the children are up and at us?'

Bridie shook her head. 'I couldn't eat it, Aunt Ellen. I was glad of the tea though. It revived me. I think I should go along to the factory first.'

'But it's down, Mary told you that.'

'Aye, I know,' Bridie said. 'But there's bound to be someone about.' Added to the worry of the raids, trying to keep the children safe and the thought of poor Jay in hospital, was the thought of Peggy McKenna carrying out her threat if she didn't have a pound for her that week. If she wrote the dreaded letter after the children had gone to live in Ireland, the shame would rebound on them too. It didn't bear thinking about. If her and Mary's old jobs were gone, she'd have to find a new one, and quickly, just as soon as she made sure the children were safe.

Bridie found the factory just as Mary had said, with men and women milling around in a quandary, not knowing what to do. She talked with some of them, but so far no one knew anything. She also found quite a few of her fellow workers had been bombed out the previous night and had lodged in a variety of places. A fair number were taking themselves to the council offices to see if they'd made arrangements for the bombed out and homeless. 'We need clothes as well,' said a young woman about Bridie's age. 'All we have, my two children and myself, is what we are standing up in.'

Bridie was the same: her clothes were only fit for the rag bin, her coat had a rip right down the side of it, and her lisle stockings had been in such a state she'd thrown them into Ellen's fire and came out barelegged. Her dress and cardigan beneath her coat were grey with dust. Dust was everywhere, swirling and gusting about them in the dark November morning so that you smelt it in your nose, tasted in your mouth, on your lips and the back of the throat. 'Come with us,' the young woman said.

'I might later,' Bridie said. 'Now I have to make arrangements to go across to Ireland to see my parents and ask if they'll care for my children and my two nephews while the bombings are so bad.'

'Don't blame you, ducks. No place for kids this,' another woman said.

'But not everyone's got relatives in safe places,' the first woman retorted. 'And what's safe about sending your children to live with strangers?'

'I couldn't have done that either,' Bridie said soothingly. 'In fact I don't like the thought of them living so far away, but . . . Well, after last night.'

'You do right, lass. Will your hubby mind?'

'No,' Bridie was able to say definitively. 'He'll

be all for it. He was at me to send them at the beginning.'

'Yeah, mine's the same,' put in another woman. 'Says he has enough to worry over as it is without fretting over my safety, or the kids. You're not coming then?'

'No, not yet. Once I get some money out of the post office, I'm off to New Street to see how soon I can go.'

'New Street Station was hit,' a man called across. 'My brother's a signal man. Says it's closed.'

'The ticket part might be open though,' someone said. 'And they'll have the trains up and running before you know where you are, mark my words.'

Bridie hoped he was right. In any case, she made her way to the post office. It was half past eight and she didn't mind the wait till nine; she wanted to be first in the queue. She didn't know what to do about Peggy McKenna though. There was nothing she could do until she had the children safely in Ireland. Then, she imagined, she'd get another job quickly enough. Anyway, the safety of the children was her paramount concern. She'd have to take the risk that Peggy would hold off telling anyone straightaway, thereby cutting off her source of easy money.

'You'd not think to take the children with you?' Ellen said when Bridie told her she was leaving for Ireland the next day. 'Surely Sarah would not turn them away? Didn't Mary tell me that when you were over for the funeral that time your daddy told the two of you you'd be welcome?'

'Aye,' Bridie said. 'Daddy did and that's the point, isn't it?'

'What is?'

'Mammy said nothing. God, Aunt Ellen, she loathes me still,' Bridie cried. 'She was barely polite. I wouldn't ask her to look after the children at all if I were not desperate, but their safety is more important than my pride. I'll get down on my knees to Mammy if I have to.'

'I see that, girl, but surely to God she wouldn't refuse to have them?'

'She might well,' Bridie said. 'You didn't see how she was with me. I couldn't just foist them on her. It would be another black mark against me that she could make the children suffer for later.'

'She wouldn't do that, not to weans.'

'To mine she could,' Bridie assured her aunt. 'She didn't even glance at the photographs I took. She asked nothing about them at all and if Daddy did, she got up and began making tea, or clattering crockery, making it quite clear she wasn't interested really in anything I had to say.'

'But it would be different now, I mean the war hadn't begun then,' Ellen said. 'It was just a rumour, good rumour, but now with the bombs and all . . .'

'That's what I'm banking on,' Bridie said. 'I'll tell her how bad it is. I'll make her see.'

'And what if there is a heavy raid while you're away?' Ellen asked. 'Have you thought of that?'

'Of course I have,' Bridie said. 'It's the one thing that terrifies me. I know you and Mary will see to the children and keep them as safe as you're able to, but God, I will worry all the time I'm away. I can't think of doing anything else though. At least, this way, in a few days time, they'll be completely out of it – I'll not leave until I have Mammy's agreement.

'I could write, I've thought of that,' Bridie went on. 'But a letter would take too long and she'd probably not answer anyway. I mean after the funeral, though she was so bad with me, Mary said maybe I'd broken the ice and to try writing to Mammy again. I did, you know how many times, and you know too that she didn't put pen to paper to reply, not even the once, and if you mentioned me in your letters she never commented on anything you said.

'She acts as though I don't exist and because of me that my children don't exist either. How then can I just arrive with them beside me?'

'No, you're right – the only way is to actually go and plead with her. I can understand how you feel, Bridie,' Ellen said. 'That sister of mine has put you through it over the years.'

'It isn't totally her fault,' Bridie said. 'She doesn't know the full story.'

'Well, we'll keep it that way,' Ellen said. 'Now let's start on these clothes for you. We can't have you go to home in these rags you have on.'

While Bridie had been out, Ellen had sorted through clothes of hers and Sam's that could be altered to fit Bridie and Mary, or cut down to make things for the children, and the two sat and cut and pinned and sewed as the house began to rouse itself, as first the children, and then Mary, came downstairs.

Bridie began to yawn as the afternoon wore on and eventually Mary persuaded her to have a rest before tea.

However, Bridie had only just dropped off when she was woken again by the siren piercing the night. With a heavy groan she got up and dressed and grabbing up the quilts and blankets, she hauled them down the stairs after her. She looked in on Ellen, knowing she wouldn't leave Sam. 'D'you want anything?'

Sam smiled a wan smile and shook his head, while Ellen said, 'All we want is to see you safe down in the cellar. Go on now. Stop wasting time.'

Bridie handed her sister the quilts to settle the children on and Mary said, 'We'll have to take our chance with the gas and stay here – the other shelters are too far away to get to.'

Bridie nodded and hoped that the children hadn't got to take that risk for long.

After the previous night, everyone was nervous, but though the raid went on for some hours and some of the bombs fell remarkably close, close enough to make the children jump and cling to their mother, the raid lacked the intensity of the one before.

It strengthened Mary and Bridie's resolve, though, that the children must be moved to a place of safety and as quickly as possible.

The next morning, Bridie bought a *Birmingham Post* as she passed the paper shop in Bristol Street on her way to the station. It was not surprising that so much damage had been done, Bridie thought, when she read in the paper that three-hundred and fifty bombers had attacked Birmingham on the 19th November, the first of them dropping flares and incendiaries to light up the targets. Nine major factories had been hit that night, and many smaller factories had been targeted too. It was a severe blow, for all the factories had been working for the war effort in one way or another.

The city centre had been gutted, few areas escaping some form of damage either from bombs, parachute mines or incendiaries, and many of the major department stores were no longer standing.

Bridie was used to craters, disruption and mounds of rubble, but the extent of the destruction of Birmingham shocked her. When this war is eventually over, she thought, what in God's name will be left?

She was glad though that, despite the bombing and destruction at the station, trains were still in operation: people had been working hard all that day to repair tracks and clear blockages and most regular trains, including the boat train from London to Liverpool, were working as normal.

The train was already in and she climbed aboard and lay back against the train seat. She was more than just tired: every bone ached and her eyes smarted and felt as if they had grit in them. She dreaded the ferry trip on that cold and windswept day, certain she would be as sick as a dog.

She wasn't disappointed and when she alighted from the rolling ferry, she felt light-headed with hunger and lack of sleep and her stomach ached from vomiting. She was thinner than ever and her face looked gaunt, as white as lint and lined with strain. Her two eyes were like pools of anxiety standing out, ringed with red and with black bags beneath them.

And this was the picture Sarah saw that evening as she looked up from the hearth and saw her daughter standing by the door. She took in other things: the ill-fitting coat and the lack of gloves, scarf and hat on such a raw day and, glory be to God, bare legs stuck into shoes that had seen much better days. Resentment and anger towards Bridie faded at that moment, for this was her child and in need, desperate need by the look of her. 'Mammy,' Bridie said plaintively, for she was near collapse, and Sarah ran across the room and enfolded her daughter with her own good arm, shocked at her thinness.

'Dear God, what ails you?' Sarah said, drawing Bridie towards the chair by the fire and automatically hanging the kettle on the hook above it.

'Oh, Mammy,' Bridie said again, and she put her head in her hands and wept. She wept for the fear and helplessness she'd felt and the worry and the strain of the last few days. Sarah didn't urge her to stop, or ask her what the matter was. She had the feeling that Bridie needed to cry, hadn't done enough of it, being brave in front of the children most likely, and that she had reached breaking point.

Bridie's sobs were easing and she felt the strain seeping from her. When she raised her head, her cheeks were wet, tear trails running down them, and her eyes brighter than ever, but the heart-rendering sobs had stopped.

'D'you want to tell me about it, Bridie?' Sarah said, for though her anxiety was primarily for the state Bridie was in, she wondered what had induced it. Was something wrong with Ellen maybe, or Mary, or, God forbid, one of the children.

But before Bridie was able to answer, Jimmy bounced through the door. There was no other word for it, but bounced. He'd been checking the stock in the fields when a neighbour had hailed him and told him he'd seen a girl, the spit of their Bridie, alighting from the rail bus just a few minutes before. Jimmy had known the man was not codding him; no one would over such a matter. 'Was she alone?' he had asked.

'Aye, I saw none with her,' the man had said. 'And she only had the one bag.'

Dear God! Fear had run like ice in Jimmy's veins, for though he longed to see Bridie, he wondered what had brought her alone, headlong from Birmingham. He had thanked the neighbour, called to the dogs and almost ran back to the cottage.

He stopped at the door and stared at Bridie in shock. She looked ill, very ill, and he was filled with terror so acute that he felt his heart banging against his ribs. He was across the floor and holding Bridie tight in seconds.

Bridie proceeded to tell her parents how it was in Birmingham. She didn't just describe the raid on 19th November, but from when it had all started. Jimmy and Sarah sat and listened to a catalogue of events they could barely comprehend, for all they'd read the papers and listened to the news bulletins on the wireless Jimmy had insisted they buy at the beginning of the war. No report was any substitute for hearing it first-hand from their own daughter who'd been living through it. Neither Ellen or Mary could tell them anything in the few letters they wrote during the time; besides the censor would have cut such things out anyway.

But now Bridie spared them nothing, because she couldn't. The words spilled from her lips once she'd begun. They were appalled by the number of deaths and those injured and then Bridie finally came to the last raid. She didn't think she'd have the words to describe the horror of that night and their terror, but she needed few words – her face said it all. Her sensitive eyes spoke volumes, as did her tremulous lips and shivering body that rocked slightly backwards and forwards as she spoke.

And so Jimmy and Sarah knew it all. Wee Jay in hospital and Bridie and Mary without a home or possession in the world. 'That's the reason for these clothes,' Bridie said, pulling at the coat she still wore. 'This is Ellen's – she altered it for me. Mine was nearly in rags, dust laden and stinking with smoke.' She stretched out her legs. 'Between us, Mary and myself, we didn't have a decent pair of stockings to our name. Ellen offered us hers, but . . . Well, she needs them, she's an old woman – I didn't want her to take a chill. Uncle Sam relies on her now. He's virtually bedridden and Aunt Ellen can't afford to be sick.'

'Oh, my darling child,' Jimmy cried. 'What can we do to ease this for you?'

But it was to Sarah that Bridie spoke as she said pleadingly, 'Will you take the children? Will you look after them until the bombings eased? Mary's as well as mine? And will you love them as if they were your own?'

Sarah was ashamed that she'd not offered a place of sanctuary earlier, at least for the children. Whatever Bridie had done was hardly their fault and so, though her eyes shone with tears, she answered, firmly enough, 'We will, Bridie,' she said. 'And we'll be glad to do it.'

Bridie sighed in relief and looked from one to the other with gratitude, certain many of her troubles were over.

Bride slept like a log that night; she was tired out anyway, but she slept well because there had been no raids in Birmingham the previous night, at least there hadn't been one up until the time Bridie went to bed, according to the reports on the wireless.

She was woken by the sound of the garrulous Beattie talking to her mother and remembered it was Friday, one of the days that Beattie and her husband came to help out in the farm and in the house. She looked at her watch and was horrified to see that it was ten o'clock. She'd never slept so late in her life and she told herself she should have been up earlier, helping her mother but when, later, she opened the door sheepishly, Sarah beamed at her. 'You look better already,' she said. 'God, Beattie you ought to have seen the cut of her last night. Hadn't slept in nights with the bombing and all.'

'And your Mammy tells me you and your sister were bombed out.'

'Aye, the whole area was flattened,' Bridie said, and gave a shudder at the memory of it. 'I thought we were all going to die. Mammy is going to see to the children while things are so bad.'

'Aye, it's no place for children,' Beattie said. 'And aren't they better with their own flesh and blood when all's said and done? Jesus, haven't your parents this fine farm and all for them and isn't it a grand place for weans to grow up? Won't they be delighted so at the space and freedom and fresh air after the city streets?

'My man was over there before we married,' she went on, 'and he said the air in the city would nearly choke the life out of you. And that was before any war. You're doing the right thing, bringing the weans to your mammy. I mind when I was . . .'

The woman continued to talk as Sarah drew her daughter to the table and put a steaming bowl of porridge before her, with a jug of cream to one side and a dish of sugar to the other. Beattie continued to talk, but Bridie found she had to contribute little, but nod and make the occasional grunt, for Beattie liked the sound of her own voice best. But, for all that, Bridie sensed she was kindly and Sarah got on with her, as well as she would with anyone who took control in her kitchen.

When there was a gap in Beattie's monologue, Bridie asked where her father was.

'He was away to town in the cart just as soon as he'd had a bite after milking,' Sarah said. 'I gave him a list of things to get as he was going in, but he really went to get the battery charged up for the wireless. You mind it was losing power last night?'

Bridie did and was glad that her father had thought of it. She really needed the wireless to find out what was happening, especially when she was away from everyone. 'When d'you plan to leave?' Sarah asked.

'Tomorrow,' Bridie said. 'I want the weans gone from the place as soon as possible and I'll return with them straightaway. One thing, Mammy – they haven't many clothes to bring. Everything was destroyed, you see.'

'I'll see to it don't worry.'

'I'll give you some money and Mary will too.'

'You'll do no such thing.'

'I will, Mammy, I must,' Bridie said. 'You don't know how you've relieved my mind in agreeing to take them in for a while. I don't want you to be out of pocket. Everything will have to be replaced.'

'If it eases your mind I'll take a wee contribution,' Sarah said. 'But there's no need of it. Let's talk about it again when you return and the children are safe.'

Aye, that was the one important thing, Bridie thought. She wished she could be back with them now with a click of her fingers, for every minute away she worried.

That evening, with the meal over and Bridie packed and ready to be off first thing in the morning, she settled before the fire between her parents. As usual Jimmy turned the wireless on for the news. The news was of Irish issues initially, and Bridie took little notice, but then it switched to the raids in Derry. Derry was in the six counties belonging to

England and as ships were stored and made in the docks there, they suffered much enemy damage.

Then the broadcaster switched to the news from Britain, concentrating primarily on the nightly raids over London and the damage incurred. But he then said words that made Bridie's heart almost stop beating,

> *Reports are coming in of a large body of enemy planes attacking a Midlands town. Approximately two-hundred and fifty bombers are involved. All areas of the city are being targeted with incendiary flares, followed by ordinary bombs, parachute bombs and land mines.*
>
> *The raid is continuing with great intensity. There is much damage reported and a great deal of casualties expected . . .*

'Oh God!' The roof of Bridie's mouth seemed suddenly very dry.

'No saying it's Birmingham, pet,' Jimmy said, seeing the blood drain from Bridie's face. 'A Midlands town. You heard him. Could be anywhere.'

'It's what they always call Birmingham in any national paper or BBC broadcast,' Bridie cried. 'No one really knows why when they name other cities. Only the Birmingham papers called it Birmingham. He's talking about where my sister, my aunt and uncle and all the children are. I wish now I'd brought them all with me.'

'You weren't to know.'

'I'm not stupid, Mammy,' Bridie snapped. 'I ought to have guessed. God, I might have known Hitler would have something like this planned. He's done this before, giving us a day or couple of days' respite. It does no good. You lie awake for hours, waiting for the shriek of the siren and then you're struggling into clothes, and away in the cold inky black night. 'Only now, of course Bristol Street shelter is gone and so they'll have to take their chance in Ellen's cellar. We stopped using them because we heard of people gassed in their cellars when the pipes were fractured by bombs.' She turned horrified eyes upon her parents. 'What if that should happen to them? What if I go home and find they've been choked to death?'

'Bridie, stop it!' Sarah said. 'This does you no good. You all survived before and you'll do it again.'

'Only just, Mammy,' Bridie said plaintively. 'That raid! God, it was the worst I've seen and many times that night I thought we'd die, all of us. I prepared for it, I held the children close, so close that if we were going to die, it would be together. Who's holding my babies this night?'

'Bridie, what are you thinking of?' Sarah said. 'Dear God, won't Mary care for them as if they are her own and Ellen's there too.'

'Ellen doesn't leave Sam now,' Bridie said. 'She's stopped using the cellar and stays with him in the bedroom. And Mary, she has Jay in hospital. What if she were visiting him and the raids were so bad she couldn't get back?'

'Bridie, stop torturing yourself like this.'

'Mammy, you've no idea.'

'Maybe, I haven't,' Sarah said. 'But I don't believe in crossing bridges before I come to them.'

Really Sarah and Jimmy were as worried as their daughter and yet they felt powerless to help. But Sarah doubted if Bridie even heard what she said, for the hourly news reports brought her little ease as they stressed the raid continuing unabated in 'the Midlands town', and said there was much damage and many casualties.

Bridie turned to look at her mother after one of these reports and said, 'If they die, if anything has happened to my children, it will be my fault.'

'No, Bridie,' Sarah said. 'It's the people dropping bombs that will have hurt your children.'

But Bridie shook her head. She thought to herself that if they were dead it would be another two deaths laid on her door. Peggy McKenna would have her wish at last and Bridie wouldn't care any more, for her reason for living would be over.

And what would Tom do then, if he lost them all, and after urging Bridie to take the children to a place of safety, long before the war began in earnest? What now if it was too late?

Sarah was worried about her daughter, what she'd find back in Birmingham and how she'd cope with it. She already looked far from well and more than thin, gaunt almost, so that her ill-fitting

436

clothes hung on her frame. But it was the look on her face that worried her most. It was her face, white as snow and her eyes, which seemed to stand out in her head, looking huger than ever and filled with terror, with blue smudges beneath them.

Sarah so wished she could enfold her daughter in two good strong arms and tell her everything would be all right, but the time for such things, such assurances, was passed. She could do nothing but wait, for she was worried herself. Hadn't she another daughter and a much loved sister going through it, not to mention her grandchildren?

Sometime in the long night, Jimmy went to his bed, exhausted beyond measure. But rather than disturb the women folk grouped around the fire, he undressed behind the curtain. Sarah was also tired, but she stayed as support for her daughter.

Bridie's eyes felt gritty and sore, but she knew there would be no sleep for her that night. The extreme terror she felt had made everything around her of no importance. She drank the seemingly endless cups of tea her mother pressed on her, and was aware that they knelt at least once and said the rosary together. Time had no meaning for her and she sat hunched forward, gazing into the fire, her hands clasped and between her knees, immobile except for the odd shudder that ran through her. Every hour the newscaster spoke of the raid continuing and the whole of the city centre blazing out of control.

*   *   *

As the raid began that night, back in Bell Barn Road, Ellen watched her husband's laboured breathing and knew he hadn't long to go. Dear God, she thought, this war was no place for the young, the old and anyone vulnerable. It was no place for anyone, but not everybody could run away. There comes a time when people have to stand and fight evil and this was one of those times and, if she'd been younger and hadn't had Sam to consider, she'd have been alongside of them.

But, Sam, dear Sam, her husband of many years was on his way out. It had been a good and happy marriage, the only disappointment being that they'd not had children. And yet with Mary and then Bridie and their families living around the doors, she'd not felt the lack so keenly. Still, she thought, Bridie was right to get the children away. She listened to the whistle and whine of the falling bombs and the crashes, thumps and crump of impact and shivered, especially at those falling close, and imagined the children's fear.

Sam had seen the shiver and it bothered him. He was no fool; he knew his days were numbered. Hadn't Father Shearer given him the last rites earlier in the day. Heard his confession too. That had made Sam smile. 'God love us, Father,' he'd said. 'You can't get up to much wrongdoing tied to your bed. This is probably the most sinless time in my life.'

Father Shearer had smiled and gave Sam absolution, followed by Communion and then the last rites to prepare him for the afterlife. Sam wasn't afraid of dying – he was prepared for it – but Ellen had years ahead of her yet. 'Go down to the cellar,' he urged now.

'I will not.'

'Ah go, Ellen. To please me.'

There was a catch in Ellen's voice as she said, 'Not even to please you will I leave you alone in this bedroom tonight.' She caught hold of his weather-beaten hand and said, 'We'll stick it out together, as we always have.'

Sam smiled, glad of the comfort of that hand. 'We've had a good life together haven't we, Ellen?'

Ellen didn't insult Sam's intelligence by telling him they had many more years yet. Her voice was little above a whisper as she said, 'Aye, lad. A grand life.'

'There was never anyone but you,' Sam continued. 'I loved you from the first moment I saw you.'

This was unusual talk. Ellen and Sam never spoke of the love they shared. And yet, the words brought a glow to Ellen's whole being. And so, uncharacteristically, she said, 'I loved you then too and I love you even more today,' and, still holding his hand, she leaned over the bed to give the paper-thin skin, stretching over his hollowed cheeks, a kiss.

As she did so, there was a whizzing sound and for a split second it was as if all the air had been sucked from the room. Ellen opened her mouth to scream, but no sound came out. There was an ear-splitting explosion, the room went black and Ellen knew nothing more.

The raids still continued and Bridie sat up all night, with Sarah keeping her company, as they listened to the growing list of targets. There were many other armament factories, big and small attacked, and the broadcaster said many hospitals has also been hit, with many casualties and doctors, nurses and patients killed. Bridie worried about Jay; the General in the centre of the city was probably one of those damaged.

At midnight, she heard of more bombers approaching and, at three o'clock, another raid. Bridie knew what they'd all be going through and wondered when it would end. She desperately wished for morning so she could go back and check her loved ones were all right.

The raid didn't finish until almost six o'clock, but by that time Bridie was aboard the rail bus. Her anxiety was such she hadn't been able to eat breakfast and her mammy had given out to her gently.

'No food, no rest! What good will you be to them if you fall ill?'

'Mammy, food would choke me,' Bridie said. Sarah, seeing how dreadfully worried she was, and with reason, didn't argue further. Instead she'd said, 'I'll wrap up a few pieces of soda bread with some lumps of cheese and a few apples. Maybe you'll fancy it later.'

Bridie let her do that, knowing she'd be unable to eat the food. She felt as if a lead weight had filled her stomach and she knew it wouldn't shift until she was home and held her children in her arms.

CHAPTER NINETEEN

It was dusk by the time Bridie emerged from the station and she could see that the high street and New Street were still ablaze. Water streamed along pavements and gurgled in gutters, but while many fires just smouldered, others blazed merrily. Plumes of black smoke swirled over the city and mingled with the orange and red flames filling the winter's sky. Black dust stung her eyes, went up her nose and in her mouth and settled on her clothes, mixed with the smell of smoke and gas.

She didn't bother waiting for a tram or a bus. She'd heard of areas where the tarmac had been set ablaze, or others where it had melted enough to slide into the gutters, thereby lifting the buckled and twisted tram tracks. Buses were always being re-routed too, for many roads were impassable due to great craters, or piles of rubble, and just occasionally because an unexploded bomb had landed close by, so trying to get anywhere by bus was just as fraught.

She wondered if she should first go and see if Jay was all right as the General Hospital had been hit, but she had a great longing to be home and so she set off quickly. She went up Bristol Passage and then stood still, more stunned and horrified than she'd ever been in her whole life. One side of Bell Barn Road, the side Ellen's house had been on, was one giant mass of rubble: not one house remained standing. She suddenly felt light-headed from lack of food and sleep and the horrifying sight before her, and she staggered and would have fallen to the filthy littered ground if it hadn't been for an ARP warden who steadied her.

The warden, Gillian Pearce, had just recently been drafted into the area to help with rescue work, after working all night in Hockley. Not that there were many survivors expected, they had told her. For the first time that night, low level attacks had been carried out and they'd also used some naval mines, which had exploded near the ground to maximise the damage caused. So she asked Bridie gently, aware that she may have to impart bad news, 'Was this your road?'

'Aye,' Bridie answered, looking bleakly about her. 'At least it was after I was bombed out of Grant Street. I . . . I went to Ireland then to ask my Mammy to take the weans in. I left my sister minding them while I was away and there was my aunt and uncle as well. They were in the cellar of number 78.'

She looked about her. In the growing dark, the

rubble looked like a big, black mound and not far away, she could see a rescue party moving the debris by hand with the help of shaded flashlights.

Suddenly, there was a cry. 'They've found a survivor,' Gillian told Bridie. 'Come on. It might be someone you know.'

Bridie hurried after the woman, anxious to see if it was a neighbour or possibly one of her relatives, for it was difficult to say where the house had been. Minutes later, she was looking down into the bruised and battered face of Peggy McKenna. Grey dust covered her face and her lashes, coating her cheeks and lips, ingrained in her hair and mixed with the blood seeping from a head wound. Her whole body was covered in dust too and one leg was at an odd angle. With a sickening lurch, Bridie saw the bones sticking through the flesh.

But it was Peggy's eyes that held her, bored into her. 'God will have his revenge,' she said in a hoarse whisper, each word spaced out as if it was an effort to speak. No one but Bridie appeared to have heard, but Peggy's meaning couldn't have been clearer.

And then, Peggy coughed and spluttered. It was obviously painful for her, for her eyes glazed over. Two wardens rushed to raise her, but it was too late, Peggy's head rolled back and blood pumped from her mouth in a stream, so that Bridie had to leap out of the way of it. She stared at the eyes of the dead woman and felt relief seep all through her body. She was dead and could hurt her no more, but when all was said and done, nothing could hurt her more than the loss of her loved ones and she had no way of knowing if they were alive or dead.

But maybe they weren't lost. Maybe just now they were being cared for in some hospital or other. 'Where were the survivors taken?' she asked as they carried Peggy away.

A man answered. He didn't say that those caught in the epicentre of a parachute mine, or blasted by a bomb, often came out in pieces. Nor did he tell her that bags of human remains had already been delivered to funeral directors to clean and try to assemble to help with identification. 'Many were taken along to the General Hospital,' he said, 'and then directed wherever they had room.'

'Thank you,' Bridie said. 'I'll go along to there now.'

But the man, who knew what she might find, told Gillian to go with her, but softly so that Bridie wouldn't hear. 'She looks very near to collapse to me,' he added. 'And I don't think what she will find there will help her any.'

Bridie was glad of the warden's company; she seemed unable to function properly and doubted she'd have even found her way without help. The hospital was packed, both by victims of the raid, some of those buried in the rubble only coming in now, and relatives and friends trying to trace them. Bridie looked at the press of people helplessly. 'Stay here,' Gillian said. 'I'll ask about your relatives. What are their names?'

Bridie told her and a little later she was back. James Coghlan was there and not injured further in the raid of the 22nd, although the ward next to his had been caught in the blast and his own ward had a huge hole in the wall.

'And my children?'

The warden shook her head. 'No sign,' she said. 'Your sister's here though, but she's in a coma.' She didn't add that the nurse had said Mary Coghlan would be unlikely to survive the night and that if Bridie wanted to see her alive, it wouldn't do to linger. She asked Bridie instead if she'd like to see her sister.

Gillian didn't tell Bridie what the nurse had said, but she did ask her if she wanted to see her sister. Bridie considered it, but a coma didn't sound that serious and anyway she was in the right place to be treated. Surely it was better find the others first. Her overriding concern was for her children and so she shook her head. 'No, not yet.'

Gillian bit her bottom lip and wondered if she was wrong to keep the seriousness of Mary's condition from Bridie. But, just at that moment, Bridie turned and said, 'I must find out how everyone else is before I see Mary. You must understand that? It's the children I'm worried about mostly.'

Gillian knew Bridie would not rest until she found out what had happened to the children, good or bad, but Gilliam felt her heart lurch at what she might discover.

'I also need to find out about my aunt and uncle,'

Bridie said, and with a sigh went on sadly, 'I don't really think they will have survived such a devastating raid. They never used the cellar you see, my uncle was ill and bedridden.'

She looked at the concerned woman before her and suddenly asked, 'What d'you think has happened to my children?'

'I don't know.'

'You were working there.'

'No. No, I wasn't,' Gillian said. 'I'd just been drafted into the area to help with the rescue work when I saw you. Last night and all day today I've been over Hockley way. Shall we try Lewis's basement? They said at the hospital some of the injured were sent there.'

There they found Mickey, lying on a makeshift stretcher, and he was as delighted to see his aunt as she was to see him. His eyes were panic ridden, but they shone as he caught sight of his auntie's face. 'Oh, Auntie Bridie, I've been so scared,' he said with a sigh of relief, as Bridie bent and kissed him on the cheek.

'How are you?'

'All right,' Mickey said. 'I mean not bad. Mom sort of threw herself over us, me and Katie and Liam.'

Hope leapt inside Bridie. 'So where are Katie and Liam now?'

'I don't know,' Mickey said. 'I blacked out. First I knew I was waking up here. Have you found Mom?'

'Aye, she's in the General Hospital,' Bridie told him. 'She's in a coma. It's like a deep sleep.'

'She'll be all right though?'

Bridie, ignorant of the severity of her sister's condition, said reassuringly, 'I'm sure she will be, Mickey. We must hope so. Jay's doing fine too, though the hospital was hit.'

Mickey was pleased Jay wasn't hurt further and was so glad his mother was going to be all right that he sighed again with relief. 'I must go, Mickey, and get news of Katie and Liam and Ellen and Sam,' Bridie said.

'Will you come back?'

'Tomorrow,' Bridie promised, and though she felt sorry for the young boy, left alone, she knew she must search until she found out what had happened to her own youngsters. Mickey sensed the restlessness in his aunt and could even understand it. He drew on all his reserves of courage and gave his aunt a hug and watched her walk away. He knew he had to try to be brave, but he also knew if the bombers came again that night, he'd bawl his head off like a baby.

Bridie was glad to be away from Lewis's. The dust-filled, smoke-laden air was preferable to the stench from the basement where Mickey was found. Bridie hadn't been aware that blood smelt, but she knew it now all right, like she knew the smell of charred flesh made you want to vomit. But it wasn't that alone. It was the smell of human misery, of fear and death, decay and hopelessness.

And the sounds tore at your very soul, the heartrending sobbing, the long drawn-out moans, the cries of pain, the odd shout or scream, and the nurses moving amongst them trying to sooth them and make them as comfortable as they could while they waited to see a doctor.

Gillian knew most of the undertakers used and so she led the way over the rubble-filled streets where fires still smouldered. 'If they turn out tonight, them German bombers,' she remarked to Bridie, 'Brum is done for.'

'Why?'

'No water. Three trunk water mains were smashed up in the raid last night. They drained the canal and everything, but couldn't contain the fires. God, if the wind had been in the wrong direction last night, there wouldn't have been anything of Birmingham left. As it is, if there's a raid tonight – well, let's just say, I bloody well hope there isn't.'

'Dear God,' Bridie said. 'What if I've found Mary and the boys only to lose them tonight?' And what of her own little ones? Where the Hell were they?

Gillian couldn't see Bridie's face, but heard the sigh and thought what a depressing job she did. What the Hell was she doing anyway, touring the city, looking for Bridie's people when she longed for a hot sweet cup of tea and her bed. She couldn't leave Bridie, though, for she knew her sister and nephew were probably all she was going to find alive and she sensed she needed someone with her when that realisation dawned.

Two hours later they found Ellen and Sam in an undertakers. Their bodies and faces had to be pieced together, but Bridie had no doubt the pain-riddled faces were of her aunt and uncle. There was no record of the children in any of the funeral directors, or in the city morgue, or in any of the hospitals and emergency rest centres they visited around the city centre. Bridie knew then that her children were dead. Maybe their bodies where blown into such small pieces she'd never know for sure, or maybe they were still buried beneath the bricks, wood and glass in the ruins of Bell Barn Road.

The shock of it, the realisation that her children, her beautiful children that she'd have given her own life to save had died, struck at her like a knife in the stomach and she doubled over with a cry of deep distress.

Bridie didn't feel herself falling to her knees, nor the other woman's efforts to lift her, for her misery was too intense for anything, or anybody, to touch. Flashing through her mind were memories of the children that she knew were all she would have to sustain her in the years to come.

Staggering, and with great difficulty, Gillian got Bridie back to the General Hospital, worried about her state of mind. The nurse she'd spoken to earlier recognised her struggling with a woman obviously in some sort of semi-collapse and hurried over. They sat Bridie on a chair and the warden said, in explanation of her condition, 'She's had a belly full of bad news today.'

'Oh God,' said the nurse in a whisper. 'I can't lighten it for her. Her sister, the one you asked me about, died a few minutes ago.'

'Oh no!'

Bridie didn't hear the words, but caught the tension and the warden's reaction to whatever the nurse had said and came to a little and leaned forward. Gillian hesitated to tell her and yet she had a right to know. Maybe it would be as well to let her have it all in a place where there were doctors and nurses on hand and where she wouldn't be on her own. And so, she said, 'Your sister, Bridie, she never regained consciousness. She slipped away just minutes ago.'

It was the final straw: her lovely, beautiful sister, her rock as she was growing up, the one who'd loved and sustained and helped her in her bleakest moments, was dead and gone. Mary was the very one she hadn't worried about. She'd thought she was all right at the hospital, and would get any treatment necessary while she found out about the others, but now she was gone and Bridie hadn't even had the chance to say goodbye. Suddenly, it was too much for her and she fell from the chair and keeled over in a dead faint.

Bridie came round, lying on a trolley in the hospital corridor and wished she had stayed asleep as the memories came flooding back. There was no sign of the warden and she saw by the hospital clock that it was half an hour past midnight. She struggled to rise as she realised with a jolt that Jay and Mickey would have to be told they were motherless. Tom and Eddie would also have to be sent for and the funerals arranged. She knew she'd have to push her suffering aside for a moment to help Eddie and the boys. After that, she could grieve properly for Katie and Liam.

But, she thought, how can I send telegrams or make arrangements for things when I have no idea where I'm going to live?

A nurse, seeing movement, scurried forward. 'Doctor would like you to stay overnight,' she said. 'He thinks you're suffering from shock and wants to keep an eye on you.'

'I can't stay here. There's things I must do,' Bridie protested.

'Oh, I really think . . .'

'It's impossible. There is no one left to see to things,' Bridie said, and then a thought struck her. 'My sister. We're Catholics and . . .'

'We know,' the nurse said. 'She had a rosary around her neck. A Father Flynn gave her the last rites. He's the priest that gives Communion and so on for the Catholics we have in here. He's from the Mission hall.'

Bridie felt somewhat comforted for she truly liked the man and she knew Tom had thought the world of him. He'd probably recognised Mary, if not by her appearance, then by her name, as he'd met all the family.

'He's not still here, I suppose?'

'Yes, I think he is,' the nurse said. 'He was with a dying man on the first floor a few minutes ago. Would you like to speak with him?'

'Aye,' Bridie said. 'Tell him Bridie Cassidy would like a word. He'll know me. Before the war my husband worked alongside him at the Mission hall.'

The nurse found Father Flynn, who was heart-sorry he'd recently given the last rites to Bridie's sister. Not very long after she'd spoken to the nurse, Bridie saw him hurrying down the corridor towards her, where she'd sat on a bench waiting. The priest thought she cut a tragic figure, so small and slight and still in the ill-fitting coat and bare legs and feet thrust into battered shoes. A wave of sympathy and tenderness washed over him as Bridie rose to greet him.

She'd been trying to compose herself, to push aside her devastating loss so that she could organise the funerals and contact Tom and Eddie and her parents. However, when Father Flynn came, the sorrow in his eyes began to melt her stiff resolve and when he said, 'Oh my dear, dear, Bridie, I am so, so sorry,' it opened the floodgates. She sank under a paroxysm of grief, so profound and overwhelming she couldn't see, and she groped for a hand, any hand, craving contact with another human being.

Father Flynn held her hand for a brief second before releasing it and putting his arm around her. She didn't resist, she was not capable of resisting, but later, when the weeping had died away to hiccupping sobs, she was embarrassed at being held so close and intimately by a priest.

Father Flynn, however, showed no embarrassment and passed his handkerchief into Bridie's hand and as she wiped her face, he pulled her down beside him on the bench. 'I know of Mary,' he said. 'And young Jay injured a few days ago. What of the others?'

Bridie, her voice still trembling and husky, told the priest of finding Ellen and Sam dead, and Mickey injured in Lewis's basement. There was a pause and Father Flynn read the raw pain in Bridie's eyes and the bleak look upon her face and, dreading the answer, he asked, 'And the little ones, Bridie? What of Katie and Liam?'

'Dead, Father,' Bridie said. She shut her eyes against the pain of it and said again, as if she couldn't quite believe it, 'Dead! But I'll have no grave to mourn at, Father, for there are no bodies. They are either in bits at some funeral directors, waiting to be assembled, or crushed under tons of masonry.'

Father Flynn felt tears trickle from his eyes. Bridie had adored those children. Oh dear God, how ever would she stand this? And Tom, the devoted father, as yet unaware of his loss. 'We must send a telegram to Tom,' he said. 'And Eddie, of course.'

'And my parents too, Father. But I have nowhere to stay; Tom won't be able to find me.'

'Why, you must stay at the Mission,' Father

Flynn said. 'There is no question of you going any-where else. And,' he added, 'We have clothes banks there. We have volunteers touring the richer areas as yet unaffected by the bombing and it's amazing the quality of some of the clothes they bring back.'

Clothes were the least of Bridie's concerns, but she knew the priest was trying to be kind and so she said nothing, but followed him into the dark night, grateful that she had somewhere to lay her head, though she doubted she'd sleep.

Bridie was given a room in the priest's private quarters, the room that Tom had used in fact. She was fed too, for a meal had been left for Father Flynn and he readily shared it with her. It was a vegetable stew, with a hint of meat – the normal wartime fare – and though she couldn't remember when she'd last eaten she still didn't feel hungry. She felt marginally better though with food inside her, but she was so still so deathly tired her whole body ached, despite the scant hour or so's sleep she'd had at the hospital, 'Get yourself to bed now,' the priest said. 'Try not to worry about anything. I'll see to the telegrams and make the arrangements for the funerals. I'll contact Father Shearer in the morning'

'Oh thank you, Father,' Bridie said gratefully.

'Not at all,' the priest said dismissively. 'It's my job to help. Anyway, Tom would expect me to look after you. You go up and try and sleep, my dear, and let's hope Jerry has a night off tonight.'

*　　*　　*

When Bridie had fainted at the hospital, Gillian had sat beside her for some time. By the time the clock struck eleven, she had realised she'd been sitting there for nearly an hour and had dozed herself, despite the hardness and lack of comfort of the chair. She was bone weary and full of sadness and she'd already been on duty for well over twelve hours. She had known if she was going to be any use to anyone, she needed to sleep and eat. She had also felt confident leaving Bridie in the safe hands of the doctors and nurses in the hospital and so she headed for home.

By eight o'clock the next morning she was back at Bell Barn Road for she knew the rescue and levelling work there would take some time. She been there about an hour or so when she was hailed by the man who'd suggested she accompany Bridie to the hospital the previous evening. 'How did it go with the woman looking for her people?' he said.

'Ah, I felt so sorry for her,' Gillian said. 'She found her sister at the General, but she never recovered consciousness and died. Her one nephew is in the same hospital and the other one was in Lewis's basement. Her aunt and uncle were killed too, but what's really cut her up is that there's no sign of her children. It's hard to think of two wee children in bits or buried alive.'

'It is indeed,' the man said, casting his eyes over the stack of rubble. 'How old were they?'

'Little,' Gillian said. 'The girl's six, and the boy four. Not much chance with that lot on top them.'

'There were two little uns taken out early on,' the man said. 'Before you got here. They were so small, I think they was took up the Children's Hospital. Don't know for sure, like.'

'A boy and girl?'

'Dunno, didn't dig them out myself. Someone told me about it. Said they looked in a bad way. Didn't look like they'd make it. But they might be her kids. She ought to know.'

Gillian agreed, but when she went back to the General Hospital, Bridie was gone and no one knew where. The staff had changed shifts, and the new staff didn't know Bridie, nor of her meeting with Father Flynn.

She could be anywhere, Gillian told herself outside the hospital once more, and really she shouldn't be away from her post for too long, for every hand was needed. She certainly hadn't the time to check every rescue centre for Bridie, especially as she probably wasn't in a proper one, but holed up in a church hall or some such. Anyway, she told herself as she made her way back, they mightn't have been her kids at all, or if they were hers they might have died of their injuries. What was the point of raising her hopes only to have them dashed again? Things were probably best left as they were.

In a room off a hospital ward in the Children's Hospital a couple of days later, a small girl and boy were being discussed, for the hospital didn't know what to do with them when they were ready to be discharged. 'No relatives that we know of,' the hospital doctor told Dr Havering from Oakengates orphanage. 'I've checked with the authorities. As far as they know everyone in the house was killed except, for one young boy, obviously a brother. He'll be another problem, I should think, and certainly not able to look after these two. They can't seem to tell us their names or their parents' names, or anything at all.'

'Shock and trauma,' Dr Havering said. 'And quite common and understandable in such a case. We have psychiatrists on hand to deal with this sort of thing. As soon as they are physically fit to be moved, we'll take them along to the orphanage. It's right out in the countryside, the other side of Sutton Coldfield, no threat of bombs there and once the children recover from the shock of that dreadful night, I'm sure they'll be very happy.'

The hospital doctor was relieved there were two less children he had to worry about. His workload was already enormous and the orphanage sounded ideal. The last thing those two young children needed, though, was to experience another air raid and that could happen anytime. It might send them over the edge completely. 'Have you any hospital facilities there?' he asked. 'The children just need basic nursing now, but it will be a fortnight or so before they can be allowed out of bed and really I'd be afraid of the effect on them if we get another raid before they are fit to leave us.'

'We have an excellent medical wing,' Dr Havering

said reassuringly. 'With qualified staff, of course. I'll enquire first thing tomorrow. If we have the space, we'll move the children immediately. I quite agree about the damage another raid might do to them.'

The two men shook hands amicably, glad the situation was resolved so satisfactorily. In the small room behind them, Katie lay with eyes wide open. She wanted her mother, needed her so badly, but she was frightened. She'd been terrified of the bomb blast on their house, and could remember her aunt throwing herself over the children as the walls began caving in around them.

She couldn't have said how long it took for people to dig her out, or explained how lovely the cold air was on her face. She'd closed her eyes, scared of the shouting people and the screams and cries and the crash of explosions and crump of buildings falling and the rat-tat-tat of the anti aircraft guns.

But what frightened her most of all was her little brother that lay so still on the stretcher that she knew her instincts in that black hole were right. She knew she'd killed him.

She was afraid of the men that lifted her onto a stretcher and took her to a place where people prodded and poked at her. Then someone washed the grit and dirt from her body and stuck a needle into her leg that made her go into a deep sleep.

When she awoke the next morning there was much she wanted to ask. What had happened to

Ellen and Sam and Mary and Mickey and where was her mammy and why hadn't she come to find them? But, when she opened her mouth to say this, she found she couldn't. Intense fear had taken away her voice.

Liam wasn't dead, though she didn't find that out for twenty-four hours and then she saw he was in a worse state than she was. He didn't seem to know or care what they did to him and even when his eyes were open they looked odd and that frightened her too and she waited hour upon hour for her mother to come and find them.

CHAPTER TWENTY

Tom and Eddie came to the Mission hall, white-faced, the smudges of black beneath their pain-filled eyes telling its own tale. Both were in shock, one bereft of a wife, the other his children. Tom, having been told how this tragic occurrence came about, knew that had Bridie not been in Ireland at the time, he probably would have lost her too.

How would he have borne that? To lose his beloved children caused him deep pain and he imagined that pain would always be with him, but to lose Bridie as well . . . And yet in a way, he *had* lost Bridie, for her spark, her vitality, her very essence had gone. She seldom heard him when he spoke and even when she did, she often didn't bother answering, her eyes vacant and her movements heavy and ponderous.

Father Flynn told him to be patient, but he couldn't afford patience; he only had ten days' compassionate leave. Father Shearer called to see Bridie because Tom was so worried and in the end he called in Doctor Casey as well. Both told him time was a great healer. 'You can't expect anyone to bounce back after a tragedy of this magnitude, Tom,' the doctor said, grave-faced. 'If she doesn't buck up after the funeral, I'll give her something.'

With that Tom had to be content. The one person Tom didn't mention his worries about Bridie to was Eddie, for he had his own anxieties. As well as mourning the loss of his wife, he had his sons grief to contend with too. Jay's sorrow had turned to anger which he directed at his father. Mickey, on the other hand, felt guilt. If his mother hadn't tried to protect him and Katie and Liam she might well be alive.

Mickey had been transferred to the General Hospital to be with his brother, the staff and Eddie hoping it would help. It had done little good, though, because for each boy the pain was too intense and raw and personal and they each tried to deal with it their own way. So, while Eddie worried what would happen to his sons when he went back to fighting and they were out of hospital, Tom fretted about Bridie.

The funeral was well attended by friends and neighbours and flowers almost filled the hearses. There was no representative from Ireland though. Sarah and Jimmy had wanted to come: they'd lost a beloved sister and brother-in-law, a daughter and two grandchildren, and wanted to be there to pay their respects. Bridie had urged them not to, though:

Birmingham was too dangerous a place then and the family had suffered enough loss already. And with the housing shortage worse than it ever had been, there was nowhere for them to stay.

Instead, they sent Mass cards as well as more wreaths of flowers. Mass cards came too from Catholic friends and neighbours, both from Donegal and Birmingham, so many they virtually covered the coffins of Ellen, Sam and Mary lined up in the church. There were no coffins for Katie and Liam for their bodies had never been recovered.

Father Shearer could hardly say the Requiem Mass, so saddened was he and nearly blinded by tears. He'd conducted many funerals in that war-torn city and each innocent loss of life affected him, but this . . . this was such a tragedy for the families to endure. But at least there would be a grave for these three who would be buried together. Maybe to stand and pray at the graveside would be a comfort in years to come, especially for Mary's two sons.

What of Bridie and Tom though? Their children could be in a million pieces spread all over bombed ruins. How could any parent stand that thought? He was desperately worried about Bridie. Tom had openly wept and was still weeping, one of many attending that service overcome with grief. Bridie, however, hadn't shed a tear – not in front of him anyway.

Her ravaged face showed the level of her sorrow though, especially her lifeless eyes and the lines pulling down her mouth. Tom sneaked a look at Bridie through his own streaming eyes as the funeral began, marvelling, but almost frightened, at her self-control.

He too wished he had a grave to visit where he could go to remember and mourn the death of his darling and petite little girl and his wonderful, boisterous son.

Maybe in time, he and Bridie could talk about their children, take comfort in remembering them, regretting that the few short years they'd shared hadn't been longer. But, now their deaths were too new, the pain too raw, to take comfort in anything. He wished he could hold Bridie's hand, but he knew if he did, it would give him no comfort, for she'd not respond in any way, just allow her hand to be held as if it mattered not a jot to her.

He couldn't risk rejection like that. He knelt down, covered his face with his hands, and tried to pray for the repose of the souls of his children.

The funeral did not help Bridie at all. A funeral was a saying goodbye, a coming to terms with the fact that a loved one was dead, and death was a gravestone, a place to mourn, to cry and pray, to cover with flowers so that the person is never forgotten. She could do that for Sam and Ellen and Mary but she had nothing for her own children. How could she say goodbye when there wasn't even a coffin to slide into the brown earth? Peggy McKenna had got her wish at last, but why had God punished her children? She was the one that had sinned. Why had she been spared and the children taken?

Dr Casey called to see her the day after the funeral, for he'd been there himself and saw the behaviour that so worried Tom. 'How are you, my dear?' he said, recognising himself what a fatuous thing it was to say.

Bridie turned deadened eyes upon him. 'How would you expect me to be, Doctor?'

'Quite,' the doctor said. 'Can I say I'm very, very sorry for this tragedy, Bridie?'

Bridie didn't answer that and the doctor went on, 'I could give you something to help.'

'Help? Will it return my children to me, hale and hearty?'

'Bridie . . .'

'If it won't do that, Doctor, I have no need of your pills and potions,' Bridie said.

'Tom is worried. Everyone is worried about you.'

'I can't help that.'

There was no more to say and so the doctor got up to leave. He did write a prescription for a mild sedative, which he said might help Bridie sleep at least, but when Tom gave her the bottle, she tipped the medicine down the sink.

Two days later, Mickey was given the all clear to leave hospital. 'Can he come here?' Eddie asked Bridie. 'Can you see to him?'

'No,' Bridie said sharply. She hated being near children now, even her nephews.

'Please, Bridie,' Eddie pleaded. 'I've heard that once your children go into care, you never see them again.'

'There's no need for talk of care,' Bridie said. 'Mammy will have both of them. It's what Mary wanted. Take Mickey to her.'

'Your mother will not mind?'

'Of course not. It would be a comfort for her,' Bridie said. 'She's lost a lot too, don't forget.'

Sarah had been beside herself with sadness and regret that for years she'd refused to communicate with Bridie, refused to meet her husband, denied herself the pleasure of her grandchildren. And now they were gone, blasted to kingdom come. But there were still Mary's two sons and she was well aware that any day a bomb like the one that had killed Mary, Sam, Ellen and Bridie's children could wipe out Mary's boys just as easy and so she welcomed Eddie's suggestion to bring Mickey to her. She'd keep him safe and he was, after all, part of Mary. The reply she sent back by telegram told Eddie to bring Mickey straightaway and Jay too, as soon as he was recovered.

On Tom's last night at home, he tried again to talk to Bridie. It was hard work – they were like strangers these days – but he persevered. The priest and doctor had both advised him to talk about the children with her. They said though they'd lived

466

such a short time, they could, while lamenting their tragic deaths, remember the good times they'd enjoyed and it was a therapeutic thing to do.

But Bridie wasn't ready for that. She'd locked herself behind a wall of pain and sorrow where nothing could touch her and when Tom tried, she cut him off. 'I don't want to talk about the children I failed to rear,' she snapped out. 'Not now, not ever. Peggy McKenna got her wish at last.'

'Peggy McKenna?' Tom repeated, bemused. 'What has she to do with this?'

'Everything,' Bridie said flatly. 'She's cursed the children since the day they were born.'

'But why?'

'Why? Because I had an abortion that's why,' Bridie said. 'She knew of it and said God would punish me by allowing something to happen to them and he did.'

The desolation was evident and deep in Bridie's eyes and Tom wished he could pull Bridie towards him and wrap his arms around her, but knew it would do no good. Bridie was empty of any emotion but sorrow, and could accept comfort from no one and most definitely not him. 'Our God is a God of love, Bridie,' he said gently.

'Love!' she spat out. 'You talk of a God of love that allows this carnage: the innocent, the old, women and children, murdered in their homes, crushed, or blown into pieces and you talk of love.' She turned from him in disgust. 'Peggy McKenna said God would demand retribution. I sinned, Tom, and never atoned for it, not really. I went on to marry you and have another two children. I couldn't go unpunished. She knew that and, deep down, I knew too that it was only a matter of time.'

'Mary said that woman was never away from the house,' Tom said. 'No wonder you hardly let the children out of your sight and couldn't sleep at night and barely ate enough to stay alive. For God's sake, Bridie, why didn't you share this worry with me?'

'What would you have done if I had?' Bridie asked.

'Why, had a word. Tell her to leave you alone.'

'That's why I told no one,' Bridie said. 'Because then she would have done what she said she would do and write to Mammy and Daddy and tell them of my pregnancy and abortion. The one thing she didn't know was the father of the child, but she knew enough to destroy them.'

'It was a threat, that's all,' Tom assured her. 'She wouldn't have done it.'

'I couldn't take that risk,' Bridie said. 'I gave her money most weeks to be sure.'

'Money?'

'Aye,' Bridie said wearily, and added, 'Some I took from the Post office book when I was short. And when I began work, part of my wages went to still Peggy's tongue.'

'Oh Dear God, Bridie,' Tom cried, and he drew Bridie into his arms. She allowed him to do that, but kept her own arms hanging by her side. After a moment, Tom released her, tears running down his face, as he thought how Bridie had suffered for years for a disgusting episode in her life that was not her fault.

'My life's over now, Tom,' Bridie said suddenly.

'No, no,' Tom cried. 'That can't be true. You're a young woman still. We can . . .'

'Don't say have more children,' Bridie cried. 'Not that. I've had three pregnancies and nothing to show for it. That's enough for me, I have nothing to remember of the first child I aborted, but memories of the others will never leave me. I'd not risk another child – what if God was to wreak his vengeance again? I feel I could die from the pain inside me. I couldn't cope at all if it happened again.'

'God isn't . . .'

'Don't say what your God's like,' Bridie said. 'No one knows and I'm not risking him getting his claws into me again. He can do what he likes to me – I can't hurt anymore, but I will have no more children.'

Her voice was implacable, and Tom was saddened and desperately worried about leaving Bridie with her mind in the state it was in. 'Won't you think of going home to your mother?' he asked her.

'No, Tom,' Bridie said. 'Not while my children's remains are here.'

'But, Bridie, you'll be all alone.'

'It's how I like it.'

'Go on, for a wee holiday at least.'

'No,' Bridie said. 'Leave me alone, Tom.'

'Oh God, Bridie,' Tom implored. 'Help me, I'm crumbling away inside, desperately worried about you and brokenhearted about the children. Tomorrow I go back. Hold me, for God's sake. Kiss me.'

Bridie seemed unmoved by Tom's distress and eventually she said, 'I have nothing left for you, Tom. Inside I am empty, but you can hold me and kiss me if it will help.'

But it didn't. Hugging Bridie was like hugging a piece of wood and the kiss was sterile and chaste, reminiscent of their courtship days. At least then Bridie loved me, Tom thought. Now, he wasn't at all sure.

He returned to his unit a broken man, not at all certain that if he were wounded or killed and a telegram sent to Bridie, that she had enough inside her to even care. He couldn't load any of this onto Eddie when he'd lost his own wife, so both men coped as best they could, alone and saddened.

Bridie watched Tom go with relief. She knew she'd hurt him by her indifference, but she hadn't been able to help herself. She'd promised Eddie she'd visit Jay, but she had to steel herself to do so. But at least the ward he'd been moved to after the raid of 22nd November housed mainly adults; she could cope with that.

Bridie was visiting Jay the day after the men went

back when the sirens went off. She read the panic and alarm in Jay's face and fully understood it, especially as he couldn't be moved into the basement with his foot suspended as it was. Instead, they pulled out a heavy-duty wire bed protector to put over the whole bed. They wanted Bridie to go down to the basement, but at the look in Jay's eyes she refused.

She got under the bed protector with him and held his hand while bombs whistled down, crashing all around the city centre, and she saw him flinch and felt the pressure of his hand tighten, his fingernails digging into her, when any exploded close at hand. She searched around for a topic of conversation that wouldn't be too distressing for him, but strangely enough Jay asked about his mother. 'What about her?' Bridie asked.

'Everything. Tell me what she was like.'

'She was the greatest big sister in the world,' Bridie said simply and sincerely and, as she spoke, the depth of her loss hit her afresh. Mary had been so important to her and she told Jay that. 'She was always there for me, she was like another mother,' she said. 'She was good and kind and patient and loving. I don't know how I'm going to go on without her – I will miss her so much.'

She couldn't prevent the tears squeezing from her eyes and trickling down her cheeks and Jay put his one good arm around her neck and cried too. But it was somehow comforting to mourn Mary's death together.

When they were both calmer, Jay said, 'I wish I had a picture of Mom. When I close my eyes now I can see her, but I know one day I won't be able to. It will be like she doesn't exist.'

'I'll find you a photograph, Jay,' Bridie promised. She held the boy's hands and felt the emotion running all through him. Around them was the crump and crash of falling bombs and the explosions when they landed, but Bridie and Jay barely heard them, caught up as they were in memories of Mary.

Instead, Bridie told Jay of the childhood she and Mary had enjoyed in rural Ireland, and what it was like growing up on a farm. She went on to tell him of her brother and sister that died of the flu when they'd only been children.

'Mammy and Daddy were so upset, I didn't like to add to their problems,' Bridie said,' but I was only wee myself. It was Mary who saw to me then. She made sure I was washed and dressed and fed. She was the one who held my hand and that of my cousin the day of the funeral, when the whole town and half the county seemed to be in the church and nearly all of them weeping.

'Even later, when I got upset thinking of wee Robert and Nuala and their dead bodies up at the churchyard, she didn't urge me to stop crying, or tell me not to be silly, or expect me to get over the children' deaths by a certain time. She would comfort me and often would cry too, for God knows she was sad enough herself.'

Her face hardened as she remembered her uncle

taking advantage of that grief. But that something she could share with Jay. Jay have asked her about the look that had co over her face if a particularly loud bomb hadn't then exploded with an ear-splitting crash nearby. It caused him to jump in the bed and he jarred his leg. The spasm of pain took all thoughts of the look on Bridie's face from his mind. Bridie saw the boy wince and his eyes glaze over, and so, to take his mind off it, she attempted to take him back to Donegal.

'Your mammy always liked the springtime best,' she said. 'She always said she liked everything fresh and new. The lambs are born then too and sometimes we'd come into the kitchen in the morning and there would be a baby lamb before the fire that we'd have to feed with a bottle.'

'Oh,' Jay said. 'I'd love to do that.'

'It didn't happen that often,' Bridie said, 'and it wasn't usually for very long, but Mary and I loved to look after the wee things. I loved the summer too when I was allowed to run about barefoot. My cousin Rosalyn would go off, leaping the streams and climbing the hills and thinking up all manner of games so that the days weren't long enough for all we wanted to do.

'Mary wouldn't be with us then,' she said, 'for she was older and began working at the factory in the town when she was fourteen.' She had a sudden mental picture in her head of Rosalyn and her sitting on the five-barred gate at the head of the farm, waving to Mary as she cycled down the road. She felt so terribly sad that she would never see her again.

Mary had been so important to Sam and Ellen too. Yet, though she'd been sad at their deaths, the colossal tragedy of losing her children and not even having their bodies to bury had overshadowed the loss of the others. She knew that Jay and Mickey would always miss their mother and both had been devastated too by the news of her own children, particularly Jay who had adored his little cousin Katie.

She hoped and prayed that Jay would recover sufficiently as soon as possible before anything happened to him, for the raids had not lessened. This one that they were sitting out now continued with the same intensity and the walls shook and the windows rattled. Bridie squeezed Jay's hand and told him how she'd missed Mary when she'd gone to England to their aunt Ellen's and how she'd resented his daddy for stealing Mary's heart, which meant she would stay there.

'I came to visit,' she said. 'I was just a wee bit older than you and frightened and unnerved by everything: the traffic, the noise, the people. God, what a scaredy cat I was then.'

'Why did you come back then?'

Bridie had no intention of telling Jay the truth. 'Well, I was only scared at first,' she said. 'Your mammy and daddy too made sure I enjoyed myself. We went to Cannon Hill and Calthorpe Park, the

Botanical Gardens, the Lickey Hills. We went to Sutton Park on the train once and I paddled in the stream and took a boat out on the lake. Nothing was too much trouble and every fine day we were away somewhere. And then, some evenings, we'd go to the cinema.

'Best of all though, I liked talking to Mary, I hadn't realised how much I'd missed her. Sometimes in the evening we'd all listen to a play on the wireless together. Your mammy was expecting you then and she was so happy about it.' Bridie was grateful to see a vestige of a smile on Jay's face at her words, but then an explosion near at hand caused him to jump in the bed and he gave a groan as he jarred his leg again.

The explosions were all around them suddenly, and they heard the whistle of the bombs hurtling downwards and the thundering roar of the explosions. The walls of the hospital swayed and somewhere there was the sound of glass splintering behind the tape. The ack-ack guns continued to bark into the night, but the bombs kept on coming.

To try and distract Jay, Bridie told him of her journey from her home the second time. She didn't touch on the reason for it, or explain the cycle ride to Strabane. She told him only of meeting Tom on her way over and how she met up with him again in Birmingham.

'I felt sorry for Dad and Uncle Tom when they came home,' Jay said, and Bridie saw the tears glistening in his eyes. 'They looked sort of lost.

And I shouted at Dad, I told him I hated him and that it was all his fault. I don't know why, but I was sort of angry with him. I sort of blamed him.'

'That's natural,' Bridie said. 'You want to blame someone. Don't worry, Jay, your daddy knows all this, he won't take anything you said to heart.'

'Are you sure he won't hate me for saying those things, Aunt Bridie?'

'I'm sure,' Bridie told him.

'Oh God,' Jay cried. 'I feel so miserable.' He began to cry again and Bridie held him as close as she dared, stroking his head and telling him to go right ahead and cry and not to worry or feel bad about it.

Bridie wasn't sure how long the two stayed entwined, but when Jay had stopped crying he was embarrassed. 'Sorry, Aunt Bridie.'

'Never be sorry for crying. When something so horrific has fractured your life, you need to cry.'

'I miss Mom so very much.'

Bridie felt her heart lurch. 'So do I,' Bridie told him with feeling.

'Will you come again and visit me?'

'Of course I will,' Bridie said.

She meant it too, for both sympathy for the child, and knowing her sister would like her to take up the role of substitute mother, meant she would visit Jay as often as she was allowed to.

She didn't feel the same, though, about the children at the Mission hall. She found it very hard to take being around so many young children.

Their plaintive crying, giggling laughter or just loud chatter affected her badly and in the early days, a child only had to cry, 'Mommy,' for her to turn around automatically.

Father Flynn suggested she help mind the children and give the young mothers a break, but she found she couldn't do that. They had tried to be friends with her at first, but she'd not responded and so now she was mainly left alone and she preferred it. She was so envious of those with children and if she saw a child cuddled close to its mother, she felt a throbbing ache in her arms and an actual pain in her heart.

Eventually, she found she could stand it no longer and she moved out of the Mission hall into an attic room of a large house in Belgrave Road that she'd seen advertised. She told no one where she was going and when her absence was discovered, Father Flynn was worried, for he'd promised Tom he'd look after her. He contacted Father Shearer, but he had no idea either of Bridie's whereabouts.

Bridie's new home was shabby; the paintwork peeling, the wallpaper hanging in strips, the lino ripped and pitted and thin moth-eaten curtains hung at the windows, which the blackout shutters covered in the evening. Grey-looking sheets and even darker grey rough blankets covered a stained mattress with springs poking through that sat on top of a dilapidated bed frame. An old wardrobe stood at the foot of it. Before the miserable old gas fire, that lent little heat to the room were two armchairs, as well worn as the rest of the furniture, with sagging seats and shiny arms. Two cupboards were set into the alcoves and behind that a small wooden table and two rickety chairs. A grimy curtain was pulled across the corner opposite the bed, in an attempt to hide the sink, gas ring and cupboards in there.

Bridie didn't care about the state of the room. It suited her mood. She put away the few clothes she'd brought with her. She had no food, but it hardly mattered: she wasn't hungry. But she was incredibly tired and cold. Bed would be the warmest place, she decided, and she crawled in between the uninviting sheets and fell fast asleep.

Over the next few days, Bridie only left her room to visit Jay or, if hunger threatened to overwhelm her, she'd go out to one of the centres selling food for the homeless. Soup and a chunk of bread cost only three pence, but between twelve o'clock and two o'clock, a two-course meal could be bought for eight pence. Bridie had her ration book with her, but hadn't bothered to register with a new grocer. She had no money either except that which was in the post office, for Tom, not knowing she had left the Mission hall, still send his pay notes there.

Father Flynn thought about telling him Bridie has disappeared and if he'd known where Bridie was, he might have done. But how do you write to a serving soldier and say his wife had disappeared? He presumed Bridie would write to Tom and give him her new address. However, Bridie couldn't face writing to Tom – there was nothing she wanted to say to him, or anyone really. She was better alone, wrapped in misery.

Father Flynn knew she hadn't when Tom's letters continued to arrive at the Mission hall. He and Father Shearer decided in the end that Tom must be told.

Eventually though, Bridie wrote to her mother. She felt she owed it to Mary to keep her mother informed about Jay and ask about Mickey. But Sarah was more worried about her daughter than her grandson. The tone of the letter would have alerted her alone, but in addition, she'd had a worried letter from Tom. He wondered if Bridie had gone back home as he'd urged after all, because she hadn't answered any letters and just the day before he'd heard from Father Flynn saying she'd left the Mission hall. 'Something's up,' Sarah said to Jimmy. 'Losing the children that way, and Mary, Ellen and Sam too, has turned her brain.'

'Small wonder.'

'Aye, I know that well enough, but something must be done.'

'Well, I don't know what,' Jimmy said. 'Write to that husband of hers and give him her address, maybe he'll think of something.'

'Aye,' Sarah said with a sigh. 'I'll do that. If he could get a spot of leave, it might help.'

'They're fighting a war, woman,' Jimmy snapped. Worry making him irritable.

'You think I don't know that,' Sarah screeched. 'This war has robbed me of my sister, her husband, my own daughter, left two boys motherless and two other grandchildren crushed into pieces. D'you think I don't know there's a bloody war on? D'you not think I understand it and am more heartbroken than I ever remember being? I'm so scared for poor tormented Bridie, too.' And at this, Sarah covered her face with her apron to hide the tears streaming from her eyes. But she couldn't hide her shuddering body, or the gulping sobs coming from her.

Jimmy put his arms about his wife, glad that young Mickey was away at school and it wasn't Beattie's day for coming in, for Sarah would have hated to have given way like this in front of them.

And yet, he told himself as he patted his wife consolingly, you can't keep a stiff upper lip all the time. Sarah had barely grieved for the family members dead and gone and never after Mickey came to stay with them. The boy's presence had helped them both in one way, but in another meant she'd been unable to cry or talk about her unhappiness but now it burst from her like a dam.

He suddenly remembered that there was one person who might get through to Bridie, someone who'd just arrived at Delia's only a few days ago. It might not work, but then it could hardly make the situation worse, and when Sarah was calmer he decided he'd talk it over with her.

CHAPTER TWENTY-ONE

Over the next few days, Bridie felt depression enfolding around her until it was an effort to rise from her bed in the morning. It was only because she knew Mary would expect her to visit Jay and the child's own loneliness that kept her going there. She couldn't remember when she had last washed, changed her clothes or eaten. She didn't know of the rank odour that came off her, and the grey tinge to her skin, or that her clothes were dirty and crumpled and her hair hung in greasy strands. She wouldn't have cared if she had known. As for food, she was seldom hungry now.

None of it mattered anyway. She'd had letters from her mother and more recently from Tom, but they didn't touch her. They were like people she had once known vaguely in another life. Once Jay was out of hospital, delivered to her mother's home in Ireland, her purpose for staying alive would be at an end.

She'd not even left her bed when the siren had

wailed out on the 11th December, but only covered her head with blankets, with the blasts and explosions all around her, hour upon hour. The walls had shook and the smoke and dust from the melée outside had seeped into the room through the ill-fitting windows and caused her to cough, but still she'd not felt the tiniest frisson of fear.

The raid the following night and the one after that were mild in comparison, but the one days later was another massive assault, which caused much damage and loss of life. Bridie was glad she was at the hospital with Jay when it began. This time Jay, who now no longer needed the weighted hoist for his leg, was put into a wheelchair and taken down to the basement. Even if Bridie could have left, the raid was too fierce to get home and Jay was nervous and jumpy anyway, so she spent the night in the shelter with everyone else.

The next day, Bridie didn't get out of bed until the evening when hunger drove her on to the streets to buy a sandwich and a cup of tea from a WVS van. The woman who served her was cheerful and encouraging and Bridie wondered what made these valiant women come out night after night to feed the destitute and homeless, as well as the rescue workers and emergency services.

Maybe she should find something to do, make a useful contribution to the war effort, even if she would win no medals as a mother. It would fill the days too until Jay was better and her job would be over. She'd talk to him tomorrow, because it would mean she would probably visit less often, maybe just in the evenings.

Jay, however, thought it was a good idea. Secretly, he thought if his aunt went for a job, she'd have to look after herself better and dress more decently.

But what should she do? Everywhere she would be welcomed, whether she offered herself in a voluntary capacity, or went back into a factory. But wherever she went, she reminded herself, she'd have to meet people, answer questions. They'd talk about their families and ask about hers. She wasn't sure she was ready for that yet, maybe she'd never be ready. She wrestled with the problem all the following day. If only she could summon up more energy, she thought.

By the time she visited Jay the next day, she hadn't come to any decision, but he didn't ask as his thoughts were centred on Christmas, just six days away. Bridie had almost forgotten about it; it would be easy enough to do, she thought, for there wasn't much evidence of it anywhere else either. The remaining windows of the shops still standing were very sparsely decorated, very little tinsel, or artificial snow, and few lights ringing the windows.

Of course there was little incentive to do more when the windows would have to be shuttered close before dark. No lights were strung across the streets now, nor were there lighted decorations above any shops and no huge Christmas tree in St Phillip's churchyard.

But the festive season had definitely come to the General Hospital and in Jay's ward, streamers were strung across the room and between the beds, and a giant Christmas tree stood in the corner. Jay had Christmas cards paraded on his beside cabinet. 'I've had one from Dad, and Uncle Tom,' he said. 'Grandad and Grandma sent one too, and Mickey. The other one is from the nurses. They send a card to everyone.'

Bridie was ashamed that she'd never even thought of sending a card to the lad herself, never mind getting him some gift, however small. She decided to remedy that as soon as possible and also to spend as much time as she was allowed with Jay this Christmas, the first after all without his mother, and leave the problem of getting a job for the New Year.

She'd not risen from her bed the next morning, although it was eleven o'clock, when a knock came to the door. She stiffened. Nobody ever knocked on her door. She paid her rent every week to the landlady on the ground floor, but the woman had never mounted the stairs to the attic. No one did. Whoever it was at the door couldn't want her. It must be a mistake and she didn't have to answer it.

But the knock came again, louder and more insistent this time, and with a sigh, Bridie heaved herself out of the bed. She had no nightwear and slept in her clothes, but she drew a stained cardigan over her jumper for the room was like ice. She had to steady herself for a minute or two, her hand on the bedpost until the giddiness had passed, before she shambled across the room.

Bridie recognised Rosalyn straightaway, for she still had the same mop of auburn curls that she had as a child, though her hair was cut shorter than Bridie remembered, and her eyes were the same, deep-set and dark brown. And yet Rosalyn was the last person in the world that Bridie would expect to call. She lived on an entirely different continent, for Heaven's sake. She looked at the smart woman in the black, fur-trimmed coat, with matching hat and gloves that looked so out of place in that dingy doorway, and said hesitantly, 'Rosalyn? Is that you, Rosalyn?'

Rosalyn was glad Bridie had spoken for she'd not been at all sure that the dirty drab that had opened the door to her was her cousin at all. She was sure now though and also glad that Bridie's parents had been worried enough by her letters and behaviour to ask her to call as it was obvious that Bridie needed help. She smiled at her. 'Hallo, Bridie,' she said. 'I bet you're surprised to see me!'

Bridie was surprised to see Rosalyn standing at her door all right, but she didn't know whether she was pleased or not. Hadn't her father been the start of the whole thing? But Rosalyn had been unaware of it and had been her friend for years before that.

Before Bridie had recovered her wits about her, Rosalyn, not waiting to be asked, had stepped over the threshold of the door and only then did Bridie notice the case she had with her.

Rosalyn looked about the room, wrinkling her nose with distaste at the state of the place and the stink of neglect. It was so cold her breath was escaping in whispery vapour. She'd been shocked at Bridie's appearance and demeanour, but recognised depression when she saw it. Her aunt Maria had had a touch of it after the last child's birth and, God knows, Bridie had suffered enough, losing so many loved ones, to depress anyone.

But that was over now. She was going to take her in hand. She'd come to stay for a few days, though the thought of spending any time in that dreary place did nothing to lift her spirits. 'How . . . How . . .' Bridie began. 'I . . . I thought you were in America?'

'I was,' Rosalyn said. 'When war was declared, my husband Todd was annoyed that America didn't side with Britain. He's always been mad to fly anyway and he joined the American Volunteer Air Force. He did just basic training in the States before coming here. There a company of them sharing the base at Castle Bromwich aerodrome with the regular RAF guys.'

'So you came over with him?'

'Well, I followed him,' Rosalyn said. 'He wasn't best pleased either. I arrived in Birmingham in early December, just after you had those really bad November raids, the first one that robbed you and Mary of your houses and the one days later, the other one that was so tragic. Of course, I didn't know that then. Aunt Sarah only told me of it when I went back to Ireland. Todd was worried stiff about me and he convinced me to go home to Mammy while the bombings were so bad and after spending a week with him I agreed, mainly because I didn't want him fretting about me when he needed to keep his wits about him.'

'So how come you're back here now?'

'I'm here because your father came to see me. Bridie, you have your parents both frantic over you. They knew you weren't right by the tone of the letters you sent. I promised I'd come and see for myself.'

'So now you can go back and tell them you've seen me and I'm fine,' Bridie said truculently.

'No I can't, because you're nowhere near fine,' Rosalyn said. 'But why should you be? Bridie, don't shut people out and try to deal with this terrific tragedy on your own.'

She put her hand on Bridie's arm and said, 'Let me at least try to help you?'

Bridie shrugged her arm off. 'Leave me be, Rosalyn.'

'That's the last thing I'll do,' Rosalyn said. She crossed the room and lit the gas fire with the matches above the mantelpiece and turned it up full, then she pulled the curtain of the small kitchenette and opened cupboards and drawers. She turned to face Bridie. 'You've no food in the house.'

'It doesn't matter. I don't get hungry.'

'Bullshit, Bridie!' Rosalyn cried.

'Leave me alone,' Bridie pleaded. 'You don't know what it's like at all. My life's over.'

Rosalyn bounced before Bridie in impatience as Bridie remembered her doing when they were growing up together. It stirred a memory and the affection, no, love, she'd once had for the woman before her. 'Listen to me, Bridie McCarthy, or Cassidy or whatever you are, your life's not bloody well over. Don't be so bloody selfish.'

'Selfish?'

'Yes, selfish. I know what you lost and I know it hurts like Hell. Pain like I've had no experience of and hope I never have, but you're not the only casualty. How d'you think your husband feels? And have you given any thought to your parents, your mother in particular who's lost a daughter and her sister? And Mary's boys? Mickey, I know, is still going through it, because Mammy said so. They have no mother. Are you going to deprive them of an aunt too?'

'I can't . . .'

'You can,' Rosalyn said with force. 'We're going out to have a meal somewhere, but you're not going like that. Is there a bathroom in this dump?'

'Yes, next floor down. But you have to put money in the geyser.'

'That's not a problem,' Rosalyn said. 'Nor are clothes because I have a caseful here. These you have on really should be burnt.'

'I had nothing after I was bombed out,' Bridie protested. 'These were from the Mission hall.'

'Well, I daresay they were decent enough at the beginning,' Rosalyn said. 'But you don't have to wear them till they walk off your back.'

Bridie was no match for Rosalyn in this dominant and assertive mood and within minutes she was immersed in a bath. The government told everyone to use no more than five inches and a line was drawn around, but the water from the geyser, mixed together with cold, barely reached the line anyway. This time, though, it was filled with bubbles and fragrant oils from Rosalyn's collection of toiletries and she washed Bridie's hair three times, kneading at her scalp till it squeaked with cleanliness and her head tingled.

Bridie stepped from the bath to be enfolded in one of Rosalyn's thick towels and dried and powdered like a baby. The underclothes Rosalyn handed her reminded her of the ones she'd worn under her dress the night of the Harvest Dance and for a moment the memory made her stiffen. But Rosalyn, with no idea what had happened that night to cause Bridie such pain, was impatient with her.

'Hurry up, my stomach thinks my throat's cut,' she complained, handing Bridie a soft wool jumper in a deep red and a blue serge skirt. The jumper hung down nearly to her knees and she had to roll the waistband of the skirt over and over, yet they were the nicest clothes she'd worn in ages. Then there was black high-heeled shoes and Rosalyn thanked her lucky stars that for her size she had fairly dainty feet and that they were only a little too big for Bridie. Then she gave her a suspender belt and, wonder of wonders, nylon stockings, which Bridie put on almost reverently, for she'd only ever had one other pair in the whole of her life.

She surveyed herself in the mirror in the attic and, despite herself, felt her spirits lift just a little. Because her hair was still damp, even after the towelling Rosalyn had given it, she coiled it around and piled it on the top of her head. The effect was stunning.

It was a shame she had to pull her old coat on over such clothes, but Rosalyn hadn't another coat. 'I'll get Maria to send some parcels for you,' she promised. 'Lots of women in America want to do something for you all over here. Most, like me, have more clothes than they know what to do with. They can donate some of them to a worthy cause – my cousin.'

'Oh Rosalyn.'

'Now, Bridie, don't start to cry on me,' Rosalyn admonished, but gently. 'I imagine you've done plenty of that.' She put her hand on Bridie's arm and said, 'They're gone, pet, and you have to accept it. But you're alive and you must stay that way for Tom, your parents and Mary's sons.'

'It's hard, Rosalyn,' Bridie admitted. 'Some days I can't see the point of getting up.'

'That's because there's nothing to get up for,' Rosalyn said. 'Before I go back, I'll give you a reason, just see if I don't. But for now, we must eat. Where shall we go? Name a place?'

'The city centre, I suppose,' Bridie said uncertainly. 'If there's any place not burned to the ground. Tom and I didn't eat out much. But at least if we make our way there, we're near the General Hospital for visiting Jay.'

They ate a slap-up meal in a small hotel in a side street off Colmore Road. It had sustained bomb damage and some rooms were closed off, but the restaurant was open and doing good trade. Many ate out if they could afford to in the war, for it saved the rations for the rest of the family. Rosalyn, used to American lavishness, and Ireland – the land of plenty – thought the meal rather tasteless and was appalled at the small amount of meat she had on her plate. But Bridie, used to rationing, thought it wonderful.

She'd told Rosalyn she'd not felt hungry and it had been true, but that had been linked to her mood. Feeling moderately better, she'd felt hunger stirring in her as they went into the restaurant and the different smells assailed her nostrils. When the meal was put in front of her, she felt saliva in her mouth and attacked the dinner as if she hadn't eaten for a week and indeed she might not have done. She knew it had been a long time.

Feeling full and knowing you look good gives a lift to anyone's spirits and as Bridie made her way to the General, she began to feel a little more self-confident. Rosalyn, following behind, was devastated by the state of the city centre after the sustained attacks by the Luftwaffe. There were gaping holes in roads, where buildings had once stood, filled with rubble.

There were no lights, no festivity at all. You'd hardly credit it was nearly Christmas, Rosalyn thought, and wondered how many families were without a home that year. And the children, many deprived of their father, without presents. We could do more in America, she thought to herself. I will write to Maria as soon as I have a chance.

She said none of this to Bridie, who barely noticed the bomb damage now. She'd become inured to it.

Jay was in pretty good spirits and was delighted to see Bridie looking so well. He'd been worried about her lately, and he had to admit he'd been slightly ashamed, for she'd looked such a mess and smelt a bit like rancid cheese.

He was also pleased to see Rosalyn. He'd not seen her for years and didn't recognise her, but remembered his mother talking of the great friendship between his aunt Bridie and Rosalyn. And Rosalyn amused him, telling him tales of America, entertaining stories to make him smile and laugh.

It was when there was a lull in the conversation that Jay said to Bridie, 'That's Syd Bradley over there,' motioning to a bed to the side of his. 'He's been moved up from the orthopaedic ward this morning.'

Syd Bradley had been a neighbour of Ellen's in Bell Barn Road and Bridie said, 'I'll go over in a minute to say hello.' But when next she turned, his wife was with him and she came across when she spotted Bridie. 'Terrible business that night. Fancy coming home to that,' she said. 'My heart went out to you when I heard. Course, Syd will never be the same, but we've had a good innings. I think it's hard to take a person dying when they're young. And a child, now, that's a double tragedy.'

Rosalyn, seeing the effect the woman's words were having on Bridie, wished she'd go away and attend to her own man. But then, the woman asked Bridie directly, 'Did the wee ones die too?'

Bridie, her voice too choked to speak, gave a brief nod and the woman said, 'Ah well, they looked in a bad way.'

Bridie, agitated and upset, didn't realise the significance of the woman's words, but Rosalyn did. Her mother had told her Bridie's children's bodies had never been discovered: she said they'd either been blown to smithereens, or crushed to pieces. So what did this woman mean, they 'looked in a bad way'?

'When did you see the bodies?' she asked.

'When they was fetched up,' the woman said. 'They was still, but I think they was breathing then, 'cos when they put them on the stretchers they didn't cover their faces like. Mind, they did look bad. Took them away sharpish.'

Bridie felt as if she'd been kicked in the stomach by a donkey. 'You say my children were taken out of the rubble?'

'Yeah.'

'Are you sure?'

''Course I'm sure,' the woman said. 'I was shook up and cut and bruised, but all right apart from that, not like Syd what was buried, like. I was sitting on this pile of rubble while a woman patched me up like and I saw them bring your kids out.'

'Where did they take them?' A flicker of hope was penetrating Bridie's confused mind.

'Gawd knows. Thought they'd be here.'

'They weren't here, we checked,' Bridie told Rosalyn. 'And we checked Lewis's basement and the other emergency centres set up. We tried all we could think of. I had a warden with me and she knew of places used that I didn't know – we trailed the streets looking. We went to the morgue too and the funeral directors. There was no sign of them.'

'Then where?'

'I don't know,' Bridie said helplessly.

Jay raised himself on his good elbow. The woman's words had knocked him sideways too. He'd been nearly as upset about his little cousins' death as he was about his mother's.

'Go and find out about it,' he urged his aunt. 'Go now, I'm all right. Come and tell me when you know anything.'

'I promise we will, Jay,' Bridie said, anxious to be gone and search again for her children.

As she left the hospital with Rosalyn, she faced the fact her children could still be dead. 'Surely to God if they weren't, I'd have been informed, for they'd be able to give their names.' Maybe they'd been taken to hospital and died there and were taken to the morgue afterwards; she'd only been the once. Perhaps there were too many dead bodies for the morgue to cope with and they'd opened up other centres that she knew nothing about.

But whether her children had lived or died, she needed to know. They'd been pulled out of the rubble alive and in one piece, that much she knew. She hardly dared hope she'd still find them living. That would be wonderful, tremendous, her wildest dreams come true. But, realistically, she had to face the likely fact of them dying from injuries sustained during the blast. Then, however, she could have them at least buried respectably, with a Requiem Mass for the repose of their soul and she'd have a grave to tend and visit. A place for her to remember their lives and at times be filled with sorrow because it wasn't longer.

The short winter's day was at an end when they reached the Children's Hospital. None of the hospitals they'd visited so far could recall having any children so young sent to them during the raid in question, but it was Rosalyn who asked as they left the Orthopaedic Hospital in Broad Street, 'Is there a hospital just for children nearby? They might have been taken there.'

'Of course, I can't believe I hadn't thought of that already,' Bridie said. 'We'll try there next.'

However, the porter had just come on duty there and knew nothing about admissions from a month before, and had no intention of being helpful enough to find out. Bridie pleaded with him, telling him why it was so important, but he was unmovable. They would have to come back in the morning.

It was as they made their dejected way homewards that the siren's wail sounded about the city. People began streaming from houses, carrying blankets and bags of provisions and small children, and Rosalyn looked at Bridie helplessly. 'What do we do?'

'Follow the people,' Bridie said. 'All we can do; I wouldn't know where to find a public shelter here.'

An ARP warden appeared before them suddenly, marshalling people forward, urging them to hurry, and Rosalyn and Bridie fell into step with everyone else. A little later, crushed into a shelter with Bridie, Rosalyn smiled wryly to herself. She'd intended staying a few days with Bridie, but when she saw the state of the room, she didn't fancy sharing it, but it would have been better, she conceded, than this cramped and uncomfortable shelter.

Bridie, while not content, was stoical about it all. The raid was light and she was amazed how jumpy and scared Rosalyn was of the general cacophony of noise, the crashes and explosions and the tattoo of anti-aircraft guns.

'How d'you stand it?' she said to Bridie in a voice that trembled.

'You get used to it,' Bridie answered. 'Ellen's Sam was for ever saying the British fight better with their backs against the wall. It's a sort of stubbornness. Hitler is trying to frighten and demoralise us, and so we refuse to be. Anyway, at least we are near to the hospital for the morning.'

Rosalyn couldn't feel the same way about it. The sanitary arrangements in the shelter were basic and so were the washing facilities. To arrive anywhere unwashed and in crumpled clothes she was unable to change was a real trial for her. And to arrive at the hospital where they had to persuade professional people to help them in their quest for two children – well, she would have felt better if they could arrive clean and more respectable looking.

There was nothing for it, however. By the time the 'all clear' sounded it was too late to even make for Bridie's flat, never mind tour the streets looking for lodgings somewhere, and so they bedded down where they were and slept away the few hours till dawn.

The next morning, Bridie was up first, anxious to return to the hospital. 'I need food,' Rosalyn complained. 'And a cup of coffee.'

'Coffee might be difficult,' Bridie said. 'But we can get tea from any WVS van – we passed one on the corner of the street on our way here. They do toast too and a bacon sandwich if you're really lucky.'

Rosalyn wasn't a great lover of tea, but that morning it tasted like nectar and with it and a couple of slices of toast inside her, she was ready to start the day. They made their way back to the Children's Hospital. The matron was also new to the hospital and knew nothing about admissions the month previously. 'Yes,' she said in answer to Bridie's question, they kept records, but they were not open for anyone to see. Could Bridie even prove she was who she said she was?

Of course she could, Bridie replied calmly. Everyone had to carry an identity card, which she produced. The matron scrutinised it and then said, 'I don't recall anyone of that name.'

'Surely there's someone that we can speak to,' Rosalyn said. 'And perhaps give us access to the hospital records.'

'You'd have to see the doctors for that,' the matron said stiffly, annoyed that her authority was under question. 'But I don't know when one will be free to see you. The wards are almost over-flowing and the doctors start their rounds about ten o'clock. It will possibly be a long wait.'

It was, and on a hard, hospital bench it seemed longer. They had nothing to do but watch the clock going round slowly. 'I hope the children's wards are brighter than this,' Rosalyn said, looking with dismay at the grim, grey and beige walls. 'It would put years on you if you have to spend much time in here.'

Bridie couldn't help agreeing; the place was very dull indeed and she wished the time went quicker. Every minute seemed like an hour to her.

Now and again people passed, porters pushing children in wheelchairs or on trolleys, young nurses scurrying beside them, or anxious-looking young doctors, their stethoscopes hanging around their necks, hurtling along. Some of the children cried or screamed in fear and pain and the sound pierced Bridie's soul. Others bore it all without a sound, too scared to cry or more worryingly appeared unconscious. 'God, a true seat of misery this,' Bridie said in a whisper to Rosalyn.

But then the silence was broken by the loud chatter and laughter of hospital cleaners – their shift over – stacking their brooms and mops and cleaning cloths in a cupboard and ribbing one another all the time. They smiled broadly at Bridie and Rosalyn, smiles of sympathy, and Bridie wondered how many people they'd seen waiting just like them.

The matron passed them just the once, after they'd been sitting there a couple of hours. She gave no sign of recognition, nor gave them any further information. Bridie watched the woman march down the corridor, her back ramrod straight, and remarked to Rosalyn, 'I think you've really upset the matron. They like to think they run the hospitals.'

'Well, it's ridiculous,' Rosalyn said. 'All we want to know is did two children come in here the night of that raid.'

'Rosalyn, you have no idea of the severity of some of the raids,' Bridie replied. 'The night of the 23rd I went looking for them. The General Hospital and Lewis's basement were littered with the injured, some dreadfully injured too. There were people coming in all the time. In fact, as the General Hospital had been hit itself, people might have been ferried anywhere across the city.'

Rosalyn could see what Bridie meant and wondered if there was even the slightest possibility she'd ever find out what happened to the children. Maybe the doctor knew no more than they did either.

But thankfully the doctor did, although he told Bridie that from the minute the raids started, he'd had many injured children arrive in his wards and some he couldn't save. He often had a further problem with those who had survived, for if they had no known relatives they had to go into one of the city's orphanages run by the authorities.

'But my daughter, if she survived, would say who she was, where I was,' Bridie said. 'She was six and bright.'

'Even so, if there'd been no one to take her . . .' the doctor said. He rifled through the sheaf of papers he held in his hand. 'The raid of 22nd/23rd, you said. I had twenty-five children in that night and the following morning. Two of these died, four are still with us – three boys and a girl between seven and ten – and the rest were eventually re-united with family or relatives or were taken in by the social services.'

'Where did those ones go? How many children were there?' Bridie persisted.

'I'm not sure,' the doctor said. 'It amounted to about six, I think.'

'And were there two young children amongst them?'

'I have the names and ages here,' the doctor said, checking his notes again. 'Most of the children were able to tell us themselves.' But something struck a chord in his memory and he said, 'There were two, a boy and a girl, who didn't seem able to speak a word. They weren't dumb as such, it was trauma-related. But neither of those children were six. We estimated three to four years. We have it on the file here. The ambulance driver told us they were taken from the ruins of a house in Bell Barn Road.'

Bridie gave a gasp. 'My children!' she said in an awed whisper. 'They'll be my children.'

'Steady,' Rosalyn said gently. 'That's not absolutely concrete fact. There might have been more than your children buried in that road.'

Bridie knew that was true and yet she had a gut feeling about these children. But then she asked herself whether it was just a flicker of hope, clutching at straws even. 'I know where those two children went,' the doctor said suddenly. 'They weren't really well enough to leave hospital, but wc were worried about their mental state as much as their physical injuries. They were taken to Oakengates Children's Home. It's on the edge of Sutton Coldfield and has a fully staffed medical wing with trained psychiatrists on hand.'

'Have you the address?' Bridie demanded. 'We'll go straight up.'

'I have,' the doctor said, 'but they don't encourage impromptu visits. In fact, they don't like the children disturbed in any way – many of them are damaged, you see.'

'They told you this?'

'More or less,' the doctor said. 'The children were moved from here after only a few days. They thought if they had relatives they would have turned up to claim them before then. So did I. It's taken you almost a month, Mrs . . .'

'Cassidy,' Bridie said. 'I wasn't here for the raid, I was in Ireland, seeing if my parents would take my children in while the bombing was so bad and my sister, Mary, was minding them. When I came back, I found my aunt and uncle dead and my sister and two nephews injured. My sister never regained consciousness. No one knew about my children and I searched for them everywhere. I thought they'd been blown to pieces. We even held funeral services for them. It was only a chance remark from an old neighbour the night before last, when

I was visiting my nephew in hospital, that got us to this point.'

'Such things happen in war time,' the doctor said sympathetically. 'I suggest you phone Oakengates and arrange an appointment with the supervisor of the place – a Dr Havering – and tell them what you have told me.'

'I'll do that,' Bridie said vehemently. 'Thank you, Doctor,' and she took the phone number and address the doctor had copied from the file and walked out of the hospital with Rosalyn, so happy she felt like she was floating on air.

CHAPTER TWENTY-TWO

Bridie would have gone into the first phone box they passed the minute they'd left the hospital and phoned, but Rosalyn stopped her. She had the feeling that the phone call, the first link in the process to Bridie getting her children returned to her, had to be planned carefully. Bridie was in such a state of nervous excitement, she might give doctors the impression she was a gibbering idiot.

As it was nearly lunchtime, Rosalyn treated them both to lunch and while they ate, they discussed what Bridie would say to the doctors at the orphanage. 'We can go up straightaway instead,' Bridie suggested, but Rosalyn shook her head. 'We can't, Bridie – look at the state of us. If you want to prove to them how capable you are of looking after your children, we both need to wash and change and look slightly more respectable.'

'What d'you mean, prove I'm capable? They're my children.'

'I know that,' Rosalyn said. 'But it's how these

people work – they'll need to see you're a fit person to look after children who have been through such an ordeal.'

'If you're sure . . .' Bridie said doubtfully.

'I am. Trust me,' Rosalyn said. 'Make the phone call. Ask if we can go over tomorrow.'

It was torture for Bridie to wait another day and yet she saw the sense of what Rosalyn said. The person she eventually spoke to was none too keen on Bridie visiting at all. Visitors were not encouraged as they upset the children, the woman told her.

'I'm not any old visitor,' Bridie said. 'I have reason to believe two children taken in to your care on or around 25th November are my children.'

Even that didn't move the receptionist at the other end. 'Perhaps,' she said, 'but you must understand that that is something I couldn't possibly discuss on the telephone. Most of the children we have with us are sick, mentally ill in some way, traumatised by their experiences. We have to be extremely careful not to disturb their emotional balance and at the moment they are highly excited by Christmas. Maybe if you left it to the New Year?'

There was no way on earth Bridie was going to leave it a day longer than necessary. Knowing she was in no position to insist, she resorted to pleading her case. Eventually, Dr Havering was brought to the phone and he agreed to see Bridie the following morning.

When Bridie put the phone down, her hands were shaking. What a performance just for the chance to possibly see her own children! She remembered the horror stories she'd heard about the care agencies getting their hands on children and refusing to return them, and remembered how frantic Eddie had been not to risk that with Mickey.

Rosalyn thought the whole thing ridiculous, but when she thought of the dingy, depressing room Bridie had, she felt her heart sink. Bridie though, she knew, looked no further than having found her children and bringing them home.

She said nothing about this until she and Bridie had stripped and washed in the kitchenette of Bridie's attic room and changed into clean fresh clothes, then she said carefully, 'I think we need to find you another place – a better place – if you want your children back.'

Bridie looked around the room dispassionately. When she'd moved in there, she hadn't cared about anything or anyone, but now she saw it would never do. 'I can't afford much,' she said. 'Though I see this isn't right.'

'What about the money Tom sends you?'

'That probably still goes to the Mission,' Bridie said. 'I didn't tell them I was leaving, I just walked out.'

'Oh Bridie,' Rosalyn said in exasperation. 'They are probably worried to death about you. Tom knows where you are, I suppose?'

'Now he does – Mammy wrote and told him,'

Bridie said. 'He sent me the one letter, but no pay cheque, and I never wrote back. That time there was nothing to tell him except I had nothing to live for and wanted to die. He'd not want to hear that.'

'No, of course he wouldn't,' Rosalyn said. 'Let's hope after tomorrow you'll have good news to give him. But for now, we must go back to the Mission and tell them how and where you are. Maybe you can stay there for a wee while. If not, having Tom's money will give you a deposit, which you will need for a better place.'

Father Flynn was delighted to see Bridie, though he saw from her white, strained face, sunken eyes and extreme thinness that she'd been far from well. He welcomed Rosalyn warmly too, glad that Bridie had some support. He listened with excitement to match her own about the news of the children, but when she asked if she might bring them there eventually, he shook his head sadly. 'The place is more full than ever now,' he said. I couldn't squeeze you in with a shoehorn. Father Shearer took some of my overflow just last week and now the presbytery is also bursting at the seams.'

There were three pay cheques of Tom's at the Mission which Father Flynn gave Bridie. She said she would write to Tom and ask him to continue sending his money there as she wasn't at all sure where she'd be living. However, the search for more suitable accommodation proved fruitless and increasingly depressing as they toured street after street. Sometimes there were rooms available, but they forbid pets and children, or were far too expensive. Most reasonably priced places were chock-a-block and many private houses had more than one family living in them.

'Maybe I could get a job,' Bridie mused as the two made their way home from the General Hospital where they'd been to tell Jay the news. 'Then I could pay out more. I had one before in munitions. I'd get another one easy enough. I was thinking of it anyway.'

'And then how would you care for the children?'

'I got Liam into nursery last time,' Bridie said. 'Katie was at school all day.'

'And you had people by to help you,' Rosalyn reminded her. 'How would you get Liam off to nursery and Katie to school and be on time for work? And what would happen at half past three when Katie left school? Who would see to her until you came home? What about holidays? And how d'you think they'd fare anyway, being pawned off with strangers after all they've been through?'

Bridie, listening to Rosalyn, knew she was right. If her children were at the orphanage and were returned to her, they would need her to care for them, her constant presence to reassure them.

'It's a bit like the chicken and the egg,' Rosalyn said.

It was depressing stuff all right, and Bridie told herself to take one day at a time. If the children at Oakengates were hers, then surely anyone could see they'd be better off with their natural mother, whatever situation she was in.

As they sat on the train on the first leg of their journey the next morning, Bridie told herself not to be so downhearted. God, more people than her lived in unsuitable accommodation in that war-ravaged city and they got by. She was sure she'd make the superintendent of the place see that she could cope.

Rosalyn had insisted they get up early and have a bath and change into fresh clothes. She said that looking smart would give Bridie confidence. 'You're going to run out of clothes at this rate,' Bridie said, struggling into another outfit of Rosalyn's.

'I might,' Rosalyn agreed. 'I shall have to buy more. I'll give Todd a call and tell him to release some money into my account.'

She didn't, in fact, need to call her husband for that; she could withdraw money at any time herself. But she was in a quandary over Christmas arrangements and she needed an excuse to phone Todd. He hadn't been happy with her returning to bomb-riddled Birmingham at all just because a friend she'd not seen or heard of for years was in a spot of bother. But as she seemed set on it, he expected her to spend the festive season with him. How could she leave Bridie to fend for herself? And yet her husband stared danger in the face night after night. She owed it to him to be by his side.

Todd certainly saw it that way and told Rosalyn

so forcibly. Rosalyn, however, said nothing to Bridie, feeling she had enough on her plate. When the ordeal at the orphanage was over, she'd perhaps have a better idea of how things stood.

The train soon left the city behind and they passed wide open countryside with fields of cows and others of sheep. Occasionally horses looked over the farm gates, watching the train pass. Except for the lack of hills, it could have been Donegal and Bridie felt a tug of homesickness.

The train pulled into Sutton Coldfield Station, and from there they had to take a Midland Red bus to the terminus past Four Oaks, where the conductor directed them further. 'It's a tidy step,' he said, pointing ahead. 'You go along that lane there for a mile or so. The place is on the left. Can't miss it.'

Rosalyn made a face. Her shoes were not made for trudging along muddy, country lanes in December. She said nothing, however; Bridie was already curled up as tight as a spring and so she took her arm and strode out boldly.

The conductor was right. No one could miss Oakengates, a huge and beautiful English manor house set in its own grounds. At the entrance to the drive, Bridie looked at Rosalyn a little fearfully. The sheer size and beauty of the place daunted her already fragile self-confidence.

Rosalyn gave her arm a squeeze. 'If your children are here, it's through no fault of yours. Hold on to that.'

'Do you know what struck me on the train?' Bridie said. 'You remember the doctor saying they had two children in after that raid who died? I so didn't want them to be mine that I never asked questions about them. Maybe this is all a wasted exercise – maybe they did die after all.'

'And maybe they didn't,' said Rosalyn, catching hold of her arm. 'Come on.'

The gravel crunched beneath their feet and to each side of the path, where once Bridie imagined had been green lawns, were vegetable patches. The house looked even more imposing close up and they went up the three white steps that led to a terrace that ran along the front of the house and tentatively rang the bell.

They were expected and were ushered straight into the Superintendent's Office. As they entered the room, he left his place behind the desk to welcome the women with a hand outstretched. 'I'm Doctor Havering,' he said. 'Which one of you made the phone call?'

'Me,' Bridie said. 'My name is Bridie Cassidy.'

'And you have reason to believe your children might be here?'

'Yes. The doctor in the Children's Hospital told us about the two wee children you had taken in here a day or so after the raid on 22nd November. A boy and girl, he said.'

'And what makes you think they're yours?'

'Just a feeling.'

'Wait a minute,' Rosalyn put in. 'Are they or

aren't they? Don't play cat and mouse with Bridie like this. Surely the children were able to tell you their names?'

'I'm not playing cat and mouse, believe me, Miss . . .'

'Mrs,' Rosalyn told the man firmly. 'Rosalyn Flemming. I'm Bridie's cousin.'

'Ah, well, Mrs Flemming. The problem, you see, is that the children have not yet spoken.'

'Not spoken,' Bridie said, aghast. She recalled that the doctor at the hospital had said the same, but she'd put that down to shock. But shock surely didn't last a month? 'They can't speak at all?'

'They can speak,' Doctor Havering said. 'Their vocal chords are intact. It's trauma that's brought it about.'

'Trauma!'

'The effects of the raid,' the doctor told her. 'Eventually, with treatment and time, they will recover. We have a psychiatric wing in the hospital annexe. Many children we take in are damaged in some way.'

'Wouldn't returning the children to their own mother help them?' Rosalyn asked.

The doctor ignored Rosalyn and directed the next question to Bridie. 'Mrs Cassidy, forgive me,' Doctor Havering said. 'But I have no proof you have any connection with these children at all. Have you any photographs, anything to prove your claim?'

Bridie took out her shelter bag and pulled out

the children's birth certificates and the photographs Ellen had taken. 'These are a little out of date now,' she said. 'Katie is six and Liam is just four.'

Doctor Havering knew that he was looking at the two children that he'd had in his psychiatric wing. The girl was so fine-boned and the boy so sturdy yet he'd thought them to be twins for they were the same size. He'd worked solidly to try and unlock their tortured minds, but while their physical injuries had healed, he'd been unsuccessful so far.

After almost three weeks they'd been physically well enough to rejoin the main wards of the hospital wing of the orphanage and he had hoped being with other children might help them to speak. To aid this process, he'd suggested separating the two and so Katie went into the girls' section and Liam to the boys'.

He had to admit now that this theory hadn't worked and if anything they'd become even more withdrawn. They sat, hour after hour, immobile and silent. The other children were puzzled and unnerved by them and so left them alone but not even that appeared to bother either of them. They seemed to be locked within themselves and he was sure they were in need of full-time professional psychiatric help. He himself was a doctor of psychology and if he'd had no success, what chance would a layperson have with them? But he needed to tread carefully – he could tell Bridie Cassidy was a desperate woman. 'Why has it taken you so long to track down your children, Mrs Cassidy?' he asked, returning the photographs and certificates to her.

'Is it them?' Bridie cried, barely hearing the man's words.

'Answer the question, please.'

Bridie sighed and began her story again, just as she'd told the doctor at the hospital. His reaction when she had told him how everything had happened had been sympathetic, but she could read no sympathy in Dr Havering's eyes. He just sat and looked at her until eventually she cried out, 'Now, for pity's sake, Doctor Havering, have you my children in your care?'

'I have two very sick children similar to those in the photograph,' Doctor Havering answered. 'It's hard to believe your little girl is six – she's so small – though now I can see the resemblance to you it's more understandable.'

The breath that Bridie hadn't been aware she was holding left her body in a great sigh of relief and she leapt to her feet. Her heart was singing. The man had spoken trauma, but she was sure anything could be cured once the children were back with her, where they belonged. She turned to Rosalyn, her face alight with joy. 'Rosalyn, they're alive! Alive! Oh God above, I can hardly believe it. All these days and weeks thinking of them as dead.'

Rosalyn ached for her. She and Todd had no children. They'd been married in March 1938, and when Rosalyn had raised the subject, Todd had said the world was too unstable to bring a child into. In 1939, when war was declared,

Rosalyn realised he'd been right, especially when he applied to join the Volunteer Air Force almost immediately. She didn't know how she'd have coped with what Bridie and many like her had endured. The rationing and the blackout were bad enough, but then so was the dilemma of what to do with your children. Some sent them to live with perfect strangers to try and save them, while others kept them at home, suffering the raids together. And what raids, what terror, what destruction!

She knew how Bridie was feeling now – the elation, the extreme joy – and yet she feared for her. She knew she had looked no further than finding the children alive and well and assumed then that she would take them home. Rosalyn very much doubted that this would be the case. Doctor Havering's next words confirmed her fears. 'Your children are not well enough to leave the orphanage yet,' he said. 'Now we have names for them we might make more headway, but for the time being you must leave them with the professionals.'

'Leave them?' Bridie said incredulously. 'But I can't leave them. They're my children – they should be with me.'

'Would you risk their mental health because of a selfish whim of your own?' the doctor rapped out. 'I don't think a court would uphold your claim.'

Bridie sank defeated into a chair. 'What are you saying?'

'I'm saying that, for the moment, your children are better left where they are,' the doctor said.

'When they are deemed fit for release, this will only be done if you are able to provide a suitable home for them.'

Bridie stared at him. 'A suitable home?' she replied incredulously. 'In a war-ravaged city? Don't make me laugh.'

'This is no laughing matter, Mrs Cassidy,' the doctor said gravely. 'That is the criteria which must be fulfilled before your children can be released from our care.'

Bridie stared at him and noticed the coldness in those blue eyes. He was authority and power – his word was law. She knew it and he knew it. 'Can I see them?' she pleaded.

'Would that really be fair?' the doctor said. 'That could do more damage than ever, I feel.'

Bridie's bleak eyes sought Rosalyn's sympathetic ones and Rosalyn stepped forward and held tight to Bridie's arm. 'Can we come again?' Bridie asked.

'I hardly think . . .' the doctor began as Rosalyn hissed at him, 'For God's sake, if you've a heart at all, use it.'

''Phone us after Christmas,' the doctor said. 'And we'll tell you how things stand.'

Rosalyn was aware how despondent Bridie was and to cheer her a little on the way home she said, 'You'll have good news to tell your Tom now anyway.'

Bridie turned sorrowful eyes to Rosalyn. 'Have I?'

'Of course you have,' Rosalyn said impatiently.

'Up until a few days ago, you thought your children were dead, crushed or blown to pieces. Now you know they are not. Okay, they're damaged by their ordeal and no wonder, but they'll recover. Children are very resilient. Tom has the right to be told his children are alive.

'All right,' Bridie conceded. 'I know that really and I will write to him tonight. I just wish I had something more definite to tell him.'

That evening, as promised, she sat down and wrote a letter to Tom she'd hardly dared imagine she ever would.

> *Dear Tom*
> *I have some amazing news for you. Our children are alive! Can you believe it after all this time? They were taken out of the ruins of the house before I got there and with them being so small, they were taken to the children's hospital rather than the General. They were sent from there to the hospital wing of an orphanage in a a place called Four Oaks, where I tracked them down. The children have been ill, traumatised from their ordeal and not yet ready to leave hospital, but I thought you should know as soon as possible. I will write more later. Tell Eddie the good news if you can.*
> *Love Bridie*

Rosalyn scanned the letter before Bridie sent it and

could understand why she'd told Tom so little. She said nothing, but as if she had spoken, Bridie said, 'If I'd told Tom how it really is, what could he do but worry? I don't want him to do that. Christ, hasn't he enough to worry about as it is?'

'I know,' Rosalyn replied. 'But this is bound to buck him up.'

It did more than buck Tom up. He gave a whoop of joy as he read Bridie's words. Tell Eddie she had said. Tom had the desire to tell the whole damned world, have it announced all over the camp, stuck to the notice board at the NAAFI. But the news filtered through the camp anyway and every one of the men was genuinely pleased for Tom. Most were family men themselves and they all worried about their loved ones back home, knowing in this war it wasn't only fighting men at risk. When Tom and Eddie had returned after their funerals, both men broken by tragedy, many suffered with them and now they rejoiced with Tom.

The following day, as they ate dinner in a city centre café after visiting Jay, Rosalyn broached the news to Bridie that she would be staying with Todd for Christmas. At first, Bridie had been horrified that Rosalyn was to leave her over Christmas: Rosalyn had been the one who'd pulled her out of the mire, bullied her into cleaning herself up and evaluating her life, before helping her search for her children. But when she heard Rosalyn's voice as she talked of Todd and saw the light shining in her eyes, she realised she was selfish to expect Rosalyn to spend Christmas with her when her husband, who she so obviously loved, was just a few miles away, especially as her man was in the front line. The Battle of Britain might be won, but young pilots were losing their lives daily.

Wouldn't she have given her right arm to have Tom beside her this minute? But the memories of Tom's few days with her after the children's presumed death disturbed her. She'd pushed Tom away instead of drawing him to her so they could take comfort from one another. She'd make it up to him, though. She'd write a letter as soon as possible and tell him how much she loved and missed him, before telling him of the children's survival.

But that was for later. This was now and Rosalyn was looking at her with wary, anxious eyes, awaiting her response. Bridie knew she had to lie and make it seem as if she'd already made plans for the Christmas period and say it in such a way that Rosalyn would believe it. 'Well, that's just grand,' she said to her cousin. 'For I've already made arrangements to help out at the hospital. I thought it would help Jay too to have one of his own beside him. It will be the first of many Christmases without his mother. I know my parents will make it special for Mickey, but I'd not like Jay to be on his own.'

In fact, Bridie had made no such arrangements. Before Rosalyn's arrival, she'd viewed the Christmas with dread. She'd been determined that she wouldn't take part in the festivities, but stay in bed in her dreary room and let the season go on without her. Now, she saw she could do as she'd claimed and lend a hand at the hospital. They were always glad of help, especially at holiday times when there was less staff in.

CHAPTER TWENTY-THREE

Bridie went to visit Jay in hospital early the next day after Rosalyn had left. They'd told him all that had transpired at the orphanage the day after the visit, playing it down so that he wouldn't get too upset. But it was obvious he'd been lying in bed thinking about it because his first question to her was, 'Why didn't Katie and Liam say who they was in the beginning? Then they'd have found you, like, wouldn't they, and you wouldn't have been so sad?'

'They were in shock and couldn't speak, Jay. That was part of the sickness,' Bridie said.

'You mean they was sick in the head?' Jay asked.

'In a way.'

'And they still are?'

'Aye,' Bridie said with a sigh. 'They're still sick.'

'Daint they even speak to you?'

'I wasn't allowed to see them.'

'Why not?'

Bridie shrugged, and Jay saw her eyes glistening

with unshed tears and heard the catch in her voice as she replied, 'They said . . . the doctor said it would upset them too much.'

That was daft, anyone would know it was daft and yet to say so would only upset Bridie further and that was the last thing he wanted to do. Besides, he told himself, at least Katie and Liam are alive and that had to be better than being dead. However sick they were, they'd recover in time.

And so he said nothing more about the children and instead revealed proudly, 'They're dead pleased about my arm, by the way. They say I might have the plaster off in the New Year, then I can have crutches and get about a bit more.'

Bridie knew being still didn't sit well on Jay's shoulders and so she was pleased.

'When that happens, I can go to Ireland to my grandma and granddad's,' Jay told her eagerly. 'You'll take me, Auntie Bridie, won't you?'

'Aye, of course I will,' Bridie assured him. 'As soon as the hospital say you are fit to travel. I promised your daddy and it's what your mammy wanted too.'

Jay didn't want to dwell on his mother. He still wept about if he thought about her too much. He decided to steer the conversation around to Ireland. 'I can't wait to see them all again on the farm,' he said. 'I bet our Mickey's getting dead spoilt. He needs me there to knock him into touch.'

Bridie laughed. 'You and whose army?' she said.

'He'll soon have you off those crutches if you start throwing your weight around.'

'Huh,' Jay said with a grin. 'Like to see him try.'

'What can you remember about the farm and all?' Bridie asked. 'Not much I expect. You were quite small last time you were over.'

But Jay surprised her, for he remembered a great deal and she recalled how he used to trail after her father as she'd done as a small child.

'I loved that place,' Jay said now with a sigh. 'I used to ask to go every year. I'm going to live somewhere like that when I grow up.'

'Who knows where any of us will be by that time,' Bridie said. 'The war will be over certainly and your daddy and Tom back home and, please God, the world will be a better, more peaceful place altogether.'

'Do you believe that?'

'I have to believe it, otherwise all those who died did so in vain.'

'I know,' Jay said glumly.

'Come on, cheer up,' Bridie said, wanting to lift his despondency. 'It's Christmas Eve tomorrow. For one day at least let's believe in 'Peace and goodwill to all men.''

'Even Germans?'

'Even them at Christmas,' Bridie said with a smile. 'The angels didn't make exceptions.'

'All right,' Jay said. 'When you come over to the hospital, I'll be all sweetness and light.'

He was incredibly grateful to Bridie for offering

to help out at the hospital on Christmas Day and Boxing Day and the nurses jumped at the chance of an extra pair of hands. Jay knew they worked hard and would do their best to make the day special, particularly for the younger patients, and they had already made the ward looked very festive indeed. And yet he didn't want to spend Christmas alone just with the nurses. He knew it would be a time when he would remember his mother and he would be frightened of crying in front of everybody and spoiling their day too. He had to remember that some kids had more to put up with than he had.

When his aunt left that night he lay back on his bed and thought how good she had been with him. He didn't know if he'd have coped so well if she hadn't been to see him as often as she had. It was a pity, he thought, that she wasn't really happy and that having found her children alive and well, after thinking them dead for a month, they were still being kept apart. He shut his eyes tight and prayed earnestly that things might work out well for his aunt – for all of them – in the New Year.

On the way home, fired with enthusiasm, Bridie bought a lot of cleaning materials, plus her rations from the grocery shop near the Mission where she'd eventually registered. She arrived in at the attic out of breath, her arms nearly pulled out of their sockets, and shut the door behind her with a snap. She looked about the room: the whole place needed painting and repapering and although she wouldn't be able to do that, she could give it a thorough going over. She felt ashamed of the way she'd let it go.

She made herself a cup of tea and then set to work with a will, boiling kettle upon kettle of water, which she had to fetch in buckets from the tap on the landing below. She didn't stop until the place looked brighter and fresher and the musty smell had been overridden by one of polish and cleaning fluid.

She made herself a Spam sandwich and looked around again, wondering how she could make the place more suitable for her two children if she could get nothing better. With the furniture rearranged, she could possibly squeeze another bed in – they could sleep together while they were small – but would they deem that satisfactory enough? She didn't know.

She got up and fingered the flimsy curtains at the two windows and her fingers came away grubby, but she was afraid to wash them – it was probably the dirt holding them together. Maybe she could make new ones now she'd had Tom's pay. She remembered the bright curtains she'd made for the house in Grant Street and the cushion covers she'd made to match with the remnants left over.

It seemed a lifetime ago. And there wasn't the incentive now when the windows had to be shuttered for hours on end, sometimes from the afternoon if the day was dark enough to need the lights on. Anyway, she couldn't see the authorities or anyone else being swayed in their decision by bright curtains alone.

After she'd eaten, she seemed filled with energy again, unable to sit still, and so she began to wash the clothes Rosalyn had left in a heap in the corner of the kitchenette, draping them around the room to dry them off. Tomorrow, she promised herself, she would get something to hang the clothes properly. Then she'd go along to the Mission hall and look through the clothes bins – she couldn't wear Rosalyn's clothes for ever and dared not embarrass Jay by turning up at the hospital on Christmas Day in rags.

She had a wonderful day at the Bull Ring and found a collapsible clotheshorse in the Rag Market. She then queued for two hours for one orange and a banana, which she would take to Jay in the morning. She'd already bought him a couple of comics and a copy of the book *Kidnapped*. Jay was no keener on reading than he ever had been, but it would be some time before his leg was healed enough to give him full mobility. Anyway, she hoped the adventure story would appeal to him because there was precious little else in the shops to buy.

She called into the Mission hall on the way home. Father Flynn was delighted that she'd found the children alive, but incensed that they couldn't be returned to her. 'They explained that they're still ill,' Bridie said.

'And wouldn't any wee child be ill separated from its mother?' Father Flynn said. 'By rights they should have been taken to the Roman Catholic Home, Father Hudson's in Coleshill.'

'They didn't know they were Catholics, nor anything about them, not even their names until I called,' Bridie said. 'They've not spoken, you see. They say they are traumatised, in shock.'

'After Christmas is over I will try my hardest to find somewhere more suitable to live and then, if Katie and Liam are better, they might be returned to me. Until then I've told everyone to address their letters here. Is that all right?'

'Of course it's all right, my dear,' the priest said. 'And I'm glad you said that for I have some here for you delivered this very day and I might easily have forgotten to give them to you. I have a memory like a sieve these days.'

Tom had sent another pay cheque, together with a card and a little packet, and her mother a card which had a note inside saying how well Mickey had settled down and asking for news. There was another from Terry with a twenty-dollar bill and a note urging her to buy something for herself to cheer her up.

'If only it were that easy,' Bridie said, with a rueful glance at the priest. 'I'll have to write to him and the others too and tell them about the children being found alive. Mammy wrote and told them the tragic news of that night. They all sent cards – condolence cards as well as Mass cards.

Tom read them out to me, but I couldn't look at them.'

'Aye indeed,' Father Flynn said. 'By the way, do you want to look in the clothes bins while you're here?'

'I intended to,' Bridie said. 'But I honestly don't think I could carry much more.' She eyed the bags doubtfully and the clotheshorse tied with a small piece of string.

'Well,' he said at last, 'I'll help you carry them back. Come on, my dear, let's find you something to wear for the festive season.'

Bridie was grateful to the priest helping her and yet she was embarrassed of her attic room, for all it was now clean. 'Sorry about the clothes draped everywhere, Father,' she said, snatching up the damp things. 'I had nowhere to put them to dry, you see, that's why I bought the clotheshorse.'

'Don't worry, my dear,' Father Flynn said. 'I'm not here to inspect or judge you.'

But he knew with a sinking heart that others would and doubted Bridie would ever have her children returned to her while she lived there. He communicated none of these thoughts to Bridie, however, for in his opinion she had enough on her plate already.

There was no festive cheer in the place at all, bar the three cards which she had placed on the mantelpiece near the one Rosalyn had given her before she'd left. He thought of the people at the Mission and of the children so excited at the thought of Christmas. They'd spent ages festooning the place with paper chains they'd made and he'd unearthed a tree from pre-war days that they'd decorated with all manner of baubles.

But in this cold bare room there was no sign of Christmas. Thank God, Father Flynn thought, Bridie was spending two days at the hospital; spending any length of time in that drab attic would depress anyone.

The next day, after Mass, Bridie went straight to the hospital. Under her coat she wore a woollen costume in deep lilac which had been left in the clothes box for it would fit no one else. Fashionable black boots over her dainty feet covered up her heavy duty lisle stockings. At her neck she'd fastened the brooch which was Tom's present to her, bought because the bronze stone in the centre had reminded him of the colour of her hair, he'd explained in the letter.

Jay was overjoyed to see her, and so moved by the orange, banana and book that he felt tears well up in his eyes. Bridie found Father Christmas had already been around the wards with a present for each child, donated by American children, and Jay had received a paint box, brushes and a sketch pad.

Bridie had a wonderful Christmas Day and Boxing Day in the hospital and she was honoured to be part of it. She'd helped wherever help was needed, awed by the stoical courage and cheerfulness she saw in people, and especially in the children badly injured, some of whom had lost all those dear to them. It helped put her own life in perspective and she decided from that point to concentrate on those she had left to her, primarily Mary's sons and her own children, her dear husband Tom and brother-in-law Eddie, and her parents. She was well blessed.

Having decided that in her mind, she shelved her problems for the next two days and threw herself into the festivities planned with such enthusiasm that one young nurse remarked, after seeing her organise a children's game, 'You're a natural, you are. Don't suppose you could come on a regular basis?'

She could, but at that time all Bridie's thoughts and energies were concentrated on Katie and Liam and getting them home where they belonged and so she had to shake her head regretfully.

She returned to her attic room on the evening of 27th December and found a letter from Tom on the mat. She'd intended to write to both him and Eddie that night before she went to bed but was pleased to find another letter from him had arrived before she had the chance to do so.

> My dear, dear Bridie
> What wonderful, marvellous news. You're right – I can scarcely believe it. People at the camp say I'm going around with a permanent smile on my face, like a dog with two tails, but

I can't help but be overjoyed. I know how hard
everything has been for you – you've had to
bear the brunt of it all.

There are not words enough to tell you how
much I love you and how I long to be with you
this minute and hold you and our children in
my arms and never let anything bad happen to
any of you again.

All I can do though is fight this damned war.
Tell the children I love them and write and give
me news of them when you can.

My love now and always,
Tom

Bridie sat with the letter in her hand as the tears
seeped from her eyes and she put her head down
on the table and let the sobs overtake her. Oh God,
she thought, he'd like to hold his children, well so
would I.

She was too sad after she'd finished weeping to
write to either Tom or Eddie, feeling sure that Tom
at least would pick up on her mood. She couldn't
run the risk of him fretting. This was something she
had to deal with, without involving Tom at all. She
was glad though that Rosalyn would be joining her
again the next day and knew she would give her all
the support she could.

By the time Rosalyn arrived, Bridie had all her
clothes ironed and folded, ready to pack, and a
stiffer resolve to accompany her to the orphanage.

How dare anyone dictate to her when she would see her children!

That night, though, she cowered with Rosalyn in a public shelter as a raid pummelled the city and wondered if she'd dared bring the children back to this danger. Maybe they were better where they were for now. But in any case she should be allowed to see them. She ached for the sight and sound of them and the chance to hold them close against her.

'I don't think I'd bring the children back to this sort of thing, even if I was permitted,' she told Rosalyn. 'If I did and anything else happened to them, I'd never forgive myself. Peggy McKenna would have had her way at last.'

'Peggy McKenna?' Rosalyn said and, unaware of the hornet's nest she had disturbed, went on unperturbed. 'Wasn't she the eldest daughter of the Maguires? Her husband was in a bit of bother after the partition of Ireland, wasn't he?'

Bridie confused, tried to parry Rosalyn's questions. 'I don't know, I can't remember.'

'You must, Bridie. She was older than us, even older than your Mary, but it was the talk of the place when she just upped and left one day, and her in line for the farm and all,' Rosalyn said. 'Then the Garda went after them – you must remember that – and then the army, and everyone was saying someone had tipped the Maguires the wink and good luck to them, whoever they were.'

'I was but a child, Rosalyn.'

'I was only a year older and I remember it,' Rosalyn protested. 'Mary told me one time when she was home that she'd ended up living near her in Birmingham and her name was McKenna now. You even mentioned her yourself after you were at Mary's that first time. Why did you say she'd get her way at last?'

Bridie looked around the shelter. The 'all clear' had sounded and people were streaming out, but still Rosalyn and Bridie sat facing each other.

'Not now,' Bridie said, but Rosalyn knew if she left it there, Bridie would never speak and she knew what she had to say was worth hearing.

'We'll never get a better chance,' she said.

'I don't want to tell you.'

'I know that,' Rosalyn said. 'But I feel you must.'

'You don't even know what I am to say,' Bridie cried in agitation. 'Leave it, for God's sake, as it's been left for years.'

Rosalyn leaned forward and grasped Bridie's hand and felt the shudder running through her cousin. Something dreadful had happened to her and suddenly the blood in her own veins ran like ice and she felt a thread of apprehension trail like a frozen finger down her spine.

The shelter was almost empty now, and Rosalyn leant forward and whispered to Bridie, 'Has this business anything to do with my father?'

The panic with which Bridie jumped and the cry that escaped from her lips told its own story.

Rosalyn's arms went around Bridie's shaking body as she said urgently, 'Tell me, Bridie, for God's sake. I need to know.'

Bridie looked at the friend she'd known all her life, that she'd cast aside because of her father, and knew she ran the risk of throwing away her friendship and support and for ever if she did as she urged. She was frightened. Rosalyn was all she had now and, oh, how she needed a friend. 'Rosalyn, I can't tell you,' she cried. Tears poured from her eyes as she said brokenly and almost in a whisper, 'I'm frightened to tell you.'

Rosalyn was moved beyond measure by her cousin's distress, but still she insisted, 'I need to know, Bridie.'

Bridie looked steadily at her cousin and knew that now she'd gone this far, she had to tell her the rest. Neither woman bothered about the all clear continuing to sound its reassuring noise through the city, nor the people streaming past them in the shelter. Bridie at last began to speak.

She started from as far back as she could really remember: the death of Robert and Nuala and the consideration and love shown to the grieving little girl by her aunt and uncle. She went on to recount little instances in their lives, growing up together.

And then Bridie's voice changed. It became wary, watchful, even scared, as she described Francis's first advance towards her and the next and the next.

Rosalyn didn't doubt a word of what Bridie

said. Wasn't that really what she'd been dreading hearing all these years?

But Bridie went on, anxious now to unburden herself of a weight of guilt and shame that she felt unable to bear alone anymore. When she described the rape, she scarcely felt Rosalyn's nails dig into her skin, for she was back in the wood in the North of Ireland, fighting and pleading with her uncle. Rosalyn felt her pain, revulsion and shame.

Worse was to come: Francis's denial of any guilt and then Bridie's subsequent realisation that she was pregnant, her flight to England and her panic-riddled abortion. And then to cap it all, Peggy McKenna finding out about the unwanted child and the years of blackmail because of it, the money she'd extracted from her and the curses she'd put on the children, which Bridie thought had come true when she'd feared them dead.

'She's dead herself now,' she said. 'But with her dying breath she told me that "God will have his revenge." Rosalyn, the woman was evil.' But she wasn't the only one; Francis too had been evil and whatever else he'd been he was still Rosalyn's father. She lowered her head and muttered, 'I'm sorry, Rosalyn.'

Rosalyn lifted her head up and Bridie saw the tear trails running down her cousin's face and replied, 'Don't be.'

'Do you believe me?'

'Every word.'

Bridie relaxed for a moment, and then thought

of what Rosalyn had said. Francis was her father – if anyone had made a similar accusation against Jimmy McCarthy, Bridie wouldn't have believed it, not in a hundred years would she believe it, and so she asked hesitantly, 'Why do you?'

'Because it's not the first time,' Rosalyn said. 'Oh not with me, don't think that, but with other girls, young girls, I mean as young as you were. Mammy knew, but – well, she was married and in the Catholic Church and had standing in the community. If she'd admitted Daddy had strayed since the day of his marriage, many would think it must have been her fault.'

Bridie digested all Rosalyn said and knew it to be the truth. 'I can't believe she knew and did nothing.'

'What could she do? You know what it was like back then?'

'But I . . .'

'She never knew about you,' Rosalyn cried in distress. 'Oh she never, ever thought that you were in any danger. She thought your relationship to Daddy would protect you. She never imagined for a minute . . . Oh God, Bridie, I don't know what to say, how my family can ever make up to you for what you've suffered.'

'Did you hear what I said, Rosalyn? I was having a baby and I had it aborted – I am sinful.'

'Don't talk bullshit!' Rosalyn cut in. 'The only bloody sinner in this is my bugger of a father. Don't you see you're the victim here, you bloody fool!'

'Do you mean that?'

''Course I mean it,' Rosalyn said. 'Christ, Bridie, Mammy would rather have cut off her right arm than to have that happen to you. She wrote and told me about Daddy when I was settled in America, no details you know, just that he was unfaithful and had been so from the first day of their marriage and that he liked his conquests young. I suppose she just had to tell someone and with me being married and all, perhaps she thought I'd be the best person. Anyway, for whatever reason she told me about Daddy. Then in the early winter of 1938 she wrote again and told me Daddy had been interfering with young Connie since the spring. She wasn't fourteen until the autumn and had suffered for months before plucking up the courage to say anything. Mammy wrote to me straightaway. I suppose I was the only one she felt she could confide in.'

Bridie was shocked to the core. For a man to do that sort of thing and to his own daughter! She sensed there was more, but Rosalyn seemed to hesitate. 'Go on,' she urged.

'I will,' Rosalyn said. 'But you must promise to tell no one. Mammy's life hangs in the balance.'

'When have I ever told secrets on you?'

'Never,' Rosalyn said. 'You're the one person in the world I can always trust. And I'll trust you with this. Mammy has told me since that she went about like a mad woman. The whole tale spilled out of her when I came home in mid-December. I think she was glad to have someone to tell, for she was too ashamed to share the news of her husband abusing his own daughter. Anyway, as things turned out, it was better that she'd confided in no one.'

'Why?'

'I'll tell you why,' Rosalyn said. 'All the years of her marriage, Mammy had turned a blind eye to Daddy's philandering but never in a million years did she think he'd do that to one of his own. Daddy was often out at night. We were all well used to it, but the night after Connie told Mammy, just after she'd written to me, she tailed him to McCluskie's barn and saw him in there, lying in the straw, himself and the young girl with him only half-dressed. She was the daughter of a neighbouring farmer and young too, not much older than Connie. Mammy said a rage built up inside her, both for the years of torture she'd endured and the lives of the young girls he'd interfered with and worse, many may be traumatised or damaged for life, and now too for her own violated daughter. It was the final straw.

'He hadn't seen her, she's made sure of that, so she started in the direction of home and laid in wait for Daddy. She knew roughly the time he'd be back, and because she was no match for him, she had a branch of wood in her hand. Daddy was taken unawares. He was lilting a tune to himself and staggering a little, because he'd taken more than a drop, and when the branch hit him full in the face, he overbalanced and fell in the ditch. She said there was blood everywhere. He was only semi-conscious and she fell upon him, punching him and scratching his face.

'She left him lying there alive – groaning, she said, but alive – and expected him to stagger home later. But the branch must have done more damage than she'd thought, or he was too drunk to climb out, but either way, next morning, his stiff, dead body was discovered still in the ditch.'

Bridie's mouth dropped open. 'Aunt Delia killed him!'

'Aye, she did,' Rosalyn said. 'But she didn't mean to kill him. She wanted to teach him a lesson just. But you see what people would make of it if they knew what had really happened. His infidelities would be passed off as a man's weakness. You'd never get girls to publicly say what he'd done to them, for their names and their families would be mud after it. If she'd confessed, Mammy would have hung. And for what? A pervert who preyed on the young? I didn't know it all when I heard of his death, of course, but I knew enough; I knew about Connie and the others by then. I couldn't bring myself to come home for his funeral. I couldn't have borne everyone saying how great he was. If I'd known of Mammy's part in his death, I'd have come to give her some support, but I didn't find that out until much later. Didn't you wonder at my not being there?'

'Aye,' said Bridie. 'Mary and I thought you'd got above yourself. Now I understand.' But she couldn't really credit her aunt Delia with doing such a thing. To kill a man – God! 'Did no one suspect her?' she asked.

'Apparently not,' Rosalyn said. 'When he was found dead the next day, Mammy was beside herself with guilt which everyone put down to grief. The gypsies were seen in the area and that was that. The blame was laid at their door and Mammy got away with it.'

'Who knows?'

'No one,' Rosalyn said. 'No one but me and you. She hadn't even confessed to the priest – well, she could hardly go to Clar Chapel, or even Donegal Town. I mean they'd know who she was talking about. There aren't men dying every week over there, like there are in New York. I know they cannot tell anyone, but they'd know Mammy was responsible and she couldn't have borne that. That was the only thing that worried her.'

Bridie knew she'd worry over that too. 'What did she do?'

'She came with me as far as Derry when I was coming here to see you – told them all at home she fancied a day shopping with me before I caught the train to Belfast. Instead, we toured around the place until we found a Catholic Church that took confessions that day. Mammy was in and out like a dose of salts. The priest tried to give her a hard time, she said, but she wouldn't answer questions. He couldn't have followed her, for he had queues waiting on him, but we hightailed it out of there as soon as he'd given her absolution.'

'What a thing, though, to have on your conscience.'

'Aye,' Rosalyn said. 'And yet she'd come to terms with that by the time I'd come home. I never knew a thing about the way Daddy was until she told me. I loved him dearly, we all did, but for Mammy it must have been Hell for years.'

'My Mammy told me one time that Francis wasn't an easy man and that Delia had a time of it. I asked her what she meant, but she clammed up. She'd sort of let it slip out and regretted it straightaway.'

'Maybe Mammy confided in her?'

'Maybe.'

'Now that's what you must do.'

'What?'

'Tell your mother what happened and from the beginning, like you did with me.'

'I couldn't.'

'You must!' Rosalyn insisted. 'Set the record straight before it's too late.'

'But, Daddy . . .'

'Let your mother be the judge of whether to tell him or not,' Rosalyn said. 'But tell Auntie Sarah, for there's a constant sadness behind her eyes and Mammy said it's been there since you left. She can't understand it and it's left her hurt and confused. Don't leave her like that, Bridie.'

'She'll not believe me.'

'She will,' Rosalyn persisted. 'And Mammy and I will back you up anyway. She really needs to know.'

'You don't think she'll hate me?'

'Not at all. Why should she?'

'Oh, you know.'

'I don't know,' Rosalyn burst out. 'Stop blaming yourself and put Auntie Sarah out of her misery.'

Bridie remembered the love her mother and father had showered on her for years and now, though her mother was friendly enough, there was still a reserve that had never been there before.

'I'll do it,' she told Rosalyn. 'I'll tell her everything when I take Jay over to stay with them. But now I must make arrangements to see the children.'

A week later, Bridie was no nearer seeing the children. Any attempt she made to arrange a visit was blocked and she was at first angry and then despondent.

Twice that week the sirens had disturbed them and this stiffened Bridie's resolve to look for somewhere on the outskirts of the city to live once she'd delivered Jay into her mother's care. She visited him every day, and was as pleased as he was when the plaster from his arm was removed. After a week's physiotherapy on the arm, he was given crutches. 'Won't be long now till I go to Ireland,' Jay told her, his face shining. 'I'm going to practise every day.'

'You do that,' Bridie said encouragingly. 'I'm sure you'll soon get the hang of it. I bet by the time Rosalyn comes back you'll be getting along faster than either of us.'

She was glad she'd made Jay smile, she thought as she returned to her depressing room that evening. She missed Rosalyn already and she'd only been gone a few hours – off to visit Todd – before returning to help Bridie transport Jay to Ireland when the doctors gave him the 'all clear'.

'Don't come back here,' Todd told his young wife. 'It's just too bloody dangerous. God, I'd rather have you in back home in the States than here, much as I'd miss you.'

Rosalyn didn't argue with her husband. She knew he was concerned because he loved her and she didn't want him worried about her. She'd heard inattentiveness led to lack of concentration and that could sign a person's death warrant in the skies. Yet she didn't know if she had it in her to just up and leave Bridie. But she wouldn't spoil the precious time she had with Todd arguing about it either. She decided that when she got to Ireland, she'd see how the land lay and make her decision then.

Bridie was finding time hanging heavy on her hands that night and before she went to bed, she made a decision. The following morning she would make her way to the orphanage. She wouldn't ring for an appointment she'd never get, she'd just turn up and then see what they'd do about it.

CHAPTER TWENTY-FOUR

Dr Havering faced Bridie across the desk. He was furious with the woman for just turning up like this and wouldn't have agreed to see her at all if he'd been given a chance to think about it.

He was worried enough about her children, as they'd seemed to have gone backwards since the New Year. They'd had no sessions with him until then, when he'd seen them both, but separately, and for the first time used their names.

Katie's eyes opened wide and her mouth dropped, but she didn't speak.

'Well, that is your name isn't it, Katie?'

There was no answer, no response of any kind, and so the doctor said, 'I know it is. Someone told me.'

Katie wondered who that was, who would know, but she wouldn't ask, she'd say nothing to this man with the hard, cold, blue eyes that the smile never reached. She refused to play his stupid games and she fixed her eyes on the wall and clamped her lips tight. The doctor had the feeling that Katie had climbed into a glass box and pulled the lid down. She could be seen, but not reached; it was as if she'd switched herself off.

Liam's reaction had been even worse. He was terrified of the man and had begun to shake violently when he'd called him by name. He didn't dare cry – he didn't know what they'd do to him if he cried – but since then he seemed to have lost control of his bladder and bowels. He'd also started to suck his thumb again and rock from side to side, wherever he was.

Dr Havering began to wonder if he had the specialist skills to deal with such disturbed children and whether they wouldn't be better being committed to the children's wing of an asylum, such as Moneyhall. Now here was the children's wretched mother pushing her way in, uninvited. 'This is very irregular, Mrs Cassidy.'

'So is not allowing me access to my children.'

'We are not denying you access. Your children are under our care. They are showing severe behavioural problems at the moment. It is my professional opinion that it would be detrimental for your children's health if they were to see you now.'

'Do they even know I'm alive? That I've been searching for them? That I visit this place and beg for a glimpse of the children I bore?' Bridie's voice rose hysterically.

'Please calm yourself, Mrs Cassidy. Hysteria will not help the problem.'

'What will?'

'Let us approach this logically,' the doctor said. 'If these sick, disturbed children should be released into your care, where would they live? Where do you live at present?'

'I rent an attic room in a house. I've measured it and if I rearranged everything, I could get a small bed for them to share.'

'Children need more than a bed, Mrs Cassidy.'

'I know that,' Bridie said. 'It would only be for a wee while. I'd really like something on the edge of the city and I will go on until I get somewhere decent and safe.'

'Have you a husband?'

'Yes. He's away fighting like plenty more.'

'So your funds are limited and your housing inadequate for the children's needs. What good will it do seeing them? You can promise them nothing and when you go again, they will be more bereft than ever.'

Was he right? Bridie wondered. It sounded so plausible the way he said it. She didn't know that the children were unhappy here and at least they were having treatment and were safe from any bombing raids. Was she selfish to wish to see them when at the end of it she'd have to leave them behind? Would it actually be as detrimental as he claimed?

So many conflicting thoughts filled Bridie's head, but the uppermost one was that she must do nothing to make life even harder for her children so that when Dr Havering said, 'Come, come now, Mrs Cassidy, as I've said before leave it to the professionals. Believe me, it will be in the children's best interests in the end,' she found herself not only standing up, but actually shaking the man's hand.

It was as the front door closed behind her that she felt angry. Just how feeble was she? However professional these people were, did they love her children like she did? Every time she thought of them, she felt the pain of loss, her arms ached for the feel of them and her heart felt as heavy as lead. She was only half a person without them.

There was no access to the orphanage from the front without being seen and Bridie knew, at that moment, she was probably being watched by Dr Havering to see that she actually walked up the gravel path and out of the gate.

Once there, though, she stood and pondered. The house was in its own grounds, but those grounds must end somewhere: abutting farmland maybe, onto a lane, or perhaps the outlying houses of the village. Somewhere.

She began to skirt the hall and at the end of a lane she found what she was looking for, enclosed by a chain link fence with a large notice claiming that 'Trespassers would be prosecuted'. That didn't worry Bridie; she didn't want to break in, just look, and so she followed the fence around.

Eventually she came to a grassy hill. Above it on a Tarmacked yard, boys rushed about playing football, all dressed in blue jerseys, short blue trousers, long grey socks and black boots. Bridie shivered inside her coat and wondered why none of the children had one on themselves. People said children didn't feel the cold but Bridie knew that was rubbish. She'd felt the cold all right when she was younger. All the boys were much bigger than Liam and Bridie assumed the little one's playing area would probably be nearer the house.

There was a brick wall cutting the playground in half further on and on the other side of this were the girls from the orphanage, dressed similarly to the boys in blue jerseys, skirts, grey socks and black boots. They all looked so alike, Bridie wondered if she'd recognise Katie even if she was there.

But she did. She stuck out like a sore thumb. Some of the girls were skipping or hopping, or playing with balls, or participating in a variation of tag. Katie just stood there. No one went near her. She was totally alone. She was so still she might have been a statue and looked as if she'd stood for hours in the raw cold. Bridie's heart ached for her child, who was exuding unhappiness and confusion. She hadn't meant to speak – she just wanted to catch sight of them – but Bridie's lips formed the word 'Katie'.

It was so softly said, yet the child heard it and swung around instantly. For a second, their eyes met. Bridie asked herself afterwards what she'd expected: that Katie rush towards her with an exclamation of delight? Probably. What she didn't expect was for Katie to open her mouth and let out a piercing scream and another and another.

It stopped the children's games. Most screams would do that but for that sound to come from the silent Katie made it even more interesting. Nurses and attendants came running from the house and neither they nor the children saw the figure tear herself away from the child screaming at the sight of her, tears streaming down her face.

But Katie hadn't screamed at the sight of her mother; she'd screamed because she knew it couldn't be her mother and it was in her imagination. If her mother was there, wouldn't she take her and Liam away from this place? When she had looked again there was no one there. And so she had screamed and went on screaming until she fell to the floor in a faint. The doctor pushed his way through the cluster of children grouped around the child lying on the ground. 'Come away! Come away!' he said crossly. 'Nurse, do something with these gawping children.'

The children were shooed from the scene and then he picked up the inert child and took her to the infirmary. Leaving her in the nurses' care he went into his office and dialled the number for Moneyhall.

Bridie said nothing about visiting the orphanage. She couldn't bring it to her own mind without thinking of the reaction she'd evoked in her own child and she felt she couldn't tell that to anyone.

She told Jay, when he asked, that the children were coming along fine now and would probably be leaving the place soon. Had Jay not been so excited about leaving hospital himself, he'd have realised she was lying.

She decided, for Jay's sake, that she would try and put her worries and frustrations about her own children on hold for the time it took to take him home and settle him in. She wouldn't let her sadness intrude on what she was sure would be a traumatic time for him.

It was very emotional time that day in mid-February when Jay said goodbye to the nurses and doctors who'd cared for him for so many weeks. The doctors were content to shake him by the hand, but many of the nurses gave him a hug and one pressed a comic into his hand; two even gave him a bar of chocolate, scarce since rationing. He passed the things to Bridie so that he could use his crutches to get to the waiting taxi, spurning the wheelchair he was offered.

Bridie looked across as Jay eased himself along the taxi seat. 'All right?'

'Sort of,' Jay said. 'I'm all messed up inside. I mean I really wanted to leave the hospital – I've been thinking about it, dreaming about it for weeks and now, but . . .' He struggled to explain. 'I'm kind of scared of leaving. I still want to go to the farm and Ireland and that though.'

'It's bound to be a wrench, Jay,' Bridie said consolingly. 'After all, you were there weeks. You must have got to know the doctors and nurses quite well.'

Jay nodded. 'Yeah, I did. But it's not the same as being home.'

Both Bridie and Rosalyn saw the shadow pass over Jay's face at the word 'home' and Bridie also noticed how bright his eyes were behind those long black lashes. She guessed the word home brought back thoughts of his mother but also knew to sympathise with him wouldn't help. It might even make him cry and she knew he'd hate to do that in front of Rosalyn.

So instead she said, 'You'll be fit and strong in no time now you're on the mend. Daddy will be glad of an extra pair of hands. He'll have you at the milking before you know where you are, let me tell you.'

Catching Bridie's mood, Jay said scornfully, 'Huh, our Mickey does that already because he wrote and told me. He also said it was dead easy and he'd show me how it was done. He's getting real cheeky.'

Both Bridie and Rosalyn smiled at the boy's outraged face, but were not able to make a reply because just then the taxi pulled up outside the station. It was harder and more painful for Jay to get out of the taxi than it had been to get in it and when he'd done it eventually and stood, supported by his crutches, on the windy platform Bridie noticed his face was grey and had deep score lines on it. 'You'll feel better on the train,' she said, and Jay just nodded.

His leg was throbbing badly and he was feeling very tired too; he'd slept little the night before, filled as he had been with excitement and slight apprehension at leaving the hospital. If his mother had been alive it would have been different altogether, but kind though Bridie had insisted her parents were, he barely knew them. He'd just been a little boy when he was last there and that had been with his mother and for a holiday only.

Then there was their Mickey, already installed and part of the place. He knew it couldn't be helped, but it made him feel funny, like he was an outsider in some way. And he had no one to tell. He and Bridie had become good friends and could talk about most things, but how could he tell her this? It was like speaking against her parents.

But Bridie was no fool and thought it perfectly natural that the boy would feel it strange. She knew too that he was worn-out and in pain and once in the carriage she said, 'Stretch out if you want, Jay. I shouldn't think for a minute the train will get packed. Only idiots like us travel to Ireland in February.'

Oh, Jay thought, how much more comfortable it was with his leg raised up and he wasn't able to suppress the sigh of relief.

'Have a sleep if you want to,' Bridie continued. 'I'll sit beside you and make sure you don't fall off. It's a through train so you can have a fine old rest till we get to Liverpool.' And thank God for that, she thought to herself, for the less walking about Jay had to do the better.

Jay didn't answer. He was too tired to bother. His eyes fluttered closed and shortly afterwards his even breathing told Bridie and Rosalyn he was asleep.

He looked so young and vulnerable asleep that Bridie felt her heart lurch with sadness that Mary wasn't there to see her two sons grown into manhood.

Rosalyn saw the look and gave Bridie's arm a squeeze. 'We can't bring Mary back,' she said. 'But we're doing what she wanted. It's the next best thing.'

Bridie sighed. 'I know,' she said, and then with a wistful smile at the memory of her sister went on, 'Ellen always thought Mary would never rear Jay, he was such a daredevil. He was always up to some mischief or other.'

'I wouldn't have said that,' Rosalyn said.

'He isn't now,' Bridie agreed. 'There was a change in him after the men came home from Dunkirk. I didn't see it at first, but he definitely matured after that. 'Course, he's turned thirteen now, he's growing up fast.'

'How long will he have the plaster on?'

'Some time yet, I believe,' Bridie said. 'The doctor told me the break to his arm was minor, what they call a greenstick fracture which usually heals completely, and the head injury too wasn't too serious, though the gash was long and deep enough to need stitches. It was his leg that caught it mainly. It was broken in three places and he'd also ripped through sinew and muscle. He might always have a limp.'

'Dear God, that's nothing,' Rosalyn said. 'Anyone can live with a limp.'

'Aye,' Bridie said. 'I know. If that's all he's left with, we can thank God for it.'

'I'll tell you what though,' Rosalyn said. 'I'm not looking forward to the ferry journey. I was as sick as a dog coming over.'

'I'm not a good sailor either,' Bridie said. 'Though the times I've travelled have never been the best. One day, maybe I'll travel across the Irish Sea with the sun shining and the sea itself like a millpond.'

'That's as unlikely as the thought that they might apply to have Hitler canonised after this little lot is over!'

The two women laughed together and then impulsively Rosalyn grabbed Bridie's hand. 'I'm so glad we're friends again,' she said. 'Are you?'

'Aye, I am,' Bridie said. 'It was nothing you'd done, you do understand that?'

''Course I do,' Rosalyn assured her. 'I would have reacted the same if such a dreadful thing had happened to me.'

Bridie made no reply to that. She didn't want to start the whole thing about Francis again. Waiting for her at the journey's end was the need to tell her mother and the thought of that was enough to tie her stomach in knots, she didn't want to rehash it here.

Rosalyn seemed to understand, for she said nothing else about that, and instead they reminisced over their lives together when they were young. Rosalyn also described her life in America, an alien place to Bridie, despite the American films she'd seen at the picture house with Tom before the war, and Terry's letters. Rosalyn's life sounded colourful and exciting, just what she always wanted, and though Bridie knew it would never have suited her, she was glad her cousin was happy.

Then in a lull in the conversation Rosalyn asked, 'How long are you stopping?'

'A week,' Bridie said. 'No longer, I need to get back. You know . . .'

Rosalyn knew all right. She knew every minute Bridie would be fretting to go back. Rosalyn was very worried about her, for she hadn't said a word about the children since she'd returned from seeing Todd and that in itself was ominous. She knew they'd never be far from her mind. She wondered if she'd faced the fact that those children might not be allowed to live with her again until Tom returned, whenever the damned war ended and they were allocated somewhere half-decent to live in.

Whatever Todd said, she decided she'd go back with Bridie – she badly needed support – and so she said, 'Let me know what you decide and I'll go with you.'

'I thought you'd be staying here now?'

'No, I can't imagine what gave you that idea.'

'Didn't Todd say you should?'

'Todd says many things and many times I take no notice of him,' Rosalyn said with a laugh. 'I'm my own woman and I'll make my own decisions. Anyway, I've known you years longer than Todd and with the two of us, we're bound to come up with some better place than that attic eventually.'

Bridie was too relieved and grateful to argue further and she took hold of Rosalyn's hand and squeezed it. 'Oh Rosalyn.'

'Now don't start blubbering,' Rosalyn said briskly. 'Jay will know you've been crying when he wakes up and he'll go for me for upsetting you.'

Bridie smiled, knowing Rosalyn had a point – Jay was quite protective of her – and she said, 'Rosalyn, I don't know what I'd ever have done without you. I'm very grateful to you coming over and taking me in hand.'

'Think nothing of it,' Rosalyn said airily. 'Isn't that what friends are for? Anyway, you know I've always been a bossy cow.' And she leaned across and kissed Bridie on the cheek.

As the boat ploughed its way through the choppy, churning water of the Irish Sea, Jay proved as poor a sailor as Bridie and Rosalyn. That day though, they had to ignore their own queasy stomachs to deal with the child, especially as he couldn't stay on deck for any length of time as the sea spray and damp mist in the air were no good for his plaster cast.

'I don't remember being as sick as this the last

time,' Jay complained, wiping his mouth.

'You were just wee, you'd hardly remember.'

'I'd remember being this sick, anyone would,' Jay said indignantly. He shivered suddenly and Bridie realised how thin his coat was. The first thing she must do before she left she thought was buy some suitable clothes for the boys. But that was for the future; Jay would freeze to death if he stayed up on deck much longer. 'How are you feeling now?' she said. 'We'd be better inside.'

'I'm all right,' Jay assured her. And with Rosalyn's help they moved slowly across the deck to the saloon.

A cacophony of noise greeted them as the door was opened: voices rising and falling, someone singing, a group arguing and gales of loud laughter coming from the four large men at the bar. The room smelt of a press of people, damp clothes, a hint of vomit, all over ridden by the smell of Guinness and the smoke from the cigarettes that hung in the air in a cloud.

She remembered the time she'd come over with Tom and he'd bought her a brandy to settle her stomach. 'Did it work?' Rosalyn asked when she told her.

'Depends what you mean by work,' Bridie said. 'I went to sleep when I took mine with my head on Tom's shoulder and when I woke up he had his arms around me. I was too embarrassed then to think of a queasy stomach.'

Rosalyn smiled. 'Maybe we could all be doing

with a bit of that,' she said, and going to the bar brought them back two large brandies and a ginger beer for Jay, which the barman had assured her would make him as right as rain in no time.

He did feel better after he'd drunk it, he said, and so did Bridie, though she liked the taste no better than the first time she'd had it. But even with the help of the brandy and ginger beer, they all breathed a sigh of relief when the boat docked in Belfast.

By the time Jay had been carried off the boat and made his way to the awaiting train, his leg had begun to throb worse than ever. He remembered the doctor saying that he wasn't sure he was up to such a journey and that his leg was far from well enough for such an arduous trek, but Jay had got so distressed that, in the end, he'd reluctantly given permission.

Jay didn't complain about the leg, though the pain was getting worse as they changed trains at Derry and then again to the rail bus at Strabane. Both Bridie and Rosalyn had noticed the child's face, which had been stripped of colour on the ferry, turn grey with pain and caught him catching his lip and wincing more than once.

He'd not spoken much either and his replies to anything they'd asked him had been short and to the point. Bridie would be glad to get him home and hoped he hadn't done himself any further harm, for it was not an easy trip, even for people with two good legs.

*   *   *

Jimmy was waiting for them as the rail bus pulled to a stop at the bottom of the farm. He had been devastated by the death of Mary and indeed Ellen and Sam, and more especially when Bridie's children were feared dead too.

He'd had to rouse himself when Mickey arrived – a poor, wee, motherless child, confused and deeply unhappy – and then just after Christmas came the startling news that Bridie's children were alive, sick, but alive, and in some hospital. And now Jamie – or Jay as he must remember to call him now – was coming to join his brother.

But when he saw the child in the murky half-light of a winter's evening he was shocked. He swung the lantern he carried and it took in Jay's face creased with pain, his bottom lip pinched and his eyes glazed over. 'Dear Almighty God,' he cried. 'Let's get you all indoors and quickly – this child needs his bed.'

He wished he could carry him, but the child was too tall and he was too old himself for that. He took much of Jay's weight, however, and placed an arm about him as they hobbled towards the cottage, Rosalyn and Bridie lagging behind with their baggage and Jay's abandoned crutches.

The warmth of the cottage hit their frozen bodies like a hot bath and caused fingers and toes to ache and tingle. The smell from the pot of something wonderful simmering above the peat fire made Bridie feel faint, despite the sandwiches they'd had on the train from Belfast to Derry.

Jimmy half-carried Jay to the fire, while Mickey, such a different child from the one who'd left Birmingham, was dancing behind him, crying, 'What is it? What's the matter with him? What's he done?'

Sarah stepped away from the fire. 'Leave your grandad,' she said. 'Your brother is tired and sore by the look of him. Come away out of that.'

But her eyes took in Bridie as she spoke and she crossed the room and enfolded her with her one good arm, kissing her cheeks. 'Rosalyn,' she said, turning from Bridie at last and hugging her niece. 'Are you stopping for a bite? We have plenty.'

'No thanks, Aunt Sarah,' Rosalyn said. 'Mammy will be expecting me.'

'You're sure now?'

'Aye, but don't press me too much,' Rosalyn said with a laugh. 'I might just sit and have a big feed for it smells delicious – oh dear God, Mammy would roast me alive, though, for she wrote that she'd have a meal ready too.'

'Ah. Leave it so then,' Bridie said.

'Aye. See you all tomorrow.'

'Bye, Rosalyn.'

'Glad to see you two are friends again,' Sarah remarked to Bridie as she laid cutlery on the table.

Bridie looked up from where she was hugging Mickey, who'd wrapped himself around her knees, and replied, 'Aye, Rosalyn's been just wonderful. I'd forgotten how great she was.'

'Delia was over earlier – she's glad to have her at home, for a wee while at least. Come on now, take off your coat and sit up to the table. Mickey will take your bags to your rooms, won't you, Mickey, and then we can all eat.'

Jimmy had laid Jay in an armchair by the fire and pushed another one close to it to rest his leg. He gently removed his one boot and his coat and said, 'The only place that child is going to move to is his bed. I'll take his dinner over to him on a tray.' And then he was before Bridie, and he knew she was more precious than ever to him now – his only remaining daughter – and, his voice broken with emotion, said, 'How are you, my bonnie girl?'

'Oh, Daddy!' Bridie cried and they clung together. Bridie felt as if she was wee again and her daddy could protect her from everything and everybody, that she was safe and secure and need never be afraid. He smelt as he'd always done; of the outdoors and the animals, the peaty smell that had always clung to his clothes, and a hint of the pipe tobacco he smoked. It was blessedly familiar.

She had told her parents and Tom that the children had been injured in the raid and were in hospital and this is the story she stuck to over tea. Jay knew more, but she'd asked him to say nothing. She said she'd tell her parents what she thought they needed to know, and there was no reason at all to distress Mickey. He was still a young boy, she said, and could do nothing about it. Jay saw his aunt's point.

Jimmy, with Mickey's help, had done the milking before they arrived, so apart from washing the pots there was nothing for them all to do, but sit around the fire and talk together.

Bridie was glad to see Mickey so well and happy now, though her mother had told her in letters how he'd initially had horrific nightmares and even now sometimes cried for his mother. None of this was discussed in front of him though and Sarah only told of the positive things; what a good and helpful boy Mickey was about the farm and how well he'd settled in at the village school. 'That's why he won't be allowed to stay up late tonight,' Sarah said. 'In fact . . .'

'Ah, Grandma not on Jay's first night,' Mickey protested.

'Jay's not up to conversation tonight, Mickey,' Jimmy told him. 'There will be plenty of other nights. Now do as your grandma bids you and go on down to the room like a good boy.'

Mickey went reluctantly, dragging his feet, and Bridie smiled. She'd hated been sent to bed herself as a child, but now she thought longingly of settling down to sleep.

She could see Jay was also worn-out and Jimmy, also noticing this, said to Sarah, 'I've a mind for Jay to sleep in our bed tonight. I've a feeling his leg might well be painful after today's exertions. Mickey might kick out in the night and accidentally hurt him.'

'What about you?' Sarah asked.

'I'll do well enough in the bed chair beside the bed,' Jimmy said. 'I'd feel easier if I was beside the boy, for tonight at least. You don't mind, sure you don't?'

'I do not,' Sarah said emphatically. 'I'll share the bed with Bridie so.'

Bridie, although she knew her father was right for Jay looked far from well, was apprehensive about sharing a bed with her mother. But there was no alternative so, pleading tiredness, she went to bed not long after Mickey, intending to be asleep before her mother came to bed.

Once in bed, however, though her eyes were smarting as if they had grit rubbed into them and her limbs ached with fatigue, sleep would not come.

She lay this way and that, tossing about in the bed to find a comfortable spot. She told herself to relax, but she couldn't. She shut her eyes and counted sheep, but eventually she gave up and opened her eyes again.

Empty your mind – she'd heard that expression somewhere and now thought it a crazy one. So much had happened to her and her loved ones over the last weeks, months and years – how could you sweep those memories and worries away like so much rubbish? And in the night, when you're in bed, alone, enjoying a bit of peace for maybe the first time that day, the anxieties gained a foothold and hammered at your brain.

And Bridie had many worries – sorrowful

remembrances and problems that seemed unsolvable – that when Sarah came to bed, she was more wide awake than ever. She shut her eyes quickly, pretending she was asleep, but Sarah was not fooled. 'I know you're awake, Bridie, I heard you tossing about till just a few minutes ago.'

With a sigh, Bridie opened her eyes. 'I am tired,' she said. 'That's no lie, I just can't seem to get off.'

'Things troubling you, maybe?'

There was a pause and a sigh before Bridie said, 'Aye.'

'Need to talk about it?'

It wasn't how Bridie planned to tell her mother, but now with the two boys in the house, one at home all day and Beatie coming in on them in the morning, as well as her father's company in the evening, it might be her only chance.

She took a deep breath and began.

Sarah lay in the dark beside her daughter and listened to her telling her of her uncle's interference with her when she was but fourteen years of age. Dimly, Sarah remembered Bridie, telling her a tale of Francis touching and kissing her in a way she found upsetting. And how she had reacted? Had she given her sympathy, understanding, even asked her to explain further?

No, Sarah thought, she hadn't and yet she knew then of Francis's philandering. She'd known of it for years because once Delia, depressed beyond measure by her sham of a marriage, had told her of it.

Sarah knew also of Francis's preference for young girls, and he had the charm, wit and good looks to attract them. So why, knowing this, did she not question her daughter further? She thought she was safe, being family. But did she, really? Sarah admitted to herself that night that she hadn't wanted to face the fact that Francis had behaved inappropriately with her daughter.

Bridie had only had Mary to confide in, Sarah realised, but she waited, for she knew the abuse that Mary dealt with so adequately when she came over to visit was nowhere near the end of the story. And it wasn't, though Bridie burned with embarrassment at the things she had to describe and was so stiff with tension, she lay beside her mother like a block of wood.

Rosalyn said Bridie must spare her mother nothing, but Bridie had never spoken of intimate things with her mother and it was hard to do so now. Many times she would pause and try to gather the courage to continue. This was never more so than when she was describing Francis trailing her into the woods and the ensuing rape. She knew then, whatever Rosalyn had advised, had they not both been hidden by darkness, she couldn't have told her mother, especially when she heard her sharp intake of breath.

Sarah was feeling various emotions as she listened to her daughter: shame and regret that she'd done nothing about this when she had the chance; disgust and revulsion that Francis should do such a thing. It was obscene to violate any young, innocent girl, but when that girl was your own niece, who had looked upon you as a father figure, it was a vile abomination.

Bridie had stopped talking again and so Sarah said, 'My darling child, there aren't words enough in the whole English language to say how sorry I am – I let you down and I'm bitterly ashamed. Was this what made you flee your home? Did you felt you couldn't trust Francis?'

'In a way,' Bridie said. 'But it was worse than that.'

Sarah lay stock still in the bed, knowing for a young, unmarried girl there was only one way things could get worse. She suddenly remembered how she commented to Jimmy that the upset over Rosalyn leaving had stopped Bridie's monthly cycle and recalled that she'd heard her being sick in the chamber pot in the mornings. But never in a million years would she have guessed that her young daughter was pregnant. She hadn't even a boyfriend at the time.

It was hard for Bridie to go on and Sarah's hand sought hers. She knew there was more, and she needed to know what it was, but she also needed to let Bridie know she was on her side. 'Go on, my love,' she said as she squeezed her hand.

That encouragement gave Bridie the courage to continue. She hadn't fled to England because she couldn't bear life with them, or even because she couldn't stand Francis's proximity. She'd fled

566

to England because Francis had made her pregnant. Bridie said she knew that the knowledge of this would have destroyed them all, ripped the families apart, and Sarah felt bitter shame flow through her.

Every word Bridie spoke was true. Would they have stood by her if she'd come to them for help? Wouldn't she have felt in some way that Bridie was to blame? So her child, and she was still a child then, had borne it alone, running to her sister, the only one who'd believed her, to save the family from disgrace.

And because she'd run away to save their shame, their standing in the community, and preserve the links between both families, Sarah had cast her off, had declared her not to be a daughter of hers, ignoring the letters she wrote day after day. How in God's name could she ever make this up to her daughter – the one she'd loved more than life itself, the only one she had left, and the one who'd suffered the most?

The words poured out of Bridie: the panic she'd felt, the dilemma she was in and she told of the cycle ride in a cold, dark and rain-sodden winter's night to Strabane. Sobs overtook her as she spoke and Sarah lay beside her, mortified with shame for her part in it, and thought it was a pity Francis was dead, for she'd like to kill him by her own hands, slowly and be damned to the consequences.

Bridie was still afraid to tell her mother of the abortion, but Sarah had almost prepared herself for that – what else could she have done for there was no child. An aberration in God's eyes, the Church called abortion, but where was God when her child was violated?

Sarah sensed Bridie's hesitation and again urged her on. 'Go on, pet. Tell me all.' Bridie told her how it was – the pain afterwards and the loss of blood that caused her to be taken to hospital, and how she'd been blackmailed for years from one whose family lived not far from them at all.

'She threatened to tell you all unless I gave her money,' Bridie said. 'She didn't know it all, not who the father of the baby was, but I was still scared. You would have been destroyed and all I'd done would have counted for nothing. Dear God, I couldn't have borne that.'

Sarah was in shock; this turn of events was totally unexpected. What a thing to happen to her own dear daughter!

'The money was bad enough,' Bridie went on, 'especially when I had to borrow it from Mary and she'd give out to me for being a bad manager. Sometimes I'd have to take it from the post office account Tom put by as our nest egg, and occasionally I pawned something, but that was money just. What I lost sleep over was what she said about Katie and Liam, cursing them and prophesising that God would have his revenge and something would happen to them because of my wickedness,' Bridie said, her voice not much more than a whisper.

'D'you know, Mammy, her last words on earth were that God would have his revenge. I'm glad she died then. At that moment I had the urge to choke her to bloody death. But I thought she was right then too, because I thought my children were in pieces, spread all over the bomb site.'

Bridie began to cry at this point and Sarah held her and wept with her. She thought Bridie had finished but after a few minutes she went on, almost angrily: 'They're alive, Mammy, and I thought my troubles were over, but they are as far away as ever. Mammy, oh Mammy, I don't think I can bear this pain anymore.'

Sarah was confused. 'But didn't you tell us that they were in hospital, child? You'll have them home again when they're recovered, surely? Isn't that the way of it?'

'No, Mammy, not quite,' Bridie said. 'Some of the raids are dreadful, and there are so many injured, the hospitals are often chock-a-block. They've drained swimming pools and emptied basements to use as emergency centres and the injured are redirected all over the city to where there is room. Mine were apparently taken to the Children's Hospital first – because they were so small the ambulance driver thought if they could fit them in there, they probably had better facilities to deal with them. The doctor told us this.

'Everyone was dead but Mickey, and they had no idea the children had any living relatives. By the time Rosalyn and I tracked them down, almost a month later, they'd been sent to an orphanage out in the countryside with a specialist hospital wing attached to it. The hospital specialises in trauma-related injuries of the mind. When the children recover sufficiently they are transferred to the main orphanage.'

Sarah digested this and then she said, 'What's wrong with the children, Bridie?'

'They're mentally ill, Mammy,' Bridie told her mother. 'Scarred emotionally, maybe for ever by their incarceration under tons and tons of rubble in the pitch black, all on their own for hours. They've sort of closed their minds to it and the shock has caused them to lose the power of speech. That's why it took me so long to find them. Neither of them could say who they were.'

'Dear God, this is dreadful,' Sarah said. 'But surely to God they'll recover in time?'

Bridie shrugged. 'Who knows, Mammy.'

'Don't they even speak to you?'

'I wouldn't know, Mammy. 'I haven't been allowed to see them yet.'

'Not been allowed to see them,' Sarah repeated in horror. 'But, child, you are their mother!'

'I know, Mammy, but every time I say that, they remind me that the children are sick and having treatment and I could make them worse by seeing them. How can I risk that? It isn't as if I can even promise them anything, for I know even if they recover totally, they will not be returned to me.'

'Of course they will.'

'No, they won't.' Bridie said firmly. 'They've told me that. I live in this awful attic, Mammy, it's truly dreadful. There is no room in it for the children and they wouldn't deem it suitable anyway. I've tried and tried to find somewhere better, but with no luck. I'd also hesitate to take them back into the city. I mean what if there was another raid and something else, something worse, happened to them?

'Anyway,' Bridie went on dejectedly. 'It's probably just as well. I don't have contact with the children.' And she went on to tell her mother about the day she'd called at the orphanage and, after being shown the door, she'd traced the fence around the perimeter of the grounds. 'I came to a place where the children were playing,' Bridie continued. 'I didn't see Liam, but I did see Katie. And she saw me and screamed, Mammy. Screamed and screamed and screamed. I'm worthless as a mother if that's what my child thinks of me.'

'Of course you're not worthless,' Sarah told Bridie, holding her tight against her. 'You're a wonderful mother. You frightened Katie, that's all. You didn't speak to her?'

'I called her name, that's all.'

'Well then.'

'What d'you mean, well then?'

'She was probably unnerved at seeing you, even frightened perhaps,' Sarah said. 'Leave it now, darling, till the morning and we'll talk again.'

Bridie said nothing, but though she lay nestled

571

in her mother's arms she didn't think she'd sleep. But eventually she did. Sarah, holding her daughter, merely dozed and in between made plans in her head.

CHAPTER TWENTY-FIVE

Bridie opened her eyes, but the room was in darkness and for a moment she was disoriented. Then the memories of the previous evening came flooding back. Dimly, she saw her mother clamber out of bed, strike a match and light the lamp on the table, bathing the bed in a soft orange glow.

'Mammy,' Bridie said, struggling to sit up.

'Ah, pet!' Sarah said. 'Did I wake you?'

'I don't know what woke me,' Bridie said. 'I didn't think I'd sleep.'

'Well, you did,' Sarah said with satisfaction, struggling into her clothes. 'How d'you feel now?'

How did she feel? Better. The heavy burden of shame and guilt that had lodged between her shoulder blades was gone. She'd become so used to the heaviness over the years, she'd barely noticed it, but she knew it was gone all right. 'I feel grand, Mammy,' she said. 'Grand, so I do.'

'Good,' Sarah said. 'Now I want you to rest yourself and not think of a thing.'

'I was going to give Daddy a hand with the milking.'

'You'll do no such thing. What d'you think we pay Willie for?' Sarah said. 'Mickey has begun to help him in the evening, but I'll not let him get up at this hour. He's just a wean yet.'

'Aye,' Bridie said. 'Poor Mary.'

Sarah sighed. 'Aye indeed, poor Mary. God, I thought I'd die myself when I heard the news. And then Eddie came with the young boy and I saw how they were. My heart went out to them. Eddie had no time to grieve, he had to go back to the army. And Tom, thinking his own children dead, would be no real help to him. But because Mickey was in our care, we had to buck up. It was the saving of the two of us.'

'Aye, I see that.'

'It could be the saving of you too.'

'What?'

'Darling girl,' Sarah said, grasping her hands. 'There is no need for you to stay in Birmingham now. There is no home for Tom to return to, no Ellen, Sam or Mary to fret over. Come home here with your children. We have a more than adequate home and plenty to love them and provide for them.'

Bridie was stunned. She'd been so worn down with sadness and desperation, she'd not seen the solution that her mother held out to her. 'Oh, Mammy, do you mean it?'

'Of course I mean it,' Sarah said. 'I haven't

mentioned it to your father, but I know he'd jump at the chance of having you live here again and he'd love to get to know your weans.'

'Will you tell him about Francis?' Bridie asked. 'The things I told you yesterday?'

'I must tell him, darling girl,' Sarah said gently. 'I can't keep such things from him. But don't worry, you'll not be blamed.'

'Oh Mammy, how can you be so sure? He loved Francis so.'

'And he loves you more,' Sarah reminded her. 'He knew what manner of man Francis was. Such a thing cannot be kept quiet in a small place and I know he spoke about it to Francis more than once. But never in his wildest dreams did he imagine Francis would violate his own niece.' Sarah thought for a moment and added, 'Did he do the same to Mary? I only ask because she believed you so readily.'

'Aye,' Bridie said with a sigh. 'I'd have denied it if Mary had survived that raid, because that would be what she wanted. It wasn't rape, or anything like it, just touching and ... well, you know. It was around the time that Sally McCormack's father named Francis as the father of her unborn child. He denied it, Mary said, and was believed because Sally was just a gypsy brat, though no one expected her to drown herself.

'Anyway, Mary told Francis she'd shout out what he'd done to her if he didn't stop and then questions might be asked about Sally McCormack and she frightened him into leaving her alone.'

'Dear God, girl, I feel so ashamed that we weren't aware of it.'

'It began the summer after Robert and Nuala died, Mammy,' Bridie said. 'Neither you or Daddy were in any fit state to notice anything. I was just wee, but I can remember how lonely I was. I remember telling Mary once that you were both still there, but it was like there was nothing inside you. Mary knew what I meant. Without her, and Rosalyn too, of course, I'd have been worse. When I thought my children were dead, I understood, probably for the first time, the intense grief you and Daddy were going through. I wanted to die too and had no time or understanding for either Tom or Eddie.'

'I know, girl,' Sarah said. 'But things will be different now and for all of you, please God. Through my own stiff-necked attitude, we never knew your children and yet we grieved for them too. Now, you pull up the blankets around you for the morning is bitter. I'll wet the tea for your father and Willie and bring you a cup in, all right?'

'I'll get up, Mammy.'

'Let me do this for you,' Sarah said. 'I feel I won't live long enough to make it up to you.'

'I don't want any of that sort of talk,' Bridie said sharply. 'You owe me nothing, but it you want to bring me a cup of tea in bed, I won't stop you, just this once.'

With her mother gone, Bridie lay back and

thought about the proposal she'd been offered. She'd be happy to live back in Ireland again; she'd not been like Rosalyn. She'd found the workload heavy, but she'd never really wanted to leave and she'd love to rear her children in a place like this. She knew Tom would have no objection, at least through the war years. After it, they'd discuss the future together.

However, there was one stumbling block. How could she force the orphanage to release her children? Dr Havering claimed they were too sick to leave and she couldn't stand against medical opinion. Anyway, he could be right, must be right. Why would he say it if wasn't true? And she had to admit Katie hadn't been overjoyed to see her that time she'd spotted her through the fence. Her reaction had been anything but normal then. But now there was a lifeline held out to her, to the children. She sipped her tea and fantasised about them, happy, fit and healthy, running the fields as she'd done as a child, and knew she needed help and advice if her fantasies had any chance of coming true.

Later that morning, Bridie went round to see Rosalyn and tell her what her mother had suggested. When she went into the kitchen, for they never knocked on doors, Delia was at the press. She turned, and seeing Bridie, her face flamed beetroot red and she lowered her eyes immediately. 'I don't know what to say to you, Bridie,' she said. 'I can hardly bear look at you. Can you ever forgive me? When Rosalyn told me last night . . .'

Bridie reached out and grabbed her aunt's hands. 'Aunt Delia, there is nothing to forgive.'

'There is. I knew what the man was like, by Christ I knew! I thought you being his niece and all . . . but then why did I think that when his own daughter wasn't safe? If only I'd killed the bugger before he'd done such a thing to you.'

'Hush,' Bridie consoled. 'No one knows your part in that and it wouldn't do you any good for them to know either. Don't go to pieces now.'

'No, I won't,' Delia promised. 'I'm happier than I've ever been. But, believe me, if I'd known about you, had just a hint, I would have killed the man stone dead and not been a whit sorry.'

'I know that, Aunt Delia,' Bridie replied. 'In my opinion you did the world a service anyway. But now let's have no more talk of it.'

She was glad that Frank came into the kitchen at that moment, for she knew Delia would say no more in front of him. He didn't know the truth about his father and that is how she wanted it to stay. After exchanging a few words with him, Bridie went in search of Rosalyn.

On the way back she met her father. His face didn't break into a wreath of smiles as it usually did seeing Bridie, if anything his head sank lower. 'Daddy, what is it?' Bridie cried.

Jimmy raised his weather-beaten face and Bridie saw his eyes brimming with tears. 'Daddy!' Bridie

578

rushed towards him and put her arms about him. 'Tell me what ails you?'

She could barely hear the words, mumbled and made husky with tears, and then she made out some of his disjointed sentences – 'Wee Bridie. The light of my life. For such a thing to happen.' – and she understood.

She broke from his hold and said, 'Mammy's told you?'

'Aye, she told me,' Jimmy replied. 'She took me to the room so Jay wouldn't hear, for all he was sleeping. She told me first of Mary.'

'You didn't disbelieve it?'

'No, why would I?' Jimmy said. 'Who ever would make up such a thing? Anyway, I know what Francis was like. I'd let him have it time and again. I was sorry about the gypsy girl. In fact, if I'd been more myself that time, I might have done more about it, but I definitely didn't want to upset your mother further, or Delia either, dealing as she was with another miscarriage, so I did nothing. But, by God, if I'd known about Mary, I'd have torn Francis to pieces, much as I loved him.'

'She never said anything,' Bridie said soothingly. 'She wouldn't have told me if I hadn't suffered the same way.'

'Ah God, girl, that I'll never get over,' Jimmy said. 'If I had Francis before me this minute, I'd put a bullet through his skull and another into that McKenna one who did all she could to destroy you.'

'It's over, Daddy, Peggy McKenna is as dead as Francis. No point raking over it again and again. Let it lie now.'

'Aye, you're right,' Jimmy said. 'For your sake, nothing will be said or done about it. One thing that's always puzzled me, though, was how you got away that time without half the neighbourhood knowing of it. I broached the subject with your mother a time or two, but she'd never discuss it. I always wondered.'

'Didn't Mammy tell you that bit? I cycled to Strabane.'

'Cycled all the way to Strabane?'

'Aye, I unearthed Mary's old bike,' Bridie said. 'It was rusting away in the barn there and I did it up and set off in the middle of the night. I knew I couldn't go to a station nearer because of the risk of being spotted. I didn't know what story you'd give to the neighbours afterwards, and I didn't want anyone to see me fleeing my home.'

'We told them you'd been ill and gone to Mary's for a wee rest,' Jimmy said. 'Everyone knew that wasn't true – you don't just disappear overnight from a place – but we kept up the pretence. That McKenna one did write home that you'd arrived at Mary's, so everyone knew that bit was true. But I still can't believe you cycled all that way in the pitch black.'

'I followed the rail tracks as much as possible,' Bridie said, and admitted, 'it was pretty bad. At first it was just bitterly cold, but then the freezing rain came down. Tom was wonderful. I met him at Strabane and he loaned me his coat and fed me his breakfast for I'd not thought to take anything with me. I'd left in a bit of a state. Then he cared for me on the boat when I was as sick as a dog. I'm not a good sailor and I don't suppose expecting helped.'

'I can't bear hearing what you went through,' Jimmy said. 'But now we need to look forward and get those weans of yours over here where they belong.'

'It might not be as easy as you think,' Bridie said.

But neither Jimmy nor Sarah could see a problem. They were the children's grandparents and Bridie their mother, and so when the children were released into her care she'd bring them to Ireland. Whatever ailed them, Sarah was convinced could be cured as soon as they were where they belonged. 'All this psychiatry mumbo jumbo,' she said scathingly. 'They may be very clever, these people, and do all sort of tests and examinations, but has anyone thought of loving the children? Has anyone put their arms around them or picked them up and given them a hug? If they haven't it's no wonder they've gone inside themselves. The sooner they leave that place the better.'

Sarah said a lot of the things that had been battering around Bridie's own head and she thought back to the forlorn figure standing alone in the playground and knew her mother was right. They had to be taken away from Oakengates, but she had no idea how that could be achieved.

It took the combined arguments of Rosalyn and Bridie to convince Sarah and Jimmy that there might be a problem getting the children's release from that place. 'Look at it from their point of view,' Bridie said. 'I could just say I have a place for them, I could say anything. They're not going to take my word for it. And if the children really are as sick as they say, they're even less likely to release them.'

'I think we need the advice of a professional in this,' Sarah told them. 'Bridie, tomorrow you and I will go into the town to see Doctor Monahan, and you can tell him the whole story. After all, he's my cousin's son, and he'll help us if anyone can.'

Doctor Monahan surveyed the two women across the desk. He'd listened while Bridie told him of the raid robbing her and her sister of their homes, their lodging with Ellen and the subsequent raid while Bridie had been away in Ireland. She'd told him how Ellen, Sam and Mary had been killed and Mary's youngest son injured, and that she'd assumed her children to be dead too until a chance remark by an old neighbour changed everything.

It was a tragic circumstance, but one the doctor imagined would be happening in many British towns and cities. He knew too of the difficulties of getting children out of local authority care once they were in, especially as Bridie told him they'd been so traumatised they'd been too afraid to speak and were having psychiatric treatment.

'I could write you a letter, verifying that your parents are who they say they are and giving an assurance of the suitability of the home, but somehow I think you might need more than that.'

'Aye, I know,' Bridie said resignedly.

'This home isn't a Catholic one, is it?' Doctor Monahan asked.

'No.'

'Is there one in the area?'

'Father Flynn said something about Father Hudson's Home being in Coleshill. That's not far away,' Bridie said.

'Well, that's the angle I'd use,' the doctor said. 'Tell Father O'Dwyer all this and go from there. Meanwhile, I'll write the letter because it might carry some weight.'

For the first time, Bridie had a glimmer of hope. She remembered Father Flynn saying although the children were Catholics they was no point in making an issue of their not being in a Roman Catholic Home. The thing to do was release them into her care. But maybe this was the way that objective could ultimately be achieved.

After that, things moved speedily and three days later, Bridie and Rosalyn alighted from the train at New Street Station, weary, hungry and cold, to be met by Father Shearer. 'Father Flynn thought I should come with you to this place tomorrow since

I've known you longer,' he explained to Bridie. 'We have an interview with Father Phillips who runs the place at twelve o'clock tomorrow. So if you call around to the presbytery about ten o'clock we'll be in plenty of time.'

'So soon?'

'I think sooner the better, don't you?' Father Shearer said. 'I'm of the same mind as Father Flynn that the children must feel they've lost everyone belonging to them. Surely to God the first thing would have been to reunite them with you and see if that would unlock their tongues and still many of their fears.'

Bridie fervently hoped Father Phillips thought the same way as they left the priest and made their way to Bridie's attic. Rosalyn, remembering the previous state of Bridie's kitchen shelves, said, 'I'm starving – have you any food in?'

'I had, but I gave anything left to the landlady before I went to collect Jay from the hospital,' Bridie said. 'I kept a bit of tea and sugar back, though, and we have the soda bread and tub of butter Mammy pressed on us.'

'Good job she did,' Rosalyn said. 'But I think I need more than bread and butter.'

'We can get chips somewhere,' Bridie said. 'Let's just dump our stuff first.'

As they went into the house, the landlady's own door opened. 'Oh you're back,' she said to Bridie.

'Aye, I said I would be.'

'Well, I wasn't sure,' the landlady said. 'I've

had someone else after the place. After all, you owe rent.'

'Only one week and I'll give that to you now.'

The landlady wasn't so easily mollified. She cast a malevolent glance at Rosalyn and said, 'I hope you're not into subletting? I'd never agree to that.'

'She's my cousin,' Bridie explained. 'And just staying a night or two.'

'Aye, well, she's stayed before. I've seen her.'

'I only stayed a night or two then as well,' Rosalyn said. 'You can hardly charge extra rent for that.'

'I can charge what I like, it's my place,' the landlady snapped, but brightened a little when Bridie put the rent money into her hand. 'Yes, well, I'll let it go this time,' she said. 'But be warned, you disappear again and there will be someone else in your place when you come back.

'And another thing,' she went on. 'There's a big bloody parcel come for you and I've had to have it in here cluttering up my place – I couldn't cart it up to the attic with my back.'

'A parcel?' Bridie repeated.

'That's what I said, weren't it,' the landlady said. 'A great big bloody parcel.'

Bridie had to admit it was a great, big, bloody parcel after she and Rosalyn had manhandled it to the attic. Bridie had never had a parcel in her life and she cut the beeswaxed string with a knife, too impatient to untie the knots. Rosalyn rescued the brown paper before Bridie ripped it to shreds, noting the sender's address, which Bridie hadn't seen.

Rosalyn had done what she'd promised before Christmas and contacted her friends in the States, telling them about the situation in Birmingham in general and her cousin Bridie in particular.

Bridie pulled open the cardboard box and lifted out jumpers, dresses, cardigans, coats and even trousers with delight. They were better quality and of more style than the few utility garments available in British shops and they'd also included children's clothes and shoes. Rosalyn was glad of those. She was good with her needle and she knew she could adapt most of the things to fit Katie and Liam. Bridie wouldn't want to take the children to Ireland in orphanage charity clothes.

But there were more things in the box: tins of condensed milk and sausages and beans and two tins of peach halves in syrup. 'Oh boy,' Rosalyn cried, her mouth watering. 'We'll have a feast tonight, Bridie. I'll go for the chips, while you open one of the cans of sausages and another of beans and we'll have one of the tins of peaches to finish.'

'Aye,' Bridie cried. 'We will. And we've even got milk for the tea.'

After a fretful night, in which Bridie and therefore Rosalyn who shared the bed hardly slept, Bridie was up at the crack of dawn. When Rosalyn opened her bleary eyes it was to see her making tea for them both in the kitchenette. 'What are you doing, Bridie? It's the middle of the night.'

'No it isn't,' Bridie said. 'Anyway, I'm too excited and nervous to sleep.'

Rosalyn was about to snap back that she was too tired to be excited about anything and flop back into bed when she caught sight of Bridie's face. She couldn't take that light of hope from her eyes; it would be like whipping a puppy. So, with a sigh, she struggled out of bed and began to dress quickly, for the room was like an ice-box.

They were ready far too early. Bridie collected her letters – one from the doctor and the other Father O'Dwyer had insisted on writing too – and looked at the clothes she had sorted from the box and had folded on a chair, waiting for the children to fill them. 'I hope this Father Phillips is as helpful as Fathers Shearer and Flynn,' Bridie said to Rosalyn.

'Well, we'll soon find out,' Rosalyn said. 'We're ridiculously early, but you'll turn into a nervous wreck if you stay here a minute longer. Come on.'

They called for Father Shearer at the presbytery and he left hurriedly, watched disapprovingly by Father Fearney and the hatchet-faced housekeeper.

'I know it's easy for me to say,' Father Shearer said, 'but try not to worry too much. I had a long chat with Father Phillips on the phone last night and I can truthfully say that I think he's on your side in this.'

Bridie took comfort in the priest's words as he

hoped she would and did find Father Phillips to be a compassionate man when she met him, and one who intended to be fully supportive. After his long talk with Father Shearer, he'd phoned Father Flynn and discussed the case. Both men spoke highly of Bridie and within minutes of talking to her, he too liked the woman. She was respectable and kindly, a good, devout Catholic, and her parents were more than willing to offer them all a home with them back in Ireland.

'I'll phone Oakengates straightaway,' he said.

'Every time I ring they make excuses, or say it's not convenient to visit at the moment,' Bridie said dejectedly.

'Well, they won't say that to me,' Father Phillips promised.

Nor did they. When he explained who he was and enquired about the two children, he was told they had severe emotional problems and Katie was awaiting assessment from a psychologist from Moneyhall. He didn't share this information with Bridie – it wouldn't be helpful – but he made an appointment to speak with Doctor Havering the following morning.

'Can I go with you?' Bridie asked.

'Not this time, my dear,' the priest said. 'They mustn't guess there is any sort of collusion between us.'

Bridie realised she had to be patient. 'I will come to the Mission hall afterwards to save you dragging out here again,' he said. 'Wait for me there.'

They said goodbye to Father Shearer in the city centre and then Rosalyn, knowing the rest of the day would drag for Bridie, readily agreed to go and collect her rations with her and go around the Bull Ring to kill time. Rabbit meat was on sale in one butcher's, but the queue for it was so long, it snaked in and out the stalls. Rosalyn noted each person only got a very small amount and yet Bridie joined the end of the queue without thinking about it. 'See if you can get hold of some vegetables,' she advised her cousin. 'If I get a bit of rabbit before they run out, we can make a stew. It's what you need in weather like this.'

Rosalyn did get vegetables – potatoes, swedes, parsnips, carrots and onions – the things grown on British soil and in every available space now the 'Dig for Victory' campaign was taking effect. After a wait of more than an hour, Bridie managed to procure a small supply of rabbit meat, which she was ridiculously pleased with.

They went to the Mission hall before returning home to tell Father Flynn of the latest developments only to find Father Phillips had already phoned him and put him in the picture. They arranged to go to the Mission hall at half past ten the following day to hear what the priest had to say.

Early the next morning, Father Phillips travelled to the orphanage, full of misgivings. However honest and trustworthy Bridie was, she'd not seen or tried to speak to the children in all the time following the raid. Maybe they'd been so mentally damaged by the raid, they would never fully recover.

However, he would see the children himself and make up his own mind, he decided. But that was the one thing he sensed the doctor was loath to let him do. 'They are sick children, Father.'

'I understand that,' the priest said, 'but I wish to see that for myself.'

'Do you propose to remove two distressed children from a unit where they are having specialist help?'

Father Phillips smiled. 'Your orphanage is not unique in having specialists work with damaged children,' he said. 'And those two children Katie and Liam Cassidy are baptised Catholics, born of devout parents, and belong in Father Hudson's Home, not here, however good the establishment is.'

The doctor wished he could tell the priest to go to Hell, but knew he couldn't do that; the man could make life very awkward for him. Now when the children were in charge of social services, he could fight anyone else, including the natural parents, for custody and probably win his case, but against the Catholic Church, he was powerless and he knew it.

If he was to try and block the priest in what he wanted to do, he knew he would bring bishops and the rest of the Church hierarchy down on his head. It wouldn't be the children's physical state they would be worried about, but their spiritual welfare, their immortal souls. He'd met many Catholics and knew that they considered their Church was the one true one, founded by the apostle Peter, and anyone who worshipped in any other faith was destined for Hell. He personally thought this a load of rubbish, but Catholics believed it and therefore as children baptised into the faith, their souls were at risk if left in his orphanage. This Father Phillips would take them away and there wasn't one damned thing he could do about it.

'I understand the children are distressed and traumatised,' Father Phillips said. 'For that reason I would have no problem in yourself, or someone else from the orphanage who they are familiar with, sitting in with me, but I must insist on seeing the children today.'

Father Phillips didn't see two severely disturbed children when they were brought in to the room, he saw frightened ones, scared by what life had thrown at them. He left his chair and crouched down on his haunches, knowing an adult's height often intimidated children. 'Hallo,' he said. 'My name is Father Phillips.'

Katie and Liam had been spoken to by many strangers over the last few weeks, and they'd learned to ignore most of the questions fired at them, but no one had crouched before them before, nor spoken so gently.

None of them had been priests either. Priests belonged to their other life, before the tragedy that had robbed them of their mother, along with everyone else. Priests were familiar and safe. Katie smiled tentatively at the priest and Liam, watching his sister, smiled too, though his smile was even more tremulous and hesitant.

Father Phillips heart ached for those two frightened children. He understood they'd been separated, and knew that sometimes there was reason to separate children from one family, but surely to God not when they'd lost everything else. Mindful of the doctor in the room, he had to be careful what he said, so he just talked to the children, telling them who he was and of the home for Roman Catholic children not far from there at all. He asked them if they'd like to see it and after some thought, Katie nodded and Liam copied her.

Doctor Havering was astounded and annoyed. He'd worked with these children for weeks, no months, and not got anything like the response this man had got in a few minutes. He couldn't remember the children ever smiling at him or nodding to a question asked. 'Take them away, Nurse,' he barked at the attendant who'd brought them in, and Father Phillips saw the children jump at his harsh, loud voice.

Liam, however, didn't obey. Despite his fear of consequences, he launched himself at Father Phillips' legs, wrapping his arms tightly around them like a vice. 'Come, come now,' the doctor said sharply, pulling at Liam in an attempt to dislodge him.

'Leave him,' rapped out Father Phillips. He shooed the nurse away and lifted Liam gently into his arms and felt his heart melt as the child, desperate for love in this terrifying world, wrapped his arms tight around him. 'It's all right, Liam,' he whispered in the child's ear without anyone else hearing the actual sounds. 'I'll come back soon.'

It was a promise and one Liam recognised as such. He released his hold and Father Phillips placed him gently on the floor where he put his hand in the nurse's without protest. The priest had made him a promise and he believed it. Katie knew the priest had said something to Liam that had consoled him in some way and that made her feel better as she followed her brother from the room.

Father Phillips left a worried man. The two children he'd visited had affected his heart in a strange way. He knew that well intentioned as the staff at the orphanage were, they were affecting the children with their attitudes. The sooner he removed them the better.

He told Bridie only the bare bones of the visit, and none of his misgivings, but he stressed the fact that he thought that in his opinion the children would make a full recovery with lots of love and patience. Though he wasn't a medical man, Bridie was comforted by his words.

CHAPTER TWENTY-SIX

Two days later, the children left the orphanage bound for Father Hudson's Home. Father Phillips himself went to fetch them, knowing how unnerved they could be about yet another change in their lives.

All the way, he talked to them, pointing out things of interest as they passed, and telling them of the children they'd meet at his orphanage.

He wasn't surprised at their lack of interest. He knew they hadn't been happy at Oakengates. The staff had been hard working; not harsh or cruel, but to most of them it had just been a job and the children had sensed that.

Doctor Havering had been upset they were leaving. He'd told the priest he thought himself a failure because of it. The priest knew that that had been part of the problem. The man thought of the children as some sort of case study to test out his theories and treatments, forgetting they were flesh and blood, little children with fears and worries of their own.

No one had seemed to understand their grief when they'd arrived or had tried try to explain what had happened to their relatives. When their mother had turned up, she'd been viewed as an unwelcome intrusion to their work.

He intended to bring the children together with their mother as soon as possible. Firstly though, the children had to be isolated until they had been examined by a doctor who was coming that afternoon.

He pronounced them physically fit, though he commented on Katie's small stature. Father Phillips himself had been surprised that she was so small, for she was barely as tall as her brother.

'Not that she isn't fit enough,' the doctor said. 'Rum do this not speaking, though I have heard of it before.'

'And I,' the priest agreed. 'But this has gone on for some time already.'

'Still, they're young enough to get over it, I'd say. Time, that's the thing.'

'I thought to re-unite them with their mother as soon as possible to see if it helps,' the priest said. 'That's who Katie takes after, I would imagine. She too is small and slight.'

'They have a mother then?' the doctor asked in some surprise.

'Oh yes. A wonderful woman too,' the priest said. 'She was away from home at the time of the raid and came back to complete devastation. All the family dead but one young boy and no sign of her children. She thought them dead for a month until she met one of her old neighbours who'd seen the children taken away.'

'Do they know she's alive?'

'No, she wasn't allowed to see them in the last home for fear of upsetting them.'

'Bunkum!' the doctor said emphatically. 'Plain daft idea. Get them together, Father. Buck them up better than anything, if you ask me.'

Bridie was on her way to Coleshill the following morning with her cousin for support and Father Phillips met them at the door, with a smile. 'They're here and have settled well,' he told them. 'They've been examined by the doctor and proclaimed fit and well. I think it's time for them to be re-united with their mother now.'

Bridie felt her stomach lurch and suddenly her mouth was incredibly dry. This was what she'd longed for, prayed for, but now she was suddenly afraid. Oh God, if they should reject her, she thought. She'd never be able to cope with that. 'Can I . . . Would you mind if I saw them alone?'

'No,' Father Phillips said. 'I'll have them brought up to the staff sitting room. It's empty now – you'll not want to meet them for the first time in an office.'

Katie and Liam didn't know where they were being taken or why. They didn't protest, knowing there was no point. They seemed to have no control over anything that happened to them anymore. Father Phillips followed them into the room and dismissed the nurse who'd brought them. He bent down to their level and said, 'Now there's someone I want you to meet.'

Katie suppressed a sigh. They were always meeting people, people who fired questions at them, or peered at them with frowning eyes, or shook their heads about them sorrowfully.

'I think you'll like this person,' the priest said, and though Katie said nothing, she doubted it very much. When the priest left the room, she saw the fear on Liam's face and reached out and held his hand tight.

And that's how Bridie saw them, her two wee, unhappy and confused children standing hand in hand. Her doubts and apprehensions fled. These were her own flesh and blood, her reason for living. She wanted to rush over and take them both in her arms, but knew she must proceed slowly.

She watched as realisation dawned on the children. It was their mammy in the doorway, the mammy they'd thought to be dead, who had to be dead or she would have come for them. She was the woman at the fence who Katie thought she'd imagined.

Now a million questions teemed in her brain, but she was unused to speaking and her mammy stood so still as if she were afraid. Liam was afraid too. She felt the shivering go all through his body. She wanted to squeeze his hand and tell him everything was all right.

Liam, however, was past anything Katie could

do. So many frightening things had happened in his young life and now here was the mammy he'd cried for at night when he'd been alone, and longed for every minute of the day, and she stood like a statue in the doorway, saying nothing. It was like his mammy had turned into a stranger.

It was too much, the last straw, and with a cry, he dropped Katie's hand and sank to the floor, tears streaming from his eyes, his whole body shaking.

His action had unlocked the terror that had rooted Bridie to the spot and she went over and bent down to her small son, while her other arm encircled her daughter. She tried to turn Liam to face her, but he wouldn't. He had his knuckles in his eyes and tears seeped between his fingers as he gave great gulping sobs.

Katie felt tears pricking the back of her eyes and her throat becoming unaccountably tight. Bridie saw tears glisten on Katie's lashes and wondered if she was doing any good coming here and upsetting her children like this.

Father Phillips could have told her that the tears were a good sign, releasing the tension that for so long had stilled the children's tongues. But Bridie didn't know that. All she knew was that she wanted to hold her children, but Liam had curled himself into a defensive ball and Katie held herself stiffly in Bridie's embrace.

'Darlings, please,' Bridie pleaded. 'Please stop

crying. Please let me explain everything to you.' And then as the crying failed to ease she sighed, 'Oh God! How I've searched for you.'

Katie stared at her mother. What was she talking about? They weren't lost.

Bridie saw the look and though she didn't fully understand it, she began to talk, telling them of hearing of the raid on the wireless in Ireland and the sights that greeted her when she returned. Father Phillips said they must be told the whole truth; much of it, he'd said, they would already have guessed but they deserved to be told of the death of their loved ones and be allowed to grieve for them.

And so Bridie told them how she'd found Ellen and Sam and Mary dead and Mickey in hospital and no one could tell her what happened to Katie and Liam. Liam's sobs eased as Bridie talked, for this was the mammy he remembered. Her voice was the same and he began to relax.

Then Bridie said, 'I thought you were buried under the rubble.'

Liam gave a moan and a shudder passed through his whole body. He was back again in that inky black dust-filled space that he'd fallen into while the house above him creaked and groaned and bits kept falling into his face. He couldn't move either, for his legs were held fast by something.

In all his life, he'd never been so scared, too scared even to cry. His hands had run over the ground around him, hoping against hope that he wasn't there alone, that his aunt Mary was there and she'd make everything all right.

But the hand he had connected with had been small and slight. 'Katie,' he had said, his throat husky with the dust, pleased he wasn't alone. 'I'm scared, Katie, and there's dust down my throat and up my nose.' He had begun to cough and couldn't seem to stop until tears ran from his streaming eyes.

Eventually the coughing had eased and Liam had run his sleeve over his eyes and nose and had said, 'My throat's sore, Katie and I don't half want a drink.'

'And me,' Katie had said. 'Try not to think of it. Can you come over to me? My hair's caught somewhere at the back.'

'I can't, my leg's stuck.'

'Wriggle a bit, try and pull it out!' Katie had said, as desperate for the feel of another person next to her as her brother was. Liam had tried, twisting this way and that, until the stack above him had tilted and more bits trickled down on him, including one large lump of wood which hit him squarely on the head and knocked him out.

Katie had heard the thump and had called, 'Liam, are you all right?'

But there had been only silence and, horror struck, she had slithered over the ground towards her brother, nearly pulling her hair from its roots as it was held by a pile of debris.

Liam had lain still, though she had pushed at him and spoken to him incessantly. He was dead, she had thought, and by telling him to wriggle and move, she'd killed him.

That was what had rendered her speechless. And then she'd lain in the pitch black alone, but for her dead brother beside her, until rescue came some time later.

The memories had come flooding back for her, too, and Bridie looked from her son to the bleached white face of her daughter and could only guess how much they'd suffered.

'I went a little crazy when I thought you were dead,' Bridie said. 'Daddy came home, and Uncle Eddie, but they had to go back and I was alone and very unhappy. Then Rosalyn came. She's my cousin, yours too. She'd been in America, but was over in Ireland and my daddy asked her to come and see me. She saved me from going mad altogether. My darling children, I love you so very much.'

That broke both children completely. Liam tightened his arm around his mother, while Katie sagged against her.

Bridie hugged them to her with a sigh of relief. It had been three long months since she held them that way and her arms had ached for the feel of them. She staggered to her feet, still holding them, and sank into an armchair with the children nestled each side of her and told them how she'd heard of their rescue. 'Though the person didn't know whether you were alive or not, Rosalyn and I began to search all over again. That eventually led me to Oakengates.'

Why didn't you take us away then? Liam's eyes said. It was as if he'd spoken. 'You were ill then,' Bridie explained, 'and I was told it would be too upsetting for you to see me.'

Liam glanced at his sister and they both stared at Bridie disbelievingly. Grown-ups weren't told what to do.

'Believe me, it's true,' Bridie said. 'And I had no home for you then. I lived in one bare attic room. It was all I could get and there would have been no room for you there, even if I could have got the landlady to agree. But I'd have loved to have seen you.'

So, Katie thought, what was her mammy saying? They couldn't go home with her, was that it?

But then Bridie told them of their grandma and grandad in Ireland who they'd never met but who would love to have them all stay there. She told them of Jay and Mickey already there, and described the cottage and the farmlands and hillsides around until she sensed their excitement. It was another new place, but this time their mammy would be with them and they'd see their cousins who they loved. Liam and Katie smiled at one another.

The smile felt strange to them; they'd not had much to smile about for some weeks. Stranger still was Katie's voice, which came out husky and hesitant as she asked, 'When do we go?'

Bridie hardly heard the question. She'd been told her children were mute and now she held Katie slightly away from her in amazement. 'Katie, you spoke!' she exclaimed delightedly, hugging her. Katie's mouth felt strange, her lips tight, but she smiled at her mother. Though her mammy looked happy, there were tears trickling down her cheeks. Katie couldn't understand it and neither could Liam; he was worried by the tears. He turned around, put his little arms around her neck, and said, 'Don't cry, Mammy.'

Now Bridie cried in earnest and almost tumbled the children to the floor in her haste to get to the door and summon Father Phillips and Rosalyn to hear the good news.

The children were still hesitant to talk much, and Father Phillips advised Bridie not to rush them, but Bridie was content to wait. She'd seem glimpses of the old Katie and Liam and knew that with love and time they'd soon be back to normal. They got on well with Rosalyn too and she was enchanted by them.

'I don't think the psychiatrist will find much wrong with them,' Father Phillips said to Bridie. 'He's coming tomorrow.'

'Is he the same one they saw at the other place?'

'No, I didn't think that at all wise,' Father Phillips said. 'But he'll have all the old notes.'

The psychiatrist arrived expecting to see severely

traumatised and mute children, but the two children he met were anything but unbalanced. He thought it entirely natural to have been traumatised after being buried beneath the rubble of a house and thought they were coping rather well and though neither of them were chatterboxes, they answered all the questions he asked them and he was satisfied.

He made a diagnosis that the children had suffered fear so extreme, it had caused a temporary loss of voice. Being reunited with their mother had obviously had a beneficial effect on the children's wellbeing and general health. He recommended that the children be released into their mother's care, especially as she had a home they would be welcomed into, well away from the horrors of bombing raids.

This, together with the character reference from Father Shearer and the letter from the doctor and the parish priest in Donegal, led that the board of trustees which operated the home voted in favour of accepting the psychiatrist's recommendation.

It was an emotional moment the morning they actually left, for Bridie realised how much she owed Father Phillips, and Father Shearer and Father Flynn too. They waived away her thanks and said they'd been glad to help, but Bridie wasn't at all sure she'd have got her children back without their help. Katie and Liam, though, were anxious to leave, terribly excited to be starting on this adventure to see their grandparents and cousins.

Rosalyn, who'd gone to spend a few days with Todd after the children's future had been secured, met up with them all at New Street Station. 'It was quite a wrench saying goodbye to Father Phillips this morning,' Bridie said to Rosalyn as they boarded the train. 'He's been such a tower of strength to me. Well, they all have.'

'Aye, they have,' Rosalyn agreed and then added with a smile. 'Bet it wasn't such a wrench to say goodbye to your room?'

'You can say that again,' Bridie said. 'And it gave me great pleasure to tell the landlady I was leaving and wouldn't be back and she could let it to who she liked if she could find someone mug enough to take it.'

'Good for you,' Rosalyn said. 'Mercenary old cow.'

'Ssh,' Bridie whispered. 'Liam has ears on him like a donkey and repeats everything. I don't want him coming out with that in front of Mammy.'

'Sorry, I forgot,' Rosalyn said, and added with a little laugh, 'wouldn't have mattered what he heard if he was still mute.'

'Oh aye,' Bridie said. 'Then wouldn't he have a fine store of bad words to let rip with when he began to talk again?' The image of Liam standing before his grandmother, spewing out one obscenity after another, was so funny that both girls burst out laughing, bringing the children's attention from the comics Rosalyn had brought them. 'What's funny?' Katie asked.

'Nothing,' Rosalyn said. 'Nothing you need worry your little head over anyway.'

Katie shrugged. When adults went on like that you were wasting your time talking to them, you'd never get a straight answer, but she was too happy and excited to care much.

Katie and Liam took to travelling with aplomb, changing trains at Crewe as if they'd done it all their lives. The ship enchanted them and they insisted on exploring every nook and cranny of it. Bridie was constantly up and down the narrow metal stairs, inspecting the saloons, and up on deck, both front and back, or to the prow or astern as one sailor, amused at the children's interest, told them. They were impressed by the thick hawser he pointed out that was tying the boat to the concrete bollards at the docks and reassured by the lifeboats he showed them that were slung above them. 'Just in case the ship should strike a rock and sink,' he told them solemnly.

Bridie wondered if that thought might have made them nervous, but not a bit of it. 'It would be all right,' Katie told her confidently. 'We know where all the lifeboats are, you see, and the sailor said he'd make sure we all got into one.'

'That's good,' Rosalyn said. 'But if it's all the same to you, I'd rather not put it to the test.'

Katie's reply was drowned out by the screech of the hooter. It was so loud and shrill that everyone had their fingers in their ears. A cloud of black smoke escaped from the funnel as the engines throbbed into life and then the children were hanging over the rail, tightly held onto by their mother and Rosalyn. They saw the gangplank raised and the ropes unwound from the bollards and they waved wildly to the grinning sailors as the ship pulled away from Liverpool, moving slowly through the sludgy grey water.

Once in open water, it picked up speed, riding over the white-crested breakers, churning and seething before the ship. The sky was the colour of gun-metal and the clouds low and dense and yet Bridie felt as light as air.

Despite her own churning stomach, Rosalyn, she noticed, had become quite green as the ship hit the open water. The children, cavorting about on the deck with other travelling children, under Bridie's watchful eye, had obviously never heard of sea-sickness, but Rosalyn was suffering.

'Do you want to go inside?'

Rosalyn shivered. 'God no! It would be worse in there.'

Bridie had to agree with her, but the February day was raw and cold with biting wind and a dampness in the air. 'I suppose being pregnant doesn't help,' Rosalyn said.

'Pregnant! You're pregnant?' Bridie cried delightedly. 'But you said Todd . . .'

'I know,' Rosalyn said. 'He didn't want children till after the war, but I talked to him at Christmas. I want to have his child, Bridie. Heaven forbid anything should happen to him, but . . . I want his child.'

Bridie knew how she felt. She was so glad she had her little ones and while Katie resembled her, Liam's likeness to his father was startling, now he'd lost the chubbiness of babyhood.

'Your mother will be over the moon,' she said.

'I can't tell her yet, not till I'm sure, and then not until I've told Todd first. You're sworn to secrecy, Bridie.'

'I shan't say a word,' Bridie promised. 'But don't be surprised if your mother guesses.'

'I hope it will help her,' Rosalyn said in a low voice. She glanced around to see the children were not in earshot before saying, 'She was devastated over what had happened to you.'

'I know, she told me,' Bridie said, 'God, Rosalyn, she could barely look me in the eye and if she said she was sorry once, she said it thirty times. Try and convince her I don't blame her in the slightest, will you?'

'Aye, I will.' Rosalyn promised.

Bridie hoped so: Francis's wife had been a victim too and had been forced in the end to drastic measures. She didn't want her beating herself up for what had happened to her, for she'd had no hand in it.

By the time the children had disembarked from the ferry onto a tram to Derry and then a narrow gauge train to Strabane before a rail bus for the last leg home, weariness had overtaken excitement. Katie climbed on Rosalyn's knee and Liam on his mother's and both went fast to sleep.

Bridie was nearly home and safe and felt she was starting life afresh. 'This will be so different,' she said. 'There'll be no Francis, no secrets, no Peggy McKenna. I'll be able to bring the children up decently and in safety and give a hand rearing Jay and Mickey too.'

'What about after the war?'

'At the moment, that's like saying when the sky falls in as Henny Penny would say,' Bridie said. 'After the war and, please God, Tom and Eddie and your Todd will come home safe from it, then we'll see. But for now, this will do me fine.'

'I hope you're happy,' Rosalyn said. 'You've suffered so much and mainly through my father.'

'Oh for God's sake, don't you start feeling bad about it now,' Bridie urged. 'That part of my life is over and done.'

'Okay, I know how you feel,' Rosalyn said. 'And I won't go on about it, I promise. And now shall we try and waken the children, for we'll be passing the farm in a few minutes?'

Katie did wake up, but Liam slumbered on. 'I'll carry him,' Bridie said. 'Daddy will be there to help carry the bags and packages.'

And Jimmy was there. The conductor had helped them down the steps of the rail bus, unloaded their baggage and begun to chug away from them towards Donegal town before Bridie noticed the man standing slightly behind her father.

The man was a stranger, not one of their neighbours certainly, and instinctively her arms tightened around Liam, worried even at this late stage that her children might be whisked away from her. Liam whimpered in protest at being held so tightly and that brought the man's eyes round to him. Bridie noticed they were a strange yellow in the light of the large torch her father carried. Before Jimmy was able to introduce him, Bridie heard the man say, 'Glory be to God. Sure he's the spit of him.'

'This is Sean Cassidy, Tom's father,' Jimmy said to Bridie 'This is my daughter, Bridie, and a cousin of ours, Rosalyn.' Nothing had prepared Bridie for anything like this and she'd stared at the man incredulously.

'And that's Tom's son?' the man asked Bridie, indicating Liam.

Bridie barely heard the question. This was the man that Tom had told her had run up tick in the pub because his son was to be a priest and who obviously cared more for that than his son's happiness, judging by the letter Tom's mother had sent before they were married. She wondered what he was doing there. Both he and his wife had given up any right to be involved in their lives. And she didn't have to be polite to him either. This man had badly hurt her lovely Tom and that damned him in her eyes.

Katie was tired, confused and cold and she wondered what her mother was doing standing in the dark without speaking, especially when the man had asked her a question about Liam. So, before Bridie was able to gather her wits to make any sort of reply, Katie, who reasoned that if the man wanted to know about Liam, he might be the grandfather her mammy had told her about, looked into the eyes of Sean Cassidy and asked, 'Are you my grandad?'

Bridie wanted to tell her daughter the man was no part of her, that he didn't even know she was born for Tom had refused to tell his family, but before she could say anything, the man nodded slowly. 'I imagine I am and this here is your other grandaddy,' he said, indicating Jimmy beside him. 'He's told me all about you.'

Katie's eyes opened wider. Her mammy had never said there were going to be two granddads and then Jimmy lifted her into his arms. He felt tears prickle the back of his eyes, although he fought to control them for the sake of the child before him. But the sight of the wee girl had affected him so much, for it was like looking at her mother all over again.

'Hello, darling girl,' he said, and he hugged Katie close and she smelt pipe tobacco on Jimmy's jacket and other smells she didn't recognise: the smoke from a peat fire, the hay he'd been feeding the sheep earlier and the general smell of the farmyard that had clung to him. It wasn't an unpleasant smell, just unfamiliar, and Katie liked being hugged that way and snuggled closer. She liked this man, she decided. She liked the words he said in his gentle, lilting voice and the way his eyes twinkled in the light of the torch he'd handed to Rosalyn before lifting her up.

Jimmy loved the feel of the child in his arms, the thing he'd longed for all those years, and over her head he addressed Sean. In a voice made husky with the tears he was fighting, he said, 'This here is little Katie.' And then, because he knew Bridie was still suffering a form of shock from seeing the man there, he went on, 'And that is Liam. These are both Tom's children.'

Sean went forward and peered closer at Liam and, like Jimmy, he had the feeling he was looking at his own child as a youngster and felt a yearning to hold him in his arms as Jimmy was doing with the wee girl. 'They are fine children you and Tom have,' he said to Bridie. 'Could I carry the boy for you? He looks a weight.'

Bridie felt as if her arms were being pulled from her sockets, but she had a reluctance to hand her son to this man. 'No,' she said tersely. 'I'm fine.'

Sean wasn't surprised at Bridie's reaction. It was what he might have expected and certainly what he felt he deserved. 'Ah, cutie dear, I know how you feel,' he said. 'I've been a stupid, proud fool and I'm prepared to admit it and so is my wife Annie, who's up at the house now.'

'But how, why . . . ?'

'We got to thinking, the wife and me,' Sean said. 'Aye, we were puffed up with pride at Tom going in for the priesthood, but as your wise father said we can't live our children's lives for them. We've missed our son and worried over him, especially when the war started, and in the end we swallowed our stupid pride and wrote to your parents just a few days ago. They told us you were coming back home today and invited us down to meet you.

'When we arrived here, your father told me of the raid that killed his wife's sister and her husband and their own daughter, and that your two weans were buried in the rubble of the house. God, that was dreadful altogether. We were smote with guilt, Annie and I. We're here to beg your forgiveness and, if you'll let me have Tom's address, we'll write to him the same way. Can you forgive us, Bridie?'

Bridie knew it had taken Sean a lot of courage to say he'd been wrong and that he was sorry and she could tell he was genuine. She had no wish to alienate Tom from his parents – it had never been her intention – and their children deserved two sets of grandparents. She smiled at last at Tom's father. 'I'm pleased to meet you,' she said. 'Tom has told me much of the farm you have, and his sisters. Maybe we could come over and visit you one day?'

'You'd be welcome,' Sean said sincerely.

Jimmy let the breath he'd been holding leave his body gently. He had no idea how Bridie felt about Tom's family, no idea either whether she would welcome Sean or not. That is why he advised the man to come with him to meet the rail bus and why he would let neither Jay nor Mickey come with them – he'd left the two of them straining at the bit in the farmhouse, mad with excitement. Remembering them now, he said to Bridie, 'We must be away. There's two young boys who will be plaguing the life out of your mammy. Two boys who've been longing to see you all.'

Bridie suddenly felt surrounded by love and contentment stole over her. In the farmhouse beyond there was a family waiting to greet her. Delia and her family, who now held no horrors for her, would live beside her as they had all the days of her growing up, and now too there was Tom's family to welcome her. It was more, much more, than she'd ever dared hope for in those dreadful days after the raid when she thought she'd lost nearly everyone belonging to her.

Katie suddenly stirred in Jimmy's arms, pulling herself from his tight embrace, and said accusingly to her mother, 'You didn't say nothing about two granddads.'

'I didn't know either,' Bridie said. 'Aren't you the lucky girl?'

'Have I two grandmas too?'

'You have,' Sean answered the child. 'And they are both up at the house this minute waiting for you, along with your cousins Jay and young Mickey.'

'Maybe we'd better go then,' Kate said and she wriggled in her granddad's arms and Jimmy laughed as he set the petite child on her feet. 'If you're half as good as your mother, you'll do well enough,' he said. 'And now will you do an important job for me,' and at her eager nod, he placed the torch in her hand. 'You light our way up the field,' he said, 'while we carry up these bags.'

Then Jimmy turned and embraced first Bridie and then Rosalyn. 'You're a treat for sore eyes,' he said. 'The pair of you. Now let's be away before we stick to the ground, the night's cold enough so.'

'Wait a moment,' Bridie said, and she approached Sean and gently placed Liam in the man's arms. 'He is heavy,' she said. 'Will you carry him for me?'

The man didn't have to speak, the smile that lit up his whole face spoke for him, and they were off, following Katie's wavering torch. Sean Cassidy after her, his grandson in his arms, and then Jimmy, laden with bags.

Bringing up the rear were the two cousins and friends and whatever distance they were from each other now, Bridie knew it didn't matter; they'd always keep in touch. Between them they gathered up the rest of the packages and made their way towards the house over grass crunchy with frost and Bridie felt as if her heart was as light as air.

She thought of the letter to Tom she'd almost finished writing. She'd told him the children were being released from hospital, not the whole story yet, and she'd left the letter open in order to describe the way the children took to the journey and the welcome waiting for them at the farmhouse.

What a wonderful postscript she could now add, she thought. She knew Tom had often felt guilty about his parents, knowing they'd given up a lot for him to train in the seminary, and his doting sisters taking up the jobs on the farm that should have been his duty, and all without a word of complaint.

He'd not said any of this to Bridie, but she knew Tom so well there were things he didn't have to say. She could visualise his reaction when she told him who was waiting for her to alight from the rail bus.

If it wasn't for the shadow of war looming over their lives, then it would be perfect, Bridie thought, but as it was, they had to make the best of what they had and hope for a better future. As she turned the corner of the farmhouse, she felt her heart skip with joy. It was good to be finally home.